Three months ago, Rex discovered a world-shattering truth about what it means to be a Liquid Onyx survivor and experienced devastating losses in the process.

Rex, momentarily gripped by raw fury and freshly torn grief, committed an act of shocking violence and was re-forged by it.

Unable to face his new, fractured reality, he ran away from everyone who loved him and threw himself into the life of a morally grey vigilante.

Every choice Rex makes pushes him one step closer to embracing his father's legacy. But there are other legacies who won't let Rex fall into that darkness without a fight.

At his lowest point, will Rex find the strength and courage to step out of Alex Nova's shadow and finally become the man—and the hero—everyone needs him to be?

BLOOD WHICH BURNS

Liquid Onyx, Book Five

BL Jones

A NineStar Press Publication

www.ninestarpress.com

Blood Which Burns

First Edition, May 2025

ISBN: 978-1-64890-860-6

Also available in eBook, ISBN: 978-1-64890-861-3

CONTENT WARNING:

This book contains sexually explicit material that is only suitable for mature readers, violence, death, guns, breath play.

Prologue

Andy

I was six the first time I broke into my mum's lab.

Even at that age, I knew I wasn't allowed in there because it was full of dangerous and fascinating things.

I had to break into the lab at least two dozen times before Mum gave in and simply took me down there with her.

She would sit me up at a table and give me work to do. Just simple things at first, calculating equations and mixing low-risk substances as required.

When I watched my mum move through her lab, I marvelled at her intellect. She knew so much, understood so much of the world that I did not.

It seemed to me she was one of the most brilliant people alive, and I wanted to be exactly like her.

Then there was my dad, a man like a natural disaster, unrelenting and inexplicably dangerous, his unique genius as captivating and destructive to watch as a tornado tearing across continents. His mind was unrivalled, a man destined to change the world.

And he did. With my mum's help. My parents were the creators of Liquid Onyx, the gods of superheroes, the killers of children.

But, in most ways, Alex Nova was the man who taught me how to swim at our local pool and how to do a cartwheel, who took me out for ice cream when I did well on a test in school. He was the man who tickled me until I cried with laughter and dried my tears away when I got hurt falling off my skateboard. He was the man who told me I could do anything I wanted with my life because I was brave and clever, when all anyone else did was call me pretty.

My dad was my hero, not because of his extraordinary mind or the things he could do with it, but because he was my *dad,* and I loved him desperately.

When he died, my world crumbled and my heart broke. A piece of my childhood was set ablaze, never to be recovered from the ashes.

From then, it was just Mum and me. Mum became my everything; there was no one else, really. She didn't want me to have any contact with my dad's side of the family, and her side didn't want anything to do with either of us.

Mum tried to make up for it by always being there when I needed her, by being my best friend. She came to all my science competitions and supported my academic dreams with all the attention, energy, and money she could spare. She bought me enough books to sink a ship and took me to museums all over the world, encouraging me to seek knowledge wherever I could find it.

I came out at fifteen and Mum made me a cake with the pansexual flag colours, which we ate together in front of the TV, watching our favourite 80s eighties films, quoting lines from *Top Gun* and *Back to the Future* in terrible American accents.

For a very long time, all I had in my life was my mum and my work.

Then there was Dru, who was too easy to love, and through her I met my little brother for the first time. Rex. A boy I'd been thinking about for too many years, imagining what he would be like and all the things we might have in common. Shared DNA doesn't have to mean much, I know that, but it still felt like a connection I couldn't pass on the potential of. I was too curious, have always been too curious by nature. Mum used to say that was how she knew I'd grow up to be a scientist like her and Dad.

Now, Mum is dead, and it was Rex who murdered her, and all I could do was scream for him to stop. Useless. Fucking stupid. As if my pleading would mean anything to him at that moment, after what I saw in that factory, what happened to Damon North. After what happened to our uncle Roux.

Thing is, I was right about how it would feel to meet Rex. There was a connection, instant and visceral. I felt it wind around my heart like barbed wire the moment our eyes met across the university lawn. Eyes the exact replica of our dad's. He looked so much like Alex Nova, my breath had caught in my throat, threatening to choke me up. It had been a long time since I saw our dad's face, and seeing it reflected back at me, albeit in an undeniably younger and angrier iteration, was bizarre. It's like there was an edge there in the cut of my brother's cheekbones, in the sardonic twist to his mouth that I can't remember our dad ever possessing. Almost too much to deal with. But when he looked at me, I felt something, a tether pulling taut between us, and I'm certain, even now, that Rex felt it, too.

That's what makes hating him so hard.

"What are you doing?" Dru asks as she sits down next to me at a table in what was my mum's lab.

It's been weeks since Mum's death and Dru hasn't left my side for more than an hour at a time. I feel shame over how deeply I'm grieving my mum, after what she did to Dru. Every time my eyes catch on the faint scars around Dru's mouth, I can't help an internal flinch.

Turns out, my mum was the villain of this story, and you're not supposed to mourn the villain. You're not supposed to hate the hero who stopped them. You're not supposed to cry every night in your girlfriend's arms over the person responsible for maiming her.

But this isn't a story, this is my messy, brutal shit stain of a reality.

"Going through Mum's files." I nod at the computer screen in front of me.

I've spent the last few days reading through my mum's electronic journal entries. They were password protected, but Dru helped me to hack into them. I wasn't sure why I wanted to read them at first. Rationally, I knew nothing in them would fix what happened. But the more I dig through my mum's tangled psyche, the more I understand why she did what she did. There's not a thing on this earth that would make me agree with her resolve to kill all the Liquid Onyx survivors, but it's become obvious to me that she genuinely thought it was the only way forward.

In her mind, she was saving the world. More than that, she was fixing what she believes she broke when she and Dad created Liquid Onyx.

Dru scoots closer to me on her stool and reaches over to press her hand to the back of my neck. My blonde hair is up in a messy ponytail, leaving the skin there exposed. She wraps her warm fingers around my neck and squeezes gently. "You've been down here for hours, babe."

Her implication is clear. It's three in the morning and I should be trying to get some sleep. That would be pointless, though. All I ever do when I fall asleep is have nightmares about that night at the factory. I keep replaying Mum's death over and over again. I hear myself screaming. I smell fire, overwhelmingly hot and sharp, from the warehouse explosion. I feel the freezing-cold rain soaking into my skin.

I dream of my brother's face—my dad's face—as it hardens in response to my begging. I dream of his mouth forming the word, "No". Uncompromising. Cruel. There was so much anger in him that night, so much pain. It hurt to look at, like staring into the heart of an infant volcano just as it's erupting for the first time.

I'd rather live with my exhaustion than see any of that again.

"I'm all right." A standard lie that I don't even pretend Dru will believe.

"You're not, though." Dru exhales tiredly, moving even closer, resting her chin on my shoulder as her thumb rubs soothing circles into my neck. "And that's okay, Ands. I don't expect you to be all right after everything. But staying down here all the time, surrounded by your mum's work, can't be helping."

"Not sure anything would help," I murmur, but lean into Dru, steadied by her presence. I truly think that if it weren't for her, I'd have lost my shit and given in to the urge to do something terrible and reckless, like confront Rex. What a bloody, traumatising mess he and I have got ourselves into. Sometimes, when that clawing, furious hatred roils through me at the thought of him, I contemplate the idea that I might never be able to talk to him again, which feels like a loss all its own.

Dru doesn't contradict me, pressing a light kiss to my bare shoulder instead, soft lips a sort of balm to the blend of dread and bitterness swirling around inside me on a near constant basis. Both of us are in our pyjamas, chequered bottoms and vests, a hers and hers matching set some of our friends got us for a joke at Christmas, having been asleep before I gave up and came down to the lab.

She turns her head and squints at the screen, reading out loud from one of my mum's journal entries. "None of the Liquid Onyx survivors have made it to twenty-six alive. And, whether I succeed in my mission or not, none of them ever will." Dru shakes her head, expression deeply disturbed. *"Jesus Christ."*

Neither of us speaks for a while, the gut-punch of

those statements too much to absorb all at once.

I keep forgetting that Dru has a personal connection to all this. She was friends with Rex and Damon, and she's mentioned working closely with the scientist, Rohan Sathe. She said it was Jamie Moon, the older brother of another Liquid Onyx survivor, who saved her from being imprisoned by OI, convincing the director to hire her to work for them instead.

She knows these people. Cares about them. They aren't just faraway tragedies to her. When they die, she will be affected by it in a very real way.

"It was me, you know," I say, voice too loud in the eerie quiet of the lab.

Dru pulls back to frown at me apprehensively, no doubt reading something in my tone she doesn't like. "What was you?"

Sighing wetly, I raise a hand to rub at my tired eyes. "She got the idea to use a blood ritual to kill the Liquid Onyx survivors from something I said. She wrote about it in here." I nod my head at the computer. "I had no idea at the time, but she made it sound like we were discussing a project from work."

When I first read that entry, it took me a moment of searching through my memories to pick out that day. The two of us sitting on my sofa with cups of tea, talking about how she was struggling with a problem, and me, being so eager to help her. It makes me feel physically sick to think I was even peripherally responsible for the suicide of Damon North. I've thought about him non-stop since that night. He was younger than me, not even twenty-two. Far too young to die.

Bursting into that room to find Damon's lifeless body crumpled on the dirty factory floor, and Rex chained to the wall staring with horrible, dead eyes at his equally dead boyfriend, isn't something I'll be able to scrub from my memory any time soon.

But, as my mum's journal entries suggest, all the Liquid Onyx survivors will die young.

Dru affords me the respect of not trying to convince me it wasn't my fault that my mum used what I said to hurt people. She squeezes my neck again instead, offering comfort rather than reassurance.

"I found something else as well," I tell Dru, shifting away from her and getting off my stool. I move towards the pair of large lab fridges, where Mum stored chemicals that needed to be kept at a certain temperature.

Dru slips off her own stool and follows me. I open one of the fridges, a gust of coldness causing goosebumps to rise along my arms, and gesture at what I discovered when I was going through the lab earlier. Dru moves to my side and bends slightly to see where I'm indicating.

Sitting on the second shelf is a small, black safe.

"What's in it?" Dru asks, brows pulled together.

Shrugging, I move closer, going down on one knee so I'm at eye-level with the safe. "I don't know yet, I got distracted by Mum's journal, but she mentioned the safe in one of her entries. She didn't say what was in it, only alluded to its importance."

"To one of her Obsidian Inc projects?" Dru goes down on her knees beside me, her own curiosity piqued.

I brush a long strand of hair behind one ear, a nervous habit. "I think it's something to do with Liquid Onyx."

Dru's eyes widen slightly, and she leans forward, peering at the safe with more acute interest. "Did your mum mention the passcode to get into it?"

Rather than answering, I reach out and punch in the code Mum buried within her journal entries. It took me a while to figure out the pattern, but once the first few numbers revealed themselves, figuring out the rest was easy. I recognise the date she used.

It was the day my dad died.

Once I've put in the code, there's a soft couple of beeps and the little door pops open. Sitting at the very back of the safe, hidden partially from view by shadow, is a vial full of some dark chemical. I exchange a quick look of apprehension with Dru before reaching inside to take out the vial. I bring it up into the light so we'll both be able to see what it is.

Dru lets out a short gasp, but I'm unable to tear my eyes away from the vial to see what her expression is doing.

The chemical inside the vial is a pure black, like ink or oil.

"Holy shit, Ands!" Dru exclaims, disbelief thick in her voice.

A faded label is plastered on the vial, with two words printed on it.

In hushed awe, I read, *"Liquid Onyx."*

Chapter One

Rage, Rage Against

Three months later

I'm starting to regret the decision to let Rohan choose which car to take from the lot tonight. His tastes usually lean towards eclectic, but rocking up to an Obsidian Inc facility in a Rolls Royce Phantom is pushing it a little far. They're going to think we're mocking them, which would be fine if we actually were mocking them, but we aren't. Rohan is just a gothic princess with no sense of ego regulation or base-level shame.

At least the car is armoured and has bulletproof windows. If something goes wrong again and we end up with a host of OI goons chasing after us, we'll have more protection than last time. We barely made it out alive in that stolen panel van. Bloody thing had more bullet holes in it than a First World War helmet thrown dramatically into no man's land.

I turn to Rohan, who sits in the driver's seat, dressed all in black, his hood up and mask on. I'm similarly decked out in my new Wrath suit and mask.

Rohan finished working on it a month ago and presented the modified suit to me just before we were due to set out on one of our missions, in much the same fashion as he gave me the first suit.

I didn't ask Rohan for an upgrade, but he said he'd been working on it before...well...*before*. And he didn't see the point in wasting the work he'd already put into it.

Apart from the increased dexterity and strength of the material used to create the outfit, he made some changes to the general appearance of it as well. My new suit is still mostly white, but the symbol on the chest has switched from daggers to the depiction of a blue and black supernova.

Rohan also added a hood feature to the suit, with what he calls his "shadow-shield" technology built into it. The shield can only be activated or deactivated by my voice, and once pulled up it creates a shadow effect over my face, making it look like there's nothing inside the hood but pure darkness, as if you're staring into the depths of a cave.

I probably don't need to wear my domino at all any more. But I still do. Tradition and all that.

Rohan doesn't react to my looking at him. He rarely does lately.

It took us a while to get into a good rhythm working

together. We were both too used to either working alone or operating under circumstances requiring a different form of vigilance.

Over the last three months, we've learned to share the responsibility of paying attention to our surroundings. It seems a basic thing, but making sure one of us is always taking account of what's going on around us, while still focusing on each other enough to notice problems or communicate effectively, is vital, especially for the work we've been doing.

"How sure are you that the intel we need is being kept in this facility?" I murmur without inflection, making it sound more casual a question than it is.

Rohan can get a bit testy when I doubt his mysteriously gathered intelligence. I'm sure he's getting it from FISA. After every mission, he speaks to someone through his comm unit and relays information about the results of our endeavour, for good or bad.

I don't know who it is he talks to. Rohan calls the person our handler, despite the fact I quit FISA three months ago. The person who Rohan reports to must know I'm involved, though, because Rohan includes me in his mission reports.

When I left FISA and Rohan offered to let me stay in his flat until I got myself sorted, it was only supposed to be temporary, but after we started going on these missions, my leaving date became a question mark.

Living together makes it easier to share any information we've gathered and plan strategic raids on Obsidian Inc labs.

At least, that's what I tell myself. In truth, I don't

know where I would go if I left Rohan's flat.

I can't go home to Colbie yet. I'm nowhere near ready to face it, all the people and the questions and the torrent of well-meaning sympathy. I just can't deal with it, not even after three months of dwelling and grieving.

If grieving is what I've been doing. The general tone of the conversations I've had with Green over the phone would suggest I've been doing nothing of the sort. She keeps indicating I should either come to the agency or go home for a while. She wants me to rest, to stop going out as Wrath, to stop going out on missions entirely.

I'm honestly charmed, more than angry, that she thinks I have the kind of restraint it would take to set aside my Wrath persona for longer than a handful of hours.

These days, I spend more time in the suit than out of it.

I think I'm beginning to worry Green. But that's all right. She'll learn. I stopped worrying about myself months ago. Hopefully she'll find the same damning freedom in it as I did, although perhaps not as destructively. A supervillain Green would likely be a horrifying thing to contend with. I'd stand no chance, I don't think. She knows me too well at this point. Could be the most dangerous thing in the world; a psychiatrist gone rogue.

Rohan answers my question with an infuriating shrug, and an even more infuriating verbal response. "As sure as I was all the other times."

I puff air out through my nose, containing a sigh by the grip of my fingernails. He's like this, Rohan. He's so ridiculously nonchalant during our missions. No matter what happens during them, and sure as shit some panic-worthy stuff has gone down, he just shrugs his way through it like we're living in a video game and we'll both come back to life if someone shoots at our car with a grenade launcher.

The only reason I let Rohan drive is because otherwise he'd just be there hanging out of the window, laughing manically and spraying the OI vehicles chasing us with bullets from the multiple machine guns he seems to have stored in every one of his cars. I swear he only has a hanger full of cars because he needed somewhere to circumspectly store all the various and seemingly unending number of weapons he owns.

Dr Sathe, the somewhat shy man I met six months ago, has officially dropped the act and raised the curtain. I can now see him for the out and out lunatic he truly is. Trust me, you've never seen a man take as much pleasure in carnage as Rohan.

It makes me wonder if maybe that's why he likes me so much, since I'm currently the human equivalent of a forest on fire. I thought I was before. Before the factory. But these past few months have taught me otherwise. I didn't even know what that much heat and smoke felt like until I got up the nerve to press my face into the flames and take a deep breath.

My lungs are swollen lumps of flesh. They feel it, too. I haven't taken an easy inhale since the night at the factory. I'm starting to believe I might not get to exhale without choking ever again. I think one day my oxygen will just be cut entirely and I'll go into respiratory failure in the middle of an op. Or maybe in the fucking shower, which is where I've designated my formal crying area. I don't do that shit anywhere else. Cliché of me, yes, but some things are overdone for a reason.

It won't be at night, in bed. That won't be where it happens. Because I don't use the bed in Rohan's guest room. Because I don't sleep. I think my brain has forgotten how to sleep. I wasn't aware you could forget things like that. I thought sleeping was like blinking or breathing, possible to control but mostly automatic. It's your body doing what it needs to do to keep working as it should.

Turns out, though, if you've managed to piss off your mind enough with your constant fucking trauma and lack of respect for your mental health, it will enact vengeance. It will give you nightmares conjured from the very worst shadows living inside your head. It will offer no respite from the memories you so readily downloaded, playing them out on a screen at full volume and picture clarity.

"Yes. Exactly," I drawl to Rohan, discarding my pretence of indifference. "All the other facilities we've been to didn't have the file we were after, did they?"

Rohan doesn't react to the irritation in my voice. He just sits there, looking out of the window at the Obsidian Inc facility we'll be infiltrating tonight, completely unbothered by me or my very valid concerns.

What makes it more annoying is the fact that before a mission, when we're hammering out our strategy of attack over the dining room table, he's a manic pop rock of a person. He dashes around, jittering and vibrating like a faulty electric toothbrush, snapping at me when I ruin his file system by touching his computer, and practically pulling his hair out over every tiny detail of our plan.

Also yes, Rohan has a dining room table in his insanely massive flat. We'll get into all that nonsense later. Suffice to say, though, Rohan has been keeping more than just his status as a Liquid Onyx survivor close to the vest.

I make a sound in my throat, voicing my frustration without words.

Rohan keeps his own voice unaffected, if slightly withering, when he finally replies, "Fine, fussy. I'm marginally surer about this one."

He's a pain in my arse, I swear. It's like trying to work with a tween who has a superiority complex. Meaning any tween alive. Although that might be a bit unfair to Jatin. I think I'd genuinely prefer to be out on this op with him right now. He's mouthy, yeah, but at least he'll give me the satisfaction of sparring with me over any disagreements. Quite happily, I'd imagine.

Jatin won't be a tween for much longer, though. He's turning thirteen soon. I'll need to do something for his birthday. Maybe pull the trigger on the taser gloves I had Rohan make for him. I'm not sure Rani would approve. Actually, nah, that's a lie, I know for a fact she wouldn't approve. But the kid has earned something for his months of steadfast good behaviour and dedication to his training.

We're still doing that, the training. There was a gap in there at one point, right after...everything. But Jatin had more dedication than I gave him credit for. Both for the training and being my saving grace.

In the end, it was an easy decision to make, giving in to him a second time.

I might have let nearly every other person in my life down, including myself, but I refuse to do that to Jatin again. He's a kid, a special one to boot. Maybe a little bit damaged, like I was. Like...him. *Damon.*

But you don't let kids like Jatin down. That kind of shit sticks to them like wool on Velcro. They can't shake it off like kids with two parents and a soft life would be able to. It's partly my responsibility now to make sure Jatin gets to adulthood with minimal wear. To give him skin thick enough to take a punch, not a bullet.

"I am so very reassured by your not at all obvious lie regarding the likely success of our forthcoming operation," I throw back at Rohan with enough sardonic undertone to scathe, if he had a less honed sense of dignity than he does.

"How dare you," Rohan drawls, the lackadaisical fuck. "My lies are never obvious. That, before, was sarcasm. Not the same thing."

I suppress another sound of exasperation. He's been especially cagey the last few ops. He hasn't even told me what intel we're supposed to be going after, just that it's information OI should not be in possession of for the sake of all Liquid Onyx survivors. I could guess at what it might be, but it doesn't really matter until we've got the data file in hand.

I'm not the kind of person who needs high stakes to take a mission seriously. I rescued a snail from being crushed on the wet path yesterday. Unlike Rohan, my sense of dignity is non-existent. I quit my job, therefore I have no paygrade.

"I'd just like to know the excessive amount of

property damage and murder I'm going to commit tonight will be for a higher purpose than my own sense of flawed justice," I tell Rohan, only partially joking.

I've spent the last three months bombing OI facilities all over Europe. With my power, I mean, not literal bombs. But the end result is the same, so I suppose it doesn't really make a lot of difference. It's just there, in the fine print. In case anyone wants to make a case out of it someday, which they very well might.

I have killed a fuck load of people. Obsidian Inc agents. People who made their choice, as I did. I don't feel bad about it any more.

Maybe it's because all my guilt reserves are being used up on other things. Like how Damon slit his throat open for me. Or how Roux took a knife to the chest for me. Or how my father is still killing people over fifteen years after his death.

That was also for me, apparently. I have yet to figure out why. Mostly because I haven't asked. Maddox might know what Mia meant, or Snow. But I haven't asked them. I haven't spoken to either of them since the night Roux and Damon died.

I can't even think about Mia without also remembering my sister and how much she must hate me. I haven't seen or heard from her since the night at the factory. It seems just a matter of time before she comes back into my life and either forgives or condemns me for my actions. I killed her mum, and I can't pretend it was justified when justice was the last thing I was thinking about when I did it. That was all heat of the moment fury. A revenge killing in the extreme.

It's as if I'm waiting for her. My sister, Andy, I mean. It'll either be her or Liquid Onyx. Both of those threats feel like a conclusion, an ending waiting to happen.

Dru is missing, too. She was there, that night, I was told later by Rohan, and she convinced Andy to leave with her before the FISA agents could get themselves together enough to arrest anyone.

Nobody knows where either of them is. Dru must have put her well-known disappearing skills into practice.

The optimistic view would dictate that Dru is just helping Andy to grieve for her mum, somewhere off the grid where they won't be disturbed by OI or FISA. That they'll come back one day, or maybe not at all. I like to imagine my sister and Dru starting new lives, away from all the agency and superhuman bullshit. I don't believe either of them knew about Mia's plans, which means they were as innocent in all this as Damon was. They deserve some peace, if that's possible.

As for using my power to blow up OI labs and bases of operation, Rohan says it's also far cheaper, so there's that as well.

"Why?" Rohan asks, faux quizzically. Openly mocking me now. "Have you started a programme? Are there steps you're supposed to be following? If I'm going to be getting a letter from you, just know, I expect cotton paper and *professional* level calligraphy. Don't write your apologies on a piece of toilet paper with an eyeliner pencil. I have standards, Rex."

"Cotton paper?" I raise both my eyebrows at him, despite the fact he can't see it with my hood up and my shield switched on.

Rohan gives a concise nod.

"Yes, the kind you use for wedding invitations."

I have to press my lips together so I won't laugh. He's using his posh voice again. I'm almost certain he only uses it to amuse me, not because it's natural.

"Is that a rich person thing?" I ask wryly.

"What? Twelve-step programmes or wedding invitations? In either case, no." Rohan shakes his head a little. "I've heard you lowly peasants have addictions and occasionally marry each other sometimes."

"Ah, yes," I intone sarcastically, "we gather around our bin-fires and sing our peasant songs about either being poor, or maybe, one day, not being poor."

"Sounds perfectly marvellous," Rohan says in that same exaggerated posh knob voice. "I'll make sure to wave at you from my golden carriage next time I ride by to observe the rabble and remind myself why I was born your better."

I give a quiet snort.

"More like to remind yourself not to blow your money on insane rubbish like the life-size Doctor Who-themed chess set you keep taking in and out of your Amazon cart."

"Also that, yes."

"You don't even play chess," I say, mildly incredulous, but also just a little bit fond.

My original assessment of Rohan as an unrepentant Strange Person was absolutely on point. My other instinct—that he had real potential to become a proper mate—was similarly correct.

"Of course not." He's aghast at the mere suggestion that he would entertain engaging in such an activity. "In my house the chess sets were only ever decorative. Like the piano we had that no one ever played or the bookshelves filled with books no one ever read."

I'm never quite sure what to do when Rohan brings up his childhood. I understand completely, now, why he wouldn't want to discuss it. But there are times when he mentions things from his past, before he came to FISA, and I'm almost certain he's trying to gauge my reaction to what he tells me. It feels very much like I'm being tested. For what, I'm still not entirely clear on.

Perhaps Rohan wants to see if I'll judge him for his upbringing or try to fix the numerous issues it carved into him. If I'm right about the reason for it, I hope Rohan will eventually see I have no intention of trying to mend what's broken in him. I'm barely capable of holding the shredded pieces of my own mental stability intact. That shit is more duct tape and gum at this point than it is anything else. Can't depend on it to keep me steady like I used to.

It took a while for me to figure out Rohan was testing me with his out of nowhere reveals. I was confused, and honestly a bit pissed, when I figured out what he was doing for the first time. But then, the more I ruminated over it, the easier it was to see how someone like Rohan would have been taught, probably from birth, to conceal the damage done to his internal circuitry.

You grow up in a cold place, filled with sharp edges to cut yourself on, a place where you're constantly getting backed into darker and darker corners, and you probably learn how to create shadows in whatever amount of light you get shining in through the cracks.

I can't blame Rohan for how he's trained himself to protect all his soft parts. At one time in his life, it was probably necessary for survival. Might still be, with other people. People with ice running through their veins and hearts chilled for later use.

Far be it from me to rebuke someone for scratching at old wounds until they bleed and bleed and bleed. I've got so many of my own, wounds and scars both, that the only way to conceal them from the people I care about is to wrap myself in shadows and remove myself from their line of sight.

Since coming to understand Rohan's odd dance of now-you-see-it-now-you-don't, I've worked out the best reaction to any admission, big or small, is not reacting to it in any significant way at all. If I call attention to what he's said, he often comes at me with an acid whip of scorn in unspoken punishment. Jokes sometimes work, but not always. Only if he's in the right mood. Right before a mission, when Rohan is on the brink of donning his apathy like someone else might armour, is a bad time to poke the razor blade bunny that is Rohan and his neuroses.

I'm determined not to let Rohan off the hook. "Also, why am I apologising to you with toilet paper?"

"You aren't," Rohan replies disdainfully. "You're doing it with wedding paper and artisan penmanship."

"I mean, why am I apologising to you at all?"

At this, Rohan does look at me. I still can't see his face, but somehow, I'm able to tell he's glaring at me. His displeased tone of voice suggests I am not wrong about the glare.

"You're apologising to me because I'm the one who's

had to deal with your entire family constantly badgering me for Rexley updates ever since I made the colossal mistake of letting them know we were in contact. Every bloody day a group of them will stampede into my lab and bother me, asking stupid questions like if you're still alive and when I think you'll be ready to talk to them and could I maybe suggest you should call Lady Mars before she gets desperate and starts putting some real effort into training Maddie, your bloody duck, to carry messages like a giant, incompetent pigeon."

I ignore all of that in favour of a less emotionally charged topic.

"I don't think they do a twelve-step programme for murder anyway."

Because that is my life now. Where murder addiction is less charged a topic than the reasons why I'm not talking to my own family.

"Shame," Rohan laments. "Guess you're just going have to live with it, then."

I keep prodding. "Be real, did you even know murder was considered a super bad thing by general society until you joined FISA?"

"Nah. In my house the only edict was, succeed. The 'by any means necessary' was never said, but..." He shrugs.

"It was implied?" I guess.

"Heavily." He pauses. Then adds, an unmistakable wince in his voice, "Painfully."

With what I now know about Rohan's parentage, it isn't difficult to imagine the kind of upbringing he likely suffered through. No matter how much he downplays it, growing up as he did, with the father he had, I'm impressed on a daily basis that Rohan is here at all. Let alone still thinks the world worth risking his life for.

Or maybe I'm wrong about what I'm capable of understanding. I really can't imagine what it was like for Rohan, how truly awful and frightening it was to have no one he could trust to care about him as they should.

My own childhood was messy and non-traditional in the extreme. But it was mostly good, and I was never short on people who cared whether I was safe and happy. For all that I lost, I can't discount what was given to me by Lady Mars and The Parents.

They tried. They tried to fill the holes shot into my future, to patch over the grooves clawed into my mind by memories of lifelong horrors, which is more than most people like me get.

When I look at Rohan, sometimes, I think he is what a lonely child eventually becomes when no one intervenes on their behalf. He reminds me of Damon so much in those moments, I can barely stand to be near him. It's a painful thing, to see those marks raked across another person's skin with such clarity.

Rohan and Damon did not grow up wandering through the same thatch of spindly trees, scratched by the same sharp branches, but they were in the same wood, and both were equally as alone as they scrounged their way through the dirt and darkness surrounding them.

I wasn't equipped to help Damon then, not as much as I thought I was, and I'm even less equipped to help Rohan now. But I still want to. I want to slice up whatever part of me is left which could be of use and offer it up for Rohan to take or leave as he chooses.

Neither of them asked for my hack-job attempts at kindness, I know, and maybe I have no right to try to offer anything to anyone when I've failed so badly before. With Lewis and Julia. With Damon. I tried, and I fucked it up. I really fucked it, didn't I?

I'll do it again, though. The trying part, I mean. I'll keep making this mistake until I die, which, to be fair, might not be too long in coming.

Poison in my veins, remember. Bubbling under my skin, it is. A ticking time bomb. A clock running down to zero, fast.

I might not make it to twenty-five. None of us is supposed to make it to twenty-six. At the rate I've been going, there's a chance I won't see my twenty-first birthday. I've taken too many bullets lately, taken too many hits in general of both the physical and the mental variety. I've thrown myself into the pit and I'm not even trying to drag myself out.

If I don't get a fucking grip, I'm gonna die before Liquid Onyx has a chance to dig its hooks in any deeper.

Problem is, I'm really struggling to feel like that matters any more, which, trust me, is more nauseating for me to think than it is for you to hear. I want to be better than that. Stronger. Nihilism isn't something I've ever particularly aspired to. But I can't force myself to care as much as I know I should.

It's one thing to stop being afraid of dying, and it's another to stop being afraid of the pain that goes hand in hand with living. I've reached the stage where I'm not scared of either, which is how I know I'm well and truly fucked.

Fear is a survival instinct. I need it back, as strange as that might sound. Fear gives the world colour. I can't live with all this grey, it's driving me mental, making me do shit just so I won't have to think about anything other than immediate concerns, like a bullet to the head or a stranger's hands tightening around my throat.

I'm officially one of those arsehole adrenaline junkies who take risks just to "feel something". Yeah, I know. It's awful. You can feel free to hate it. *I* hate it. Want to punch myself in the face for being this person, someone who Damon and Roux would both be so bloody disappointed in.

With my limited willpower, I push my own darker thoughts aside. They'll still be there later. We'll have more fun with them after this op is done, and people aren't shooting at me any longer. We can look forward to that together.

I hope we don't get into another car chase tonight. OI agents drive like drunk grandads zigzagging across golf courses in those little cart things. No respect for road safety, those lawless fucks.

Since Rohan brought up his father more overtly than he usually does, I think maybe it's okay this time to directly address the issue.

"You know where your dad is?"

All Rohan gives me a simple, crisp, "No."

Here's where I make the offer. For Damon, it was giving him a family who gave a shit about him. For Rohan, it's this.

"If you ever do know, tell me."

I know Rohan is frowning at me, even though I can't see the pinched expression on his face.

"Why?"

I would give him a beatific smile if my own face wasn't covered in shadow. He'd appreciate that. Rohan always does.

"So I can rip his throat out for you. What's the point in having a killer for a partner if you don't let him murder your bastard of a father for you? It's like dental. Make the most of your benefits."

There's a short beat of silence, then, where Rohan just looks at me. I feel his eyes pinned onto me like darts in a board.

"Careful, there, Rex," he warns, a good dose of humour in his voice. "Keep talking like that and...well...I might fall in love with you or somethin'."

Since there's about zero percent chance of that happening, I can only laugh.

"Like hell. You deserve better than even the man you think I am, let alone the one I actually am."

Rohan snorts in apparent disagreement. "You're dead wrong about that. Know who else would think so? Jamie. You should really call him when we get home. That boy is sick with missing you. It's embarrassing. Him and Caleb. They're both moody tossers all the time and people are getting fed up with it. Seriously. Return to the fold and save them from getting banished or mutinied. Or fed to bears. I don't know. The masses are thinking and that never ends well."

"No." I shut him down hard. "I'm not ready."

I want to be ready. I wish I felt even two percent less like I'm coming apart at the seams than I did three months ago. But I don't, so I can't go back. It's selfish of me to keep my family at arms' length when they all lost Roux as well, not to mention the news they've undoubtably been told about the life expectancy for Liquid Onyx survivors.

If I was a better person, I would be able to get over myself, force the bad shit aside, the guilt and the grey, and focus on helping my family deal with what's happened.

But I'm struggling to keep my head above water, and until I can find a way of setting my mind back on an even keel, I'd be nothing to my family except another weight dragging them under.

They wouldn't see it like that, I know. They would want me home, with them, no matter how badly I was acting. For that reason, it's my responsibility to protect them from their own kindness.

I will go back. Soon. I will.

Just not yet.

Rohan doesn't sound impressed with my response, but he doesn't try to push me on it either.

"You're thick in the head is what you are," he grumbles. "But, fine. I'm not your keeper, do what you like."

Catching onto Rohan's opening like the lifeline it is, I resettle myself in my seat, preparing to get this op underway before we get sighted by OI for lingering too long outside their facility. OI send out regular patrols as a matter of course, and they're likely to pick up on any car that stays too long in one place close by.

We're parked a good distance away, but the facility is set up outside the city of Bristol, sectioned off from the road. It's not quite in the countryside, although the surroundings are more rural in appearance. There aren't any buildings near the facility, just empty fields.

The facility itself is rather large and modern, all silver metal and brightly lit from within, illuminating the otherwise pitch-black area. Most of the windows are around the front of the building, likely because all the interesting things are happening further back inside the facility.

There isn't a car park we can see, which means they probably have an underground parking area only OI employees have access to.

Clearing my throat, I go to instigate a more dynamic course of action than just sitting around bleating at each other all night.

"I bloody will. Now shut it 'bout feelings and let's get on with it. I'm not fucking dressed like this just for your personal aesthetic enjoyment. We have actual shit to do."

Rohan does his usual thing of pretending he had no intention of getting my ire up by talking about my family. He likes to do that. Poke at my soft spots and quickly back off to hide in a bush before I can take a swipe at him for it. I can't decide if it's another way of testing me, like he's trying to make sure he still knows where I'm vulnerable, or if he's having flashbacks to being at boarding school with a load of future vipers in striped ties.

"Ah, pushed a button, did I? Okay, then. We're going. Please try to contain your excitement, or any other erroneous emotions you may be feeling at this time."

In an effort not to flick him directly in the eye, I turn my head away from Rohan and look out of the windshield at tonight's target. It's not as big a facility as some of the others we've hit, but I've found sometimes the smaller OI bases are the ones with better security.

We don't have as much information on this facility as I would like.

Rohan and I have staked it out for the better part of the early evening. It's a risk to do too much on-site recon with OI facilities because of how camera-heavy they tend to be.

Other times, we've had a basic layout of the facility or lab, so at least we'd have a general idea of where things are going to be and where we need to go. This op, however, we'll be going in mostly blind. With no clue of the layout of the building's interior, we were not able to plan as much as we usually would. We'll be working on the fly in a way I'd much prefer to leave for patrolling only, where I'm mostly dealing with two-bit criminals who put about the same amount of planning in as I did, meaning the bare minimum.

To make up for this, Rohan is going to be taking up his role as "man in a van" rather than coming into the facility with me.

For a limited amount of time, Rohan will be able to hack into the camera security system inside the facility and guide me through it manually.

As if prompted by my thoughts, Rohan reaches into the back seat and grabs his laptop. He pulls it onto his lap and opens the lid. On the screen, once he's banished the generic snowy mountains screen saver, is a whole load of symbols and numbers on a black background, all of which mean less than nothing to me.

Rohan begins tapping away at the keyboard, creating a series of codes and complicated formulas that will allow him to get into the OI security system undetected. Or at least he'll be temporarily undetected. It's unlikely I'll have long to get into the facility and find what we need before every alarm system starts blaring. Rohan will give me as much time as he can, and whatever that is will have to be enough.

"They're getting wise," Rohan mutters, more to himself than to me. He's still furiously punching buttons on the keyboard. He directs the next part to me, a slight apology in his voice, "You're going to have around half an hour, maybe."

Yeah, about what I thought. I was prepared for a limited window, but that doesn't make me feel any more reassured about my likelihood of success.

I don't respond, mostly because there's nothing I can say. This needs to be done, so I'll do it, and if everything goes to shit, then I'll cross that bridge when I come to it.

"Remember," Rohan tells me rigidly, "you're looking for the file called 'CTRL.'. It'll be saved with all their most recent projects."

"Got it," I say, putting my hand on the doorhandle and pushing down.

Rohan doesn't respond as I climb out of the car and slam the door shut behind me. I take off towards the facility with hastened steps, all too aware of my limited time.

Once I'm closer to the facility than I am to our car, I press two fingers to the earpiece that will allow me to communicate with Rohan.

"You hear me, T-6?" I check.

Rohan's voice comes through the earpiece loud and clear, if a little annoyed. "We're all good, Wrath."

He hates his call sign, which is too bad because it amuses the hell out of me. It was his fault for saying I could choose the name we use over comms. Why he thought I wouldn't choose something he'd hate is beyond me. Further proof Rohan hasn't had a lot of mates before, I guess. Either that, or it's proof some people are nice to their friends on a day-to-day basis and my lot are just unusually mean, which could very well be the case.

Rohan's voice comes through again. "No guards at the agreed entrance point."

Since time is more of the essence than stealth for this op, I don't bother breaking in through either a window or the roof like I would on other missions. Instead, I go round the back and enter through an emergency exit on the ground floor.

As promised, there are no guards, and Rohan uses his control over the building to keep the cameras off me and open the emergency door so I won't have to kick it in. The noise I'd make doing that would doubtless draw unwanted attention to my current position.

Once inside the building, I head up the three flights of stairs to where Rohan tells me over comms the master computer system is located.

I don't meet anyone on the staircase, but Rohan does stop me from entering the third-floor hallway before I can open the door.

"Hold it," he warns. "There are three guards."

I wait for Rohan to tell me they've rounded a corner and that it's safe for me to continue.

At least half a full minute goes by before Rohan gives me the go-ahead to press on.

I silently push open the door from the stairwell and sweep into the third-floor corridor. Rohan directs me from there to the correct room. There's a pad on the wall next to the door, indicating the need for a card to gain access to the room.

Rohan bypasses security for me again and the door clicks open a few seconds later.

I enter the room, which is empty of human beings, but packed full of technology. There are what appear to be walls of machines with multiple wires sticking out of them and lots of coloured lights flashing all over the place.

This is where the facility's hard drive is stored. All the data files from the separate departments will be collated here.

At the front of the room is a large computer, where I'll be able to access all the files saved on the main database.

I sit down on the little spinny chair in front of the computer and take out the USB stick Rohan gave me to download the file onto.

Under Rohan's direction, I dig into the files, searching for the one he's asked for. It takes me a while, since there are lot of bloody subfolders to check through, but eventually I find the datafile called "CTRL".

There's another fraught period of time where I download the information to the USB stick, wary of how exposed I am in this room. I don't mind having to fight my way out, but I'd rather not have a load of gun-toting OI troopers trying to shoot my head off if there's an option to avoid it.

I'm working on a nearly empty tank of energy right

now, so if I can get away with easy, I'll take it and run.

I close my eyes for a moment when the bright lights of the data systems start to make my eyes feel funny. A small headache even begins to prick at my left temple.

That will be the lack of sleep just as much as it's all the blinking lights confusing my brain.

When I do manage to work myself hard enough to pass out for an hour or so, my dreams only come in shades of fear and fire.

Before, it felt like my mind was a glass orb with a mess of cracks, a spray of fractures marring the transparency.

But on the night Damon took a knife to his throat and Roux had one lodged in his chest, something inside my head gave way. The orb splintered from the centre outwards. I heard the spiderweb of fissures take form and spread through the glass.

Afterwards, when all the blood was shed and the fire still raged, my mind had become a far more fragile thing.

It was still whole, though, which was a shock to realise.

I thought I would shatter, shards of bottomless fury and profound grief cutting into me from the inside of my skull, jagged pieces scraping against flesh and bone.

No. Instead, it cracked. I cracked up all the way. I cracked and cracked, but I did not shatter.

Some part of me, separate from all the other parts, feels guilt for that. Losing Damon and Roux as I did should have finished me. I can't help believing they deserved it, for their deaths, the way they died, to have a larger impact on me, if not the world.

I survived the loss, barely, holding on with burnt fingertips and the human instinct to never give in. It's a lot more difficult to surrender entirely than we think. Even if we have to crawl and beg and break ourselves in half just hold on to the ability to feel all that pain, we do. We crawl. We beg. We break and break and...

Well. It's a real shitshow. Every breath and splinter of the experience. Death is hard, but life is always harder. That shit just keeps on happening. Keeps on fucking going, no matter how radioactive the world around you becomes, no matter how much of a genuine danger you become to it in return.

I'm beyond relieved when I open my eyes and see the file has completed its download.

I grab the USB stick, put it back in the pouch I have on my belt, and head to the door.

"Ready to go," I say to Rohan.

His response comes almost immediately. "Sorry, Wrath. You've got trouble. Five guards are coming your way and they're checking rooms."

Fuck.

"How close?" I ask with hushed urgency.

Rohan sounds apologetic again when he answers, "Right on top of you. Move now!"

Well, if that's the case...

I decide subtlety is for cowards, we die like men, and I crash through the door into the hallway with bombastic enthusiasm, hoping for the element of surprise to go in my favour. It's certainly been a friend to me before.

Much to my satisfaction, the guards do show a great deal of surprise. They must have been checking the rooms as part of a routine exercise, not because they were thinking they'd find something worth getting worked up over.

I am most definitely something to get worked up over.

Rohan was right, the guards were close, at the end of the hallway, just about to come trampling down towards the room I was in.

Three of the guards are fast, quick to get over the immediate surprise of my sudden existence, threatening to fuck up their shift. They have their guns out of their holsters in record time, aiming them at me and firing with prejudice.

I turn my face away so they won't hit anything other than my very bulletproof suit. The hits come, sudden pressure knocking me back. Two bullets to my chest, another to my stomach, the last barely scratching along my left bicep.

In the next second, I'm able to move quickly to the side and avoid more bullets, flickering a look at the guns and detonating them like small bombs with my mind.

I've got used to my power these months, in a way I never wanted to, but always suspected I was capable of.

The two other guards are still working on getting their guns out when their co-worker's weapons explode in their hands.

Cries of pain and shock ring out through the hallway, both from the guards who have just had their hands blown up along with their guns, and the others who witnessed it.

The three guards who shot at me are now all crumpled to the carpeted floor, blood spurting from the mangled remains of their hands. They look like bloodied stumps to me, all frayed skin and exposed bone.

You might expect them to be screaming, but shock can do powerful things to a person's mind. None of them is making any noises louder than fearful gasps and pain-filled mewling. One of the injured guards, a large man with red hair and scars on his face, vomits onto the carpet at the sight, or perhaps even the feel, of his missing hands.

The two guards who didn't manage to get their weapons out in time are now staring at me in awed horror, their guns gripped loosely at their sides.

I turn away from them, confident they won't come after me, and make a dash for the stairwell.

Rohan is silent in my ear as I take the steps in a few leaps, eager to get out now that the job is done.

When I'm out in the evening air once more, I run around the side of the building until I'm standing in front of it.

I step back slowly, and I look up at the building, waiting until I'm a safe distance away to finish this as Rohan and I previously agreed.

In warning, I press my fingers to the earpiece again, and say, "T-6, get the car ready."

Rohan curses in my ear. "Ah, shit, hurry up, people are coming out in a sec."

Peering ahead through the large panes of glass which make up the front of the facility, I can see Rohan is correct. Floods of guards are racing towards the main entrance.

After taking another few steps back, just for good measure, I choose a spot on the building to aim at. I've learned better since the factory. I've trained myself to know the weak points of a structure like this one, so I can set about bringing it down with the most devastating efficiency.

When the cluster of guards is almost at the front door, I strike.

With a single thought from me, one side of the OI facility explodes in a fiery fusion of combusted matter.

It's a rush. The bite and pressure and rippling quake of my power. It's a *rush*, every time.

Bits of singeing metal and torn-apart brick rain down from the exploded area, orange and red fire lighting up the sky above it. Black and grey smoke billows out into the air like thick blankets blowing in a ferocious windstorm.

A blast of heat billows out and hits me, like I've just got off a plane in a really hot country. It burns the skin on my face, while the rest of me is protected by the suit. I'm too far back for the smouldering heat to have any lasting impact, but the feel of it is enough to knock some of the breath from my lungs.

Seconds later, the structure begins to collapse, giving way to the pressure created by my explosion. It ripples down through the building, bricks crunching, metal grinding and bending beneath the weight of it. All the large windows crack and splinter, shards bursting outwards and spraying the ground with jagged pieces of glass.

The few guards who managed to get outside are on the ground, arms wrapped around their heads for protection. Through the smoke and the debris, it's difficult to see what the other guards are doing, but I'd guess they're on the floor as well, either on instinct or because they were thrown down by the force of the explosion.

Fire continues to rush upwards, angry flames eager to suck in as much oxygen as it can. Rigorous swathes of smoke rise from the building, coating the air with the thick smell of charred matter. It's a scent I've got used to lately, reminding me vividly of the factory and all that comes along with those memories.

If the world was less grey, I might lose my breath over it.

Op well and truly completed, I turn to sprint towards the road where Rohan is waiting, leaving the mayhem and destruction I've created behind me.

People scream. Fire rises.

I grit my teeth hard enough to cause pain. I'll be lucky if I have any teeth left uncracked soon.

As expected, Rohan waits in the car, nearer than where I left him. He still has his hood up and his face shadowed by the shielding he created.

I open the passenger side door, throw myself down into the seat, and quickly close the door behind me.

"Let's move," I throw at Rohan unnecessarily.

Rohan doesn't hesitate to put his foot down, shooting the car forward and taking us away from what remains of the OI facility.

"You got it?" he asks me, even though he knows I did.

I pat the place on my belt where the USB stick is safely nestled. "Got it, T-6."

Rohan makes an exasperated sound, probably in response to his call sign, and flashes me the middle finger of his left hand. "Fuck off, Nova," he growls, with feeling.

I let out a bright, manic laugh as we drive about ninety miles per hour along an empty road, leaving the facility in the rear-view mirror and heading back to Danger.

Chapter Two

Nightmares and Chips

Three Months Ago

"Did you know?"

Snow looks at me from across her desk, a mostly blank look flattened across her face. She's sitting in her padded swivel chair, hands twined together on the desk in front of her.

"I think you should sit down, Agent Nova." Snow speaks to me like anyone else would to a stroppy toddler.

It's incredibly brave of her, really, to still sit there looking at me with barely veiled impatience, as if I've just run late for a meeting, and now I'm taking up her precious time by talking nonsense. She looked at me the same way barely a few weeks ago when I came to the meeting with

Jamie about the Clarke family massacre. She's still looking at me as if nothing has changed between then and now, like I'm the same person.

I'm scared she thinks I'm supposed to be reassured by her thinking the person standing in front of her now is the same man who sat in her office that day. It's a horrifying indictment, if Snow really believes I was always this person.

If Snow thinks I was always capable of this—or worse, that this eventuality was truly inevitable—it makes me think she saw this coming, all the way back when I was a child.

I want to know what kind of person you might be one day.

It used to make me feel better that my father's descent into destruction was a choice, not an inevitability. The madness may have made him what he was in the end, but he took the first tremulous steps on that red-hot path all by himself.

I thought, as long as I chose to lay bricks down for my own road, as long as I put in the work to be someone else, someone better, I'd be able to avoid my father's path completely for my entire life.

Unbidden, I hear Snow's voice inside my head.

The concept of choice is subjective.

I dismissed Snow's words, once, months ago. But fuck. Now maybe I understand what she meant. I thought I understood what it meant to make the right choice, to choose who I wanted to become, what kind of man, what kind of hero.

But in that moment, when I killed Mia, it didn't feel

like I had any choice at all. I knew the possible conse-quences, what it would mean for me and for Andy, and it didn't matter. Nothing mattered except the all-encom-passing need to do something, to act.

In those few seconds, minutes, mental lifetimes, I was done. I was done trying to be a better person than my father. I was done blaming my darkness on him, on our shared blood, on what he did to me.

Killing Mia felt like it was my second metamorphosis event. The first was biological. The second psychological. One as significant as the other in terms of impact.

There's no doubt in my mind that tonight felt like a death. More than the physical deaths of Roux and Damon. Tonight felt like the end of something for me. I gave some-thing up, or maybe I gave it away, and there's not going to be the chance to take it back. You can't fight for what isn't there. You can't bring war to an empty space. You can't stake a claim on air.

I discarded what Snow said about choice, because I thought I knew better. I thought I knew what making the right choice looked and felt like. I definitely thought I knew what making the wrong choice looked and felt like.

Not now. After tonight, with all the shit I've done and compromised, the promises I've broken to people who de-served better, who would have always deserved better than that from me, I've realised I don't know anything. I thought I did. I really thought I did. But I'm just so fucked up over this, I can barely tell up from down, let alone make actual decisions involving real-life stakes.

It's like I don't feel safe to be out. I've been a time

bomb all my life, and part of me thought if I ever blew up, if I ever shattered the world down to its foundations—my world at least—then that would be it. I'd be done. I thought I would take myself down and out along with everything else.

Would that be the decent thing to do, now, do you think?

Do I even care about decent now?

The answers to those two questions are yes and probably not. Interchangeable depending on how dramatic I'm feeling from moment to moment.

It's all that numbness still protecting me. I thought it would have thawed by now. But no. The ice is still thick over my skin, the metal scratched up all to hell, but holding strong. I'm encased in it, like crystal inside rock. At some point I'll need to crack that shell, split myself right down the middle. Not yet, though. I've still got one last bridge to set ablaze before tomorrow.

"Did you know, director?" I ask again, ignoring her blatant order to sit and calm the fuck down. She might not have said that, but it was implied in every cut and slice of her expression. There's granite in her face, fused into the muscles like liquid from a syringe.

I'm leaning on one of her deviously uncomfortable chairs now, my hands gripping the back of it like I might at some point swing it up and try to tame the jaguar who is my boss. I'm almost certain, even with my power and current volatility, I would lose that fight, easy.

If Snow were anyone else, after what I've done tonight, she wouldn't want to be within the same building as me, let alone the same small, enclosed space.

Half an hour ago I blew up a factory and murdered Mia Solar by exploding her chest with my mind. You'd think someone with that knowledge in mind would reconsider their own sense of power in what amounts to a stand-off between them and an IED minefield.

But Snow didn't get to where she is by being frightened off by things like a weapon with an attitude problem.

Instead of leaning away from the crazed superhuman, Snow leans forward. She's a very jagged person, it seems. Perhaps that is where Damon learnt to zag. He had to get it from somewhere. No one is born as infuriating as he is. Was.

Was.

He was on the floor. On the...

In the grass. On the warehouse. On the factory...

Floor.

He was on the...

"Damon. Please!"

Why is there so much screaming in here? Inside my head. It's everywhere tonight. It's everywhere.

"I think I love you."

No. That's worse. That is definitely worse. Bring back the screaming. I want the screaming back, now, please.

I'm furious, though.

I'm so furious I'll never get to tell Damon how much I hate him. How much I'll never forgive him.

I'll never...

I'll...

I...

I'll never be...

"Okay, Agent Nova. Okay." Snow relents. Or pretends to.

I prefer to think that she pretends to. I need something else to think.

I don't want to think about Damon any more, so I'm not going to.

There.

Decision made.

Because that's how brains work. Always have. Historically. We just decide not to think about things and wow, all gone, bye, see you again never.

Right.

"Agent Nova, I understand that you're upset," Snow begins crisply, and I almost choke to death right there on laughter, cutting her off with a vicious maw of regurgitated sound.

I'm laughing, then, and it's a horrible racket. Worse than the screaming.

Why are so many things worse than screaming right now?

My fingers unconsciously tighten on the chair. Snow's eyes flicker to my hands and just as quickly they swivel back up to my face. There's an absence of fear in how she arches her eyebrow at me that I find both comforting and insulting in equal measure.

"I know you're dealing with a lot right now, agent." Snow's voice is so deceptively calm and quiet. Not kind, though. Snow is never kind.

I'm glad. Kindness might force me to crack that rock sooner than I'd like. I've still got things to say. I've got secrets to uncover. This is an interrogation. Not a very well-choreographed one, but still. I've had no time to plan, so I'm having to think on the fly, which isn't a very smart move when interrogating a pillar. You really need a plan if you're going to start kicking at marble to try to bring down the second Roman empire.

"Roux—" she starts again.

I must break out a reaction even Snow thinks is a concern for someone's safety, if not her own. I'm not sure if it's my expression, or the wounded noise I make at the mention of my dead uncle, but she stops immediately.

There's no apology in how she pushes the topic of Roux aside for now. Snow does not apologise. But I think it's about as close as I'll probably ever get to seeing regret in her eyes. Whether that regret stems from causing me indirect pain or the very real fact of Roux's death, I can't be sure. I'm not sure I ever want to know. I don't think I want to know if Snow truly cared about my uncle. Some things are better off left ambiguous.

"You're struggling, it's understandable. After what happened to Agent North—"

"You mean how he stabbed himself in the neck with my knife? Had a dramatic moment and killed himself, finally, the bastard. Except you've probably been waiting for that for years. Got his funeral arrangements planned for him by the time he was twelve. A miracle he lasted this long, yeah?"

I don't know what I'm saying or why I'm saying it. Words just keep pouring out no matter how much the voices in my head tell me to shut up, to shut up and stop talking about him, stop thinking about him, you failed him, you fucking failed him, you failed him like you were always going to, because that's who you are, that's who you are.

I made this choice, because I knew it was what you would want.

It should have been...

It was going to be you. For Alex.

It should have been me, then. Fifteen years ago, at the safe house. It should have been me, now. Tonight, in the factory.

For years, I've had this feeling. I've had it for so long I can barely remember what it's like not to feel this thing, this terrible sense of knowing I've been stealing time. Not borrowing it. Stealing it. Stupid expression, borrowing time. You can't give time back after you've taken it. You can give some of your own away, but you can't give someone else's back to them. It's like death, time is. Only two constants there are for us. Two sides of the same coin. Both of them take, they force you to take, then they go and go and go. There's no end to them.

It's all just middle. So much of existence is just middle. When all we really care about is how it starts and how it ends, why does the biggest part seem to mean the least?

What the bloody hell am I thinking about right now?

Bring back the screams, I swear to fuck. It's just so much better than anything else my brain has to say for itself.

Fresh grief makes me think like an indie pop music video, Jesus Christ.

I'm so tired. So fucking tired. Too bad I'm not ever gonna sleep again. Real shame, that, and just when I was starting to think about going semi-pro. And I was so young and had such promise.

"Agent Nova," Snow says for roughly the seventeenth time since I came storming into her office with the intention of being not at all reasonable for the duration of our impromptu meeting. Why I expected Snow to put up with that for more than two minutes is beyond my current understanding.

There's admonishment in Snow's voice now. She's chiding me. I'm not sure what for. It can't be bringing up Damon's death, because she took the first swing at that dead horse. Unless this is Snow's version of irrational grief. I hope not. I barely have the patience for my own bullshit. I'm not capable of the subtlety and intelligence it would take to help Snow unpick and restitch her own reaction to Damon and Roux's death.

I loosen my grip on the chair, only to realise I've bent the frame without meaning to. There are now two indents in the chair back, the metal beneath crushed by my twitching fingers. The fact that I did it so unconsciously should indicate the necessity of a strategic retreat from this possibly destabilising situation.

It would be smarter, and possibly safer, to leave now. I can come back and do this when I'm not so close to the knife edge as to be slowly cutting into my Achilles with every slip and swing of my temper. There's no rush. It's not like Snow is going to evaporate by tomorrow.

But since when did I start making sensible life decisions? Tonight does not seem like the time to start bettering myself. This decade doesn't seem like a good time.

Decade. I'm twenty years old. I'll be dead in six years, max. This thing, this blood inside my body will kill me.

More importantly it will kill my friends. Caleb. Mei. Tate. I still need to tell them.

After I did what I did outside the factory, I booked it out of there before anyone could reach me. I got in one of the vans, keys left conveniently in the ignition, and drove away from the scene of every crime I'm going to spend my life running from.

I had to go. I had to. Jamie and Steivater were looking ready to roll right over to me and...

I'm not sure what they were planning to do.

They can't have been meaning to comfort me, help me. There's no helping someone who...

I mean.

I stood there on that pavement, Damon and Roux dead at my feet, Mia murdered by my hand less than twenty feet away, my not-so-secret-any-more secret sister glaring at me like I'd just invented genocide and cancer and global warming in the same breath. She was looking at me like I just started a war.

How do you help someone who lost what I lost and took what I took? Time. Time and time and time and fuck-ing murder and I'm just still right there. Right there with the fire and the teeth and the screaming yelling scream-ing. I'm there. On the floor. He was...

I was...

I was there, clothes slashed and ruined all to shit, covered in my dried blood, fingers still smeared with Da-mon's.

Even now, there are still traces of black on my finger pads, faded into the skin like ink from an exploded biro.

Caleb used to chew biros in school. The number of

times I had to steer him towards the bathroom and help him clean up after biting too hard on the plastic and getting a mouthful of black or blue ink is ridiculous. It used to make him look like he'd been punched in the side of the mouth.

I rub at the black on my left thumb. Damon's blood is under my nails, tarred into the creases between the nail and skin. Or it could be mine. Our blood looks the same. Jet black. Poison, it is. That's what Mia told us. She said...

Well.

She said a lot of things.

"You knew," I say, not computing that it was me who spoke until I realise who that dead dead dead can't find a chord to land on dead voice belongs to.

It's quiet. It's threatening. It's surer than I have any right to be. Surer than this life has taught me I deserve.

But there's no point asking Snow any more questions. I know the answer. I've known the answer since Mia told me about what Liquid Onyx was going to do and the idea first touched my mind. Like the prick of a thorn to a thumb, or a vine causing ripple rings in a pool of water. Slow and silent, but out of my control all the same.

I didn't dwell on it because there was no time. There was too much background noise to allow for a burst of clear sound to be properly heard.

What makes it worse is that Snow doesn't even feign innocence. She just goes on looking at me, like time and death themselves, exactly how she was before. As if this changes nothing.

Although, I suppose, in some ways it doesn't. Nothing has actually changed for the Liquid Onyx survivors.

What's going to happen wasn't altered by tonight's events; we already knew how it started. What we are was decided for us a long time ago. The only difference now is that we know how it ends. All that middle has done is become pure diamond in its clarity. The game is not on. Cancelled. Solved in the first five minutes. Everyone can put on their coats and take off their hats and piss off home.

Snow does me the courtesy of not pointing out how irrelevant and insipid my declaration of knowledge is. She's being downright nice to me during this not-meeting, so far anyway, and it's unnerving in the extreme.

We can't have Director Anabelle Snow falling apart over my dead uncle-dad and my boyfriend of at least five whole minutes. I can be fucked, but she can't be fucked. I almost died tonight. I earned the right to be fucked out of my mind for the next few hours.

"You are very upset, agent," Snow reminds me, because I almost forgot just then in my indignation over which of the two of us gets to be more fucked up right now. "You're upset, and understandably so," she concedes, which is a big thing for her. She doesn't usually do that unless I have a proper reason for disregarding the invisible wall of respect her position and demeanour and overall badassery demands, which is arguably not the case here. Snow didn't kill anyone. I'm not sure why I should be so upset with her.

Yeah, she didn't tell us about Liquid Onyx. That it's poison. That it would kill us all eventually.

But why would she? Why would she tell us anything? Of all the adults who have known me since childhood, she's the one who owes me the least.

Maybe she owed Damon something, but he's dead. He's dead, so...

I mean. He's just. He's...

He's fucking dead.

"But you need to stop this, Agent Nova," Snow tells me, a sternness to her tone, borders lining up either side of the words, bracketing them in.

She leans forward, blatantly ignoring the bent chair set before her as evidence of my instability.

"Nothing you've seen or done or learned tonight changes the fundamental truths of who and what you are."

I have never, in my life, heard such a grand, family-sized packet of absolute crap.

"Has it affected anyone you know?"

We can both ignore things, look. Look at that. Go us. Snow and Nova, taking the world by static blink and grinding bone.

Snow doesn't want to let me ignore her; I can see that in how she purses her mouth ever so slightly. This insubordination, at any other time, would result in an immediate ice stare of impending doom. I've been on the receiving end of it enough times to know. But she concerns me once again by taking my lead and allowing me to evade her. It's like watching a snake play mother to a gerbil. Inherently wrong.

She's wearing a pink dress today, and gold jewellery. Not modest and thin jewellery either, but chunky stuff that you only ever get in either Claire's Accessories or Cartier. No money or fuck-off money. Her dark hair is twisted up into a sleek, fancy bun. She looks like a fashion mogul who sidelines as a warlord.

"Yes." Snow leans back in her chair, keeping her hands where they are on the desk. "There have been incidents and fatalities, both to the public and the Liquid Onyx survivors who began to deteriorate."

She's not even being cryptic. It's a travesty of monumental consequence. Next thing you know she'll be squeezing my arm and making me tea. I can't deal with that level of madness tonight; it would be too much.

"Did they die, or did you finish it before that could happen?" I ask, absently wondering which option makes me want to retch less.

Snow does not hesitate to respond, despite the ominous warning in my voice.

"I did not allow the situation to escalate." She doesn't go into detail on what that really means, but she doesn't have to.

I absorb the hit with a minimal amount of collateral damage, if only because there's so much wreckage already, crumbling and breaking apart, turning to dusty and mottled emotion.

Fighting the urge to pick up that mangled chair and throw it against the wall with every bit of force I can muster, which would be a considerable amount right now, I close my eyes and take a moment to parse and accept the implication of Snow's brutal truth.

Of course, that had to be the answer, because otherwise I would have heard something about rogue superhumans running around killing people. The media would have blown up with excitement. The internet would have swallowed it whole and choked it back out again and again. For at least a week, maybe.

If the Liquid Onyx survivors started going publicly insane and murderous, it'd be Diane Foxley's dream come true. Her superheroes-hating book would have suddenly become bestseller material, more so than it already is.

When it comes right down to it, the simple, honest, malicious truth of us is that we love to hate things. We thrive on hating the things we fear most.

Nothing pure is entirely real and nothing corrupt is entirely a lie. That is what we are. Purity and corruption. Reality and lies.

Get my poetry journal back out, people, we're writing some lines. I need a stool and a turtleneck. Make it happen or we're all just going to look ridiculous out here.

Jesus, fuck. My brain is wired all to shit, like I've sparked the wrong nerve, sent every synapse firing in multiple directions, like a machine gun spraying light. On a good day my brain is one of those static orbs. Now it feels like I've turned the fucking thing into a nail bomb, glass and shrapnel erupting from within, an internal attack set up, planned and executed by me.

What am I doing? What am I even doing here?

"Agent Nova. Listen to me." Snow looks mildly alarmed now, which is at once gratifying and disappointing. I thought she had more metal in her than this. I haven't even punched a wall yet. Maybe I should, just to make her feel better, to give her justification, to stem the flow of embarrassment we'll both feel over it later.

"You lied," I say, swallowing the spit in my mouth. There isn't much. My throat is dry. Dry like rusty iron or sand turned to rock. It hurts to swallow. But that's good.

I need pain I can actually do something about later. It's gonna make me feel like I'm being proactive. Anything that will distract me from walking into traffic as soon as I leave the base has got to be worth suffering through some relief over.

"I did not lie to you," Snow refutes, getting some of her defences back into place. She can't feel sorry for me forever. I hope not anyway. That's going to get irritating. "I withheld the truth."

I'm beyond amused that she does not even attempt to elaborate. She doesn't explain the way almost anyone else would feel compelled to. I respect her so much it's insane.

But she's wrong, so I need to correct that.

"No. I'm not talking about the Liquid Onyx is Very Exceptionally Bad and We're All Going to Go mental and Then Die thing. I get why you hid that shit from me."

Of course, I understand why she hid it. What would be the point in telling me, from her perspective? She probably thought I'd just get all dramatic about it, which is a fair cop because I am getting very dramatic about it. I will most likely continue to be dramatic about it until my blood robs me of my sanity and kills me.

I let go of the chair and move backwards, closer to the door. Snow's pale eyes dart to it for a second, like she thinks I'm going to make some sort of grand escape attempt. Would I need to escape? Is there where we're at now? Am I someone who would have to escape from her? From FISA?

We've come full circle. Here we are. Another Nova in need of redemption they don't deserve, standing in front of Director Snow. Except I'm not asking for anything from her. There's nothing I want that she could reasonably give me. Nothing she could take away that would matter if I decided to keep it. My freedom. My life. My soul, if such a thing exists, has already been given away. Thrown up into the air along with all the fire and smoke of that factory I destroyed.

Snow is making another one of those placid-but-not faces at me. Since I am not quite as respectable, I do explain. "I meant you lied about not letting the situation escalate. You did."

Snow blinks slowly, once, then twice, then three times. I think she's about as close to flummoxed as she would ever allow.

"Agent Nova, what do you mea—"

"You let us live." I scowl mockingly at her. "Not very on-brand of you, director. Never would have thought you'd be the bleeding-heart type. The rip out and stomp on type, sure. I mean we've all had that nightmare about you. But this. Letting us all live? Why the hell did you do that?"

Snow looks momentarily stunned. Her mouth purses into a little moue, and I can tell she's getting pissed off. I'm glad. It's the sort of relief I can grab on to and yank until it's all used up and I can boast the energy of a man who has gained himself the materials for a toilet paper mummy costume.

When Snow doesn't respond in a timely fucking manner, I keep on trucking.

"If you say your reason is because it would be morally wrong to kill us, then I will laugh. I will die laughing right here in your office, and no one wants that. Think of the cleaning staff. Think of them and their probable sensibilities. Why do you want to ruin someone's Wednesday like that? And I don't want to go to the morgue, anyway. Damon and Roux are gonna be there, and I've had enough of them for tonight, thanks."

Snow appears to collect herself, like a band has snapped back into place against someone's wrist. I can almost hear it twang. I can feel the echoing sting of it.

"Most of you are heroes," she says, cold and efficient with her little white lies.

I shake my head, brows drawn together, dismissing her words like they're flies buzzing in front of my face.

"We're a danger to the public. By letting us roam around freely, you're putting innocent people at risk. Why? Why would you do something so reckless?"

Snow's jaw tightens almost imperceptibly. But I'm watching her closely, so I see it. She stands up without warning and moves around her desk. She doesn't come at me, but an edge to her posture suggests she might want to.

She leans against the front of her desk, crossing her arms and presenting me with a truly magnificent wall of resolve on her face.

"I let him—" She stops, pauses like she's taking a run at an impossibly high jump.

I can't imagine Snow ever jumping. She'd break the heel of her black business stilettos right off. Or not. How sturdy are those things supposed to be? I also can't imagine Snow wearing anything easily breakable.

Snow catches my attention again when she says, "His father was my best friend." There's no doubt in who she means. Aaron North. Damon's father. The father he watched die. The father my father killed.

Snow tightens her arms around herself and releases a less than steady breath. She looks right at me. I wish she wouldn't. Not for this.

"I let my best friend's son damage and distort himself for my benefit." There's no hint of reprieve or regret in her voice. "I let that boy go out into the world and become what he was. I let him think being a hero was all he could ever be that would matter."

Snow looks away, finally. She looks away and it's not nearly enough distance to hide, to pretend not to see, not to feel this shame we can't help but share.

"I thought he was owed something for that," she says, quiet but sure. "I thought I owed Aaron his son's life. I thought I owed Damon North a whole lot more than he ever got."

And isn't that the ultimate bloody truth of all our lives.

Before, my mind was in a frenzy of emotions and colours, red rage and blue guilt and yellow fear, all of it churning in together, mixing like paint.

Now, it's one solid mass. One terrible, lifeless mound of nothing.

It's just a whole lot of grey.

"Yeah, well." I turn slightly to grab hold of the door handle, ready for my impending exit. "Guess that's one less thing you have to worry about now." I look away from Snow and wheeze out a laugh so strained it physically hurts. "You're fucking welcome."

*

Rohan Sathe's flat isn't just a flat, it's a top floor, fully kitted out penthouse. Larger altogether than some people's actual fucking houses.

Rohan's massive flat is open plan and very modern in design. He has white marble kitchen counters and sleek, silver appliances. His walls are all white and the furniture is a mixture of cream and dark wood. The leather sofa is bent around the living room like a coiled snake and probably cost more than six months' worth of pay cheques.

His flat opens onto the roof, where he has a large patio area. It's like an over-the-top garden centre display with its dark-grey slates, white pebbles, and plants which don't look native to England. I don't think they do anyway. But I'm not exactly a foliage expert. Green would know. She'd probably lose her mind over it, like she was wandering around a museum for plants.

Do they have museums for plants? Probably. Green is unlikely to be alone in her enthusiasm, bordering on obsession, for the flora and herbage of this world. I bet there are even fan sites where people gather to gush over flowers like some people do with fictional characters. The flower fans would have online names like cactuslicker98 and daisymerollin' and youhadmeataloe and putthepetaltothemetal and yes, I did spend one sleepless night scrolling through flower chatrooms from the early 2000s. Green, when I talked to her about them during our last phone conversation, agrees with me that the best online name of the lot was stoptryingtomakevetchhappen. For obvious reasons.

I am so tired.

When Rohan first showed me where he lived, I almost got right back into the private lift he'd hustled me into and absconded on principle. It was just too ridiculous, exuberant in the extreme and not at all what I expected from him.

His flat is so—I don't know. Fancy? Ornate? Boring as shit? Yeah, that one.

Rohan always struck me as being rather eccentric in his preferences, as indicated by his choice of workwear and the decor of his evil laboratory on base. I'd sooner have believed he lived in a house made entirely out of Lego than in this lavish child-unfriendly hotel suite.

But when I voiced this to Rohan, he just said it was what he felt used to and he doesn't care enough about where he lives to change anything. To be fair to him, he's barely ever at home. He spends a good deal of his life at work, although less so now that I'm living with him. He pretends to come home because he's stressed out and in need of my company to relax him, which is obviously bullshit.

I am many things. Soothing to be around ain't one of them.

I think he just comes home early to make sure I haven't killed myself by abseiling down the side of his building using bed sheets. Or accidentally offended the fridge and made it shoot balls of ice at me again. Or met his neighbours and talked to them. Rohan told me I'm not allowed to do that last one ever again, because now people think it's okay to talk to *him* and he spent years building up his reputation as a mysterious, standoffish techno-logical genius who could buy and sell all of them and might hack into their shit and ruin their lives on a whim.

Whatever Rohan might say, I only did the bed sheet thing once. Possibly twice. Okay, three times, but I was drunk for the last one and don't remember it, so it's like it didn't even happen.

Rohan would argue that, but only because he's a grumpy chicken about recreational peril. He prefers his peril to be government sanctioned and technically legal. I don't know why. Personally, I think getting permission for your mayhem takes half the fun out of it.

As soon as we got home, Rohan demanded I hand over the USB stick. I forced him to say please, just because his arrogant little rich boy behaviour needs to be challenged occasionally, and I'm the only person who Rohan likes enough not to ignore outright. He doesn't like it when I call him out on his pretentious shit, but *I* don't like that he confiscated all my bed sheets like I'm a prisoner who's been put on suicide watch.

So. You know. What is a friendship without pockets of resentment and casual vengeance sewn into it? You have someone who's nice to you all the time and pretends your flaws don't exist; that's called an acquaintance.

My stand for the integrity and ethical necessity of politeness led to, no shit, a three-minute-long staring contest. I won, obviously, as I'm the one with the specialist training in that area. I had the clear advantage due to my prior well-worn experience.

Rohan kept trying not to blink by squinting, which is bad form and a cheater's gambit, but I allowed it. His surrender was made all the sweeter for his lack of honour in battle.

Once I'd finally given him the USB stick, Rohan snatched it from me like a peeved seagull swooping down to steal an ice cream cone. There was so much pissy hedgehog energy in how he stomped gracefully away.

I didn't know it was possible to stomp like a ballerina until I genuinely annoyed Rohan for the first time. I'm nothing but impressed by his elegant stomping ability, which I presume he learned on some uber-rich person training course. I mean they must have those. People don't just go around flouncing like irate feather dusters naturally.

Rohan took the USB stick into the living room, along with his computer, and set himself up at the coffee table, sitting on the ground because the sofa is too far away and Rohan, I have learned, does not like to lift or drag things. He's not OCD about his stuff, or where it gets placed in his flat. It's more like the idea of doing something as simple as moving a table closer to the sofa doesn't occur to him as a possible option for resolving a problem.

Sometimes it seems to me Rohan refuses to entertain mundane courses of action on principle. It's like his brain is too full of complex ideas and more important thoughts to bother with simple logic.

I didn't used to think the whole "super smart person ignores the obvious solution" thing was real, but apparently it is. For Rohan, anyway.

While Rohan goes about plugging the USB stick into his laptop and bringing up the information I downloaded onto it earlier tonight, I go into the kitchen to make possibly the bravest decision of the night by taking my chances with Rohan's ridiculously fancy coffee machine.

I'm pretty sure it's formed some sort of alliance with the fridge to aid it in its vendetta against me. No matter what I do, every time I try to use it, the bastard thing randomly fires scalding hot water into my face, with what I would describe as *sadistic glee.*

I'm almost certain Rohan finagled his super high-tech fridge into hating me, somehow. The door never opens for me the first dozen times I pull on it, but it will open easily for Rohan. As mentioned before, it has fired ice balls at me on numerous occasions, and I have no idea how this would even be possible, but sometimes I'll put food or drinks into the fridge, and it will purposefully turn off the chill on my side.

Rohan thinks I'm going mental, but I swear to you it's true. He says it would be impossible for him to do what I'm accusing him of, which is rubbish. We live in a world with superheroes and platypuses and the other day, Rohan and I had a Jurassic Park franchise marathon and there's a scene in one of the newer films where someone not only tried to but ultimately succeeded in running away from a Tyrannosaurus rex in *high heels.* My suspension of disbelief has been fucking tested, all right.

I make Rohan his favourite nutmeg coffee bullshit drink, managing to get away with only second degree burns to my corneas, and grab myself a beer from the fridge. I sit down close to Rohan on the floor so that I'm able to see the laptop screen.

Rohan takes his spicy swill from me and keeps using his laptop with nimble, quick movements of one hand.

I thumb off the metal cap of my beer bottle and let it ping off to land on the dark wood coffee table. It bounces obnoxiously across the table before coming to a stop just about dead centre.

After swallowing down a mouthful of beer, I jerk my chin at the laptop screen and ask, "Are you finally going to tell me what's in the super-secret file I almost took a bullet to the face for?"

Rohan doesn't answer me at first, attention rapt on the screen in front of him. He opens the file and documents full of notes appear on the screen one after another, pages and pages of them. Rohan clicks through them, most likely to verify this is what he's been searching for.

Just by watching how his expression changes, from creased into a pensive frown to smoothed out in grim elation, I can guess this file contains the data he was hoping to find, which is a relief. Not that I minded blowing up yet another OI facility, but Rohan and I have been chasing down this CTRL file for over a month. Our hunt had begun to feel a bit like a fool's errand, at best, and a blatant misdirect to distract us at worst.

"I didn't tell you what it was before because I wasn't certain the CTRL project really existed, and if it didn't exist, then what the file allegedly contained wouldn't be relevant anyway." Rohan answers me without looking away from the laptop screen, because apparently, he took lessons from Snow on how to be enigmatic and unhelpful.

I stare hard at the side of Rohan's head, willing him to look at me and prove marginally less of a challenge to my patience.

"Well, that was a whole load of nothing. Are you trying to *evade* my question, you manipulative shrew? I hope not, because it was a really shit attempt if so, and I don't want to be mates with someone who can't effectively misdirect." I scowl at him in exaggerated disappointment.

Rohan lets out an unimpressed snort, eyes still fixed on the screen as he reads through the barely comprehensible pages of information. It all looks like gibberish to me. Just random equations followed by squiggled notes in red ink. I'm about ninety percent sure these documents were written up by a spider with a concussion.

"There are high fucking standards for being your mate," Rohan complains to me.

I take another drink from my beer bottle and put it down on the floor beside me. Ten to one I'll be accidentally knocking it over with my leg or arse later. Put your bets in now and you might win yourselves a free moment of smugness that it wasn't you who did the embarrassing, clumsy thing.

"That's because I have faith in you and your ability to friend correctly."

Rohan does look away from the screen then and eyes me with an underserved amount of condemnation.

"I think you mean I'm one of the few human beings who will put up with you and your bullshit on a daily basis."

"I mean. Yes. That is one hundred percent correct, Holmes. Your attention to detail is truly one to be revered. Now answer my bloody question before I take the nutmeg gravy back to the kitchen and pour it down the sink."

I make to reach for his purple and white striped mug and Rohan bats my hand away with a viciousness rarely seen outside of a tiger attack.

"You leave my coffee and my sink alone. You've made

enough enemies in my home as it is."

I offer up an unsettling grin as Rohan draws his mug further away from me and hunches over it protectively, shooting mistrustful glances at me.

"Are you one of them?" I ask acerbically, raising both my eyebrows. "An enemy of mine."

Rohan blows air out of his nose, considering the question with all the gravitas of a mouse deciding whether to go after a bit of cheese sitting on a trap.

"If you touch my coffee then you might get to see the beginning of my villain origin story."

That's probably an accurate supposition for him to make. He's a right crack addict about his coffee.

Last week I bought some Nescafé to replace his fancy Black Ivory coffee, which sounds like it's made of elephant tusk and privilege dust. When Rohan found it in the cupboard, he looked at me like I'd just confessed to having sex with his mother and told me to, "Remove this abominable box of gravel from my home immediately or face the consequences."

It was an easy decision to make, since I had a sneaking suspicion Rohan's idea of consequences would involve him siccing his legion of advanced tech on my person. At this point in my vigilante career, I've faced many things, but even I have limits. I don't want to get my fingers broken by the microwave door or have my face burned off by the kettle or find out how the electric shower rates my singing voice.

Rohan does the thing where he gets bored with a conversation and completely changes the topic midway through, then acts as if that was the conversation we were having all along.

He nods at the laptop screen. "Do you remember when we talked about those blue and purple drugs that Obsidian Inc created?" he asks.

I don't have to cast my mind back to remember. That chilling revelation left its mark on my memory well enough. I dip my head in a nod at Rohan.

"Okay, well, OI have found a way to turn the blue drug, the one that puts you under chemical compulsion, into a gas. These files"—he pulls up a page on the screen with a sketch of some sort of metal contraption that looks like a cross between a very large canon and a telescope—"contain the plans to build a machine that will allow them to shoot the mind control drug up into the atmosphere, allowing it to disperse over the world, therefore infecting the oxygen supply and taking control of everyone who inhales it."

What the... What the bloody hell? Obsidian Inc have been doing *what*?

Rohan's information dump is insane enough to cause me to need a mental pause to re-orientate myself in this new reality I've been drop-kicked into.

I sit back against the sofa and pick my drink back up. The bottle is still cool from being in the fridge, but I can barely feel it, like the skin of my fingers and palm has become calloused. I lift the beer bottle to my lips and drain the entire thing in one drawn-out swallowing event, keeping my head tipped back and my eyes closed as I fully digest what Rohan has just told me.

I only just manage to stave off a panic attack by biting the inside of my cheek hard enough to break skin. It's not the pain that distracts me. It's the blood. These days, it's always about the blood. My whole life revolves around that shit.

The torn flesh of my cheek leaks iron-tasting ink into my mouth. A flood of blackness spreads across my tongue and between my teeth. I swallow it, despite wanting to spit the vile substance out with every fibre of my being. There's a hatefulness in me that I have to admit I've always had, but in the last few months it has grown into something I find almost impossible to ignore.

It's visceral, this feeling. There's so much of me I want out. Bled out. Beaten out. Fucked out. Just gone. To be flayed and cut. To have it all scraped and yanked from me like the skin and bones of a hunted animal.

My blood doesn't taste any different than normal. No more venomous than before.

I keep thinking, one day, I'll get hit in the face or bite my cheek and the blood will spill over my tastebuds and I'll taste something else. Something new. A tinge of rot. And that will be when I know my blood is going to kill me.

It's a stupid thought. I already know my blood is going to kill me. I think I might have known even before Mia Solar told me outright. I think it's been there, in the back of my mind, the idea that no one gets to survive what was done to us. Not forever. There had to be a catch.

It was all too easy, even though it really wasn't.

Now I know the debt we owe for the time we were given. It's a debt none of us signed on for. But it's one we will all have to pay.

I wish, more than I've ever wished anything in my

life, that I could pay it for them. For the people I love. For the dozens of Liquid Onyx survivors who thought the worst was over.

But I can't. I can't fix this. I can't make it right.

I'll never be able to make any of this okay.

I'll never…

I'll never be…

When Roux and Damon died, I didn't wish them back to life. I didn't wish I could have saved them. I didn't wish I could fix the mistake the universe made when it let them die. When I let them die right in front of me, like my mum, fifteen years before.

I didn't wish for those things, because it would have been too hard to be denied them. Some things, it turns out, are too important to waste on hope.

Rohan allows my temporary loss of composure to go unremarked, as he's allowed it many other times since I moved in with him.

At this point, I think Rohan has seen the very worst of me, which is an odd thing to live with. It's strange, when you've peeled back the veil of civility and bared your true face to someone. Once done it cannot be undone. You can't staple the mask back on. You can't regrow that second skin thick enough for the other person not to see through it, to make them believe it's what is real.

There's both fear and freedom in not being able to hide who you are, and I can't rightly say if the second is worth the depth and frequency of the first.

I lean forward again, fixing my eyes on the coffee table so I won't have to look at Rohan. It's a pointless act of cowardice.

Rohan and I differ in many ways, but there are things we share. I don't have the monopoly on shit fathers and guilt carved in so deep it scratches jagged patterns into bone.

By all rights, neither of us should be concealing our reactive weakness about what OI have done. But I don't need to be looking at Rohan to know he'll be wearing his indifference like a shield and sword and armoured helmet in one.

We've agreed, unspoken, to pretend as if the veil was never ripped away by either of us. We act like we see brick when what we really see is glass.

If Jamie were here, he'd probably try to coax me into talking about things, just like he's always had a knack for doing. If Caleb were here, he'd demand that I talk about my stupid feelings, as he is contractually obliged to as my best friend for forever. Neither of them would let me get away with pretending to be cool, not for long anyway, the couple of pushy Moon bros that they are.

Rohan never makes me talk about anything, either because he doesn't care or because he already knows the answer, so why would he ask me to explain it out loud?

Did you know some people have respect for personal boundaries? It's bloody wild.

"Have they actually built the machine yet, or are they still in the planning stages?" I ask, keeping my voice level, somehow.

I'd much rather yell. But Rohan doesn't like yelling. He's never said so, but the few times I've raised my voice around him he's got this weird, depleted look on his face.

It reminds me of a broken horse, too tired to even be wary of the next kick. You can't fight someone who's resigned themselves to losing and come out of it not looking like the arsehole, even if you were absolutely right to take up arms in the first place.

"They haven't built it yet," Rohan says. "It won't work with how it is now. I can see where they've gone wrong. Or at least I will be able to once I have a chance to properly read through all of this."

"Is this the only copy of this file? Do you think they can recreate it?" I ask.

Rohan shrugs, his shoulder casually bumping mine. He jerks away from the touch, and I shuffle to the side to create some distance between us. Rohan still has proximity issues. He lets me get closer than he does most other people, though, and I take that as a good sign for how much trust he has in me. Not everyone is as cuddly as Tate, and that's okay.

It's possible no one is as cuddly as Tate, and it really annoys me how much I miss him and his inappropriately long hugs.

Rohan's brow furrows in thought. I'd say it's likely he's considering whether to answer honestly.

"As far as my intel goes, this is the only copy. And those scientists you've killed on our previous missions..." He allows me to fill in the obvious blanks.

"They were the ones working on the schematics for the machine," I say.

Rohan looks grimly satisfied by my deduction. "OI will have to start from scratch."

I don't prod at Rohan to cough up more details. Part

of me feels like I should be pissed that he manipulated me into killing people for reasons he didn't tell me about, but a much larger part of me is just glad no one is left to help OI build a machine that could devastate billions of people.

Snow was almost certainly the one who endorsed this plan to steal the CTRL file from OI. She would also have told Rohan not to divulge any more details to me than was strictly necessary.

Rohan is still a FISA agent. Our partnership has only worked so far because we've both respected the line between professional courtesy and divulging private information about the separate parts of our lives. Rohan doesn't ask me about my patrols, and all the highly illegal things I've been doing over the last few months. I don't ask Rohan about FISA business, most of which no longer concerns me.

At Rohan's pointed silence, I take the hint and get up off the floor, taking my empty beer bottle with me. He doesn't react other than to briefly flicker his eyes up to me and away again, dismissing me from his focus.

I wander into the kitchen and drop the beer bottle in the recycling bin. Rohan is a stickler for recycling. We are a mostly plastic-free household. Rohan is very much on the side of "we are all going to fucking die" when it comes to the global warming debate. I'm pretty sure he's more worried about greenhouse gases than he is dying via Liquid Onyx poisoning.

My hands begin twitching with unspent energy, the rush of a completed mission having completely drained out of my body.

Since Rohan no longer needs me, I can get on with

the other plans I had for tonight.

"I'm going back out, all right?" I call over to him.

It's not really a question, but I can't just leave. Rohan will notice I'm gone later, and he'll worry. The last time I left for a patrol without telling him, Rohan donned the suit he rarely uses and came after me. He hacked into every camera in the city, which there are a lot more of than you'd think, and used them to track me down. He was very huffy about it when he found me breaking up a deal gone south between a couple of arms dealers, one of who was looking to make a move into the city.

Rohan surprises me by actually acknowledging my existence. I thought he'd just ignore me, and I could slip out easily. He looks over his shoulder, catching my gaze across the back of the sofa. His eyes flick up and down my body with a strange kind of consideration on his face. It's oddly clinical, but not unfamiliar for Rohan.

His choice of response, however, is just bloody bizarre, even for him.

"You wanna fuck?"

Like, *why*? I almost choke on my own spit, and it's been a while since that happened. I like to think I'm fairly unshockable these days. But no. Apparently, I'm still an innocent little foal, stumbling around on my shaky stick-legs, when it comes to dealing with Rohan and the randomness of his brain. He can be so deadpan sometimes that it breaks my sensibilities down to crumbs.

I spend a few seconds blinking owlishly at him. He isn't joking, though. Rohan doesn't joke like that. He is dead serious right now, his voice on the level and his gaze holding steady.

Rohan catches my disbelief and does an impressive job of letting me know he would be rolling his eyes if he were a slightly less dignified man than he is.

"Just because I'm not sexually attracted to you doesn't mean that we can't fuck," he says, like the laws of genteel conversation mean less than nothing to him. Then he keeps on going, because I haven't suffered nearly enough for threatening his coffee consumption earlier. Rohan is a vengeful man, take note. Rules of life: Book to a party. Thesaurus to an interrogation. Don't eff with the borderline evil scientist. *This is what we've learned today, kids.*

"The actual fucking part, I don't mind," Rohan tells me, and I'm very unhappy that this moment hasn't ended yet. "Seriously." He glances me over again critically. "You're my friend and you look like you need it and I'm not *not* in the mood, so..."

Just to be crystal, Rohan and I have never had sex before. We haven't even had what you might call a near miss. Apart from anything else, Rohan is not a casual-sex-having person.

Before now, Rohan has not once indicated he would be open to any physical intimacy that goes beyond a hug. We don't actually hug, of course. But you know what I mean. The hug would be the epitome of what we do together if it ever did happen.

I must look really bad for him to be willing to go this far out of his comfort zone. I know sex isn't something Rohan hates, or even necessarily dislikes depending on the circumstances. But it isn't something he needs in his life for the most part.

"Wow." I arch my eyebrows at him. "You know you should really consider jacking all this secret agent stuff in and going into the porn industry. You could write the scripts. 'Not *not* in the mood'. Fuck. Be still my aching cock."

"Think you mean, be still my beating heart." Rohan's tone is openly wry.

I smile wanly at him, crossing my arms over my hoodie-clad chest. To avoid notice for wearing blatant superhero suits, Rohan and I had clothes to dress in which would cover them.

We kept the bag of clothes in Rohan's car hangar, which is situated near Danger's private airport. It still hurts my brain that Rohan has his own car hangar. Does he have his own private jet? Also yes. I've always been very lucky with money growing up, especially in comparison to a lot of other people, but Rohan's wealth is just a little bit extra. I have difficulty wrapping my mind around it.

I still have my Wrath suit on underneath my street clothes, so I can just strip them off and leave them on a roof somewhere in the city where they'll be safe to return for later when I'm ready to go home.

"You keep talking dirty to me with things like, 'The actual fucking part, I don't mind', and I'll start beating something for you. Promise."

Rohan pretends to think about it, sticking his tongue out a little and catching it between his teeth. Then he shakes his head slowly and says, "Sounds sketch, but thanks."

For my own personal sense of revenge, I flip the conversation back to something more serious.

"I really look like I need it?" I ask, genuinely wondering what Rohan is seeing when he looks at me now.

Rohan pauses for a moment, taking time to find the right words. He takes in a long breath, then releases it in a loud gust.

"You look like you need something," he says finally, eyes sliding into a sad tilt. "I used to think, when you first moved in here, that I knew what it was. But now I know you better, I feel like I understand you a whole lot less."

That hits me like a very large brick to the chest. Just bowls me right the fuck over.

I'm not sure how to respond to all the realness in Rohan's statement. I don't think either of us is built to know how a conversation like this is supposed to go. Neither of us were made to act like well-adjusted human beings, mostly because the people who raised us weren't anywhere close to decent or functional themselves, although for different reasons.

"You get me." I correct him, because he does, even though he might not be able to see that, because I don't openly show it. "It's just that the mess of a person you're seeing right now is exactly who I am. There's no better version waiting to take over."

I hope not, anyway. One thing I can't take any more of is surprises about things going on inside me. For better or worse, this is the version of me I can handle right now. Just about.

Rohan doesn't argue or try to convince me I'm wrong

about myself. He rarely does. Not one for platitudes is Rohan, especially not empty ones he doesn't believe in.

I can see the moment he chooses to de-escalate the situation. Take us back to baseline and keep moving sideways from there.

"All right, fine. Go fight crime, save some squirrels from trees and toddlers from drugs, or whatever. And bring me back a bag of chips. I'm all heartbroken now because you rejected me. I need recompense."

Rohan has a very strange idea of what I do as Wrath. No matter how many times I try to explain what actually goes on during a patrol, he just looks at me like a blank wall made up of shrugs and the occasional squint.

"Recompense?" I ask, going along with the joke. "In the form of chips?"

"Yeah, there are emotional damages," Rohan says with mock sincerity. "Also get a battered sausage, please, if you really want to make it up to me."

I shake my head at him, blowing out a low whistle. "Blimey, you're one of those teases I've heard all those creepy straight boys talk about, aren't you?"

Rohan graces me with one of his rare, wicked grins, razor sharp and wolflike. "Throw in a cup of mushy peas and I'll be whatever you want me to be."

"No need." I scoff, half turning away from him, preparing to leave. "I'm weak enough for you as it is."

Rohan lets out a snort of laughter and twists back around to face the computer screen he briefly abandoned to not flirt with me.

I smile a little at the back of Rohan's head before turning fully and leaving the penthouse flat.

Chapter Three

Passive-Aggressive Mixology

Three Months Ago

Status update: Very not good.
Location: Hiding under a table in Rohan's lab.
Standard Time: What even is time really? Also, who cares, we are all going to die.

*

Rohan might not be a field agent, but he must have received some kind of formal stealth training in his life, because he manages to sneak up on me with alarming success. I don't hear him enter the lab or make it all the way to my not-so-secret hiding spot under one of his metal work tables.

Either he's just that skilled, or I'm even more out of it than I think I am, which would be equally impressive.

Rohan drops down onto one knee and peers under the table with an expression of dry nonchalance on his face, like finding me here, curled up under his table, is not a surprise to him in the least. I don't think that should be allowed. Legally, I mean. Surprise, or at least confusion, should be lawfully warranted in this situation. I do not like to think I've given Rohan the impression I'm just like this, so the fact I'm playing a one-sided game of hide and seek right now is simply to be expected.

"What are you doing in here?" Rohan asks after a significant pause where I absolutely fail to explain myself like any other person with a semblance of self-respect would.

I also feel called out once again that he asked why I'm in his lab, but not why I'm under a worktable, looking like shit and still wearing my bloodied clothes. I probably look like someone has been throwing black paint balloons at me all night. It's an oddly comical thing to imagine, considering the reason I'm stained by so much thick, black fluid.

It takes me a second to unwind my jaw enough to speak. I've been clenching it to the point of pain without fully realising it, grinding the gears till they got stuck.

"Hiding from the masses. Contemplating my place in this big 'ol universe." I flash a pilfered screwdriver at him. "Touching your shit."

Rohan arches his eyebrows at me contemplatively. He makes a solemn request. "Don't steal anything, please."

I offer him a two-finger salute in return, leaning back against a thick table leg and wrapping my arms loosely around myself. Lazily arrogant, taking up space that isn't mine just so I'll have something to defend. Faux casual, holding on, trying to keep the remnants of this adrenaline-fuelled emotion-denial going for as long as I can get away with. Won't last. Never does, never could, wouldn't want it to. But it's working for me right now, and I'm vaguely grateful for the reprieve, however short it might end up being.

"No worries, doc, your buttons are safe this day." I hold my hands up and make a show out of looking around me, then turn a wan smile on him. "I don't even have any paper for a ransom note."

Rohan purses his lips to the left and tips his head from side to side, as if he's trying to come up with a solution for my woeful lack of A4.

"Could send me a text."

"A ransom text?" I make a disgusted face at him, because wow, he deserves it. "Is that really what we've come to as a species? Just fucking kill me now."

There's a pause where Rohan shifts position, sitting down on the floor of his lab, legs crossed. He squints at me a little, then leans back on his hands. It's a surprisingly open gesture, his upper body pushed forward, shoulders bunched up near his jaw, chest folded out like a small, bent piece of cardboard.

With earth-shattering apathy, he asks, "That an honest request?"

Rohan's lab is quite small, but every inch of it is covered in tech and scientific equipment. Computers and laptops of multiple different sizes and shapes. Tools, from blow torches to screwdrivers to shit I don't have any clue about the intended use of. He has not one, not two, but three white boards, all of which are covered in symbols and numbers. I understand about five percent of it. As in, I understand what numbers are. I can even count. Right up to one hundred and everything.

I give Rohan a judgemental once-over, dragging my eyes across his body and face like I've got all the time in the world to assess every part of him I do not like and have no desire to play nice with.

"You wouldn't know honesty if it came up and tried to chomp out your jugular." I snort dismissively. "Bloody spy. Big, fat lying liar."

Rohan appears utterly non-plussed, which is annoying. It's also a bit of a relief. There are far too many people in my life who are confrontational bastards. Including myself. Rohan's seemingly unflappable façade is unique in that I don't actually know if it is a façade. Some people probably just have more natural chill. It's not impossible Rohan could be one of those mythical beings I've only ever heard tales of—the ones who don't like to fight for the sake of fighting. Someone who wants world peace and isn't afraid to walk the walk.

Now I'm just imagining Rohan in a tiara.

I think, upon rumination, he would look nice in a tiara. I won't tell him that. Don't want his ego to inflate too quickly. I'm not here to make people feel good about themselves. I'm here to have a mental breakdown. In slow motion. Because I'm too fucking tired to have one at a normal speed.

"I didn't lie." Rohan manages not to sound defensive about it.

I flicker my eyes down to his trousers. He's wearing actual trousers today, not pyjamas. They're black cargos, typical FISA issue. He's still wearing the Uggs, though. This time, however, one of the Uggs is grey, and the other is purple. He's mixed and matched his Uggs. Like only the very sane do.

"Tell that to your flaming pants," I say.

"Please don't say pants," Rohan pleads, crinkling his nose up at the word like it mortally offends him and every one of the fragile sensibilities he absolutely does not possess.

I offer up a few alternatives. For the sake of our friendship.

"Smoking briefs. Blazing boxers. Sizzling thongs."

Rohan nods along with each option, his mouth spreading into a conceited smile. When he replies, his tone is professionally wry. Someone should be giving out ribbons for this crap.

"Any of those would be much better, thank you."

I scoot forward, testing the boundaries. Rohan, predictably, leans back, putting the same amount of distance between us. He doesn't react in any other way, which means his reaction must be, at least in part, automatic. I wonder at it again. If there is a reason behind the response. An innocent one. A dark one.

"You ever wear a thong?" I ask off-handedly.

Rohan hits back with an equal amount of rapid-fire smoothness. "I don't wear anything."

A strained grin spreads across my own face. I can feel

the pressure of it in my facial muscles, the resistance. I force it out anyway, unheeding of my body's warnings. I'm not in the mood to listen to anything sensible right now.

"Well, this took a turn." I raise my eyebrows at Rohan. "You go commando in your pyjamas too?"

Rohan shrugs uncaringly, as if it's just that easy. "I don't like underwear."

I shake my head slowly at him, keeping my voice airy and light to combat the heavy darkness raging inside me. It wants out, but that's too bad, because I'm busy talking to Rohan about his pants, or lack thereof, I suppose. Any inner darkness yearning to be unleashed into the world around me is going to have to take a ticket and wait.

Because. Priorities. I got 'em.

"You don't wear thongs. You're a secret Liquid Onyx survivor." I blow out a breath, adding sarcastically, "Did I ever really know you?"

Rohan answers with a droll, "No, not really."

I should probably try to fix that. You know your friends. Or at least attempt to, as much as they'll let you. I'm not sure how much Rohan would be willing to give up. He's closed in, like a suitcase with a padlock.

Slightly off topic. But. What normal people are buying those? Like seriously, no one is trying to steal your Hawaiian shirts and tiny tubes of factor 50 sun lotion. And even if they do want your case that badly, they'll probably go to the effort of getting a big hammer to mash it open, so it's pointless anyway.

Not sure how long that's all been bothering me, but you know? I feel better having said it.

"Huh. Fair dos," I say, shrugging off Rohan's cavalier

respect for one of humanity's joint illusions of decency. "Is there anything else you want to confess in today's sharing circle?"

Rohan seems to think about it for a solid ten seconds, gaze darting off to the side, as if he's checking for anyone who might be listening in. He looks back at me, clear contemplation in his expression. It's like he's working himself up to telling me something or perhaps deciding once and for all if I can be trusted.

Whatever it was I thought he might say, it certainly wasn't, "My father is Ian Stone."

For perhaps the first time in the last half an hour, or maybe ever since I found out about the no pants thing, I am genuinely shocked by a new piece of information. Like, to my core, I am. Like. I mean... I... He... What the fuck? Excuse me.

Did he actually just say—

"Your father. Is. He... You... Your father is Ian Stone. Ian Stone. He's... I mean... Your father. Is Ian Stone. Ian Stone, Ian Stone?" I'm choking out the words like an idiot, but I can't help it. This. This is insane. What the fuck? No. Just. Like. It cannot be stressed enough. I just... I mean... What the fuck? "The evil director of the evil organisation Obsidian McEvil Inc. That Ian Stone?"

Rohan has the audacity to quirk one eyebrow and spew sarcasm at me, like that is in any way acceptable right now.

"No," he says. "The other one."

I could strangle this man. This person. This son of Ian Stone.

Holy shit, though. I mean, God.

I do not know what to do with this.

"Shove off." It takes everything I have not to tackle Rohan and demands answers with a lot less civility than I know he deserves. "How the hell did you end up working for FISA?"

Rohan doesn't appear impressed by the question. He's still leaning in what could be misconstrued as a relaxed pose. I'm starting to think I've been had. If Rohan is a Stone, my expectations for his ability to camouflage himself as something close to safe and trustworthy has gone up tenfold. You'd have to be one hell of a chameleon to have gone from living the life of a Stone heir to where Rohan is now, a scientist working for his father's rival.

You'd have to be one hell of an actor to appear even halfway sane after what that man must have done to Rohan.

Rohan is a Liquid Onyx survivor. His father let them do that to him. Encouraged it, maybe. What else did Ian Stone do to his son? Raise him to be an agent? Raise him to work for OI? Worst of all, raise him to take his father's place someday?

How has Rohan managed to come out of that life not being some kind of psychopath?

Jesus Christ, that must have been hell. Growing up and getting away. Both. Hell.

Rohan pierces me with a sardonic look and retaliates. "How did you, son of an evil scientist who worked for the evil organisation Obsidian McEvil Inc, end up working for FISA?"

Rohan is a lot of things, it turns out. He's a genius, the scientist who created the material used to make our super suits. He's Ian Stone's son. He's real fuckin' particular about his clothing choices. He's a Liquid Onyx survivor. He's a snarky arsehole. He's a nerd. He's a spy. He's my friend.

Doctor Rohan Sathe is all those things. But, when you get right down to it, only one of them matters to me.

"All right. Fine." I wave my hand in a vague dismissive gesture. "Don't want to give me your life story? Don't then. I do not care."

Rohan doesn't bother to hide the pungent smell of bullshit he's picked up on. "You care a bit."

"I care a fucking lot," I say emphatically. "But I'm also kind of distracted by some other stuff going on in my life. You might have heard about it on the string and cup gossip line or wherever it is you spies are getting your information these days. So, I'm willing to let your dramatic soap opera reveal go for now."

"Stuff going on?" Rohan parrots back at me calmly, his gaze raking me over with deliberate emphasise. "As in, what happened to your uncle?"

Inhale. Exhale.

Again. Again. Aga—

Nope, too hard. Breathing is... It's... It's too... It's. Hard. I can't. I...

He's. He's. He.

"Ah, forget that." I make a loud, somewhat manic scoffing sound. Who knew scoffs could be manic? Not me. Did you? New information for all of us, maybe. Add that in there with the sarcastic pained sounds Jamie is capable of in his general witchery.

"He's dead," I say with lethal sharpness, causing

blunt force trauma to the soul.

Rohan would probably respond to that, but I don't care to hear whatever his response would be.

Frowning at Rohan and dismissing everything else, I ask him, "Did you know Liquid Onyx was going to kill us all?"

Rohan hesitates for a moment, like he's considering an alternative route into the danger zone. But he seems to think better of it in record time, barely seeming divided on the decision to retreat. Maybe he doesn't care to hear what my response would be to his response.

Or perhaps he's just decided he doesn't have either the emotional willpower or the high-level psych degree required to deal with me in this state.

Either way. Smart choice. Smart man.

"I knew it was toxic, yeah. It was me who told Snow about what happened to Sara," Rohan answers honestly, and without any sort of apology in his tone for not revealing this information before. He's like Snow, strong and unyielding.

But he's better than her because Rohan never used my uncle and my—Damon—to kill people, to scare or inspire them.

Inspiration can be excruciatingly noxious when it's born from something so deeply repugnant as what Snow did to Damon. What she let happen to him. What Maddox wasn't there to stop. What we all allowed that ten-year-old boy to take on.

Rohan is better than her. Whatever his father made him do. It can't have been worse than what the supposed good guys did to Damon and Roux.

"So, it's real then?" I ask pointlessly. "You're sure?"

What is Rohan supposed to say here other than to confirm everything I've come to fear about myself. The violence. The anger. The hair-trigger of destruction. All of it.

"Yes," Rohan answers simply. Unforgiving. No mercy. Honest.

He's honest, and I hate him a little for it. I don't need a lie; it's too late for a lie. But I don't want the truth either. I never have.

"Well, fuck," I say on a huff of air. "We're all gonna die."

"Nah," Rohan protests. "First, we'll all go insane. Then we'll die."

Is that cruelty? Or is he just being ruthlessly honest again? Whichever it is, I like it. No one else is going to talk to me like Rohan is, I can guarantee that. Mostly because everyone else I know is at least somewhat well-adjusted.

Down here on the floor of Rohan's lab, though, it's just us. Sons of evil. Wordsmiths of the inappropriate and sociopathic. Satan's representatives. Ravana's brand ambassadors. Recovering mental healthaholic hopefuls. Fashion icons.

"Excellent." I clasp my hands together, squeezing too tight and shaking them in Rohan's direction. "Are we trying to solve this?"

"We aren't, no," Rohan replies drily. "I have been working on a solution for the past three years."

That is true. I've been doing sweet fuck all to solve this problem since I found out about it a few hours ago.

"And?" I prod.

"Nothing."

"So then," I say with acerbic enthusiasm, tipping my head at Rohan in a show of mocking inquiry, "we're all going to go insane and die?"

Rohan nods his confirmation. "Seems likely at this point."

Well. Okay.

No point getting excessively upset over our inevitable doom, is there?

"I need a drink. You got anything in here?" I move out from beneath the table, forcing Rohan to scramble backwards and get out of my way.

Once on my feet again, I look around, hoping for the random appearance of alcohol. Rohan doesn't seem like the type to have a secret stash of whiskey, or even a sneaky flask hidden in his Uggs. But I also didn't think he was the son of a master supervillain. So.

"Not in my lab, no." Rohan sounds somewhat apologetic. It's the first hint of regret he's expressed tonight.

"Then I'm going to leave your lab and go in search of an off licence." I start walking, or possibly half-staggering with how unsteady my legs feel, towards the exit.

Rohan chases after me at an offensively unhurried pace. Less chase then, and more idle wandering against his better judgement.

"You should lie down," he says once he's caught up to me at the door.

I had to wait for him.

"Oh shit, look, he gives advice now?" I say, turning back around, but keeping my eyes averted from Rohan's face, like I'm talking to someone else. "Doesn't wear thongs. Has no alcohol. Can't save us from insanity and death. But he's giving advice."

"I have alcohol." Rohan ignores everything else and focuses on the most important thing, like a real friend. "I just don't have it in the lab."

"Where?" I ask, hoping it's far away from the FISA base.

"At my flat."

Yes. Score one for hope. Tragedy is still up by ten points, but let's not be negative when we don't have to be.

"Am I invited to raid your secret cache of alcohol?"

Rohan lets out a bored sigh and nods his assent. He quickly adds, "As long as you lie down afterward. And have a shower. And change out of those bloody clothes. You look awful. People in my building will think I've kidnapped you from a crime scene at a printing press."

"You have yourself a deal," I say. Then, "Maybe." And then, "We'll see."

Rohan surprises me by not pushing the point. Or maybe I shouldn't be surprised by that, given how non-confrontational he's been thus far.

Before we leave his lab, I ask him another question that's been burning a candle inside my brain since I realised Rohan is like me. "What's your power?"

Rohan gives me his hardest stare yet, and says with no inflection, "When I touch people, I can make them feel extreme pain."

That is…that is sort of hilarious. If you're me. And a bit fucked. In the head.

"Raised by evil billionaire. Has pain powers. Is a genius scientist. Wow." I let out a strangled laugh, widening my eyes in disbelief at Rohan. "Exactly how many supervillain backstory clichés did you have to defy not to wind up cackling in a high-collared cape while you tried to take over the world?"

"Mate." Rohan sounds wearier than ever before. "Too many."

"Well, there's still time. You're not dead yet."

"Oh, go on, jinx it like a prick, then," Rohan says, but he sounds amused.

I lean my shoulder against the doorway and cross my arms, shooting Rohan a challenging look.

"What would your supervillain name be?" I pretend to really think about it. "Ouch Man? Lord of Pain? Torture Touch? Nope, aha, I've got it, Torture Tap!"

Rohan looks horrified. He says slowly, "I really hate that."

"I know. You're supposed to," I say in mock excitement. "The media would be all over it."

"Do not call me that." Rohan narrows his eyes at me. "Ever."

I look at him in dismay. "What? It's a great supervillain name."

"Yeah. Okay. Wrath." That same drollness flows through his words like boiling honey.

I flip Rohan off, and he looks at me with the smuggest grin imaginable.

I want to tell him I'm glad he's here. I want to tell him I know what it's like to live in the shadow of someone else's actions.

I want to tell him...

"Come on, let's go get so obliterated we'll forget about

our imminent insanity and deaths," I say.

Rohan's smug grin turns into a genuine smile.

"Now that," he says, "is a plan of action I can get behind."

*

I walk a few streets away from Rohan's apartment block before slipping into a side street and climbing up a building's drainpipe. It's a Chinese restaurant which has long since closed for the night.

Once on the roof, I scope out the area to make sure I won't be seen by anyone. When I'm sure I'll be all right, I strip out of my jeans, T-shirt, and hoodie, wrap up the clothing, and store it beside the metal chimney.

I pull up the hood of my suit, casting my face in shadow, and move across the roof to launch myself from the ledge onto the building beside the Chinese restaurant. On this street most of the buildings are of the same height, allowing me to move easily, with no need to return to ground level.

For pure self-indulgence purposes, I allow myself to enjoy the sprint and flying jump from roof to roof, adding in a few springboard flips just to make myself feel that little bit invincible. It's not real, that feeling of invincibility, but it gives me a rush unlike anything else. It reminds me of the Anti-hero concert, the first one in the park. When I was standing there with my friends and Damon, our arms looped around one another as we screamed lyrics into the night air. I had the same feeling of invulnerability in that moment.

Right before all hell broke loose and a load of people were murdered. Three of them by me.

I should probably be taking some kind of lesson from that experience, but for the life of me I can't figure out what the lesson would be. Don't be happy and carefree or you'll end up having to throw knives at people's faces so they won't frostbite you to death?

Sounds a bit specific, really.

It's hardly likely to happen twice, at least not in the exact same way.

When I get to the end of the street, I take a second to think about my next move. I have something which needs doing tonight, but I won't be in the mood to patrol afterwards, so I'll need to do that first.

Since Damon died, I've officially taken over his area of the city. It's not been an easy transition. People weren't completely untrusting of me, since I had been patrolling with Damon pretty consistently for months. But I'm not their hero, and they've made their feelings on having a far less experienced replacement unmistakably clear.

No one wanted to talk to me at first. Even people who used to tolerate me just fine when I was with Polaris seemed totally uninterested in continuing to develop the relationships we had tentatively started building. They shut me down and out cold, a clean, decisive cut of ties. Without Polaris, I was just another unknown entity in a city full of potential threats.

I didn't exactly blame them for it, especially considering the lack of information on how Polaris died. Damon. Damon died.

I think about that a lot. How he died as Damon, not

Polaris.

If he'd died as Polaris, everyone would know how it happened. They would have seen it on the news, probably. Polaris was most likely to die from battling some big bad out in the open, not in some dingy factory, on his knees on a dirty floor.

Polaris would have died loud and larger than life, because that's what heroes of his calibre do.

But Damon was just a man, a single person, and people die like they're no one every day. People have nothing deaths every day.

The reason for Damon's death was still a heroic one. Saving lives should always matter. But the actual death itself was…intimately brutal, not fit for televising, too dark for consumption, a level beyond R rated.

He didn't die how anyone would *want* a hero to die.

I can't help but think it would have been better if he died a Polaris death. Maybe it wouldn't have been better for Damon, because he'd be fucking dead either way and I've got it on good authority that dying is kind of shit no matter how it happens, but for the people of Danger.

My first port of call was to hit up every one of Damon's informants. They were too valuable to lose, as much as it pained me to be so bloody mercenary. I almost checked myself and backed away from more than one of them—the shame, deserved or not, was cloyingly thick. It felt a bit like stealing or taking credit for all of Damon's hard work. He spent a decade forming relationships with people that would last.

But Damon would have been so pissed if I abandoned his people without at least dropping in on them to make sure they were all right. He helped a lot of people through the years, more than I knew about, even after months of our working together, and they are still loyal to him. Damon, Polaris, was equally as loyal to them. For his sake, as well as theirs, I had to do the rounds.

Surprisingly, the people who accepted me the easiest were the friends of Sandra Clarke. I honestly thought they would be the most difficult to win over, their distrust for strangers running deep.

It's them I go to first tonight. I haven't seen the women in almost a fortnight, and I promised to stop by at least once a week to check in on them. I have a niggling suspicion they are pretending to need my help or protection just so they can do their own welfare check on me. Those women treated Polaris like a lost boy from Neverland who wandered onto the wrong pirate ship and got thrown overboard in the middle of Danger City one night. It tracks that they would feel similarly about me now they've decided to take me on.

The women mostly work on Sinners Street, which their leader told me was chosen on purpose because she appreciates irony. Her name is, as she told me, Luna Bell, which is about the fakest name ever. When I pointed this out to her, she just told me to *prove it, child*, and since I had no way or inclination to do that we came to an impasse. I also heard Roux's voice in my head, cackling over me, of all people, calling someone else's name fake-sounding. Sometimes I forget my full name is Rexley Xander Nova, and therefore I really shouldn't be lobbing rocks at anyone's exhibitionist house.

Luna Bell is somewhere between the ages of forty and

forty thousand years old. She's very small in stature and has biceps like an Olympic gymnast. It's entirely possible she was, at some point, an Olympic gymnast. I don't know. What kind of person just casually knows who was part of the Polish Olympic gymnastics team twenty years ago?

There are only two options with that one: either you're creepy or teeth-grindingly posh, dealer's choice. Easiest way to know is if, when you watched the Olympics for the first time as an adult, you heard the word "dressage" and didn't have to google what the fuck it was.

I made up the Polish part. Luna has traces of an accent, but I can't be certain. Jian taught all of us how to pick up on the different credence of quite a few accents, particularly those in Europe. But I'm definitely no expert. Mei was always the best at picking up languages and mimicking accents correctly, a fact Jian was very proud of.

Sinners Street is narrow, set between two rows of mostly vacant old, grey-stone buildings. The road itself is pock-marked with grooves and holes in the cement, the pavements on either side equally scuffed and flecked with bite marks. It looks dirty and well used, old and all but forgotten about. Except it isn't forgotten, not by the women who work here and certainly not by the people who use the service they provide.

Luna leans against a heavily graffitied wall when I arrive, her arms lightly crossed, pushing her breasts up and further emphasising her ample cleavage. When she sees me dropping down from a nearby roof, she gives me a brittle smile and a severely arched eyebrow. She seems to have been anticipating my arrival, which can't be possible since we have no schedule for any particular times or days, but Luna is one of those people who always seem to have a plan, even if everything and everyone else around them is complete chaos.

A few other women linger near Luna, all of them far younger and brighter eyed than her. They have meat on their bones, where Luna is entirely made up of sharp edges and nasty points. Everything about Luna is shorn off at the bone; the splintered remnant of who she was as a young woman is jagged and cruelly treated.

Luna has old eyes, just like Sandra and Geoff, except hers are a pale grey rather than dark brown. Pale grey like ghosts. Ghost eyes, she has. Ancient ghost eyes. I told her that the second time we met, about her craggy old Casper eyes, and she told me to piss off and stop talking like an up himself English professor crossed with a drunk cartoon horse.

The younger women who surround Luna like she's Maleficent and they're her horde of possibly mischievous fairies eye me with wary acceptance. They used to outright blank me, pretend like they couldn't see the hooded weirdo in their midst. It was both frustrating and amusing to be treated like a child with nits, ignored with the severity and heartfelt dedication of commuters who bear witness to an alcoholic pissing himself on the train.

Once I got the seal of approval from Luna, which amounted to her *not* spitting at my feet and telling me to fuck right off, the others followed suit and started acknowledging my existence. It really felt like an accomplishment, which was very sad then and still remains incredibly sad.

"Have you eaten?" Luna asks me when I get close

enough that she doesn't have to raise her voice above a smoky rumble. She never raises her voice any higher or louder than the chain-smoking epithet anthem I first heard from her when we met. I'm not sure her lungs could stand the strain.

"Only the hopes and dreams of the general masses," I answer half-heartedly.

Luna considers me a moment, then replies, "Doesn't sound very nutritional."

I shrug. "I'm not living for anything in particular."

Luna cracks a thin smile. Her pale skin looks cold and hard, the lines on her face hidden by shadows and a swathe of dirty-blonde hair.

"Did you eat?" I ask her, trying not to sound too concerned. She doesn't like it when I treat her like she's my friend. Too familiar. Bad memories attached to that kind of shit.

She gives me the same respect by never smoking in front of me. She lit up once with a lighter she had in her bra and the flash of silver made my brain set fire to itself. I almost choked to death on nightmares morphed from shadow and smoke to flesh and flame. Blood. For a moment, all I could see was black blood spilling from a gaping wound in someone's neck. His neck. His. Damon. He's... Because he's dead. Very fucking dead.

I need to remind myself, because sometimes I forget. Sometimes I forget for hours strung together like chainlink, and I hate that, because it makes remembering the worst thing to happen to me that day. Just remembering what's real becomes the very worst thing.

"I don't eat," Luna reminds me. "Don't need to. Too

old."

"Right, course not." I nod, a smile in my voice. "You're a vampire. Gonna outlive us all, till the planet is all burned to shit and there's no one left to drink from."

Luna peers at me with slitted eyes. Accusation. Here we go.

"You sound tired. Should probably try to sleep sometime, or you'll die. Do you want to die from no sleep? That would be impressively pathetic. Might even be an award in it for you."

She's Green in a bloody tank dress, I swear. I'd introduce them if I was interested in breaking up a marriage.

"Any problems?" I ask, not responding either way about my possible sleep-edition suicide attempts.

Luna runs her tongue along her top set of teeth, baring abnormally sharp incisors at me, which is where the ongoing vampire joke came from. She tips her head to the side, her scraggle of blonde hair barely moving with how much hairspray has been infused into it over the years. I'm not even sure if she still needs to wash it or if the stiff locks have officially become more chemical plastic than living hair.

"No problems," she answers eventually. I can feel the "but" like it's a physical thing.

"*Okay*. You sure?" I prompt, which earns me a swift glare from Luna. She doesn't like to be pushed. Luna Bell is not a pushable woman.

"Depends on if you're planning on finishing the job you started," she says. At my frown, she elaborates. "We had some snowflake-sucking bastards rolling through here yesterday. Looking for information about a certain hooded super who's been causing the family they work for a whole shit ton of grief."

Anger moves in swift and cutting, singeing across my insides so fucking fast that it doesn't burn hot, doesn't have the time, so instead it just burns cold. It's the feeling you get when you press your hand to ice for too long, that powerful ache, spreading through my body at the mention of the Winters family coming to people they know I protect for information.

"Did anyone get hurt?" I ask, voice so stiff it could give Luna's hair some serious competition.

Luna hesitates, taking a moment to really look at me before responding.

"No." Her expression darkens considerably. "We know how to take care of our own round here."

Guilt chews away at my stomach lining. "I'm sorry."

Luna snorts, crossing her arms and cocking her bony hip like she wants to stab me with it. "Fuck your sorry. Are you going to deal with this or not? That's all we need to know."

"I was planning to end it tonight."

"Good," she huffs, her posture relaxing ever so slightly.

Luna isn't easily rattled, so her clash with the Winters family cronies must have been especially unpleasant.

It pisses me off to imagine those arseholes stamping through here and hurting these women just to get at me.

"Next time anyone comes around asking, you should tell them whatever they want to know about me."

Luna looks at me like she thinks I'm a very special

kind of idiot. "Not how this works, bunny. You protect us, we protect you. That's how things go in this city. That's how it was with Polaris." The last part sounds like a reprimand.

"Polaris started doing this when he was ten." My anger sparks in a different direction this time. "You took advantage."

Luna appears utterly unbothered by the accusation. "We did."

Her simple agreement sucks all the oxygen out of my fire, and I sigh, resisting the urge to rub at my aching eyes.

"I'm glad," I say, regarding Luna meaningfully. "He was worth protecting."

Luna squints at me like she's trying to work out a particularly annoying little puzzle. "And you're not?"

I shrug, suddenly avoiding eye contact with Luna, unable to maintain it and talk about this at the same time. "Polaris thought I was."

"And he died for it?" Luna prods. I don't understand her reason for poking at that wound, but it still feels obscenely raw to the touch.

"Just tell them whatever they want to know," I say gruffly, impatience taking hold of me. "I can look after myself."

"Can you?" Luna doesn't sound very sure about it, which is offensive and possibly correct.

I force some stale charm into my voice and throw my hands out to the side like a magician presenting a trick. "I haven't died yet."

"It only takes the once," Luna says dryly.

My temper frays and I take a step back from her.

"Very astute. Great commentary." I jerk a thumb over my shoulder. "I'm gonna leave now and do other stuff while our conversation is riding on an intellectual high note."

"You're being a prick again." Luna eyes me like I'm a sad, weird animal left out in the rain. "Are you feeling emotional? Have I made you feel emotions? You sound like you're feeling emotions."

"Emotions? As in plural?" I pull a face at her. "Impossible. I'm a man. We only get to feel one thing at a time and when I left the house, I was hungry. That should theoretically carry me through the rest of the night."

Luna hums consideringly. "Could go get yourself a happy meal."

"I'd need to eat ten of them, including the little toy and the box, just to make a dent."

Luna ignores my attempt at whimsy. "After you're done dealing with the snow-bastards, go home. You should eat. Maybe sleep. There will be just as many fucks to beat up tomorrow. Take a night off."

"Hey, do I tell you how to manage your freelance career? No."

Luna does crack a half-smile at that, looking me over as if in assessment. "Do you want to switch professions?"

A memory of Lady Mars flashes inside my mind.

"I've been reliably informed that I don't have what it takes to work the streets."

Luna hums thoughtfully. "You've got the ankles for it."

"I have zero desire to understand what that means. Don't ever explain. Leave me with my mysteries." I give her a two-fingered salute, backing away again. "Good-night, Luna, I'll see you next week."

Luna salutes me back with one finger. "I'll have my report ready for you, boss."

I throw her a double thumbs-up. "Appreciate that. The sarcasm, not so much."

Luna shoots me a quicksilver grin, all Cheshire cat and glittering, malevolent intent. I'm about to head off before she can best me with another epically mordant line, when I hear the unmistakable sound of someone shrieking in obvious panic nearby.

I stiffen mid-turn, straining my ears immediately to listen for any other sounds that could alert the need of my intervention. When another sound rings out, a frightened yelp of fear, I look in the direction both noises came from.

On the left side of the road sits a row of redbrick houses, a few of which I know Luna Bell's people use for their work.

Whoever is making those sounds is too far away for Luna to have heard the shout of distress, but she does seem to recognise my reaction as a sign of trouble.

"What is it?" she asks, her face instantly taking on that of an experienced veteran when it comes to dealing with the dangers of both her profession and the world she inhabits.

Instead of answering her, I begin striding towards one of the small houses. There's a wall set between the houses and the street, with wooden doors leading into the back garden of each house. I find that the gated door I need to get through is thankfully unlatched and I don't hesitate to proceed into the garden beyond it.

Luna has come after me, too slow to keep up, but clearly determined in her quick strides.

At the other end of the tiny, unkept garden is the back entrance to the house. I try the handle, opening the door with ease, momentarily glad it wasn't locked. I could have broken in, but I'd rather not. Taking any measure of safety away from these women would feel like an offensive action whether I mean it to be or not.

There are some things you just can't do without making yourself yet another example of someone unnecessarily misusing the power they naturally have and did nothing to earn.

Once I'm inside the house, I hear another shout of terror coming from upstairs. The house's layout is simple, an open-plan kitchen and a small living room with a staircase set at the back of it. I take the shabbily carpeted staircase at a dash, managing it in three lops.

There's just one bedroom and a bathroom set on opposite sides of the narrow landing. Both doors are open.

Inside the dimly lit bedroom are two people. A tall, gangly-limbed blond man who appears to be holding down an incredibly slight woman of around thirty. She has a mess of long, black hair, which the man has fisted in one large hand, and light, currently very frightened, eyes. The man's other hand is on the woman's bare thigh. Her denim skirt has been pushed up around her waist, but her underwear has yet to be entirely removed.

There's panicked desperation in how she's trying to remove herself from underneath the man who is aggressively holding on to her. Gangly, as I've mentally dubbed him, is a man who is obviously terrible at picking up on *subtle signals* of rejection. From what I've observed since taking up the mantle of Wrath, a lot of people seem to struggle with this specific life skill. Someone should maybe start up a series of mandatory training courses. Help these confused individuals out.

It takes less than a handful of seconds for me to ascertain the particulars of the situation and decide on a course of action I believe will deliver the most desired outcome by at least half the people in this room.

When I grab hold of Gangly's jacket and haul him off the woman, he makes a very high yelping sound of shock. He was so intent on his vile endeavour that he must not have noticed me coming into the room behind him.

I slam Gangly, hard, into the wall, pushing his front up against it and keeping him there with a strong grip and firm hand. He's tall, but skinny. Enough muscle to hold down a small woman, but not nearly enough to make a dent when struggling to get away from someone like me.

Gangly makes a somewhat pathetic attempt to fight my hold. He starts shouting obscenities at me. They sound muffled and pained as he has his face pressed to the beige-painted wall.

Luna comes barrelling into the room a second later. Her blue eyes make a quick assessment of the scene she finds upon arrival. She spares no more than one glance for Gangly, all her attention settling on the dark-haired woman still trembling on the bed, adrenaline due to fear most likely still running through her.

It's only when Luna goes to comfort her friend, cautiously wrapping an arm around her shoulders and drawing her up to huddle in against her side, that it becomes clear the woman has been hurt in more ways than the obvious. She hisses when Luna touches the side of her head, making it clear she's sustained some kind of wound there. Luna draws her hand away from her friend's head and there's blood on her fingers.

After a quick scan around the room, my eyes snag on the dresser beside the bed. On the corner of the dresser is a fresh red stain. It's possible she made a bid for escape before and had her head smacked on the dresser either by accident or on purpose to disorientate her.

"Shit," Luna curses, looking down at her lightly bloodied fingers.

Her friend is silent, shaking a little, but with no tears in her eyes. She seems to be holding up rather well, all things considered.

Gangly is struggling, quite unsuccessfully, and calling me some very creative names. I figure that's only fair; I did nickname him first.

When Luna looks up at me, I ask her with no small amount of seriousness, "What do you want me to do with this one?" I give Gangly an extra-hard push into the wall for emphasis.

Luna's expression becomes a cross between resigned grimness and quiet fury. It's a look of hers I've become somewhat familiar with the last few months.

She seems to consider her options before eventually settling on a dispassionate, "Just take him outside and let him do one. I'll remember his face, put the warning out for my people."

Part of me feels reluctant to comply. I'd be more than prepared to call Yasmin and let her take a report, file charges against this prick. But one look at the dark-haired woman, who nods quickly in agreement when she meets my eyes, makes the final decision for me. It's not my place to question them about this.

"If you have a first aid kit somewhere, I can take a look at her head," I say to Luna.

"A nurse now, are you? Got a little side hustle going on during the day?" Luna asks sardonically, but there's no real spite behind the words, so I don't feel the need to respond.

It doesn't take much effort to drag Gangly out of the room and manhandle him down the stairs to the front door, which sits just beyond the staircase.

"Oi, get the fuck off me!" Gangly bellows for the thousandth time as I open the door and take him out, like the almost literal rubbish he is. "I'll fucking cut you, mate, I swear."

Once we're outside, I slam Gangly's back up against the wall next to the front door, cracking his head on the brick. I hold him by the throat, a hand wrapped around it and squeezing harshly. That cuts off his torrent of useless threats and humiliation-fuelled shouting.

When I speak, I get right up in his face, growling the words with no mistake as to the threat I intend this to be.

"Okay then. I need you to listen to me, all right? You listening? Because I really don't want to be sayin' this to you again. In fact, I won't. This is the only warning you get." I squeeze his throat a little tighter. He can still breathe like this, but it will be more difficult. I see the fear bloom in

Gangly's eyes, and I barely feel mollified by it. The only reason I'm not kicking the shit out of him is because I don't want to leave the head wound of the woman he attacked unattended for any significant period of time, just in case it needs serious treatment.

"Right, I can see you're listening, that's good. Really good. Best decision you've made tonight. Possibly the best decision you've made in your life so far, yeah? Okay." I lower my voice to a deeper octave, practically snarling. "If you ever come back here, if you ever make another move to hurt any of these women, or any woman, and I promise I will make it my fucking job to find out if you have, I will *come for you*. I will come, and I'm telling you, when I get my hands on you, there is gonna be—" I blow out a huff of air, as if anticipating the prospect. "There is gonna be all kinds of hell raining down on you, mate. All *kinds* of hell. Like, every circle of that shit, right?"

When Gangly doesn't respond as quickly as I'd prefer, I squeeze the hand holding his throat just that bit tighter.

Gangly reacts to the threats, both silent and spoken, by attempting to nod. I release the pressure enough for him to cough and choke out a laboured, "Yes."

I hold on to him a few moments longer, just to get the point all the way across.

The second I release Gangly and take a few steps to the side, leaving the path for his getaway free, he doesn't hesitate to hit the bricks. He stumbles forward, almost falling to the ground more than once as he attempts to sprint from the house and down the street to whatever he considers safety.

I hope he keeps running for a long while.

Once Gangly has turned the corner and is out of sight, I go back inside the house and make my way up the stairs again.

When I get back in the room, the dark-haired woman is alone and fully dressed again. I hear noise from the bathroom, probably Luna searching for a first aid kit. I'm sure she has one. Luna is nothing if not prepared for worst case scenarios in her profession.

The dark-haired woman looks up at me from the bed. She doesn't appear nervous, not as much as I would expect anyway. She does watch me with an understandable amount of wariness, however, likely ready to bolt if I try to make any aggressive move towards her.

I sit down on the end of the bed, careful to leave a safe distance between us. The woman is scrunched up near the metal headboard. I can see where her hair has become matted around the wound on the side of her head.

"You okay telling me your name?" I ask quietly, non-combative, making it clear she is able to ignore the question and not give me an answer if she so chooses.

The woman puffs a breath out through her nose and shrugs uncaringly. "Sinead," she answers, tone blunt.

"Okay, Sinead." I nod once in thanks for the small show of trust. "Can I maybe take a look at your head?"

Sinead hesitates at that, and I stay very still, not wanting to influence her answer in the negative. She darts a glance at the doorway, possibly looking for Luna. She might feel more comfortable if her friend is here with us when I examine her.

But then Sinead starts moving down the bed. She

settles close enough for me to be able to check out her injury.

Sinead tilts her head to the side when I ask, and I keep my touch as perfunctory and gentle as I can when I part her hair to get a better look at the damage.

It doesn't seem like anything to be overly worried about. Once I clean it up a bit I'll have a better idea, but I don't think she'll need stitches for it, despite all the blood I can clearly see.

Head wounds are a bit strange. They bleed a lot, even if they're mostly superficial.

I don't ask Sinead how she's feeling, because that question should come from someone who she's comfortable being honest with.

Sinead appears to relax noticeably when Luna comes striding back into the room holding a white and green first aid kit and a glass of water.

Luna comes over and shoves the kit at me without words and goes to kneel in front of Sinead, rather than sitting on the other side of her. She probably doesn't want to crowd her any more than necessary.

She does offer Sinead her hand, which Sinead takes. They hold each other's hands tightly, reassurance given and received on both ends, I think.

I open the first aid kit and take out the cleansing wipes.

"It looks okay," I tell Sinead, indicating her head. "I'll just clean it up for you and then it should be fine to just heal on its own in a few days, a week at most."

Sinead nods and doesn't give any comment. She tilts her head again and I set to work cleaning up the wounded area.

It only takes a few minutes for me to be done. I take a box of paracetamol from the first aid kit as well and offer Sinead two pills for the pain. Luna hands over the glass of water she was holding in her free hand.

Sinead takes both the pills and the water, giving a quiet thanks. She swallows the medication along with a large gulp of water.

"Come on, you can chill out on the sofa for a bit," Luna says to her friend, getting up off the floor and taking hold of Sinead's hand again.

Sinead doesn't argue, doing as Luna said and getting up off the bed.

They leave the room together and I leave the first aid kit on the bed, taking the bloodied cleansing wipes to throw them into the little silver bin just inside the bathroom.

I follow the women downstairs and wait as Luna settles her friend on the sofa, pulling a checked blanket from the back of it and wrapping it around her.

"I'll go put the kettle on," Luna says, and Sinead nods again in assent.

Sinead looks up at me one last time and offers a placid smile. It's more than I expected, so I give her the same in return.

When Luna walks past into the kitchen, I follow her, going straight to the back door, sensing the need to leave and allow her to attend to her shaken friend.

"I'll go then, yeah?" I jerk my thumb at the door.

At first, I think Luna won't answer me, which would be fine, and typical of her when she gets into one of her more dismal moods, but she replies after a couple of beats.

"She's new," Luna tells me, her response full of meaning I both do and could not possibly understand the scope of.

"Right." Then, "Can you do something for me?"

Luna snorts, her features seeming to sharpen with open scorn. "You want a thank-you?"

"No. Just..." I dip my head, averting my gaze from Luna, finding her oppressive judgement to be too much to look at right now. "If you need me to come around more often, you know how to contact me, yeah?"

"Like I said. We can handle ourselves," Luna says obstinately, unwilling to give an inch, which is something I can understand and respect. It's one of the reasons why the women around here trust her to protect them. She adds with a pointed edge, "*More* bodyguard bullshit isn't necessary."

I turn my head to meet her eyes again when I say, "I'm sorry it's necessary at all."

Because I am, even though it means nothing in the grand scheme. I could never expect her to be thankful, or to want something she wishes wasn't required. Something that should not, in a world much better than this one, be considered almost inevitable.

"Yeah." Luna lets out a low laugh devoid of any humour at all. "Me too. More than you could ever imagine."

She's likely right about that.

I open the back door, ready to leave. But before I can step out, Luna speaks again. "Get some rest, okay."

I look around the door at her. She's watching me

from across the kitchen, a white kettle held in one hand. She's got what could be called concern on her face as she watches me. "You can't exactly come to anyone's rescue if you've dropped down dead from exhaustion."

I give her a short nod in response.

There's no reassurance either of us can offer each other that wouldn't feel like a slap, or a lie.

I leave without another word said between us.

*

My next destination would have been checking out the streets surrounding The Refuge. But Luna's information drop about people hassling the women of Sinners Street has made me too antsy to find distraction in general patrolling. In this mood, I'd be far too likely to make a mistake, and in my line of not-work making mistakes can lead to the pain and death of innocent people. I fucked up once because of the Winters family, and I learned from that error, which is the least I owe people like Lewis and Julia.

What the Winters family did to Lewis taught me something valuable, that I was too careful and not careful enough about the wrong things. I need to be clever and decisive. No more messing around, overthinking every unimportant detail. I'm not Polaris's unofficial apprentice any more. I can't afford to be less effective than he was, even if my methods differ from his in some pretty big ways.

I head straight for The Refuge, with the intention of speaking to Ben, the owner, and finding out a key piece of information from him. He was the first of Damon's contacts to relent on his distrust of Wrath. I'm still not sure if he gave in out of pity, or because he genuinely believes in what I've been doing for the last few months. If anyone would understand the why of it, it'd be Ben, after what they did to him and his brother. That's what I tell myself, to tease out the logic of it all. But I have a slight suspicion Ben's offered branch of friendship is tied up in his loyalty to Polaris, just like with Luna.

The Refuge is very much alive with music and people when I arrive, landing on the roof, keeping myself to the shadows as much as possible to avoid detection from the bar-goers drifting in and out of the building.

Ben has access to the roof, so all I have to do is wait for him to come up. On nights we agree to meet, we have an arrangement where Ben will come up to the roof every few hours. I don't like to give an exact time, partly for my own protection, and also because there's a very good chance I'll get tied up with something elsewhere and be late most nights.

It must have been a while since Ben came up last, because I only have to wait fifteen minutes for him to make an appearance. He bangs open the door without much sense of self-preservation and comes striding out. Ben is not an easily cowed man, a fact I've picked up on over the months I've known him.

However, the sight of me half-kneeling on the window ledge, my hood up and shadow filter switched on, effectively covering my face, still seems to give him pause. His confident lope comes to a sudden, screeching halt and he eyes me with a wariness I've come to expect from people.

My new suit, or perhaps my new persona, seems to be having an impact on the city's inhabitants that I should have foreseen, but somehow didn't. It was a genuine surprise to me the first time a group of quite high-ranking gang members ran from me on sight. They'd never done that before, even with my less merciful reputation. Now, though, the people of this city, and the OCG element of Danger in particular, appear to have received the message I unwittingly put out with my one-man crusade against the Winters family.

It was a threat I delivered with more ferocity than I intended, and the results are impossible to brush aside. It would take a commitment to delusion to ignore the consequences of the anti-hero role I've carved out for myself.

The obvious downside of it all is how much it's impacted the way the general public views me. Frightening innocent civilians was never something I wanted to do, but Wrath does seem to inspire fear these days. More than I'd like, to be quite honest.

It was worse at the start, when everything kicked off and I took out the highest-ranking members of the Winters family over the course of a week. I only waited long enough to find out their locations, mostly from Ben himself, who managed to extract the intel from his network of informants within the Winters's inner and outer circles, before going ahead and stunting their reign over Danger.

Three months later, the public seem to have calmed down some. The news and social media went berserk for a while, condemning me and supporting me with equal savagery. But as the city got used to their new normal, the debate settled into a more subdued pattern. Every now and again it flares up, the name Wrath rattling around the internet like a metal ball inside an arcade game, especially when Diane Foxley sticks the knife in and twists with some outrageous article or tweet.

Apart from that, though, Danger appears to have gingerly offered Wrath its acceptance. I won't be on children's lunch boxes anytime soon, but no one's forming protests to oust me either. It's a balance I can live with, a grey space within which I'm comfortable existing.

Ben speaks first, his discomfort well-hidden if not quite dismissed. "Is it just me or is your ledge-crouching getting more and more ominous every time we meet up here? Are you practicing this shit in front of a mirror?" He allows a small grin, showing white teeth, looking to me like an especially mischievous shark. "No judgement if you do." He holds his hands up in a sarcastically placating gesture. "I am very impressed with your scary roof-looming progression either way."

"How's Sid?" I ask, ignoring everything he said. I've learned not to get drawn into a battle of nonsensical bullshit with Ben. It's like trying to keep track of a fully lit merry-go-round. You just wind up dizzy and confused and unsure at what point you lost focus and why.

"Good." Ben seems willing to get distracted by his favourite employee. "They took another one of those insane mixology classes and keep trying to push obnoxious cocktails on my customers, but apart from that they're golden. You should come in as you sometime and let them make you an Earl Grey air and vodka fog martini. Because that is a thing apparently. Who knew? Not me. And I was happier back then. In the good old days. When drinks were very exclusively liquid."

I mean. There's a lot to unpack right there. Will I attempt to unpack it?

Answer: Nope.

Every bit of that luggage can stay well and firmly in the metaphorical boot for the rest of our lives, thanks. I have way too much nonsensical information inside my head as it is. As far as I'm concerned, Earl Grey is a type of tea, and all drinks *remain* entirely liquid.

"Sid only takes those classes because they know you hate posh shit like that," I tell Ben sardonically, "and they want to annoy you for sticking them with the worst shifts every week."

Ben, full well knowing this already, makes a dismissive noise and crosses his arms in a defensive gesture.

"I give Sid the busy shifts because they're the only one I trust not to fuck up if I'm not there to supervise. All my other employees are terrible. They drop shit and swear at customers, and they never clean anything ever without specific direction, and even then, sometimes they don't do it properly. They wipe something once with a dirty, dry towel and call it overtime."

I have exactly zero sympathy for Ben on this score, which he also knows, as we've discussed it on numerous visits to The Refuge's roof.

"Stop hiring sexy randoms who don't know shit about shit, and you might not have so many problems."

Ben plays along, pretending like we haven't had this exact conversation at least half a dozen times by now. "Are you suggesting there's a level of bias to my hiring process?"

It's my turn to snort derisively at the awful farce of innocence currently being acted out before me on this roof. He's a bloody nightmare, this one, I'm telling you.

"I'm not *suggesting* anything," I say with acidic pointedness. "I'm outright saying that you're a shameless simp for young, pretty himbos with no experience of working in a bar. That's the truth of it, and Sid agrees with me. Hence, the mixology classes."

Ben makes another one of those throat noises that are the vocal equivalent of a shrug, very clearly ending the conversation, for which I am grateful. This is Sid's fight. I'm sure they'll be able to irritate Ben into hiring some actual bar staff eventually. All Sid really needs to do is threaten to walk. Ben would rather hire a load of old women in kitten cardigans than lose Sid.

I take the opportunity to bring us back on point, before we end up lost along another tangent. "Do you have the information I'm after?"

Ben catches on fast, his tone returning to that of a business transaction rather than a friendly chat. He straightens his shoulders and gives a firm nod. "Yeah. He finally resurfaced this week."

A flutter of relief bats its wings against the inside of my chest. This is the news I've been waiting for ever since I made the decision to go after the Winters family. To end their reign over Danger once and for all, with as much decisive action and as little bloodshed as possible.

But I made a mistake by going after Jacob Winters first, the major boss of the Winters's bloody mafia. It caused the others to scatter, made them harder to find. I should have worked my way up, started at the lower ranking members, spread out the assassinations so as to not tip them off right away about what I was doing. I should have been more careful and thought the whole thing through.

I was still angry. No. Too small time. I was still fucking furious. Not just about what happened to Julia and Lewis. But about Damon and Roux as well. What I felt. All that I felt. It caused me to be sloppy and rash, like extreme anger almost always does.

A lot of the big ones went underground, waiting for the storm to pass. For me to get myself killed, which was, and still is, a fair possibility. I'd go as far to say inevitable. But I've lasted longer than they thought I would. I've also been a lot more resourceful and determined than they thought I would be. It's taken me a lot longer, but I've managed to find them, to dig down deep into the scorched earth and find their little hidey holes and secret nests.

Now, months since I started, there's only one of them left. Or at least, there's only one left I'm willing to enact the atomic option on. Just one.

And yeah, of course, it's the one I wanted to tear apart the most when this all began.

"You know where he is tonight?" I prompt when Ben doesn't elaborate.

He's been helping me, and I know it's not been easy for him to do that. He's been taking risks, ones I'd rather not ask any civilian to take. But I couldn't have done most of it without him. It's possible he's regretting his part in it, now we're at the end. I can't say I don't understand the feeling. Once this is done, when this mission is over, I don't know what I'll do with all this rage. I can't keep on blowing up OI facilities and killing high-end gangsters. Not because I couldn't do it either technically or morally. No. We are far past that second reason, I think.

Sustaining the blaze isn't a problem. It's making sure it doesn't breach the parameters I've set up and catch the entire city, the whole fucking world alight without me having any control over what burns.

When Damon died it was like he took all the heat out of the world. But that can't possibly be true. Because I'm still here. Burning away like mad, with no way to douse the flames as they threaten to consume every part of me not already blackened by fire and blood. Rage and poison. That's all I am, these days.

I'm scared that's all I'll ever be again before it's over.

I try to stay focused on the mission.

"Ben," I try again when he still hasn't spoken. "Can you tell me where to find him or not?"

Ben hesitates before answering. He's giving me this look. It's one I've seen before. Not on his face, but on Rohan's. Luna's. Rani's too, every time I see her, which has become increasingly less often. Mostly because I don't like seeing that face, the concern, and the slight tinge of disappointment she can't quite hide, no matter how much she tries to.

"This is the last one, yeah?" Ben finally ventures. He seems uneasy.

"Last one," I tell him solemnly. "I promise. Just him, then we're done."

Ben doesn't seem entirely convinced by my promise,

which is probably fair enough, all things considered. I'm not his hero, or even really his friend. Polaris was. Damon was. And I, as we have well established, am certainly not him.

"Have you been sleeping, kid?" he asks carefully, as if trying to coax a street cat out of a tipped-over bin.

"Ben." I don't quite manage to keep the bark out of my voice. "Just give me the address. Then I can leave, and you can go apologise to Sid and fire your entire staff. Then get drunk. If you have the time."

There's a long pause where Ben just looks at me, and I don't know exactly what conclusions he's coming to, but I really don't have time for it. "Are you sure you want to do this?"

I laugh darkly, not liking the sound. Considering how Ben flinches, I'm guessing he doesn't either. "It's a bit late for second-guessing now."

"No, it isn't." Ben takes a step towards me, looking more serious than I've ever seen him. "Won't say it never is, because we both know that's bollocks. There's plenty of shit you can't come back from, but this ain't it. You need to slow down. You've been blasting through at top speed for months."

He takes another step forward, holding his hand out like he's beseeching me to listen.

"I'm worried you're gonna crash. I'm worried you're gonna throw yourself right over a cliff and not even realise it until you're already falling. Hitting rock bottom. You're scaring me, kid. You're scaring the shit out of me."

I can't deny the rush of defensiveness I feel at that admission. As much as I tell myself I don't care, as much as I can acknowledge I brought all of this down on my own head by making the choices I have, I still want to defend myself against the inevitable negative reaction from someone like Ben. A man whose opinion I've come to accidentally respect, and not just because Damon did first.

"Yeah, that seems to be what a lot of people are feeling towards Wrath lately—"

Ben interrupts me with a loud scoff. "No, you blond twat. I'm scared for you, not *of you*. Jesus. I'm scared of letting him down."

That gives me real pause. I squint at him. "Letting who down?"

"Don't pretend not to understand what I'm saying," Ben chides, scowling at me like I'm the one disappointing him right now.

"He loved you. I could see it," Ben says on an exhale, like he's purging the truth and it's as painful as any knife wound to the heart could be to hear those words from his mouth. "I knew him. I knew him better than he did, and I saw it when he looked at you. I saw. He loved you, and he would not have wanted someone he loved to lose themselves like you are." He's getting choked up a little, the deluge of emotion drenching his voice. "Look, I don't know what happened. I'm not gonna ask. I'll never ask. But you have got to forgive yourself for whatever it is you think you did wrong. You have to do that. If not for yourself then for him. Forgive yourself for *him*."

I know you feel guilty for what happened to us—

"Ben."

—and I know you'll feel guilty for this, because that's

who you are.

"Please."

But I'm asking you, for me. For me. Just. Don't.

"Stop."

This one time. Don't.

There's a buzzing in my ears and a tightness in my chest that only seems to get worse the more I try to shove away the automatic reaction to Ben's words. His accidental kick to the black box in my head where I keep the memories of that night. Those memories are like a swarm of wasps trapped inside their own nest. It doesn't take much to wake them up, let alone piss them off.

I clench my teeth and try somewhat helplessly to breathe through my nose. The last thing I want to do is start gasping in front of Ben. He already thinks I'm a basket case on the edge of losing it completely. I don't need to be adding any fuel to that particular fire. I like Ben, and I trust him to a certain extent. But I don't want him to see how much his mention of Damon has thrown me off balance right now.

Thankfully, Ben seems to have picked up on the seriousness in my tone because he's stopped talking. There's a sadness to his expression, with more than a hint of frustration as well. He shakes his head at me, like I'm proving more work than he originally bargained for. I feel kind of bad about that. I never meant to bring so much heaviness down on him. I never expected him to care this much about me, even if it's for Damon's sake more than mine.

Once I've regained some of my composure, and I'm able to loosen my jaw enough to let oxygen pass through my lips, I try again to bring us back to the actual reason why I'm here.

"Just give me the address, and we're done," I say, some of the exhaustion I was trying to keep out of my voice seeping in.

For a moment, I think Ben will tell me to go to hell. Or just turn around and walk away from me, letting his last plea for my return to sanity be his final word in response to all this shit. I can't say I'd be surprised. I can't even say I'd be disappointed.

There are times, lately, when I feel like I'm hooked on something, drug or drink or thrills, and people like Ben and Luna and Rohan are what you'd call enablers in any other situation.

It might be a relief to have someone deny me access to the thing I've come to rely on. Fighting and violence and adrenaline. I'm fucked. I'm just so fucked up. But I can't lose it, can't let it go, because I feel like I'll crumble to a heaping mass of grit if I slow down or, God forbid, stop altogether. I can't stop, I can't sleep, I can't give myself the space and time to think, because I've gone too far to ever be what I was.

But, if I'm not that, if I'm not the person anyone wanted or thought I could be, and I'm not this new thing I've charred and hacked myself into, then what else is there? If I can't be better, and I'm scared of worse, then what choice is there other than to ride this out until either somebody puts me down, or my genetically modified blood keeps its promise to take everything I've got left?

In the end, Ben doesn't force me to confront anything about the trajectory of my life, which is a confusing mix of relieving and pressurising, as if a layer of weight has been lifted, only to be immediately replaced by another. Different film of metal coating bone, same tonnage. It is very confusing to be a person.

"He's staying in one of their safe houses," Ben tells me. "Forty-three, Anarchy Avenue."

I mentally calculate the amount of time it will take me to get there, running through four different routes, and deciding on the best one. It's not all about speed. I want the least amount of exposure possible when I reach Anarchy Avenue. There's a good chance Paul Winters will have people watching out specifically for me. I don't want to take the chance that he'll run back into deep hiding.

There have been too many mistakes, too many hesitations in the wrong moments, not enough planning when necessary. Can't keep on spinning my wheels for the sake of leaving tyre marks. I told Luna I would end this tonight, and I will.

"Should I thank you?" I ask Ben, wondering if he'd accept such a thing, now. It doesn't seem like he'd want my thanks for giving me information he thinks I'd be better off not using.

Ben shakes his head again, letting out a sigh that could bend over a full field of grass. He looks away from me for a moment, taking his time to come to whatever conclusion he needs to reach. I keep my eyes trained on him, waiting patiently for his pronouncement.

He looks good. Ben always does. Tonight, he's wearing a red mesh top and a denim skirt with braces. He's got red beads and thread woven into his dreads, as well as expertly done red eye make-up that I would probably injure myself trying to apply.

Once, I attempted something as basic as using eyeliner and I swear I almost blinded myself. It was unbelievably tragic. There was crying and smudging and, according to Tate, a post-blow job energy going on with my face. All my friends were there in the aftermath of that disaster. I asked for help from Mei, who looked at me like I was insane, which was fair, since she is one of the most make-up averse people I know. Caleb had to step in and use his unshakable artist hands to fix the mess I'd made of my eyes.

Caleb was very good, and he had me looking present-able by the end of it. The general consensus was that it suited me, but despite that, I rarely put the effort in. More trouble than it's worth as far as I'm concerned.

"No," Ben finally answers, shifting his gaze back to meet mine. He's drawn back some of the emotions, lock-ing them away behind his face rather than having them on full display. "Don't thank me for helping you prove our dead fucking friend wrong about both of us."

That, intentionally or not, hits the target his previous comments about letting Damon down failed to spear.

"He expected too much," I say in a half-choked voice, that buzzing getting louder and louder inside my head.

Ben releases a laugh that isn't anywhere near amused. "Apparently."

Seeing no good outcome to this conversation, I don't respond, instead pushing backwards and dropping down from the roof to the dark, empty side-street below.

*

It takes me around half an hour to reach Anarchy Avenue.

It only takes me twenty minutes of scoping out the area to disable all of Paul Winters's protection.

It takes me less than five minutes to break into the building where he's hiding and knock out the remnants of his personal guard.

It takes me barely thirty seconds to disarm the man who ordered Lewis's death and Julia's beating, then to twist his neck until it gives a final and resounding snap.

A handful of seconds could change your life.

A handful of seconds can change fucking nothing at all.

Chapter Four

These Tweens Are Our Future?

Two Months Ago

I've been tracking the movement of Titanus Bullet's international arms-dealing operation for weeks now. There's a corkboard up on the wall in my room at Rohan's place. I've used pins and bits of string like in those noir detective shows when a troubled police officer or PI is desperate to solve a serial killer case that has confounded the local community. Except for the alcoholism and marriage distress, that's been my energy for the last month.

It was Luna Bell who first put me on to Bullet's ongoing illegal activity. She tossed out the information with narrowed eyes and scornful words, as if I should have known all this already, which is probably true.

She doesn't trust me. None of them do. Damon's people. Polaris's contacts. This was the first time Luna even spoke to me, and I think she only did it because of how prevalent Bullet's operation was becoming in her area of the city.

I thought Bullet was serving time in a British prison, more specifically in the supermax unit. He isn't supposed to have any contact with people who aren't direct blood relations, and even that is only once a month. How he was managing to run a weapons trade empire made no sense to me at first.

A few weeks and some invasive observation of the OCG's movements later, I've come to the conclusion that his second in command has taken over the day-to-day operations since Bullet's incarceration. His second in command also happens to be his half-sister, who has monthly phone calls with her brother as protocol allows.

Those phone calls should be monitored, so it's likely they use code to converse with each other about their business.

I got Rohan to alert Snow of this likely scenario, and he said she's contacted the prison to make them aware of this possible breach in communication. Ideally Bullet should get more time for this, but that outcome is unlikely. They'd have to prove what he's been doing, and that could prove very difficult, unless they can get either Bullet's sister or Bullet himself to admit to anything.

All of that is down to the courts, though. It's for the grey lawyers and impartial judges and pipe cleaner laws to decide what happens next.

What I care about is taking down the ongoing

operation in this city. It seems to have become their linchpin. If I dismantle their business here, it should cause something of a domino effect for the other branches of the operation.

I've spent the last four days rooting out their hiding spots and destroying their product. I could give tipoffs to the police instead, but I don't trust the system to get rid of these weapons, or even to keep them purely for evidence of any future case they decide to bring against Bullet or his sister. I've seen far too many weapons, drugs, too, reappear on the street after they've been seized. It's made me cynical about trusting any powers greater than my own to properly deal with these things.

If I want Bullet's operation to crash and burn, I'll need to pour and light the gasoline myself.

Bullet's people have proven to be less of an issue than I first imagined. Most of them are hired muscle, with no sense of loyalty at all. They're nothing like the Winters's henchmen I've come across who would die to protect their boss's interests. At this point, word has got around about me, and Bullet's people bottle it and run as soon as I step into view. I don't even need to threaten them, which is sort of hilarious, but also somewhat disappointing.

It would be a lie to say I haven't been looking for more of a challenge lately. Something to distract myself from the constant sound of screaming sirens blaring inside my head. I need a reason not to think about all the things I should be thinking about. It doesn't need to be a good reason. I'm not even sure if I have any of those left to claim.

Going after Bullet's operation has not provided that as much as I thought it would.

Tonight, however, it seems I've stumbled across a group of the gang's original members, because they started fighting back immediately and haven't given up yet.

I found them down on the docks, trying to scurry away with their latest shipment of guns. It was Luna, again, who told me about the last-ditch effort being made to move the remains of Bullet's product left in this city. She even said it without glowering at me like my existence is offensive to her on several levels, most of which I could not begin to comprehend. It felt like a breakthrough.

They tried shooting at me first, which was almost adorable. If a group of arms-dealing criminals shooting at a person in a bulletproof suit can be adorable.

I think it can.

Or maybe you just have to be here.

When they seemed to get the message, once I'd walked towards them in the face of their bullets and marvelled that no one seemed to think, maybe I should shoot the place the bulletproof suit is not covering, things quickly spiralled.

To be fair to them, they did not run away. Most of them stayed and decided to give hand-to-hand combat a go. It showed enough gumption for me to feel glad I hadn't just exploded the guns in their hands straight off the bat.

I did have to do it eventually, when one of them finally decided to level up and attempt to rate this fight R. I only just dodged the bullet that otherwise would have lodged itself firmly into my left eye socket.

Thankfully I only had to detonate two guns for the gang members to drop their weapons. I would rather not kill any of these people if I can help it.

Bullet's people, unlike the weapons, I have been leaving for the police. Or, more accurately, I've been calling Rohan over the comm line, who then in turn alerts FISA to come pick them up. I trust FISA marginally more than any other government body to appropriately take care of the gang members, much like they did the Mages who worked for Mia.

There will be trials, Rohan has told me, for the Mages who were arrested during both attacks of the city and at the factory. But those trials will be private, and most likely get filed under some classified order, considering the magical component of the crimes committed.

I'm not honestly sure what the outcome of those trials should be. For those who hurt innocent civilians, the punishment should obviously be more severe. But there were some Mages who went out of their way to spare civilians. There were some who only wanted to do what Mia told them they were doing, to achieve the ultimate goal, which was, in their minds, saving the world. From us. Me.

I don't know how I feel about imprisoning people who not only thought they were doing good, but in some ways kind of were. If what Mia said is true, I can understand why some people, and the Mages in particular, would feel the need to correct the balance of natural power in our world. The Liquid Onyx survivors, what we can do, what we are, is about as unnatural as it gets. I can't expect strangers to not be scared of what a potentially insane group of superhumans could destroy if it's something I'm afraid of myself.

It's all another load of shit I try not to think about.

I started out with around twenty of Bullet's men. I've cut it down to only four still standing, the rest of whom are currently lying unconscious on the cement dock floor.

These last four are digging in their heels, though, and I'm starting to feel like a woman in a club who's slapping away the attentions of men she has no interest in.

It reminds me of Mei once "accidentally" breaking a man's fingers in a club by "accidentally" bumping into him hard enough to make him go down to the dance floor like a clumsy tree and "accidentally" stamping on his hand.

We'd both seen the man randomly groping women on the dance floor earlier that evening. He made the mistake of his life when he copped a feel of Mei's chest and arse. She didn't even go for him straight away. She bided her time until a few songs later when everyone was thrashing around even more wildly than usual, then made her move.

I think he was just lucky he didn't end up as an icicle. Or that Caleb wasn't there to break his whole arm rather than just his hand. Not that Mei couldn't have broken his arm just as easily. But she's...well...she's not more merciful. But she is less of a drama queen.

Plus, she told me once that if she were to get truly upset every time a man groped her in daily life then she'd have no time to do anything else, which was a somewhat harrowing statement.

When Mei and I go out just the two of us, we tend to go to gay clubs more often than not, so she doesn't have to deal with all that stuff.

I, on the other hand, get groped enough for both of us, and not just by the men either. It's not something I find comfortable most of the time, which is probably why I have more sympathy for Mei than I think some straight blokes would.

Not that you can't be inappropriately groped as a straight bloke, but... You know. It's a whole thing.

One of the gang members takes another ill-advised swing, and I have to try very hard not to get impatient. There is a point where personal fortitude becomes outright delusion, and this lot should have reached that point around five dropped henchman ago.

I easily block the hit and get a hand around the man's throat, squeezing hard for a second before throwing him back into the metal wall behind him. His head hits the wall hard enough to cut the lights in his brain and he drops to the ground unconscious.

We're surrounded by freight containers; the dock is packed with them. A few of these must hold the rest of the product Bullet's people were trying to ship out.

It's like I'm a cat, playing with a group of buff mice trapped inside a maze.

Now I'm down to three, it takes less than a minute to dispatch them with a quick knock to the right place on their temples.

What I don't realise until it's almost too late is the man behind me who I thought was unconscious. He must have had a gun on him still, because he tries to fire a bullet into the back of my skull.

I'm not fast enough to stop him, but thankfully someone else is.

A loud grunt sounds from behind me just as the gun goes off. A bullet whizzes past my head, the man who fired it having been knocked off balance by someone.

When I turn around fully, I see there's a hub cap lying near the newly unconscious man. Blood trickles from a wound on his head where the hub cap hit him.

"He almost had you," a voice calls from above me. It's a voice I recognise easily, and one that makes my insides twist viciously, painfully. There's a reason I've been avoiding this moment. I knew I couldn't run from him forever, but I was hoping for at least another few weeks.

I've been following Jatin and Elle around every time they come out, making sure they're okay and not getting into too much trouble. When trouble has tried to go for them, I've put a stop to it before they even knew it was coming.

I look up to find Jatin standing on top of a freight container. He's dressed all in black with his hood up, partially shadowing his face.

Jatin steps forward and throws himself over the edge of the freight container. He's briefly airborne before he lands easily on the concrete below. He doesn't stumble or tip sideways. He doesn't lose his footing at all, thanks to his natural grace, possibly mixed in with the training he's received from me. The way he moves, handles himself, is familiar to me and my family.

I ignore Jatin's comment about me almost missing the unconscious man's attack.

"Did you just fling a hub cap at someone's head? Where did you even get a hub cap? Did you steal it? Did you just throw a stolen hub cap at a gun-toting criminal?"

Jatin shrugs with the casual insolence of a grumpy teen at a family wedding.

"Excellent, very articulate, thank you. Your shrugs are eloquent and informative," I say once Jatin makes it clear he isn't going to answer me. I move on to my next item of business. "Why are you here?"

"Following you, dickhead," Jatin says plainly. "Making sure you don't kill anyone. Or yourself."

"You need to go home," I tell him, voice cool. "Your mum will be frantic if she finds out you've snuck away again."

"I'm not breaking any promises." Jatin says, shrugging again. He takes another few steps towards me, hood still up. I can't see his dark, expressive eyes. "Deal's off, remember?" He nods at me. "You decided."

I wince both internally and externally at that reminder.

"Yeah, so I'm a shit mentor. That doesn't mean you get to scare your mother half to death. She deserves better than that."

Jatin looks to the side, and I get a flash of emotion from his face. Anger. No. More than that. Hurt and rage twinned together. Grief.

He turns back to face me again, shielding his face from me once more. His voice cuts through the space between us like a sharpened blade.

"So did Blue," he says, and it's like I've been hit in the head by a hub cap ten times over. "Polaris. He told me I could trust you." There's so much furious sadness in how he says it, like he's disappointed on behalf of Damon. "He believed that we both could."

I told Rani that Damon was dead. She was the first person I went to, a couple of days after I moved into

Rohan's place. I thought she and Jatin deserved to know. They were two of the only people who knew Damon, who he really was.

"He was wrong," I say, cold and biting, guilt so strong it feels like a water current dragging me under blocking off connection to any other emotion. "Now you know he was wrong, you should go home. Make better choices than he did."

"Fuck you," Jatin growls at me, feral, like an alley cat who dares any idiot to try to pet him. He *dares* them. "You don't get to say that about him. Who are you to say Blue was wrong?"

"I get to say he was wrong about me"—my tone is harsh, frustration reaching new levels—"because *I am me.*"

Jatin scoffs like I've just said the most ludicrous thing he's ever heard in his relatively short life. He takes another few steps forward, prowling in my direction, making the hairs on my neck stand up. I can't quite describe it. But...something about him tonight feels different, on edge, unpredictable.

It seems Jatin Mehta has officially had enough of taking my, or possibly anyone's, crap.

"Bullshit," he snarls, fierce and brashly adamant. "You don't get to decide anything. You're compromised."

I blink at him in confusion. "Compromised? What the hell—"

Jatin interrupts me before I can even finish my next sentence. He is so done. I can hear it clearly in his voice. "Yeah. You're only being this way because you're pissed off at Blue for dying."

That brings me up short. It hits me upside the head. How simply he said it. The surety. As if he's thought over all the possibilities and this is the one iron-tight conclusion he can come to.

Anger mixed with a strange kind of shame forces out my sputtering response. "I'm...I'm what? I am not pissed—"

"You are," Jatin interrupts again, tone firm, like I'm a child who doesn't want to absorb a difficult truth when it's been told.

Jatin tilts his head up and looks right at me, as if prepared for more denials, but still willing to fight his corner for as long as it takes.

I can see his face, the strength and conviction on it. The resignation and the sadness. It hurts to be the cause of so much lost innocence.

When Jatin speaks, there's no apology in it. I can't be anything but glad about that. Glad someone taught him he should never have to apologise for being honest about what he believes to be true.

"He's dead," he says evenly. "He's dead and he chose it and that makes you want to hurt him. And this is how you're doing it." He gestures around us with a sweeping wave of his arm. "By proving him wrong about you. By saying, 'Fuck you, I wasn't worth it.'"

I take a stumbling couple of steps backwards, like Jatin physically shoved me rather than just dealing unmerciful verbal blows.

"Jatin—" I start, a warning in my voice I hate, but can't help.

The new opponent to my sanity does not give a flying fuck, apparently.

"But it's pointless because he's not here to be hurt by it," Jatin says ruthlessly. "I am, though. My mum is. You're taking out your anger on people like me and my mum and that's bullshit."

Why I'm bothering to try to argue with him at this point, I don't know. But I do it anyway. One last stand.

"I'm not—"

"You are," Jatin says, again, too bloody sure and blunt as hell. "I just told you that you are. Blue is dead. He doesn't give a shit if you're a bad person any more. Because he can't. Because he's. *Not. Here.*"

Right. And now we're done. Just... I swear. Eight months' worth of therapy in a handful of sentences. Jesus Christ.

With his final, life-threatening hit thrown, Jatin stops talking. He settles for standing there, arms crossed, staring at me expectantly instead. I haven't wanted anyone to get spontaneously eaten by pandas this much since I first met Damon. And here he is, the dead man's protégé, giving me grief, talking like a mind-reading arsehole wizard.

I run a hand over my face, pinching the bridge of my nose to stave off a pending headache. I pull my hand away once I've realised that I can't prevent my headache, because the cause of it is standing in front of me with hawk-like eyes and a self-satisfied smirk on his face.

"God," I say, releasing a long breath, "you are fucking brutal, you know that?"

Jatin does not seem bothered by that in the least. "I'm right, though," he says, with that same frightening confidence.

My answering sigh is loud and achingly tired. I've given up on frustration. I haven't got the energy for it any more.

"Yeah. I know you are." I look at Jatin sadly, filled with regret for how I've handled so many things, chief among them my connection to Jatin and his mum. "I'm sorry for this. For how I've been. For breaking our promise. I'm just... I'm so sorry."

Jatin narrows his eyes at me, looking me right in the face, searching for truth and, more likely, for lies. I haven't given him much reason to have faith in me.

"Maybe you are," he says finally, which is more than I expected from him, more than I could possibly deserve at this point. He steps towards me again, like he's about to make an offer of some kind. "You wanna prove something to somebody? Good. You can prove to me you're sorry."

"Oh yeah?" I can't help but smile a little at how serious he sounds. He reminds me so much of Damon, it's indescribably painful. "How am I doing that now?"

Jatin straightens suddenly, squaring his shoulders and stuffing his hands into the pockets of his hoodie.

"By talking to my mum, for one," he says gruffly, accusing, which I do absolutely deserve. "She's really worried about your stupid arse." He pauses, eyes flickering to the side and back again nervously. He takes a moment to gather the courage to go on. "And by training me again." A pause. Then, "I miss it."

I miss you, is what he means, but will likely never say out loud.

For the sake of alleviating his discomfort, I don't call

attention to the true meaning behind his words and instead choose to focus on something entirely unrelated.

"I like your earrings." I gesture at the blue studs in his ears. They're shaped like stars. "Those for Polaris?"

Jatin shrugs, gaze darting away from me again in clear discomfort. His body language is easy to read. Hunched shoulders. Looking at the ground and scuffing the soles of his trainers on the damp stone. Too still to be standing casually.

"He was our hero," I say, letting him know it's okay to be visibly upset in front of me.

My own exhaustion is the only thing stopping me from crying every day until I'm sick with it, genuinely nauseated over spent tears and racking sobs.

My antsy nature is the only thing stopping me from curling up in the shower and never moving again.

My lifetime of training is the only thing stopping me from losing it during every fight I get in.

Jatin looks back at me then, a tiny scowl on his face, like I've said something unbelievably stupid. "He was our friend," he corrects, pointedly.

And it hits, centre mass, once again.

How does he keep *doing* that?

Because I can't.

I can't... I can't do this with Jatin now. Possibly ever, but certainly not now.

"I've got to call this in." I nod at the unconscious men scattered around us.

Jatin doesn't seem to mind that his chosen mentor is a coward in more ways than one. He just nods, willing to follow my lead despite every reason I've given him to never do such an outrageously reckless thing again.

"We should put them inside one of these containers before they wake up, then call," he says, and I'm so grateful for his dogged insistence on tracking me down and smacking me in the face with reality that I don't even remark on his use of the word "we", there, because exactly how does he think he's going to be dragging any of these extremely large men anywhere?

"Yeah, good idea, menace." I step close enough to Jatin that I can clap my hand on his shoulder and squeeze. Something in my chest warms at how Jatin leans into the touch and beams up at me with all that light shining from inside him.

I hope, so badly, that he gets to keep it.

*

"Here." Rohan shoves a white plate at me, indicating for me to take it. On the plate are three pieces of toast.

I take the plate of toast from him and settle back on the sofa, blinking tired eyes at the television, making a half-hearted attempt to read the multi-coloured subtitles I put on when I muted the sound because too much noise made my head ache.

"Thanks," I say, lifting the plate.

Rohan walks back to the kitchen, waving away my gratitude.

I pick up the top piece of toast and devour the whole thing in three bites, feeling suddenly ravenous. I've been stupid with my food intake recently, forget-ting to eat and not eating as much as I should even when I do remember to.

Rohan has taken to making me food at random intervals and literally dropping plates or bowls into my lap so I can't refuse them. I'm probably still alive right now because of him. Without him I may well have dropped dead from lack of nourishment months ago.

"Mate, seriously, you look like shit. What time did you get in this morning?" Rohan drops down on the sofa next to me, a cup of coffee in one hand, his laptop in the other. He settles the laptop on his knees and immediately begins tapping away at the keyboard with quick fingers.

After getting home a few hours ago from my patrol, I didn't even bother entertaining the idea of trying to sleep, instead jumping in the shower to wake myself up a bit. It didn't work as well as I'd hoped.

I'm currently slumped on Rohan's obscenely expensive-looking sofa in light-grey jogging bottoms and a white vest, making a valid attempt not to slip into a coma by accident. That would be embarrassing, and Rohan would be so mildly annoyed. He might even raise his voice or something. Or just fully lean into the rich boy aesthetic he's got going on and hire a butler to take care of me in my comatose state.

I frown over at Rohan. "What are you, my warden? My probation officer? My *mother*?"

Without missing a beat, or a single keystroke, Rohan tilts his head to the side, as if confused, and asks drolly, "What would you know about having a mother?"

I give a fake gasp and clutch at my chest. "Oh, arrow to the *heart!* And so early?" I poke at his coffee mug. "Drink more of your civility potion before you talk to me again, please."

Rohan complies, taking a big gulp and shuddering a bit after, like an addict getting his first fix of the day. I let my eyes rove across him with more scrutiny. He looks tired and frazzled, his black hair even messier than usual. He's wearing his ratty pyjamas, too, the grey ones without any pattern and far too many holes. He only wears those when he's spent hours upon hours driving himself into the ground over a project.

It's likely Rohan got about the same amount of sleep as I did. As in none at all.

"You look shitty, too," I mutter.

Rohan grunts in response, most of his attention on the screen in front of him. "Eat your fucking toast, inmate."

I give a low snicker, picking up my second piece of toast and turning my attention back to the television.

BBC One news is already reporting on the death of Paul Winters, getting most of the facts wrong and speculating more than they should. The way they're talking about it, pretty soon a lot of the bigger gangs in Danger are going to start pointing fingers at one another. As of last night, every head member of the Winters crime family is dead. No doubt there is now a massive power vacuum due to that fact, and numerous players are going to want to fill the space they left behind.

I'll have to pay attention to what's happening out there, make sure no one grasps enough power to take control over this city. I can't end crime in Danger, but I can put in a good attempt at ensuring no single gang has the ability to reign as the Winters family once did.

Rohan looks up briefly from his laptop to glance at the television screen. It's a ridiculously large thing, far too big for this small a space. The sound system is equally impressive, but more often than not sets my temples pounding.

My senses have become more sensitive lately. It comes and goes. Sometimes I'm fine, other times I can hear, see, smell, and taste to a level that's noticeably uncomfortable. Occasionally it's painful, too, like my senses are punishing me for not looking after myself. Or perhaps they're warning me of an oncoming chemical imbalance.

I'm no longer confident in my ability to read my own body. The signs. The reactions. If I thought I felt like a walking, talking timebomb before I found out about Liquid Onyx's severely limited shelf life, it's ten times worse now.

"Was he the last one?" Rohan asks me, voice obviously hesitant. He doesn't usually ask about the specifics of my actions while out on patrol.

Rohan chose not to be a vigilante, despite his powers, and he has good reasons for not wanting to live that life. His only involvement with my vigilantism is creating my suit.

"Yeah. I'm done."

For now, anyway.

I don't say that part out loud, because I think Rohan would interpret it badly. I'd rather not give him the impression I'm looking for another excuse to go around killing people. The Winters family was a one-time deal. I need for that to be true, or I'll...

Or I...

Or.

I just really, really need to hold on to whatever vestiges of light I have left inside me. Peeking through the slats. Shining through the cracks. Illuminating the gap under the door.

I've never been afraid of the dark, or the things waiting in it. What's always scared me is the possibility of becoming one of those things other people are afraid of.

Before...before everything. It was like I'd been living inside a dream. I had this wonderful life that I didn't earn or appreciate, then it was gone. I woke up. The Winters. Obsidian Inc. Mia. They made me wake up. And it was no less than I deserved.

You know what's worse than waking up and realising the world really is as horrible as everyone told you it was? It's realising you're one of the things that make the world horrible.

"Might be time to take a step back from all that shit," Rohan offers, his tone non-intrusive, as if it's a suggestion he only just came up with and doesn't care much about the outcome of.

I know that's bullshit, but I'm not in the mood to call him on it.

"Are you asking me to settle down, Torture Tap?" I ask teasingly

Rohan throws me his most irritated scowl to date. "I still hate that," he tells me. "And no, I'm not asking you to settle down. I'm not that much of an optimist. I just think you could take some time off for a bit, that's all."

"I meant are you asking me to settle down *with you*," I say, easily ignoring the rest of what he said. "Like. Do the whole bit. Buy a house in, uh, Ripon. Get married. Adopt a child. Take in a fleet of stray dogs."

"I am not moving to Ripon," Rohan says decisively, no hesitation. He screws up his nose, possibly at even the thought of doing a such thing. "There are only, like, five brown people there. Probably about the same amount of openly gay people, too. Plus, we're both atheists, so we'd likely get burned as witches at some point."

I shuffle a bit closer to him on the sofa and widen my eyes hopefully. "But the marriage, the child, and the dogs are on the table otherwise?"

Rohan tries to hide an amused smile behind his coffee cup, but I see it. He seems willing to pretend I've distracted him from the conversation he tried to start. He wouldn't ever be so easily manipulated, not in reality. The man is far cleverer than me, in any number of ways.

The door buzzer goes off, the sound splitting through the room and causing my headache to blossom once again.

Rohan turns his head to look towards the door. "Speaking of adopting random children," he says caustically, "your travelling orphanage has arrived."

Oh shit, yeah.

Jatin and Elle are supposed to be coming over for a joint training session. I'd partially forgotten that was meant to be today. Honestly, the days are starting to run together for me. No proper sleep cycle will do that to you.

I get up from the sofa, put the plate down on the coffee table, and snatch up the last piece of toast to take with me. I eat the slice of toast on my way to the door.

Jatin and Elle have come over to the flat enough

times by now that the doorman lets them in without having to ask and they know the passcode for the lift.

For the first month after the factory incident, I was too fucked up to be anywhere near Jatin. Or anyone, quite frankly.

But then Jatin started doing his stalking thing, this time accompanied by his new partner in insanity, Elle. They followed me through the city during my patrols, getting themselves into all kinds of trouble, involving themselves in dangerous situations. I think mostly just to bait me into acknowledging them. I can't say I wasn't a bit proud—and horrified—when Jatin managed to take down a mugger all on his own.

Or mostly alone. Elle came in at the last minute with a very impressive *thwap* of a metal bin lid to the mugger's head.

After I stepped in to make sure the targets were okay and ensure the mugger would be arrested, via a call to police officer Yasmeen Mirza, it was time to face the music with Jatin.

And he really let me have it. Full blast. RIP headphone users. It was bad. But ultimately deserved.

Jatin was angry, and I think more worried than he wanted to admit to me. Heartbroken over Polaris. His hero. His Blue. His friend.

I think Elle was mostly there to give emotional support and glower at me in open judgement. I deserved that, too.

When Jatin was telling me how much of a twat I was and how furious he was with me and how I wasn't his best friend any more and wouldn't be invited to his birthday party and, yeah, you get what I mean. When he was done, I didn't apologise, because apologies wouldn't have meant shit to either of us at that point. I did, however, promise to start our training sessions up again, so long as he promised in turn to stop going out, as was our original agreement.

Jatin told me I broke my side of the agreement first, and he was right about that, too.

But he did give me another chance, which was the one thing I got from Jatin I probably did not deserve.

Since then, I've met up with Jatin at least once a week. Sometimes with Elle in tow. And it's been good, I think, for me. Having Jatin, having a responsibility I couldn't walk away from without hurting a child, something I'd never want to do, has given me something solid to hold on to, outside of the whole vigilante thing. I need that, probably more than I realised at the time.

I was reluctant to go back to Colbie, and equally reluctant to ask Rohan to let strange children into his home. Not many people inside FISA know where Rohan lives. Actually, I don't think anyone other than Snow is aware of his address. Rohan showed more trust in me than was warranted when he brought me to his flat.

But Rohan surprised me by offering up his massive patio for use without me having to ask. He offered it nonchalantly, like it didn't matter to him at all either way if I accepted. But I knew it was a big deal for him to do that. I only accepted because it seemed the safest option, and yes, admittedly it did allow me to avoid going to Colbie like I would have done previously.

Coward, I know. Selfish, I know. Callous, even, to yet

again avoid seeing Lady Mars and my friends, I know, a big yes.

Whoever said self-awareness was the first step to self-improvement was a liar.

Or just a far better person than me.

Rohan calls to me before I can open the door. "You don't let those hoodlums talk to me, Rex. We agreed on that."

"They love you," I say over my shoulder.

"I hate them." Rohan makes a disgruntled face. "Don't let them steal anything."

"Like what?"

"The silverware."

"You don't have any silverware."

"I have spoons."

"As if you'd notice if one of them took a spoon. You didn't even notice when I got rid of your plastic plates and replaced them with proper ones."

"That's not so bad. Plates are plates, how was I supposed to know you secretly replaced them?"

"We went to IKEA to get them together. And *you* picked them out."

The door buzzer goes off three more times in quick succession. Bloody tweens.

"Don't let them take my spoons," Rohan warns one last time before turning back around to return his attention to his laptop. The sound of key clacking begins again.

I resist the urge to throw something at his head and open the door, so Jatin won't give me a migraine by leaning on the buzzer.

Waiting on the other side of the door is not only Jatin

and Elle, but Rani as well. She stands behind Jatin and Elle, wearing a large winter coat and a very stern expression, which I know means I'm in more trouble than usual.

She likes to drop Jatin off if she's able to, the excuse being that she doesn't like her son wandering around the city on his own. I'm almost certain it's just because she wants to check in on me, or at least that's a big part of it.

I try not to be resentful. I try, even more so, to feel grateful she cares about me at all. There's no possible way I deserve it, just like I didn't deserve Jatin's forgiveness for walking away from him and letting his hero die in my place.

"Hey, Sky," Jatin chirps upon seeing me.

"Hey, menace, you all right?"

"Yeah, I'm okay. You?" Jatin looks up at me with judgment on his face, like he knows the answer to that already.

I shrug one shoulder. "Not bad."

"Liar." Jatin snorts, then shoves in past me, like the belligerent little shit he is.

Elle gives me her usual raised eyebrows, telling me without any doubt she agrees with her friend. I move out of the way, letting her dart in past me to wander off after Jatin, who I imagine has gone to bother Rohan.

Jatin has gained a real appreciation for purposefully bugging the hell out of Rohan at every available opportunity. It's a hobby I fully support and do nothing to curtail Jatin's enthusiasm for.

I think it's good for Rohan. Builds character to have your nerves torn apart by a tween every now and then.

Now I'm left with Rani, who comes into the flat at a

more regal pace. I think she could push me right over if she really put her mind to it, Liquid Onyx strength be damned. But the woman has far too much class, and that's just the truth.

I close the door and follow Rani into the kitchen.

As predicted, Jatin is sitting next to Rohan, far too close, and seems to have somehow stolen his laptop, which is a feat I cannot help but admire. The last time I touched Rohan's laptop, he bit me. He literally bit me. And it wasn't a nice warning bite either. I bled. There's a black spot on the sofa to mark the occasion.

Jatin appears to be reading through whatever files Rohan had open at the time his laptop was nicked off him by a twelve-year-old with surprisingly good reflexes. At this point we can only hope Jatin does grow up to be a FISA agent with all the classified information he's been made privy to since he got involved with us.

Elle sits on the other side of Jatin. She has taken Rohan's coffee cup away from him, another outstanding accomplishment to be sure, and is busy flicking through the television channels while sipping away at whatever's left of the brew.

Rohan grasps desperately onto the arm of the sofa, bunched up in the corner, looking like a trapped and extremely vexed and/or scandalised rabbit.

"Do you want anything to drink?" I ask Rani, making for the fridge.

"No, thank you. I've got to get to work soon." Rani's tone causes me to halt in my steps and turn back around to face her. That feels like a mistake.

"All right," I say, carefully.

Rani just stands there, watching me with such open scrutiny it makes me extremely uncomfortable. I wrap my arms around myself, hands clasping my hard biceps.

An unintentional by-product of my not sleeping is that I've had a lot more time to work out, in addition to more patrolling and the strenuous missions with Rohan. I've packed on quite a bit of muscle as a result, been able to hone my body into more of a weapon than it ever was before.

"How's The Caf?" I ask, mostly because I don't know what else to respond with. Small talk isn't something I excel at and doing it with Rani would be even more difficult.

Things have become awkward between me and Rani since Damon's death. It's like she knows what happened, despite the fact she can't possibly. None of the details were released to the public, and I certainly didn't tell her more than the obvious. That Damon died, and he did it to save other people.

I'm sure my sudden disappearance from her son's life didn't help, but I know it's about more than that. Rani is upset with me. I can feel it, like an undercurrent to every conversation we have. I've been waiting for that damn to break, for Rani to decide she's had enough of the evasive shit. She's lasted longer than her son did, but then she's had more experience with dangerous men who make terrible mistakes.

Rani doesn't bother to be subtle. Like son, like mother.

"How about you find out for yourself and come by later this week?"

I give my head a slight shake, hoping it will be a

simple matter of refusing, no matter how unlikely that seems given how fiercely determined Rani is looking at me. "I can't."

Rani snorts her disbelief. "You *won't*."

"I'm really busy," I tell her weakly, knowing she won't believe it. Wouldn't, even if it was true. I've burned that bridge of trust right down to the ground. Ashes in the air. Smoke still rising.

"Oh, well. Too bad." She narrows her eyes at me and takes a step forward. "I've put up with this nonsense for months"—she gestures at me, indicating that I am the nonsense she's had to put up with, which is a bit rude—"and I've had it. You're not allowed to mope around any more."

"Mope?" I squawk defensively. "I have not been moping arou—"

Rani cuts me off with very little remorse. "You've been jumping all over this city, or hiding in this flat, feeling sorry for yourself for long enough. Time's up, I'm afraid. You've had your lot." She fixes me with a steely look. "Now it's time to rejoin the human race and start trying to sort yourself out."

Truth be told, I'm not in any way shocked by this sudden one-woman ambush. I've been able to tell Rani has been reaching the end of her patience with me for a while. It was inevitable that she would try to put her foot down about my behaviour. I'm only surprised she took this long.

But, for the sake of my pride, I still need to try to put up a fight.

"Sort myself out? Rani, what the hell? I'm fine."

Rani wrinkles her nose at me and lets out another sound of obstinate dismissal. "That is so absurdly untrue, I won't even dignify it with a response. Have you looked at yourself?" She gestures up and down my body. "Seriously? You look exhausted. You look half-dead. You look like you spent the last ten years working out in prison and just got out yesterday."

Never has anyone made what could be a compliment sound so insulting.

"Oh, wow, thank you," I reply sarcastically. "That is so helpful to my self-esteem."

Rani takes a step towards me and whacks me over the head hard enough to make a definitive thudding sound which echoes around the room. She glares at me furiously and I start to think maybe I'm going to get beaten to death by a frying pan after all.

"I mean it, young man, no more joking around," Rani says, her voice hard and uncompromising. It's her "mum" voice. I recognise it from all the times she's used it on her errant son.

She goes on, an unmistakable edge of threat behind the words. You know. A *do it or else* kind of thing.

"You will come to The Caf on Sunday, or I swear to you, I will come to this flat and drag you there by your ear."

She takes another step towards me, bringing us within touching distance, and pushes two fingers into my chest. Hard. She looks up at me, fire in her eyes.

"Today is the day you get a grip. And whatever it is *you* think *I* think about what happened to Polaris, just stop. Because you're definitely wrong about that, and probably a lot of other things."

I should probably just shut up and nod. I should probably count myself lucky she hasn't been more vicious in her handling of my motherly wake-up call.

But. That last part. I just can't let it go.

"I think you blame me," I tell her, honestly.

Rani stands there in stony silence for a solid ten seconds before responding with an equally hardline, "I don't."

It's not enough.

"You should," I say, pathetically earnest, wanting it and not wanting it at the same time. Pulled in two directions. Torn between the cool balm of forgiveness, and the ferocious sear of blame.

"You don't get to tell me what to do," Rani reminds me. "I'm older than you. And wiser than you could ever hope to be, you shit."

I'm reminded vividly of the conversation I had with Caleb on the beach, months ago.

Rani. She's like the ocean. Kind of salty. Wiser than anyone. Demanding respect with every strong current and crashing wave. Every order, every action.

"You don't know what happened," I say, because I'm stupid and I don't know when to concede defeat if I've still got words in my head and a tongue to speak with.

Rani's eyes soften then, the lines beside them smoothing out ever so slightly. She moves in close again and lowers her voice, speaking to me with a quiet intimacy that I'm not sure how to react to.

"I don't need to know what happened." Her voice is a careful balance of sad and kind. "It's bloody obvious. He died for you. He loved you." She looks me in the eye, and it hurts.

It hurts so much I can barely breathe.

Rani puts her hand on my arm and squeezes lightly. A reassuring touch. It reminds me of how Phoenix used to touch me when I was upset. It's distinctly familial and comforting, the touch offering up a warmth and unconditional sense of calm I haven't felt from anyone else since her.

Somehow, such a simple thing undoes the damage of the last few minutes. It sweeps away the rising sense of panic, allowing my lungs to untangle and oxygen to pass through clear and easy.

For a single moment, I miss Phoenix Moon with such fierce longing that it pricks at my eyes, almost causing tears to blur my vision.

Rani starts talking again, giving me a reason to push down the long-standing sense of loss I feel over Phoenix and concentrate on something far more relevant to the pain I've recently been lashed with.

"You feel guilty because you cared so much about him, because you felt sorry for the boy he was, who no one cared enough about, because you thought he was a better man than you." She pauses for a moment, then adds, "And probably because you're a bit of a narcissist."

She pats my bicep consolingly, appearing a bit apologetic about the last part, but not by much. She isn't one to pull her punches. Hasn't been since we met. I guess Jatin had to get it from somewhere.

It's difficult to be offended, though, because of everything else she said.

"Wow," I huff, shaking my head, an incredulous smile spreading across my face without my permission.

Rani leans back and gives me an appraising look. She has a tiny smile on her face as well, and I think maybe we're both a little nearer the brink than we'd like. Rani is just a lot better at dealing than I am. She's a strong woman. Jatin is lucky to have her.

Damon was, too.

And, well, so am I.

"How'd I do?" Rani asks, amusement tinging the edges of her voice, letting me know we've passed through the serious part of our discussion and it's okay to make jokes again.

"Not bad," is my wry response. Because I know how to give compliments the right way. "The narcissist part was mean. But. It's a fair shout, so..." I shrug one shoulder uncaringly.

Rani's smile widens for a second, then fades away again, as if a darker thought has just occurred to her. She lowers her voice, looking up at me with a troubled set to her expression.

"Remember what I said when we had that talk in my flat months ago?" she asks. "Remember what I told you to do?"

I remember that day, when I brought Jatin back home and we sat together on her sofa. I asked her if I could train her son. We spoke about Damon.

It takes me a handful of seconds to track through my memory and pluck out the exact words Rani used, so I can repeat them back at her.

"Be nice to him," I say, slow and quiet, like we're

sharing a secret line of code.

"Yeah. That." Rani sounds a bit exasperated, like I've missed the point. She smiles at me as she would a dopey dog who accidentally ran into a glass door. "And be nicer to yourself, too. Because I think you're a good man, underneath all the darkness you've tried to cloak yourself in."

My instant reaction is to deny it. I've done so much wrong since I became Wrath. I've killed people. Some who really didn't need to die. I've hurt people. Far more than I should have. I let everyone down. Literally everyone I care about. And I still am. Every day I avoid going back to Colbie and seeing my family and dealing with my grief in some kind of way that isn't either illegal or recklessly unhealthy, I'm hurting people.

How will I ever make it up to them? I don't even know if I'll have the time to try.

After all I've done—all the mistakes I've made—it seems impossible that anyone, let alone someone like Rani, could ever consider me a good man. By anyone's standards, I am most certainly not.

But Rani seems to believe it, and I don't want to give that up for as long as she'll let me have it. Her faith. Her belief that I'm a better person than I am. It reminds me of Damon, and God, I miss him. I miss him so much.

Four months of knowing him.

Four months of stripping away the metal so I could touch the flesh beneath.

Four months of cracking open the chest to see the heart beating inside, the one he offered to me.

Four months of arguing with each other and fighting

together and trying to make him laugh.

I only really knew Damon North for four months, but I can promise with absolute certainty that I'll spend the rest of my life missing him.

Missing everything he was. Mourning everything he would never get to be.

"I'll come to The Caf."

It's the least I can offer after all she's given to me.

Rani seems to know I've reached some kind of breaking point. She doesn't push any further, instead offering me another genuine, warm smile.

"Good," she says decisively. "I'll see you on Sunday, then?"

I give a firm nod, returning her smile with a crumpled one of my own.

"I'll be there."

*

An hour later I'm outside, in my training gear, facing off against Jatin.

From our place on the rooftop patio, I can see inside the flat through the wall of large windows. Rohan and Elle are right where I left them, sitting on the sofa together, watching some inappropriate horror film that it is far too early in the morning for.

Both Rohan and Elle, I've learned, are massive film nerds. Their joint love of all things horror is the only thing that stopped Rohan from picking Elle up and throwing her over the balcony, I'm pretty sure. Elle brought up Rohan's personal Netflix list and started commenting on all the horror films in his viewing queue, most of which I would have thought Elle too young to have heard of, let alone seen.

But apparently, I'm a little old grandma and don't know anything, so I should shut up and let the experts talk.

Elle put on one of her favourite films, which also happened to be one of Rohan's favourites as well, and the two of them immediately transformed into YouTube reactors.

They were both so engrossed in the film and chattering endlessly to each other about their shared obsession that Jatin and I were able to go outside without either of them noticing.

I decided to leave them to it. So long as they're getting on, I'll take the heat if Rani finds out I'm letting Elle watch an 18-rated slasher film at nine o'clock in the morning with a billionaire genius wearing his hobo pyjamas.

After half an hour of warming up and another half an hour of sparring, Jatin is sweating and out of breath. Far too much, really. I need to up my game. Take him running a few times a week at least. He should be in better shape than this, and he bloody well will be if I have anything to say about it. I'm going to make him regret ever asking me to train him.

God knows, I hated Roux sometimes during my training. I accused him of trying to kill me almost every session we had during the early days. Roux used to snort in response and tell me if he was trying to kill me, he would just shoot me. Far less work for him than death via exhaustion. He said it would be easy because I was tiny and slow and trusted him like a little idiot.

It has to be said, Roux had a unique parenting style.

I work Jatin hard for another half an hour before giving him a break. He immediately drops down on the floor in a heap. I retrieve our water bottles and bring them back to Jatin, then sit on the floor beside him.

Jatin grabs the blue water bottle from me when I offer it and takes three large gulps from it. He follows my advice about stopping before he can drink too much. I've told him countless times not to drink a lot of water in one go, because he'll just throw it back up during training.

I learned that the hard way by ignoring the same advice given to me by Roux.

For a while, Jatin and I sit together on the training mat I dragged out for us to use. Rohan bought it especially for me to be able to train Jatin out here.

There's a nice breeze today, which ruffles through my hair pleasantly. The sky is overcast, but that's standard for British weather, so I'm not overly worried about the clouds unleashing their usual tonnage of rain down on us any time soon.

"Did you sort things out with Mum?" Jatin asks once he's done panting.

Jatin's hair is still long, and he's begun having to tie it back when we spar to keep it out of his eyes. Conversely, Elle has changed since I last saw her. She's quite dramatically cut her hair, or perhaps shorn would be the better word. It's now about an inch long, more like fuzz than hair. It makes her eyes stand out more, and her freckles. She has a lovely face, although she keeps it rather closed off most of the time. I can't really blame her, after everything she's been through.

"Yes. Your mum has informed me it's time to stop being a prick, and I've decided to do as she says."

Jatin snorts, mouth quirking into a relieved smile. "Smart man. She might have knocked you out and dragged you to The Caf if you'd said no. She's getting pretty serious about adopting you."

I shake my head, shifting into a more comfortable position and looking out over the expanse of Rohan's makeshift patio garden. It's so fancy out here.

I've got used to Rohan's obvious wealth, but I don't know if I'll ever be comfortable with it. I'm too rough around the edges for a place like this. I look like a rock sitting among pebbles, or a weed in a flower bed. My very presence makes the whole thing appear more downmarket than it actually is.

Turning back to Jatin, I argue lightly, "I'm too old to be adopted."

"Only by law." Jatin scoffs, like I'm being purposely stupid. "In reality you can be adopted at any age."

He runs a hand over his hair, which has come loose from its tie, and tucks the dark strands behind his ears, bringing attention to the holes in his earlobes. I made him take out the blue star earrings before we started sparring, against his insistence. As far as I'm aware, he's been wearing them pretty consistently since Damon's death.

I've learned since the first night he inserted himself back into my life that the earrings made an appearance less than a week after Damon died. Rather than asking for his mum's permission, Jatin got his best mate Elle to pierce his ears with ice and a hot needle. Rani came home from work to find her bathroom covered in her son's blood from their disastrous attempt to make holes in Jatin's ears.

I can only imagine Rani's dismay upon seeing that particular mess.

"Okay. Thing number one." I scowl at Jatin and hold up two fingers. "We really need to discuss your assertion that *the law* exists outside reality for some reason, because that is really not—"

"Do you have a family?" Jatin asks, interrupting me. I seriously need to break him of that habit one of these days.

"Yes, I have a family," I tell him, hesitant to open this door, knowing Jatin's ability to dig in deep and get far too close to truths I'd rather not deal with.

"Do you...like...not get on with them?" Jatin questions, then with a fierce scowl he asks, "Are they one of those weird families who don't like their kids because of who they want to have sex with?" He wrinkles his nose. "That is *well* creepy."

I can't help the snort of laughter which pops out of my mouth at the genuine disgust on Jatin's face. "No. My family are all right about my sexuality, if that's what you meant."

"Oh, okay." Jatin frowns at me, seeming thoughtful. "Then why aren't you with them? Wouldn't they want to help you if you're struggling?"

Right, cut right to the core, why don't you, Jatin? Fuck.

"It's complicated."

"That's adult bullshit talk for 'I'm being dramatic and don't want to do the hard thing, so I'm going to pretend I can't explain it'."

"You're like the annoying little brother I never wanted, you know that?"

"Classic deflection. Want to try again, or just give up and tell me the truth? I can tell you which option will work out better for you in the long run."

"Classic deflection? Have you been speaking to—" I stop myself before saying Green's name. With an exasperated huff, I start again. "You know what. Okay. Fine. But there's a lot to it, and there's loads you don't know and can't understand."

Jatin sits up and pierces me with a look which is so much like the one his mother gave me only a few hours ago that I feel immediately cowed by it.

"You don't know what I can and can't understand. Try me and we'll both find out together." His mouth twitches upwards at both corners, voice dipping sarcastically. "High stakes. *Exciting.*"

God, is this what it's like talking to me? If so, I have renewed sympathy for everyone I've ever spoken to.

"Take it down a notch," I warn him, trying to sound stern, "or I won't tell you anything."

Jatin does a terrible job of looking like he is at all repentant about his attitude. He does, however, hold his hands up in a show of defiance and presses his lips together until they fold and disappear from view, indicating he won't speak again until I'm done. He gestures with one hand for me to proceed.

The little nightmare.

If there is an afterlife, and Roux and Damon can see this, I bet they'd both be laughing their arses off at me getting continuously owned a by a tween boy.

It takes me a moment to decide what I should actually tell Jatin. I've been careful up till now to keep certain parts of my life a secret from my mentee. I haven't told him about FISA, or Liquid Onyx, mostly in the hopes of protecting him should there ever come a time when someone might ask him questions about those two things.

What Jatin is asking about now, though, aren't exactly matters of high security. He already knows I have a connection to Colbie. He's met Jamie, although I never told him exactly how we know each other. Jatin seemed willing to take what I gave him and not ask any further questions about my personal life, or my past.

Now, though, he's getting curious, which I suppose I can't blame him for. It had to happen eventually. Jatin is, by nature, a curious person. His respect for the whole secret identity thing is probably the only reason he held back before.

For the sake of keeping Jatin as safe as I can, while not closing myself off entirely from him, I'm careful with what information I share with him. Making the choice to give up answers that matter but are unlikely to come out of the shadows surrounding me and hurt him one day down the line.

"When I was five, my parents were both killed," I begin, then go on to spin the entire, harrowing story of how Damon and I met, and what happened to us back then. Throughout, my voice remains neutral. I feel oddly unaffected by those events after all these years.

Don't get me wrong, the memory of that night—it...it still gives me a pang of faded loss, a jumbled mess of fear and pain. I don't think I'll ever truly forget the flash of blue light, the searing burn on my arm, the screams. Those memories mixed with nightmares will likely play on inside my head for however long I retain brain function.

But I can talk about it now, to Jatin, in a way I haven't been able to before. I don't know if it's just because my recent losses have highlighted the stark difference between rotted and fresh grief, if old had to make way for new. Maybe there's only so much heartache a person can bear holding on to all at once.

I didn't think so, when it all first happened, that night at the factory. I thought I would collapse under how brutal the impact was, how crushing the weight. But I was wrong.

That's the strange thing. No matter how prepared we think we are for it, no matter the past experience we have, part of us still thinks if the worst happens, if the *impossible* actually happens, the world will end, time will stop, everything will come to a screeching halt. But it doesn't. It just goes. Life. It keeps on. It goes and it goes and it goes.

Turns out, you can get used to anything. We can *survive* anything. Even the seemingly impossible.

I don't know if that's resilience, or punishment. For daring to have something worth losing.

Jatin listens to me with a rapt intensity I've rarely seen him display outside of our sparring sessions. He behaves himself, not interrupting me even once as I explain how Roux came to the safe house where Damon and I were. How he saved me. How we came to live in Colbie. How I found and built the family I have now.

When I'm finished, Jatin is frowning slightly, head

tilted, like he's absorbing the information I've offered up, the little cogs in his head spinning slowly. Over the course of the last few minutes, we've both changed position. Jatin is sitting with his knees drawn up to his chest, arms wrapped around his legs, mirroring my own pose.

I've noticed he's taken to subconsciously copying my gestures and movements. Like how I make dramatic hand wavy motions when I'm getting animated about something. Or like how I rub at my face when I'm especially agitated.

It's made me aware of my body language. In particular, my tendency to draw into a ball when I'm feeling vulnerable. I thought I'd mostly grown out of that habit. But Jatin's new penchant for doing it whenever he talks about Damon, or the few times he mentions his father, would suggest not.

Is this what it's like to be a parent sometimes? To see things in your child you didn't intend for them to inherit.

It makes me feel a bit guilty, like I'm wrecking Jatin by giving him my quirks and weaknesses when he should only ever have had to contend with the ones he developed for himself.

"So, your uncle raised you," Jatin eventually comes out with, peering at me with newly curious eyes. "But he died. When?"

"Four months ago."

"The same time Blue died? Wow. That's a lot."

"Yeah. It was. Is. A lot."

"If I'd known that, I might have been a little easier on you."

"Really?" I ask, barking out a laugh of incredulity.

Jatin's mouth cuts into a small smirk. "No," he admits. "You were being really stupid about everything. You still are, with all the Winters family stuff."

"Don't start." I sigh, a heaviness settling on my shoulders again. "That's all over now, anyway." The burden of the unknown. The lack of direction. Post-mission come down on a grander scale. The more elaborate the mission, the harder the fall when it's over.

Jatin doesn't look like he believes me, but he doesn't challenge me on it either, so he must decide it isn't worth the effort. He's tried before, to talk to me about what I was doing with the Winters family takedown, but I've dodged his questioning with practiced ease.

To be fair, I think he was letting me evade most of the time. He's proven his ability to get his shot at saying something if he really wants to say it.

It wouldn't surprise me if Jatin felt conflicted over the death of the Winters family's power stronghold on his city. They were responsible for his father's descent into criminality, and ultimately his death. No matter how good a person Jatin has been taught to be, it would be difficult for anyone to defend the people who caused you so much pain.

There is, in my view, such a thing as too good. I've learned to be wary of that, almost as much as I am of the writhing decay people can too easily allow to fester within them. Darkness can grow and spread. It can be cultivated once seeded. But light can blind, it can stunt change and wilt passion. Too much of one or the other is likely to be psychologically corrosive.

I let Jatin inwardly seethe over the Winters family

dilemma, allowing him to come to his own conclusions, unwilling to sway him in any direction.

Jatin is not Damon. Jatin is not me.

It's okay for him to think what I did was wrong. Because his mum taught him so. It's okay for him to think he would never do the same. Because Blue might have been his friend, but Polaris was still his hero. And it was okay for him to be unsure and still angry and hesitate to throw himself in front of me to save people who hurt him. Because while his own actions are his responsibility, mine and those of the Winters family certainly are not.

Not yet. Because he's a twelve-year-old boy and he's Jatin and like hell will I let this aspiring hero grow up thinking he doesn't have a choice.

"Will you tell me what happened to Blue and your uncle?" Jatin asks, out of bloody nowhere. "What really happened, I mean? How they died."

He looks up at me with cautious eyes, like he knows he's treading on landmines with every prod of his toes.

But he's also got that stubborn look. The one he had the night he confronted me at the docks. I think that look has conditioned me into backing down and giving in to him, which is a truly horrifying discovery to make about myself. It's also not something I'm going to try to subvert now, when I've had no time to build up any laudable defences.

"They both died trying to save me. The other details don't matter."

"They died for you? Like how my dad died trying to save Blue?"

"I... I mean. Uh. I guess so."

"Did they both choose to do it?"

"Jatin."

"Was it their choice?"

"Yes."

"Do you think Blue should have felt guilty about what happened to my dad? Do you think I should have hated him for it?"

"No."

"Because?"

"Because it wasn't his fault."

"No. You div. That's not the reason. Why are you so thick sometimes?" Jatin rolls his eyes at me like he can't believe he has to explain this to his adopted idiot. He goes on with exaggerated slowness, "It was my dad's choice to jump in front of that gun. He had a choice. *They* had a choice."

"And no one has the right to take that away from anyone else. I know. I do know that." I literally thought it about two minutes ago in regard to Jatin himself, for fuck's sake. He might be right in speaking to me like I'm an idiot. Apparently, I really am one.

Jatin nods decisively, like we've settled something important.

"Then you really have no excuse for belittling their sacrifices by feeling guilty for stuff you can't change." He looks smug, which is possibly well deserved.

I remember the first time I told Roux I wanted to be a superhero. I remember him looking devastated by it. I remember him kneeling in front of me and staring and staring and gripping my skinny arms too tight and maybe his eyes were wet as he told me, "You can't fix everything.

You can't save everyone. And you can't blame yourself for things that are out of your control."

I was eleven years old when I said I understood and I promised him I wouldn't forget and I thought, *I'm going to fix everything. I'm going to save everyone. And when I inevitably fail at both of those things, I'm never going to forgive myself.*

After all these years, and the experiences I've had, I would like to think I've learned better. But I don't think I have. Not in the ways I should, anyway.

"You're right," I concede, offering Jatin a self-deprecating shrug. "I should have more respect. Should stop wallowing. Stop using them to justify doing bad things, even if they are for good reasons."

"I don't think you're a bad person," Jatin tells me, with a conviction that is humbling.

"No?" I ask, huffing out a quiet laugh. "After everything I've done, you still see the best in me?"

Jatin's brows draw together in a tight frown. He gently shakes his head. "Blue told me, once, that it's not so much about seeing the best in people, as it is knowing the worst parts of them aren't all that they are."

I can so clearly hear Damon saying that to Jatin. He was probably kneeling in front of him, hand on his shoulder, looking at him with all that innate sincerity he had, virtuous energy seeping from every pore.

Instead of answering Jatin with a straightforward assertive agreement or, outrageously, a denial, I recite something another incredible person once told me.

"We are people. We are not naturally good or kind or strong," I say, thinking of Lady Mars and how much I miss her, how much I wish she was here, or I was there, anything as long as the distance between us could disappear and I would feel the steady reassurance of her presence.

I give Jatin a look, then, hard and intense, much like the one Lady Mars gave me that day outside the school gates.

"Those are things we choose to be. And we have to choose them every day, again and again, even when it's hard. Because it almost always is."

Jatin gazes back at me for a handful of long, stretched-out seconds, before his mouth twitches at one side, like he might be about to smile.

"You did not come up with that." He eyes me with a fair amount of scepticism.

I let out a short bark of laughter, a flush settling over my face, feeling suddenly bashful after all the seriousness of the last few...minutes. Days. Months?

Fucking light years.

"I didn't." It's easy to admit.

Jatin screws his mouth to the side thoughtfully, his brow creasing again in the middle. "Can I meet the person who did?" he asks, quiet and sincere.

If he'd asked a week ago, I might have had a panic attack at even the suggestion. But now, in this moment, I feel differently about it. The Winters family is gone. Rohan might have a new way of stopping me from ever becoming a monster, if not saving the lives of the Liquid Onyx survivors. I agreed to go to The Caf.

None of these things are solutions. But they feel like the first real steps forward I've taken since the night Roux and Damon died.

"Yeah, menace," I say, mouth twitching up into a soft smile. "Think I can make that happen."

I still don't know what I'm ready for. But at least I know I'm ready for *something*.

Chapter Five

Fire, Dirt, Water. The Elements to Which We Offer Our Dead

I don't usually believe in fate. But when the next day comes and I get a call from Julia to tell me she's finally ready to spread Lewis's ashes, it feels like an unbelievable coincidence.

Julia had a myriad of injuries after her vicious kidnapping and assault by the Winters's lackeys. She was in the hospital for weeks. Her leg was in a cast for months, which has only been taken off recently. She's going to have to be in physiotherapy for a while, but she told me she was fine to come out today and walk to the place where she'll be scattering Lewis's ashes.

I might have argued that she needed more time to

heal, but Julia seemed determined, and I've learned not to push when she's decided on a course of action. It seems to me as if nothing can stop her when she sets her mind to something.

We've spoken a few times since the night I found her and Lewis in that conference room. I went to visit her in the hospital to check in, and I met her dad, Tony. He was a big man with a full beard and tired wrinkles at the corner of his eyes and mouth. He was soft spoken and seemed to treat his daughter with a great deal of gentleness and care, as if she was both extremely fragile and precious to him.

It made me feel glad she has someone like that, but also guilty for having been partially responsible for Julia ending up in the hospital in the first place.

I was more or less expecting Julia to chuck me out of her hospital room and tell me never to come back when I visited her the first time. But she didn't do that. I expected her to be pissed the hell off, which she was. She was pissed at a lot of people. Just not at me.

The only time she got angry with me was when I tried to apologise. She had a right go at me for being stupid and blaming myself, when it was no one's fault but the Winters family. It was difficult to argue with her when she was all banged up and still able to look ferociously resolute in her pronouncement of my innocence.

When Julia asked me to be there while she scattered Lewis's ashes, I was instinctively opposed to the idea. It seemed wrong for me to stand at Julia's side in such a moment. Not because of my part in Lewis's death, but more generally because I didn't know him all that well. I wanted to help him because he was a person who needed it, not because we were friends.

I wish I'd got the chance to know him. The person he was, and the person he could have become if his life hadn't been snatched away for no good reason at all.

But I didn't, and I won't, and pretending I have any right to grieve for a man I met a grand total of three times feels viscerally wrong.

Despite my reluctance, however, I agreed, because it was Julia who asked, and I knew she wouldn't have done so out of some mis-wired attempt at courtesy. If Julia asked me to be here, then she wants me here. I might not understand why, but that isn't the point. If my presence can, in any way, give ease to the difficulty she must be experiencing in completing this task, then I owe it to her and to Lewis.

I borrow one of Rohan's cars, a black Mercedes-AMG GT, a car he tells me I can go ahead and wreck if I need to. I was going to ask what he thinks Julia and I will be doing which would result in us destroying his ridiculously expensive car on an outing where we're supposed to scattering a person's ashes, but then I decided not to. Let Rohan keep his crazy, I don't need it. Not today.

When I roll up outside Julia's place, she's already waiting on the pavement. After what happened with the Winters family, she moved out of the flat she shared with Lewis. She's living with her dad at the moment, in a two-storey redbrick in the outer provinces of Danger City. I have a feeling that won't last, as every time I speak to her, Julia mentions becoming increasingly frustrated by her dad's constant hovering.

Julia is standing with her arms crossed, wearing tight black jeans and a bright-green jumper. Her hair has been fastened into two long pigtails. On her back is a canvas backpack.

She spots me when I roll down the window and strolls over to the car. Instead of going to the passenger side door, though, she stops by the driver's side. She leans on the window seal and looks in at me with arched eyebrows.

"Did you steal this car?" she asks without any preamble.

"Hey, Julia," I respond. I add sarcastically, "Great to see you, too. I'm feeling tired as fuck, how about you?"

She just snorts at me and shakes her head. "Seriously? There's no chance it's yours. Who did you blow to get this sick Mercedes?" She smacks the window seal with one hand, looking along the length of the car appreciatively.

"Did you want to drive?" I ask, instead of answering.

Julia looks at me like I'm stupid and makes another derogatory sound. "Do you want to be sixty percent more likely to get pulled over?"

I'm not even going to make an attempt at picking up that molten ball of lava.

"Just get in the car, snarky arse."

Julia gives me an unrepentant smirk and pushes back from the door. She goes around the side and gets into the passenger seat. She takes her backpack off and puts it down on the floor between her legs.

"People are going to think you're kidnapping me. Taking me to your creepy rich white boy mansion," she says while strapping on her seatbelt.

"I don't have a mansion. I'm not *Batman*."

Julia scoffs, replying, "*No one* is Batman."

I mean. Obviously.

"I do have a cave I could take you to if you fancy it," I offer with faux cheer.

"Are there bats in it?" Julia responds with similarly mocking enthusiasm.

"Nope. But if you're into sand and echoes, I've got a place that will blow your fucking mind."

"Just drive," Julia says in an imitation of my own voice when I told her to get in the car.

With no inclination to argue, I roll the car window back up and push my foot down, taking us away from Julia's house. She already told me where we're going to scatter Lewis's ashes over the phone this morning, so I don't need to clarify that with her now. Instead, I ask her another important question.

"How are you feeling about today? Are you sure you're ready for this?"

Julia doesn't answer right away. She just sits there for a while, hands gripping her backpack protectively. It's the only thing giving away how anxious she is. I wait for her to work out what she wants to say, if she wants to say anything at all.

A complicated series of emotions plays out across her face before her expression appears to settle on something like grim determination.

Julia looks straight ahead, eyes fixed on a point far beyond this car, possibly at our eventual destination. It's out there, barely an hour away from where we are now. Might be too close for her. Fuck. God knows, most days the fact that Roux and Damon are buried in Danger City cemetery is enough to make me want to move to Alaska just to put some distance between me and them.

When Julia answers, it's with the resigned air of someone who has thought the very same question half to death.

"I'm ready to stop waiting to be sure I'm ready," she says, voice pitched low. "Does that count?"

She's asking the wrong person. It's not a question I could even begin to answer at this stage. I'm a mess. I've maybe always been mentally cluttered, misshapen and incorrectly wired by my own unsteady hands. But now, I'm most definitely worse off than I was when Julia and I first met. Thinking about that night, roughly eight months ago, feels mad, like it's impossible I could have ever been the person I was then.

Maybe that Rex, the version of me who thought the worst tragedy of my life had already happened, could have answered Julia's question. The version of me who thought he knew what it meant to survive, to hold on and fight back and never give in to the chaos thrumming along every nerve and strand of Nova DNA.

"Shouldn't ask me about grief timelines," I tell Julia, my grip on the steering wheel tightening reflexively. "Lost so many people in my life. But—" I swallow hard, past the regret and the shame curdling inside my gut and clinging to the walls of my throat. "Still feel like I don't know shit about shit."

Julia does look at me then. Her expression is pensive, as if she's only now thinking about how little she knows me, or where I've come from. *What* I've come from.

"Hey—" she crosses her arms and gives me a reproachful frown—"are you up for this?"

No. Probably not.

Instead of admitting that to Julia, since I'm pretty sure she already knows and asking me was just a mild attempt at courtesy, I ask a question of my own.

"Did you manage to get hold of Lewis's parents again?"

Julia doesn't push me, either because she doesn't want to actually hear the answer or because I've successfully distracted her. I thought bringing up Lewis's parents would be a good way to avoid talking about my own current instability. Her reaction to the mention of them is visceral.

"Yeah." She turns her gaze away from me and out of the front windscreen again, tone gritted with barely repressed anger. "Got Dad to take me round to their house." She blows out a loud breath. "They wouldn't listen. Just slammed the door in my face and said they would call the police if I didn't stop harassing them."

What the hell?

"*Harassing* them?" I ask, unable to hide my own disbelief. "They actually said that to you?"

Julia gives her head a sharp nod. She's already trembling a little with how upset the memory is making her, and I instantly regret bringing it up. I'd rather make myself as uncomfortable as possible than cause Julia any more pain than she's already experiencing.

After Lewis's parents were informed of what happened to him, they didn't come to the hospital to identify him or make any inquiries into when his body would be released. That was left to Julia, who Lewis made his legal next of kin after he was hospitalised for overdosing.

Julia tried contacting them several times once she got out of the hospital, but they either didn't answer the phone or would hang up on her as soon as they figured out who it was calling. On the one occasion Lewis's mother did stay on the line, it was only to tell Julia they didn't want anything to do with the consequences of their son's life choices. Julia told me she was certain they weren't just talking about his drug use.

It seems Julia decided to give it one last go before scattering Lewis's ashes, which was decent of her. I'm not sure I could have been half as kind if I was in her position.

"He was the best mate I ever had," Julia says, voice hot and sharp. "He fucked up some, I know, but he was sweet, and he tried so hard to be better, and he would never have hurt anyone." Her next words come out sounding wet and thick. "And they just…" She kicks, hard, at the car floor, a muffled thud vibrating around the en-closed space. "They just didn't care. Everything he was." She looks at me, no tears in her eyes, but anguish in every too-quick blink. "And it meant nothing to them. He meant nothing."

It hurts, something in my stomach clenching in reac-tion to Julia's pain and frustration. There are no words to express how sorry I am she's had to deal with all that alongside everything else. I can't imagine losing someone and having no one to share that sense of loss with.

"Julia—" I start, but she cuts me off.

"Can we—" She lets out a shuddering gust of air from her slightly parted lips. "Can we just not talk any more?

Not until we get there."

I nod in response, pulling whatever words of comfort I might have attempted to wield back inside me. Julia seems relieved by my easy acquiescence and settles back into her seat. She uncrosses her arms, and her hands go back to gripping the bag situated between her legs.

It takes another forty minutes to arrive at our destination. A patch of woodland located right outside Danger City called Dead Man's Forest. When Julia first told me where we'd be going, I thought she was having me on. But she heard the scepticism in my voice and told me the forest was a place she and Lewis went to often, when they wanted to get out of the city for a while. Apparently, it was one of Lewis's favourite spots, especially during his recovery. Being cut off from all the noise and temptation was good for him; it made the forest a kind of safe space.

Julia said Lewis once joked that you've got a better chance of resting in peace somewhere actually peaceful.

Plus, she thought he would appreciate the dark humour in it. I had no choice but to believe her. She's the one who knows how Lewis thought and felt about things like that.

I park the car in the small, designated area near the forest. It's mostly empty and there doesn't appear to be anyone else around.

Beyond the car park is a thick mass of green-leaved trees. Thanks to the dark-grey sky above, the forest looks like it will be quiet, dark, and heavily shadowed.

A few muddy paths lead into the forest, all of which seem to have been created by years of continuous foot traffic.

I wait by the boot for Julia to give me my marching orders or at least take the lead so I can follow her.

Julia climbs out of the car and comes around to meet me. She heaves the backpack over her shoulders, her face set in a grim line, as if she's preparing herself for the arduous walk to Mordor.

"You want me to carry that?" I ask, indicating the backpack.

Julia looks me up and down steadily, then snorts, appearing vaguely amused by my question.

"Are you trying to be gentlemanly?"

"No." I arch both eyebrows right back at her. "I just don't want you to leave me stranded somewhere in the forest of death and doom. I need the bag as collateral."

Julia wrinkles her nose. "Why would I leave you stranded in the forest?"

I just stare hard at her.

After a couple of long seconds, Julia huffs and takes off the backpack. She hands it to me like she thinks she's doing me some great favour.

This must be what it feels like to get knighted by the queen. *Chills.*

I put the backpack on and wave my arm at the creepiest forest I've ever seen. Which isn't saying much because this is the only forest I've ever seen. Because I don't do nature. Nature is for hedgehogs and gingerbread-houses, not for Rex.

"Lead on, Ranger Rick."

Julia marches off without further prompting, leaving me to scramble after her.

Once inside the forest, it seems decidedly less *Blair*

Witch Project. It looks very...foresty?

I mean, there's trees. And dirt. And dead leaves both on top of and mixed in with the dirt.

I don't know. How much of a description to do you want here?

Tell you what, if I see something that isn't a tree or dirt or dead leaves, I will take note and report.

Maybe I'll even recapture my youth at some point and shade a leaf with tracing paper. What a school trip that was for my ten-year-old self.

I spent the whole time hunched inside my too-large coat and trying not to swallow a bee which kept following me everywhere. Caleb and Tate had a great day throwing muddy leaves at each other like they were snowballs.

Mei kept asking our teacher, Mrs Lott, increasingly outlandish questions about nature she couldn't possibly know the answer to. Mei knew Mrs Lott wouldn't be able to answer her questions, she just hated her and wanted to see her struggle. Mrs Lott landed herself on Mei's shit list for continuously spelling her name incorrectly on every bit of classwork she marked and always only calling on her to go up to the front and answer maths equations on the white board.

The only other time I came to this forest was when The Parents and Roux decided to take us camping. It was awful. Hector made us build our own tent, which is a lot harder than it seems. Mei tried to take over and instruct us via the overly complex directions. She and Caleb got into a dust-up about it because Caleb kept using the numbered poles in the wrong order and Caleb argued it didn't matter because all the poles looked exactly the same.

Later in the afternoon, once the tent was finally up, we chased down a rabbit to eat. Yeah. Not caught in a trap. We literally chased a rabbit through the forest, as a family. Caleb jumped on it in the end. As in threw himself wildly through the air like a maniac and landed on the rabbit. It only worked because Tate put up a shield, which the rabbit bounced off and was momentarily stunned, giving Caleb time to pounce.

Roux got attacked by the same squirrels on two entirely separate occasions, which was hilarious. Both times.

It's a good thing I have my stupid memories to distract me, because otherwise the oppressive silence hanging between Julia and me might be uncomfortable. The two of us walk together without speaking, the sounds of the forest filling my ears like I'm listening to one of those calming nature soundtracks. Leaves cracking underfoot. Unseen birds flapping their wings and singing to one another. Random buzzing from insects. Wind blowing through trees, branches scraping across one another.

Julia seems to be existing inside her own head, like you do sometimes. She keeps her eyes down, on her shoes, as if she's counting her steps.

It takes a good half an hour to reach the place that could be our destination. Julia stops in a small clearing with a thin brook running through it. There are large rocks scattered around, and she goes to sit on one close to the brook. I follow her and drop down on a rock near where she's settled, giving her space while keeping within easy speaking distance.

Julia sits forward, resting her forearms on top of her

knees, hands clasped too tightly, long nails digging into her skin.

I take the backpack off and drop it down between my legs, waiting for Julia to ask me to hand it over, or perhaps take out the box of ashes myself. I'll do whatever she wants me to. Being here, letting her take the lead, is all I can offer. It doesn't feel like nearly enough. But then, I'm not sure if anything ever could be. We just don't live in that kind of world.

Julia is quiet for so long it genuinely catches me off guard when she finally does speak. Her voice is low, grave, holding untold weight, like she's the narrator of a sad film. She keeps her eyes on the brook, not looking at me or the bag resting between my legs.

"When I first saw Lew, he...he... He was dancing in a club. Clearly fucked out of his mind. A mate of mine pointed him out. Said she'd seen him with Paul Winters, sitting next to him in the VIP section, getting treated like a cute little dog. Always off his face on whatever Paul gave him.

"I remember my mates laughing about it, talking about how this blond idiot had no idea what he was getting into.

"I remember thinking he looked really, really tired. Just like...not tired because he needed sleep, or yeah, okay, that, too. But I remember thinking he mostly looked like he was fucking tired of the whole thing. Just. Tired of being himself. Tired of everything that goes hand-in-hand with, like, *existing* in this life, you know. Not even just the bad parts. All of it. So bloody tired.

"We met for the first time, properly, months afterwards. Lew was in the bathroom of the same club. Sprawled on the floor. He was coming down hard. Looked like shit. Worse, maybe. I actually thought he was dead, at first, and it...it scared the hell out of me. My mates, they told me to leave him. He was Paul's problem. Except he wasn't, because Paul had dropped him, had a brand-new puppy sat next to him in the VIP section. I saw that before. I knew what it meant."

"What made you decide to take him home with you that night?" I ask, curious about Julia's reasoning. It feels like more than just being a good person.

Julia's brow furrows and she lets out a long, laboured breath, her shoulders lightly raising then lowering again in a small shrug.

"Honestly? Because, when I saw him before, dancing like he was having some kind of fit, making a right twat out of himself, my mates laughed at him. And I laughed, too." She squeezes her eyes tightly shut for a moment, a stray couple of tears leaking out when she opens them.

"Do you regret it?" I ask. I add quickly, "Taking him in, I mean, not laughing."

Julia doesn't respond for a moment, her gaze travelling out and across the clearing, as if she's searching for answers there. I look over there, too, but all I can see are more trees and leaves and dirt. I'm not sure what answers you could find in a place like this, so removed from the outside world beyond this forest.

She switches her full attention back to me. "My dad used to tell me when life gives you chances to make up for the bad you've done, you should aways take them."

I can't help the huff of laughter that comes out of my mouth, as I remember something Lady Mars told me. When Julia frowns at me questioningly, I say with mild amusement, "Taking a chance on a person is the worthiest risk there is."

Julia looks at me, brows raised slightly, like I've reached into her head and pulled out a string of words she had only begun to spin together.

"Right," she agrees with a deceptively light air. The left corner of her mouth hooks softly upwards. She dips her head and hunches her shoulders, spine arching as her body seems to curve inward.

It's a clear nonverbal cue. She's done showing me the scratched and bruised surface of her underbelly and wants desperately to strap her own armour back on to cover it up again.

I expected this response from her eventually. She was being far too candid, even if we are technically at a funeral of sorts for someone she loved deeply.

Julia turns to me with another frown then, and asks, "From experience, yeah?"

I give my own small nod of affirmation, willing to let Julia redirect our conversation to a place she finds more comfortable.

I'm only surprised it took this long for her to feel the need to hide away and protect the parts of herself which often prove the most vulnerable. She's far braver than I would be if our roles were reversed. I suppose in some ways, she and I have experienced a similar depth of loss, in very much the same circumstances.

Julia makes a thoughtful humming sound, her eyes

skating over me, contemplating something I can't begin to guess at.

"Was it you taking the chance, or someone else?"

I have no clue where she's going with this, but I want to shut it down regardless. I don't, though, for a couple of reasons. One, because Julia doesn't seem to be probing just for the sake of it, and two, I'm still finding it difficult to imagine denying her anything she asks of me.

It's like that day after the Anti-hero concert, when I was in Snow's office for the first time, and she was asking me to tell her about what happened during the attack. I didn't want to talk about it, but I made myself answer her question with as much detail as I could, because I owed it to the people who died, and the people who lost someone to the needless violence of that night.

Now Julia is asking for information I'd rather keep tucked away somewhere inside my mind. Locked in a box with a key I keep throwing away, only to see it reappear in front of me again every time something reminds me of what I want so badly to forget.

God, that meeting in Snow's office feels like it was a lifetime ago now. I can't believe it's possible for so much to happen in such a short amount of time, or that I would be changed so completely by it. How is it that eight months can feel like eight years?

When I first got my suit, it felt like the beginning of a whole new life. Now it's as if I've died and been transported to some alternate reality where everything has gone to shit, my foundations have crumpled, and my future has more of a definitive end than seems natural for a person to be able to see.

I keep wondering if this is what it's like to be told you're terminally ill, to be shown the path that lies ahead with a clarity you didn't ask for.

Knowing the approximate cause and time of my death feels like more certainty than anyone should have in their life.

It's honestly maddening.

"Both," I tell Julia while I still have the nerve, and the swell of acknowledged responsibility propelling me forward. "Multiple times, really. Two were the most important. My uncle, and—" I pause, unable to put into words all things Damon was to me. Friend doesn't feel right, boyfriend feels undeserved. *Light* and *shame* are what come to mind when I think of him, and those aren't titles you can give a person. "Another man I cared about."

Julia absorbs that, slowly nodding her head like she's taking my answer and turning it over a few dozen times inside her head, looking for the best angle to analyse it from. She reminds me a lot of Green, which is low level terrifying to witness. She is studying to be some sort of mind fuck expert, or psychiatrist, whatever you want to go with. If I ever feel like ruining a life, I might suggest Julia apply to FISA's training academy.

"Do you regret it?" Julia asks, eventually, her eyes slightly narrowed.

"No," I respond instantly. "Never." Because despite everything, despite what I've lost and the pain it all caused, I wouldn't give up the childhood I had with Roux. The insane meals we shared with our family, the birthdays we ruined, the stupid arguments we had, the innumerable times he was there for me in ways no one else could be, the hours he spent training me to survive this bastard existence, the nights he sat on my bed and told me stories about his life and my parents.

I'd be so much less of a person without having known him.

And even though it was different, and so much less time, I wouldn't undo the months of getting to know Damon, the laughs I dragged out of him, the anger I inspired, the impassioned touches he gave more freely than I would have thought him able.

He *mattered.*

Damon North was... He was this...this person. With pain so raw as to make you flinch away from it, a whole lifetime full of scrape and tear, and a heart he should have known was worth more than every bit of gold buried in the earth's core.

Sometimes I have terrible thoughts when I remember what he said to me from his knees on that factory floor.

almost my entire life
people have been calling me a hero
you're the only person who has ever made me feel
like I could be anything else

Damon North was so much more than just Polaris, and it kills me to think he died before he got the chance to truly know that.

He was young, he was twenty-one years old, and every time I think about it, I remember how angry I am. I'm still so, so fucking angry. I don't know what the hell to do with it all.

Julia is watching me now, like she can't see what I'm

thinking, but really wish she could. It reminds me of Green again, and I can't help how it causes my hackles to rise.

It's good thing, though, because I needed to be braced for her next stab.

"Do they regret it?"

Ah, I should have seen that question coming a mile off.

People were taken from us, from me and Julia, and part of the reason for it lands on our shoulders, whatever anyone else might say.

Julia is unlikely to ever admit it, but she's pissed off at herself for not being able to save her friend and for involving me in their situation. That's why she told me not to feel guilty for what the Winters family did in reaction to my attempt at interfering in Lewis's life. She doesn't blame me, because she's too busy hogging all the blame for herself.

"Well," I say, colder than I've been with her so far, "they're both dead. So, I'd hope they would."

"Dead," Julia echoes, brows drawing together once more, thinking it over before continuing her assault. "Because of you?"

"For me," I correct sharply, then shrug, reconsidering. "But. Yeah. That, too."

There's a long pause, where Julia attempts to find some way to respond to all that unnecessary dumping of personal baggage. Not really the day, let alone the moment, for it. Talking about other dead people when you're scattering another man's ashes. Feels like I've proposed at someone else's wedding. Which I would never do. I mean I'll kill people, but I've still got some lines I won't cross. I'm not a complete sociopath.

Julia's silence goes on for a long while. Enough so that I'm able to relax a little and take a moment to look around at the clearing again with more scrutiny.

There's a circle of trees around us of the same kind, ash, I think. All of them are full of light-green leaves with juddered edges, like bugs have been nibbling at them on a daily basis. I notice a squirrel stretched across a branch, its small nose twitching as it scratches at the bark, its brown fur ruffled and speckled with wet mud.

I watch the squirrel for a bit, waiting to see if it has a home in one of these trees, or if it's been out exploring the forest all day.

Mrs Colburn would take one look at this little fuzz ball and declare war. She is proper mental, that one. Even after we rounded up all the squirrels in Colbie, supposedly anyway, she wanted to have them shipped to Scotland in a crate.

And yes, we did have a trial about that. And yes, the squirrels got a lawyer. Sort of. It was Tate wearing the suit he uses when he goes to church with his grandparents. He looks really good in a suit, which was my only consolation for the absolute carnage I was forced to witness as I was unfortunately chosen to be part of the "jury". My name was picked out of the absurdly large bingo ball-cage we put all the townspeople's names into.

When it was asked at the town meeting who would want to represent the squirrels, Tate put both hands up and shouted with no sense of embarrassment at all, "I volunteer as tribute!" Throughout the "trial", he kept standing up and declaring "I object!" at random intervals and quoting episodes of *Law & Order* without any context. When he cross-examined Lady Mars and her gang, they reenacted, word for word, a trial scene from *The Golden Girls*.

I don't know if they planned that beforehand, and I'm sort of terrified they did not.

Caleb and Mei didn't help either. They just stood in the cheap seats with everyone else and cheered for Tate with the same amount of enthusiasm you might see in people supporting their favourite player in the World Cup final.

I swear to you, this happened. It sounds like madness, but it was real, and we should all be afraid of that fact.

These are *people* who could be living in *your world*. Now we all have to go on with that knowledge. You're welcome for the nightmares.

Julia catches my attention again by kicking at my ankle with her booted foot. I look back at her questioningly.

When I think we've finally entered the part of this where Julia is done digging into our wounds and she's ready to lean over and ask for her friend's ashes, she surprises me by going in another direction entirely.

"Did I ever tell you that your friend came to visit me in the hospital?"

My eyes widen in response, confusion taking hold and causing me to blink stupidly at her.

"What? No. My friend?"

"Yeah." Julia shrugs, like it's nothing. "He came by and asked to see me, like, a few days before you did. My doctor told me he was one of the blokes who sat outside my room the night I was brought in and stayed until late morning the next day."

She has to mean Jamie. Oh, shit.

"I know who you mean. He is...my friend. He came to see you again?" I ask, trying not to alarm her by sounding quite so confounded by the information.

Julia nods. "He sat with me for a bit. Asked—" She stops, clearing her throat. "He asked if I minded telling him about Lewis. Nothing weird. Just, like. What kind of person he was."

Bloody hell, Jamie. What in the hell. How could I not know this? More importantly, why would he do that?

"*Why*?" I choke out, unable to contain the question.

"I asked that," Julia says, still seeming unbothered by it all, "because I thought it was really fucking suspect, him just showing up and wanting to know about Lewis."

Well, yeah, it would be, wouldn't it? I'm genuinely shocked Julia even spoke to him.

She shrugs again, continuing in total ignorance of my internal freakout. "But... I don't know. He just said sometimes it's good to talk about a person you loved who died, to someone they never met. He said he does that with his mum. Said it helps to make it feel like she won't be forgotten." Julia makes a low snorting sound, pulling a face at me. "I thought it was bullshit at the time. But after I told him some stories about Lewis, it did make me feel...I don't know. Lighter?" She scowls deeply, like she's frustrated about not knowing how to explain her own feelings. She tries again. "Like it wasn't just up to me to remember him any more, because your friend knew those stories, too."

And it hits strangely, because I understand what she's trying to say. I don't feel that way about Roux, because of my family. They knew him, they loved him, and even without me there will be plenty of people who remember everything he was, the awful, the brilliant, and every bit in between.

But Damon, though. I feel like that about him. There weren't enough people who knew him, who knew the entirety of who he was. People can't be expected to remember what they didn't know. Damon let me in, whether I deserved it or not, then he died before I could give him everything I wanted to. Now there's this weight I carry, and I hate that it feels like a weight, because it was a gift. Truly. To have known him.

"Is this your long-winded way of asking me to tell you random stuff about *my* dead people?"

And yeah, "my dead people". That's how I chose to phrase it, and I'm sticking with it.

"If you want," Julia offers, her voice having taken on a kinder edge. She gives me a serious look, no jokes. "I'll listen." She means it.

"I didn't even go to their funerals," I say, like it's some kind of excuse, rather than a further indictment of my inability to deal with what's happened.

Julia presses her lips together, hard, and tilts her head from side to side, as if carefully considering her response.

"But you're here, for Lewis." She offers me a smile verging on kind, like it's a chance all its own. "And there's no rules, you know. We can think about them. All of them. Your people and mine. We can remember them, now, together. We can do that, if you want."

I'm not sure how to answer her implied question. I've already shoved myself so far outside of my current comfort zone. I haven't really spoken about Damon and Roux, not properly, with anyone other than Jatin. I didn't feel like I could. I was afraid the moment I started attempting to unravel everything I feel and think about them, I'd just collapse entirely. Get crushed beneath the weight of it all. Turn to dust and atoms, scattered and lost to any semblance of composure, of rationality.

I didn't want to throw myself over the edge before Liquid Onyx even had the chance to drop-kick me into the open air.

Sanity can be an elusive promise to keep with yourself when the string binding it to you is pulled taut and bared to a world full of sharp edges. Every stuttered step could mean another cut, another fray.

My string is thinner than it used to be. I have less confidence in the strength of it. I'm warier of how hard I'm able to pull before it snaps.

But really. In absolute truth. I'm less scared of the fall than I am of what I'll be able to do before I hit the ground.

That's pretty much always been the truth for me.

But things *have* changed. Since I finished with the Winters family, for better or worse. Since Rani kicked my arse into gear.

After I spoke to Jatin out on Rohan's patio, I felt like I was ready to accept the possibility of a new beginning. The beginning of what, I've got no idea. But something. Something better than what I have going on now. A better beginning to my end, at least. A final chapter not written in blood, black or otherwise.

With all that in mind, alongside Julia's earnest eyes and unexpectedly soft smile, I think it's probably time I try releasing the chokehold I have on my own emotions. Or at least loosening a finger or two. More baby steps.

"Okay." I blow out a loud breath. "The man I cared about, his name was Damon."

Julia nods encouragingly.

"He was the hero, right. Polaris?"

My mouth twitches at one corner. Sitting forward on my stone, I draw closer to Julia. My voice lowers without my permission, like I can't help but want to protect Damon's identity, even now.

"He was a lot of things," I tell her.

Julia nods, as if she understands what that means. All the things I haven't said out loud. "Go on then. What else was he?"

That's all it really takes to get me going. Spilling history only two people can hold between them and building a profile in her mind of who Damon was. I give her a handful of stories about the time Damon and I spent together, and the things I learned in those moments.

I tell her about how we met, in the park, not the first time. I tell her about our somewhat disastrous date in the bar. I tell her about what it was like to hear him laugh and kiss him against a sink and to stand beside him in his kitchen and bake and talk about our mothers.

Julia, in turn, gives me some of the same about Lewis. Memories gathered. Pain shared. Lazy nights and rushed mornings.

She tells me about the time they went ice skating and

came home with twisted ankles and a mutual promise never to go again. She tells me about the time Lewis tried to put their meagre kitchen to use and almost killed them both by scorching two chicken breasts to blackened husks. She tells me about their last Christmas together, which they spent at her family's home, and how many Poundland gag gifts they bought for each other and wrapped in paper more expensive than the gifts themselves.

I'm not sure how much time goes by with us talking about our people, but it must be significant, because there's noticeably a lot less light shining in through the trees.

Our conversation seems to draw to a natural close, as if in silent agreement we reach the conclusion we've shared enough of ourselves for one day. Julia hasn't struck me as a particularly open person. I think the only reason she was so willing to open up months ago about her and Lewis's situation was because they desperately needed help, and she thought I could offer it.

Julia nudges my arm and indicates the bag. I pause for a moment, reading her expression carefully before picking it up and handing it over. I don't want Julia to rush herself. She should be able to sit here all day if she wants to.

Once it's placed in her grasp, Julia opens the bag settled on her lap and takes out a plain metal box. She closes the bag again and I take it from her without being asked and put it down beside me, lying against the stone I'm sitting on.

Julia holds the metal box with both hands, looking

down at it with a somewhat inscrutable expression, like she can't quite decide how to feel about the box, or its contents.

A memory, unbidden, of Lewis hanging from the rafters of that office flashes in my mind. Skin carved up and hair matted with dried blood.

Blood. It seeps, it sprays, it dries.

His beaten face. Swollen and wrong.

Those still, brown eyes. Dead eyes. Dead, dead eyes. Brown eyes, blue eyes, his eyes. Their eyes. In the office. On the carpet. In the park. On the grass. In the factory. On the dirty floor—

Fuck. *Fuck.*

No. I can't. I...

Please, not now.

"I'm sorry." The words spring out of my mouth before I can swallow them back down where they probably belong to curdle and wither and fade.

Julia looks at me, dragging her attention away from the box in her hands. She peers at me questioningly, asking for elaboration without voicing it.

I try again even though I know I shouldn't.

"I'm sorry I didn't just do what you asked me to do in the first place." I squeeze my hands together hard and shake my head too vigorously. "I should have just killed him."

Because I've killed him now, anyway. All that philosophising I did about my own morality was pointless, meaningless. I killed Paul Winters a few days ago and it was three months too late.

"No," Julia says, surprising me with her vehemence.

"I'm the one who should be sorry about that shit. I should never have asked you to kill him. I put you in a horrible position and now you're in an even worse one because of me. My choices. Not yours."

"What?" I draw my eyebrows together in fierce confusion.

"I'm glad you didn't kill him when I asked, because Lewis would have hated it. Lew had the softest heart of anyone I've known. He would have hated someone else getting hurt because of him. He would have hated violence being done on his behalf."

I can't help but picture Damon. That night on the roof, after we found Julia and Lewis, when we fought like kicked dogs.

Don't you ever kill anyone on my behalf.

There aren't enough words to describe how spectacularly I've failed to abide by that order. I might have killed Mia, in the moment, because of what she did to Roux. But I would never have got to that point if she hadn't hurt so many people before. Elle. All the civilians who died when her people attacked the city. Dru. Then Damon, what her actions all but forced him to do to himself.

Julia reaches over and touches my arm with purposeful gentleness. Her face has become more determined and perhaps more sorrowful at the same time.

"And I should never have asked you, because I think you've got a soft heart, too. I've seen what's been going on in the news." She presses her lips tightly for a moment, as if bearing herself up. Her gaze flickers away, a slight hint of what I think might be shame crossing her features. "We haven't talked about it, but I know what you've been doing. I won't tell you to stop, because I ain't got the right to do that, especially not after I put the idea in your head. But...I'm just going to say."

When she looks at me again, there's a determined set to her expression, a fierceness having returned to her eyes. It reminds me of what I saw that night we met, in the alley, a strength she's proven herself as possessing over and over since then.

"Don't let them take that softness away from you," she tells me, the gentleness in her voice offsetting the sharp downturn of her mouth. "Because, God fucking knows, they've taken far too much already."

Julia looks pointedly down at the box containing Lewis's ashes, her meaning clear.

My mind conjures up the memory of my conversation with Green, when I discussed with her what Julia asked of me. When Green asked me why going after Paul Winters with the aim of straight-up murdering the man was different to taking someone out mid-battle. Why I could live with the second, but not the first.

I can fight in the dark. But I don't want to live there.

That's what I told her.

For months, I've tried to tell myself going after the Winters family was nothing in comparison to what I'd already done. I broke my rules. Correction: my *rule*. The only one I truly gave myself. To not use my power on a person.

I crossed that line in an epic way, and afterwards, nothing felt like it was off limits. I was already in the deep end, cast out into the middle of the ocean, with no sign of shore in any direction. Cut off from my lighthouse. No line

I could use to drag myself back in.

I thought, if I'm already lost at sea, I might as well learn how to dive down into the deep. Teach myself how to survive without breathing. To absorb the cold and accept the pressure. To live in the dark, give myself over to the pit inside my head, let it devour me whole.

As much as I want to rise to the surface, to find the light, to wash ashore. To move forward again. As much as I want that, I just don't quite know how to yet.

It was easier to fight everyone else's monsters than to face my own.

Julia doesn't wait for a response from me. Maybe she knows there's nothing I could say that wouldn't be a platitude or an outright lie. She seems satisfied she's expressed what thoughts she wanted to express as well as she could have, and whatever I take from it will be my own choice.

Minutes pass as we both sit together, once again, in complete silence. This time however, the silence feels heavier, full of anticipation.

Not, as it turns out, for either of us to speak.

Julia, without warning, lets out a huffed breath and rolls her shoulders back in preparation. She looks ready or at least seems to be putting up a good show of it to me.

She opens the metal box containing Lewis's ashes and leans forward, closer to the brook babbling on over rock and sodden dirt, the sound at once as peaceful as it is unrelenting.

I hear Lady Mars speaking in my head.

Water, the true immortal, bringer of death and purification.

I watch as Julia takes a few shaky breaths. Her hands shake around the metal box. There's no crack of weakness in the determined set of her expression. I'd expect no less from her.

On instinct, I reach over and place a hand on her back, right between her shoulder blades. I don't speak, because as before, there's nothing to say.

My touch seems to steady Julia somehow, as if I've offered to take some of the weight from her shoulders and carry it between us, as we once did Lewis.

She and I begin this together, it seems right perhaps that we should finish it as a joint effort.

Julia's hands stop shaking after a few seconds of us sitting and breathing and existing in this moment as the unit we decided to become for this short stretch of time.

When she tips the metal box and Lewis's ashes fall in a curtain of grey, only to be swallowed up by the rush of water below and carried away, it feels almost like a gut punch. A painful release of air erupting from both of us at the same time.

It's not good. It doesn't make anything better. Nothing short of resurrection could ever hope to fix this.

But it is done. The last hurdle jumped. The last gate unlocked to reveal the endless fields beyond.

Julia reaches behind her and takes hold of the hand I still have resting on her back. I think for a moment she wants me to withdraw, but when I try to, she tugs my hand back. She settles it in her lap and wraps both her own hands around mine. She holds on tight, and I realise maybe she needs a lifeline of her own.

I have my ocean. Now Julia has her open plain.

Maybe the obvious answer is the right one. To escape the dark, I'll need someone to lead me home.

Chapter Six

Cast in Broken Moonlight

Out of fear that I will lose my nerve, I don't give myself any time to change my mind, instead moving ahead with the course of action I've decided to take.

I've spent months avoiding my friends while out on patrol, somehow managing to dodge them successfully despite the fact I know they've been looking for me. The streets have been full of whispers, people, new informants of mine, telling me the other supers of Danger have been asking them for information about me. Where I am, what I've been doing, even if I'm taking unnecessary risks with noticeable frequency.

To be honest, I expected them to catch up with me way before now. But the longer it went on with them failing to pin me down, the more wary I became of the day when they finally would.

I didn't consider that it would be me who sought one of them out first.

I've only been out on patrol for a couple of hours when I pick up the trail of my best friend. From there, it takes me another hour to track Crescent down and wait in the shadows for my chance to get him when he's alone and resting between incidents. I'm able to watch him deal with three violent muggings and one case of a man stalking a young woman for reasons other than what she had in her purse.

Crescent deals with it all as a seasoned super would, quickly and without much fuss. For the most part. Although I can't help but notice a distinct edge to Crescent that wasn't there when I last saw him out on patrol. There's a certain cruelty to his hits, an extreme excess of violence he deploys on those who mean to do others harm. I'm not sure how to explain it, but he's changed. Something has changed. I'm unable to ignore the jagged rage in how Crescent is dispensing our kind of justice.

He seems, undeniably, angry. More so than I've seen him outside of a big mission, when we're going up against a supervillain who requires harsher tactics to defeat.

When Crescent finds himself alone on top of the roof of a nondescript office building, I move to reveal my presence to my friend. I'm lucky he isn't currently using his power, otherwise he'd likely pick up on my strong sense of trepidation and excitement.

As nervous as I am to see him, I've also missed my friend more than I could ever express with words. We haven't been apart, spent this long without even talking since...well...ever, actually. Caleb has been a constant part of my life for so long I can't really remember what it was like not to have him there as a permanent fixture.

Crescent is half-kneeling on the ledge of the office building, his silver suit shining brightly against the backdrop of the pitch-black sky. There's only a sliver of moon out tonight, and very few stars, the city lights likely drowning most of them out. He looks bigger in the suit, and Crescent is a large man to begin with.

Not as much as he used to be, though. It seems he's lost more weight since I last saw him. I try not to worry about that and tell myself I can't just start nagging him after ignoring him for three months. He'd probably belt me one, or ten.

I might honestly deserve it from him.

Unsure of what reception I will receive, I feel cautious about moving in too close to start with. I keep a healthy distance between us, not wanting this to turn into a brawl before I can get two words out. Crescent can be quick to anger when he's feeling intense emotion.

Crescent notes my appearance the very moment I choose to let him know I'm here. His entire body stiffens. He does not, however, turn around. He seems to be waiting for me to make the first move, or perhaps to stutter out the first set of excuses or apologies.

We're up high enough that no one is likely to hear us talking unless they're very determined about it.

Still, the urge to abandon this course of action and run away is embarrassingly strong.

Before I can bottle it entirely, I speak.

And it isn't what I intended to say at all.

"Want to make a bet on which one of us will go insane and die first?"

It's the wrong thing to say. It's probably one of the worst things I could have possibly said to him right now. I know that. I knew it even as I said it. But, somehow, I couldn't seem to stop myself from being the worst kind of arsehole, to one of the people who deserves it from me the least.

Crescent does turn then, fast. He whips around like he's been yanked by an invisible rope around his neck. He looks right at me, absolute fury burning in his eyes, the likes of which I've only ever seen directed at his father when they're in the middle of a terrible fight.

It makes me flinch back, feeling as if I've been slapped by a strong hand.

Crescent unfolds from his kneeling position, getting up and jumping down from the ledge to the roof surface. He stalks towards me, broad shoulders set like those of a professional athlete, his expression creased into something horrifically honest and difficult to look at.

I tell myself to run. I tell myself to stay out and take what comes. I'm frozen to the spot, unable to move or make a single sound in my defence.

Crescent comes at me with the energy of a raging bull, and I fully expect to be put on my arse with a solid hit to the face.

When Crescent stops right in front of me, so tall and full of pent-up rage and breathing hard like he's just spent a few hours outrunning a building about to crush him when it falls, I'm confused.

That confusion blooms into panic when my friend

literally falls to his knees in front of me, as if his legs can no longer support his weight. He grabs hold of my arms and pulls, hard. I have no choice, and no other inclination, but to go down to the ground with him.

Crescent moves his hands from my forearms up to my biceps. He squeezes them with painful desperation, his eyes already shining with emotion and unshed tears. He sucks in a sharp, shuddering breath, trying to speak, his words barely understandable with how much his voice is wavering.

"Please, don't leave me again, brother."

He sounds like he hasn't spoken in weeks, or like his throat was rubbed raw with sandpaper at some point and he's still healing from the assault.

There's so much raw pain on his face it makes me feel sick. Because this is my fault. I did this. I left my friend alone, and this is the result of that selfishness. I knew how much it would hurt him, and I did it anyway, because I was so caught up in my own bullshit.

I wrestle out of his grip, which takes some real effort, and practically throw myself at him, wrapping my arms around his neck and pulling him to me. I hold on tight, to the point of what I know must be bone-creaking severity.

Caleb doesn't hesitate to return the embrace, his arms coming around me like two pieces of metal bending around a powerful magnet and crunching inward due to some unstoppable force. He buries his face in my neck and lets out a sound I couldn't mistake for anything other than a sob. It racks through his body, causing tears to burn behind my own eyes.

I press my mouth to the side of his face, close to his

ear, speaking without any idea of what I'm really saying, letting my own fear and vulnerability show without any of my usual barriers.

"Please don't ever hate me, brother. I can't take it. Not from you."

I'm completely undone by this ferocious display of despair from Caleb. It's the most I've seen him express since we were very young, since his mum died, maybe. Caleb. He's Caleb now. I can't think of him as Crescent when we're like this.

"I need you," Caleb tells me in a rushed whisper, like a confession he's vaguely ashamed of.

"I need you, too." I give him the same truth in return, because it is the truth. Of all the people in my life, Caleb is the one I imagined standing by my side for the whole of it. It was always going to be us, no matter what else happened.

I should have remembered that.

Caleb and I stay clenched together as we are for a long time. I'm not quite sure how long, but my knees actually begin to hurt, so it must be a significant while. I probably could have gone on for an infinite length of time, I think we both could. However, there are things we need to talk about, and I'm still afraid of losing my nerve all over again if I try to articulate what I'm thinking and feeling to Caleb.

I pull back from my best friend, just far enough to press my forehead against his. Caleb's hands come up to hold both sides of my head, keeping me in place, as if I'd try to do a runner, now, after all that. I couldn't leave him alone here on this roof if I wanted to. It would break me. It would break us both, I'm sure.

Caleb is breathing a little better now, no longer sounding like he's hyperventilating, which is at least one good thing.

"Fuck Liquid Onyx," he says, suddenly, a choked laugh escaping his lips. "I told you I'd lose my mind without you. Guess what? I was not wrong."

He pulls away from me a bit more, so we're able to look each other in the face properly. Pain is still etched across his features, like someone took a small knife and nicked away at him bit by bit, leaving him with permanent scars only I can see, changing the entire scope of his face, reforming it into something sadder than it ever was before.

There are tear streaks on his skin, the wetness having spilled out over his mask and dripped from his lightly stubbled jaw. I raise my hand to wipe them way with the flat of my palm.

It reminds me of when we were children and Caleb would cry because he got hurt during training, or when his father particularly upset him for whatever reason. I used to brush away the tears from his red, stubborn-set little face and tell him everything would be okay, because we were together, and that was all we needed to be all right.

It was mostly true then, and it still is now. Except for me, it was usually Jamie I needed, too.

I always used to think, if I have the Moon brothers in my life, I'll be okay. I should have remembered that, too. If it's not been obvious already, I have not been doing well without them. I'm not in the least surprised about my own attempts at self-sabotage.

"You haven't lost me," I remind him, and it sounds just as false as it did the last time.

Caleb pushes back from me, putting space between us in a very deliberate way. He sits down on the floor of the roof, legs crossed and elbows balanced on his knees. When he looks at me it's with an old and battle-weary sorrow. It makes me regret all over again the fact I haven't been there for him the last three months.

"You promised me I never would."

Guilt swells in my gut, settling in like the slow growth of mottled rot. I copy Caleb's movements, getting my feet under me for a brief moment, then shift onto my haunches before dropping down into a seated position across from him.

"Might not be able to keep that one, Cal," I say more honestly than I want to, mouth sliding up into a self-deprecating approximation of a smile. "I'm sorry." It's not enough. Not nearly enough.

"Don't think any of us can," Caleb says, brows creasing in consternation. "Which is so beyond shit I can't even deal, you know?" He brings his hands together in front of him, clasping them tightly, as if he needs something to hold on to and the only person who he can trust to do that is himself.

If so, I deserve it. His mistrust. Leaving like I did, it was a betrayal of sorts. A betrayal of the friendship we'd built up like a bridge for over fourteen years. When I left without a word, it was like I torched the fucking thing. I can't blame Caleb for not wanting to take a chance on leaping across the distance I've created to meet me on charred foundations.

"I know."

I'm unable to contain a choked laugh of my own, then, because everything seems to be hitting me at once. The emotional upheaval of seeing Caleb again, the friend I've missed more than words could ever properly express, has taken a lethal shot at the defences I've forged these months on my own.

It's all such a load of utter shit, this thing that was done to us, this thing that's happening to us, years later, when it was supposed to be done and over and possible to move on from. What is there even to say, now, apart from this is *fucked*, every scrape and inch of it is so fucked, and there's probably nothing any of us can do about it? We're stuck on a downward spiral we didn't know we were teetering on the edge of and have no control over. Not the speed, and certainly not the final destination.

"Come home with me," I ask. Or demand. Or whatever.

Caleb doesn't hesitate like I expect him to.

"Yes," he says with a dry undertone of censure. "Please show me where you've been hiding from your family for months like a selfish prat, I want to see." He narrows his eyes accusingly. "It better not be a bush."

"A bush?" I'm marginally incredulous.

I'm not sure why, as I did pass out in a bush one night when I'd gone too long without sleeping or eating and got my arse kicked around by a supervillain who attacked Danger when all the other supers were busy elsewhere and I had to take him on my own.

The supervillain was one of Damon's usual suspects, a man named Firestorm with the power of pyrokinesis.

He escaped from prison for what must be the third time, just to cause havoc for, as Firestorm termed it, Polaris's "replacement". Danger's fire brigade and I had a glorious evening stopping that right twat from setting half of uptown Danger ablaze. It was mostly just me chasing after the red-caped clown and Sami's firefighter boyfriend, Dan, liaising with me over a walkie talkie on where best to aim their efforts.

After the battle was over, and Firestorm was doused and drop-kicked back into police custody, I fled the scene and ended up falling into a bush somewhere inside Danger City Park. It was very late at night, so no one was around to see me do it, but still. I can no longer technically claim not to have slept in a bush.

"Or something more upscale"—Caleb pretends to look thoughtful by tipping his head to one side and frowning slightly—"like a skip."

I squint at him, this idiot I've missed every single day for over three months, and respond with what I believe to be an appropriate amount of drollness. "Do you imagine me going through the process of renting a skip in this scenario?" I raise a hand, holding it cupped in front of me and gesturing forward in a shallow scooping motion. "Or have I just found a skip and claimed squatters' rights over it like an experienced man of the streets would?"

Caleb lightly shrugs his shoulders, mouth cutting up from both sides to create an amused smirk. It looks sharper than I remember, like a curved razor has been bolted on to his face. A face that looks ashen. Paler than I've ever seen it. I would say he was sick, if I didn't know better.

He's changed so much, I'm unsure if the easy, charming smile I'm used to seeing him wear would fit any more. Even his silver domino mask looks like it might be settled somewhat loosely on his face.

Everything about Caleb seems harsher than when I last saw him this close up. His features appear to have been carved from marble, cheekbones filed and reshaped with a chisel. My friend is more rock and bone than muscle and flesh. The realisation is a troubling one.

"Figured you'd use your wiles"—Caleb makes suggestive eyebrows at me—"and get some unsuspecting delivery man to 'accidentally lose' one of his skips."

"My wiles?" I snort in disbelief. "What wiles do you think I have that would work on a professional courier of high-end mini hostels?"

Caleb pulls a more benevolent expression and presses a hand to his heart. He speaks with sarcastic earnestness. "I have nothing but faith in your ability to awkwardly charm any man you set your sights upon."

It takes a great deal of my well-honed self-control not to lean forward a bit and flick him directly in the eye like he deserves.

Blimey, I've missed this infuriating twat an absurd amount.

"How about you?" I ask instead, fusing a bit of hopefulness into it for the sake of playing along with whatever this is we're doing. Putting off the inevitable, maybe. We're both quite good at that. Which is most certainly not a compliment to either one of us.

"Oh, I'm already caught in your web. Just one of many fools desperate for your attention," Caleb intones.

"My devotion is unending. Eternal. Everlasting. Infinite as fuck."

"My *web*?" I say, genuinely horrified, leaning away from him for emphasis, because. Just. No.

No.

"Please never say anything like that again. Whatever happened to not being into me?"

Caleb unclasps his hands, holds them apart palms up, and shrugs in a dismissive gesture.

"I've come around on it," he says in a droll tone.

"You're so full of shit." I scowl at him disapprovingly. "Go away."

"Nope. Shan't." Caleb squints at me, then, eyes raking over me with more purposeful intent. He changes the direction of our "conversation" without warning. "You don't live in a gym, do you?" He indicates my arms and the obvious definition of the muscle I've cultivated since he last saw me. He doesn't wait for me to answer before going on and asking, "Mate, have you got yourself some grief muscle?"

I mean. There's only one sane response to that.

"I don't even want to know what you're on about."

Caleb does not pick up on my subtle hint. "Yeah, it's like how people get revenge bodies." He nods at my left bicep. "Is that what you did? But because people died, instead of people breaking up with you."

"Because those two things are comparable," I comment dryly.

"How would you know?" Caleb asks, mostly just to be an argumentative twat. "You've never broken up with anyone."

"I'm gonna break up with *you*," I mutter belligerently. Like a tired three-year-old who proclaims himself to not be tired.

"Pretty sure you did already, but okay, I like a good rerun." Caleb frowns and adds more seriously, "But this time I want Tate, and you can have Mei. We'll split custody of Jamie."

The sound of his name tumbling from Caleb's lips hits me directly in the solar plexus. I don't know why, as this is hardly the first time I've thought of Jamie in all these months we've been apart. But something about Caleb speaking about him affects me differently. It's sort of like the space and time between us becomes more real and less figurative.

Guilt prickles at the back of my skull like pins being repeatedly jabbed into it in quick repetition. I've really fucked up by running from my family, I know that. I feel it acutely, and never more so than now, when I imagine how Jamie must have interpreted my very purposeful absence.

I don't want to think about how hurt he must have been by my choice to abandon the people who care about me, to go on a one-man crusade against the Winters and OI. Well, a two-man crusade, if you count Rohan, which I should, since I'm sure I'd be dead already if it weren't for him.

I ignore the treacherous voice in my head, the one calling out from the ever-widening black hole that everyone would have been better off if I'd gone it alone and died like I was probably meant to. Like I wanted to, in the early days, right after the night at the factory.

It makes me uncomfortable now, to think of how desperately I've longed to be free of this incessant, painful thing we have the audacity to call a gift.

Life.

A hope I couldn't accept and didn't want to grasp onto.

After everything Damon gave to let me struggle on and try to fix what I can before it's all over and done and lost. To spend more time with the family I built and no longer feel worthy of. I was so ready to throw it away, like what he gave me meant nothing, when I know it should have been my one solace.

I've failed them. Both Damon and Jamie, albeit in different ways and for different reasons.

Even though I feel as if I have no right to ask, I can't stop myself.

"Is Jamie—"

But Caleb is apparently less willing to indulge me than he once might have been. He cuts me off before I can even complete the question. "Okay, seriously? I'm not going there right now." He speaks with that same odd sharpness to him, eyes having hardened to be more gunmetal than moonshine. The chilling threat of a storm barely leashed. "You've gotta talk to my brother and sort out the shit between you. That's all I'm gonna say 'bout it."

As much as it disappoints me, I accept Caleb's rebuff without argument. I have no right to information about Jamie. If I want to know what's going on with him, I should stop being a coward and talk to Jamie in person.

If nothing else, it's reassuring to hear Caleb being so defensive on his brother's behalf. I wonder if my absence has forced Caleb and Jamie to rely more heavily on each other than they might have otherwise had to. It might be the one good thing to come out of this if that really is the case.

I think Caleb might need more people he can properly rely on in the near future, if the problems I've picked up on continue and he deteriorates further.

It's not just Caleb's outward appearance that's bothering me. It's the painfully obvious air of fake steadiness he's failing to convince me is real, and his blunt acts of deflection, to hide how badly he's struggling, to pretend he's okay when he simply is not. I can't ignore the tension he seems to carry in every muscle in his body. There's a desperate edge to him I find unsettling. He seems to be on the precipice of something. Maybe something terrible, although I can't be sure of what.

If Caleb gets much worse than this, he and I will need have a far more serious conversation than we are probably capable of. But I will have to try. We're no longer at the point where I can tell myself Caleb is just struggling with a bad break-up.

The time for that conversation, however, is not now.

"How's Lady Mars and The Parents?" I ask, instead.

"Shitty," Caleb answers honestly, his expression one of grim acceptance. "The Parents miss you. And Lady Mars. She—" He swallows hard. "She's trying to look after everyone. She's stronger than all of us put together, you know."

Yeah, I do know.

I get to my feet at a speed which mildly alarms Caleb. He follows almost immediately and comes to a stop a few feet away from me. Still within touching distance, but with more space between us than he'd usually bother with.

I make an apologetic face at him.

It was too much just then. Hearing about Lady Mars, and how much she must be hurting after the loss of Roux. They were partners in raising me, and very close friends besides. Roux's death would have left a hole in her life like few others could. I can't think she's been as all right as Caleb seems to think she's been. Not really.

If Lady Mars has managed to hold it together for the last three months, it's only because she's felt the need to for the sake of everyone else.

That isn't fair. I should have been there to take some of the pressure off her. To give her the space and time to break apart, then piece herself back together at a pace she felt comfortable with.

A renewed flush of guilt washes through me at the re-minder of how badly I've let down a woman I so admire. She deserved more from me. She taught me to be better than this. They both did. There's no excuse for it.

I have so much to make up for, and it feels momen-tarily daunting to contemplate actually trying to.

Caleb watches me warily, but with a knowing glint that lets me know he isn't completely ignorant of the rea-son for my stark reaction.

"You okay if we leave patrol for tonight?" I ask, an-noyed at how my voice cracks, as if all this excess emotion is tying my vocal cords into knots.

Caleb's expression clears and he takes a step closer to me, reaching out with his hand to touch my shoulder. He squeezes and shakes it lightly.

"Yeah. Don't worry. You've officially pulled, mate. I will absolutely spend the night with you in your seduction-earned skip."

"Back of the queue, Moon." I shrug off his hand and jerk my thumb over my shoulder. "The last person who propositioned me was a chaotic neutral genius billionaire. Fucking step it up or get out of the game."

I don't wait for his response, turning around and taking the ledge at a swift run, jumping from one roof to another. I turn my head, looking back to see if Caleb is following.

Caleb stands on the other rooftop, dumbfounded for a few moments, before he releases a loud bark of laughter and comes chasing after me.

*

I take Caleb back to Rohan's place, partly relieved that Rohan told me he would be staying at the base tonight because he had a few projects he wanted to work on in his lair.

He's told me not to call it his lair, but whatever, if it walks like a duck and talks like a duck and provides an atmosphere that lends to the planning of world domination, then it's a fucking lair and he needs to get over it and accept responsibility for the result of his own interior design choices.

Caleb balked a little when I told him we'd need to change our clothes before we went to the flat, because there's no way in other than going through the front door like normal people.

Thankfully, over the years, the SSS unit has got into the habit of stashing supplies around the city, like emergency food or medical supplies or clothes, just in case any of them needs it while out on patrol.

We make a stop to collect some civilian clothes for Caleb at one of the stash points, before going to my own hiding spot so I can pick up my things.

Caleb and I change in a dark alley a few streets away from Rohan's flat, shoving our suits into the backpacks we stored our clothes in.

We get some of the usual strange looks from the doorman who works in Rohan's building, but he doesn't say anything, since he recognises me as someone who does have the right to be here. There was some misunderstanding about that when I first moved in. I think I looked a bit too much like the general riff-raff to be accepted into a place this unapologetically posh.

Rohan had to break his cardinal rule of not talking to any of his neighbours just to reassure everyone and their tiny, yipping dogs that I was not a thief or a rent boy or a chav or anything lethally dangerous like that.

"Rex, you fuck. What the hell is all this?" Caleb asks once we're inside Rohan's flat and he's had a good chance to scan the luxurious surroundings with wide and somewhat perturbed eyes.

"A billionaire's flat. Rohan's a billionaire." I move around Caleb to stand in front of him, throwing both my arms out and gesturing at the space around us. "This is how billionaires live. I know that now. I have observed and retained the knowledge."

"Okay," Caleb says, eyeing me with no small amount of bewilderment, "when you said you were staying with Sathe, I didn't realise you meant you were living the suite life of Rohan and Rex. Jesus, fuck, this place is big and fancy and *white*. Why is it so white? Are you legally allowed to touch stuff with your grubby peasant fingers?" He squints at me dubiously. "Does he really trust you to breathe on his things?"

I really don't feel like I should ask, but the words spill out of my mouth before I can think better of them. "*Why* would I breathe on his things?"

Caleb goes over to the sofa and drops his black, canvas backpack holding his Crescent suit onto it. He turns around to look at me again, leaning on the sofa back and crossing his arms over his chest.

"I figured you were earning your keep by shining the silverware like the Alfred cosplay existence you have clearly been living."

"He doesn't have silverware." I drop my own gym bag down on the floor beside the kitchen island. "There are, like, two spoons in this entire place." I hold up two fingers. "One for each of us."

"Wow, domestic." Caleb's mouth kicks up into a teasing smile. "Hold on, are you dating Sathe? Have you married him?" He gestures around the flat again. "Like. For his money."

"No." My voice has dipped into a sardonic drawl. "I have not married Rohan for his fat bank account."

I'd possibly consider it, especially since we're both dying anyway. Imagine the kind of ridiculously extravagant wedding we could have? I've never contemplated marriage, certainly not in any serious capacity, but I'd think about it if I got to rent my own private island and fly in a fleet of elephants or dinosaurs or whatever. Rich people probably have access to the dinosaur technology, right? That is what the Jurassic Park films have taught me.

"Really? Good." Caleb nods once, firmly, as if deciding on something. "That means I'm still in with a chance."

"Oh, yeah?" I raise my eyebrows at him, curious as to his reasons.

"Yeah," Caleb says, like he thinks it's a stupid question. He presses a hand to his chest. "I want a jet ski. And a castle." He holds up his hand and flashes it at me. "And a giant rock on my finger."

I slowly shake my head, colouring my tone with sarcastic disbelief. "Didn't peg you for a gold digger."

Caleb lets out a low scoffing sound. "I live for the bling, no apologies." He scans the room once more before settling his gaze back on me. "Does he have jewels? Can we steal them?"

"I'm not stealing Rohan's jewels."

"Oh, come on," Caleb needles, still smirking playfully. "Be gay, do crime. Don't be boring. No one likes a morally upstanding gay, and you know that. The internet has spoken and will not be denied."

I snort out a laugh. "You're actually ridiculous."

"Does he have the Heart of the Ocean rolling around here somewhere?" Caleb asks, furrowing his brows in mock curiosity. He nods at me. "You could put it on, and I'd draw you like I do my French girls."

"When have you ever drawn a French girl?" I eye him

with heavy scepticism.

"Once I drew a girl wearing a beret," Caleb replies plainly, then gives one firm nod, as if reaffirming his own conclusion to himself. "I'm pretty sure that counts."

I'm reminded vividly of the time when Caleb did an honestly beautiful sketch of Mei during one particularly boring secondary school assembly. He drew it on the back of his grey English book, using the cigarette-length pencil he wore semi-permanently behind his ear, which, alongside far too much hair gel and the leather jacket he rocked around in at the time, made him look like an artsy version of some bellend from *Grease*.

Caleb made the mistake of letting another girl who was not Mei catch him sketching. Girl Who Was Not Mei insisted he do a sketch of her, which Caleb eventually agreed to do after some prodding. Unfortunately, Girl Who Was Not Mei's boyfriend, who for the sake of this story we shall call Jealousy Lad, took offense to Caleb accidentally playing the part of a boy from a sappy teen romcom.

Jealousy Lad, the downtrodden boy of great legend, had no choice but to challenge a very confused dope, otherwise known as Caleb, to a fisticuffs-at-dawn type situation.

Caleb, never one to back away from conflict *ever*, took Jealousy Lad up on his offer of a fight behind the Science buildings during lunch break. Almost our entire year gathered around to watch the epic battle between Jealousy Lad and Caleb.

Girl Who Was Not Mei cheered with unbridled enthusiasm for Caleb from the sidelines, which was bizarre.

Tate, for the sake of fairness he told me, cheered twice as loud for Jealousy Lad. Mei, conversely, ignored all of us and went to play football with a group of sixth form girls instead.

I cheered for nothing and no one, because the whole thing was stupid, if for no other reason than Caleb was a literal superhuman and therefore had a ridiculous advantage which rendered the entire situation of who to cheer for completely moot.

Suffice to say, it wasn't much of a fight, and it only went for as long as it did because Caleb is a low-level masochist and let Jealousy Lad get a few good hits in for no good reason.

Mr Wong, the headteacher for Colbie's combined primary and secondary school, came outside just as Caleb was getting bored letting another teenager punch him incorrectly, like wow. I don't think everyone should go around punching people, but I do think everyone should be taught how to punch people properly. Keep your thumb on the outside of the fist, people, unless you want a broken fucking thumb to take home with you.

Caleb and Jealousy Lad were both given a week's worth of lunchtime detention. No one in our school ever got served with after-school detention, because none of the teachers wanted to stay late to supervise it.

Caleb used to get lunchtime detention almost every other week, mostly for bunking off or spending the entire class drawing all over his workbooks.

Not sure what the male version of That Bitch is, but I'm pretty sure Caleb was, and will probably always be to some extent, That Bitch.

He was never kicked out of school, though, by some miracle. The only one of us who was almost excluded was Tate, when he and Caleb snuck into school during the night and superglued every door in the building shut. Our school caretaker said he saw Tate climbing over the school gates afterwards.

Caleb, Mei, and I, in a form of protest that somehow made sense to our thirteen-year-old selves, chose to show solidarity by sneaking into school and gluing all the doors shut again, except this time we made sure to wait around until the caretaker arrived to "catch" us leaving.

The school exchanged Tate's exclusion for a week's suspension for all of us.

"You should be careful what you say." I give Caleb my second-best warning glower. "You're already in the shit with Spain, Ireland, *and* Italy. I don't think you need to be pissing off any more European countries."

Caleb heaves out an almighty, and somewhat melodramatic, huff of frustration. "I don't know what the Italian ambassador got so upset about," he grumbles. "I rescued his wife from a giant, mutant sheep that was trying to eat her."

"You kissed her right in front of him afterwards." I feel the need to point this out.

"Like fuck I did. *She* kissed *me* as a thank-you for saving her."

I mean. What other response is there to that other than to singsong, "Pla-*yer*."

"Shut up." Caleb scowls at me. "I didn't even want to kiss her. Fuck. I didn't want *her* to kiss *me*." He makes a disgruntled face to himself, like he's trying to reorganise a bunch of thoughts he doesn't like the look of. "She tried to stick her tongue down my throat, and it was weird. We were *hanging upside-down from a building*. And it was raining at the time. Have you ever kissed anyone in the rain? Because it is not romantic or sexy at all. It's slippery and awkward. There. I'm sorry everyone. The romance films lied to us. Again."

I can't help laughing at how dead serious he sounds about it. The irritation on his face is one hundred percent genuine, which only makes it funnier.

"I'm sorry, Cal. Do you want me to type up a strongly worded letter to send to somebody? The Italian embassy. The supervillain known, still, somehow, as Bo Peep. Hollywood. Society in general. 'Cause I will. I have the time and the printer for it right now."

"You have a printer?" Caleb asks in sarcastic disbelief. "Fuck me, your highness, I didn't realise you'd moved so far up in the world."

Sensing the relentless spiral of this continued back and forth, I put a temporary end to it by jerking my head in the direction of the bedrooms.

"All right, that's enough of your backtalk. I'm gonna go to bed. You can come with me or stay out here bickering with the living room furniture about non-existent French girls and overzealous Italian women, your choice."

"Wow." Caleb says, shaking his head slowly at me, eyes shining bright. "Your seduction routine is truly shameless. None of those skip lorry drivers and billionaires stood a chance."

I don't bother to respond, knowing we'll only end up snarking at each other again, and turn to leave.

Despite his needling, Caleb does follow me from the living room, and I lead him to the room Rohan has generously let me take short-term ownership of.

My room is, in all seriousness, far too nice for me. It has cream-coloured wallpaper with a pretty, black feather design, and dark hardwood floors. There's ornate, expensive-looking furniture I'm always afraid of touching too much, just in case I somehow accidentally leave behind a mark and wreck it.

The bed is huge and offputtingly comfortable and came with four of the puffiest pillows known to man. I'm suspicious the pillows might cost more than my entire wardrobe. I tried them out for a night and halfway through trying uselessly to rest, I shoved them on the floor and tried curling up in the middle of the bed like a puppy in a too-large basket.

Caleb only pauses for a handful of seconds before following my lead to the obscenely ornate bed and climbing onto it. We lie closely beside each other, in the middle of the bed, drawn together by instinct rather than the usual expectation of a non-verbal offer and acceptance.

The mattress is very soft and luxurious. I low-key kind of hate it.

Caleb turns his head in my direction, those dark-grey eyes I know so well seeming to bore right into the very core of me. Part of me wishes, then, that I wasn't capable of seeing him so clearly in the dark of the room. I wish it was easier to hide from him. At the same time, I'm glad I can't. I've done far too much hiding already. Hiding and running away from the truth, from our shared reality.

It's time to be brave, now. Or, if not that, then at least

I should be braced for the onslaught of my worst fears coming to life, which will happen whether I want it to or not.

Even still, thinking that and believing it to be true and wanting to be better than this terror I have locked inside me, I am apprehensive about starting whatever conversation Caleb and I need to have.

Into the quiet drowsiness of the room, Caleb speaks. "Go on then." He releases a short sigh. "Which one of us wants to talk about their stupid feelings first?"

"Really?" I ask, raising my eyebrows at him. "I don't even need to hit you this time?"

"Nah. I've grown. Matured, you might say."

"Really?" I'm highly sceptical of this fact.

"Maybe. I'm twenty-one now. I can officially buy alcohol in all countries. I am old and wise, a man of great knowledge and experience."

I purse my lips, pretending to think it over. Caleb looks oddly serious about the whole thing, which is an obvious concern.

Can't be having that shit.

"Sounds fake," is my obvious conclusion.

In response, he hits me. *Violence.*

Gasping as dramatically as my soggy, tired brain can dredge up the energy for, I stare at him in mortal outrage.

Caleb doesn't look even a little bit regretful for his totally uncalled for, volatile act against my person. If anything, he looks mildly exasperated by *me*. The audacity of it, I tell you.

I'm about to wreak my valid and justifiable vengeance on my best mate, when his expression suddenly hardens into something headache-inducingly determined.

"Will you just get on and spill your stupid feelings now, please?"

It's not really a question. More of a demand, and not a soft one either.

Yes, one of the stubborn Moon brothers is officially back in my life, and it's no one's fault but my own. It's also probably the best decision I've made in months.

All in all, the admission is easier to speak out loud than I thought it would be, every time I imagined facing Caleb and confronting the many and varied ways in which I'd let him down. How I let down everyone I care about, wilfully, and without hesitation.

"I left you alone," I say, voice so quiet and low, it's doubtful he would be able to hear me if he didn't have his enhanced hearing, "and I feel like shit about it."

Caleb's reaction is immediate and characteristically ferocious, like a wild dog snapping and snarling at the hand tentatively reaching out to touch its nose. Not angry, not really, but defensive. An instinct born of loss through misunderstanding. Trying to hold on to his threadbare control of the situation by meeting vulnerability with open aggression.

"Well, I let you do it and I feel like shit about that," he says gruffly, eyes shifting away from me, like he can't quite bring himself to carry on looking at me. His guilt is plain to see on his face, the sharp spike of disappointment in your own past actions, the mistakes you know weren't inevitable, that could have been avoided, but...you just... didn't.

There's not always a good reason why. Sometimes,

we are the worst version of ourselves, either in a single moment, or repeatedly, when we make the same wrong choice with full knowledge of the remorse we'll feel for it later.

When I give in to the urge to reach across the small amount of space dividing us and knock my fist against his chest, Caleb returns his gaze to my face. Eyes of pure silver shining in the dark, the self-recrimination in them strong enough to overtake everything else, to consume and decimate, no mercy. Barren rock surface scorched and shattered. Until all that's left is a wasteland ripped apart to reveal a molten core, ironclad and bitingly sulphuric.

I'm struck by the memory of a night not all that dissimilar to this one. The concert attack, when I went back to Jamie's flat, and my friends came for me. When Caleb came for me. His anger then, at himself, and at least partially at me, was almost exactly the same as it is now.

"I feel like we've been here before."

"What," Caleb asks, brows drawing together in a puzzled scowl, "in this ridiculous bouncy castle of a bed your sugar brother has provided for you?"

I am going to regret this so much, it's unreal. But...

"Sugar brother?"

"Yeah," Caleb answers, no hesitation, like there's not several huge issues with what he just said. "Sathe's too young to be your daddy, so..."

I do not even bother to hide the insurmountable level of horror I am overcome by in this moment. I mean, come on, there's some things a person should just not say. For the sake of common decency. I should let Caleb say that to Rohan's face, and watch as he's met by the unencumbered, acerbic wrath of my roommate.

Caleb deserves to suffer for this.

"Okay, first," I say disapprovingly, "Rohan is not my sugar anything, but thanks not very much for the horrendous thoughts that put inside my head, really appreciate it, and second, no, you plonker, I meant we've both been sorry about the same shit before. I'm getting, like, déjà vu or what-the-fuck-ever."

Caleb, as per usual, misses the point entirely, and chooses to focus in on something completely irrelevant and stupid.

"*Déjà vu*? *Horrendous*? What weird rich person language has Sathe been teaching you? Do we, finally, need to take a second stab at having an intervention? Have you been brainwashed?" Caleb clucks his tongue like an idiot, making me want to flick him in the eye. He thwacks me on the chest with the back of his hand. "See, this is why you shouldn't be on your own for so long. You're too susceptible. If you'd been kidnapped by a supervillain rather than Sathe, you'd already be wearing a high-collared cape and mwah-ha-ha-ing at innocent civilians by now."

He's probably right. If Rohan had turned out to be a secret evil genius intent on taking over the world or doing something cool, like stealing the moon, I would have been on board so fast it's not even funny.

Who doesn't want to try to steal the moon at least once in their lifetime?

Boring people who have no respect for tradition, that's who.

"Rohan didn't kidnap me." Unless this has been the

stealthiest abduction of all time. It's more of an adoption, if anything. But not like someone adopting a child, more like a lonely old person adopting a mangy dog from a rescue centre because their actual children don't visit them.

I snort, unable to help it after picturing Rohan as a pissed-off old man of *Up* level quality. Rohan would absolutely be the kind of person to say fuck the police and escape forced social interaction with other old people by attaching a thousand helium balloons to his house and floating away to the other side of the world. Except Rohan would be more likely to build giant robot legs for his house and have it walk away like a massive metal chicken.

When Caleb raises his eyebrows at me in question, I make the choice not to explain what I'm actually thinking. He'd probably tell Rohan, then I'd be on his shit list again. I think we can agree I have enough problems as it is.

"I'm pretty sure I've outstayed my welcome by at least three months and twenty-nine days by this point," I tell Caleb instead.

He seems to accept this, although he huffs belligerently. "Still. He and I shall be having words." Then, without warning, Caleb yanks his serious face on again and stares at me extra hard. "I can't believe he knew where you were this whole time." He sounds a mixture of genuinely hurt and less genuinely pissed off, as if he is angry, but isn't sure what direction to funnel that anger in.

"It wasn't his fault." I defend Rohan before Caleb can decide to pin his Moon rage on the wrong target. "I asked him not to tell you. Any of you." I add the last part when Caleb looks at me all lost and sad again.

"We've been going mental without you, mate," Caleb

tells me, his expression tightening into something painfully honest. "Seriously." He swallows hard, looking at me beseechingly, like I'll understand more that way. "It was like you fucking died the same night Roux and North did."

"I'm sorry. I am." Because it's true. More true than he can ever understand. "I'm sorry for leaving. For not letting you know where I was. For leaving you alone to deal with the fallout of that night. I can't tell you how sorry I am for all of it. I'm kinda sick with how much, really."

Caleb's mouth is turned down, body taut like a bow string, ready to snap back and fire bolts of emotion at the slightest provocation. I can already feel his struggle to hold steady like a constant ripple of second-hand aftershocks.

"Why did you leave us like that, Rex?" he asks, aggressive, but quiet, and sounding even more powerful for that reason. "Do you have any idea how it... How much I— I needed you, and you just..." He's struggling to get the words out, and it's almost unbearable to hear him try to explain what I've been doing to him all these months with my constant absence from his life.

Caleb shakes his head a little, unable to continue, looking pointedly away from me. As if I could miss the sheen of his eyes. It's like looking at the moon with blurry vision, pale light bleeding at the edges.

"I'm scared," I admit to him, because there's nothing else left to do. To offer in return for all his pain. "I am really, really scared." Of what's going to happen to us. Of what's going to happen to all the people I care about. Of what I could become. Of what I might need to do to prevent that from happening before it's too late.

Caleb lets me grasp hold of his chin and jerk his head back around so he has to meet my eyes again as I attempt to explain my actions to him.

"I didn't know how to be stronger than that for you. I just... I needed to be scared and I needed not to pretend I wasn't."

Caleb scowls fiercely then, rejecting whatever it was he doesn't agree with. "You don't have to pretend for me," he states, that obstinate Moon expression on his face again. "Or for any of us."

"You needed me to be there," I argue, "to be strong for you."

"No, I didn't. I..." He falters, wincing at his own realisation. "Okay, yeah, fuck it. You're right, and I'm sorry for that, Rex. I made you feel like you had to prop me up. You thought I'd be a mess and need someone to take care of me and I've spent our entire friendship putting that on you without meaning to. I know I've done that. And..." He stops again, looking for the right words. "It was crap of me. Really crap, actually." I suppose those will do.

"Don't be unfair." I chastise him, because he can't take the entirety of our arguably unhealthy relationship dynamic on himself. I built half that shit. "You've been there for me, too, plenty." And he has, albeit in less overt ways. I frown and release a short, humourless laugh. "I'm just shit at accepting help or comfort or anything that would be good for me, probably."

It's yet another reason I've never gone after Jamie like I would have wanted to. If I'd been bolder, more emotionally courageous. I don't take the right risks, only the wrong ones. We all know it doesn't count as bravery if you flat-out do not care about the consequences. It's just a selfish idiot doing reckless bullshit because he can.

There's a short stretch of silence then, both of us acknowledging the inescapable conclusion. That Caleb did need me and, in equal measure, I was incapable of being there for him until now. He struggled without me. I would have struggled even more than I already did if I'd had to support him as well as myself.

As harsh as it might sound, and as much as I regret giving in to the flight response, it was necessary for me to take this time, to create this space between us. For the sake of my mental stability, as well as giving us both the chance to see if we could stand mostly on our own, when we've spent almost our entire lives sharing the weight of every challenge life threw at us.

And I think Caleb understands that, whether he wants to or not.

"I moved in with Tate," Caleb says, breaking the silence, an apprehensive note entering his voice. I was so deep in thought that I nearly missed the whole thing.

Momentarily stunned, I'm not sure how to respond at first, what with how out of nowhere the statement was.

"You did..." I start, then abruptly stop, the words twisting around my tongue. A few seconds tick by before I try again. "You did what?"

"Yeah," Caleb says with faux casualness. It doesn't sound believable at all. He bites his bottom lip and nods a few too many times for it to be natural. "We got a flat together."

"Just the two of you?" I ask, making a valid attempt not to sound either astonished or suspicious. Or nosy.

Actually, no, that's asking too much of myself. Of course I'm being nosy. I have *questions*. I must *know things*.

"Just the two of us," Caleb answers, doing that fake nonchalant voice again. It's so bullshit. There will be no Oscars given out today, everyone. Not even a fucking BAFTA.

Also, yes, I am a tiny, weensy bit jealous.

It was meant to be the four of us. That was always the plan we had when we were growing up together. We were supposed to become adults, move into Danger, join FISA, and get our own place. This was meant to be our time. Our chance to be free of any constraints and find out what we're truly capable of.

But I guess things never work out like you think they will, no matter how hopeful you might be.

The more important thing to focus on is what's got Caleb acting all squirrely about moving in with Tate. It can't be just because he's worried how I'll react to the news. There has got to be more to it for him to be acting this weird.

"Is something going on with you and T?" I ask him, doing a way better job of sounding casual than he did. I could absolutely win a BAFTA. I'd wipe the floor with those other professional fakers.

Caleb stares at me in surprise for a moment, as if he didn't expect the question from me at all, not because he doesn't know what I'm talking about.

"It's... I don't... It... We're kind of..." He scowls, huffing out an exasperated breath at his inability to articulate what he wants to say.

Because I'm feeling especially warm and nice about

him after so long spent apart, I let him off the hook for this one.

"Okay, stop." Collaborate and listen. "Let's table the Tate conversation for another time." Caleb looks immediately relieved, which is too bad, because I'm almost certainly going to ruin that with my next line of inquiry. There are other things that need to be addressed.

"Do you want to tell me why you look like you've dropped down a weight class?" I ask warily, knowing I'll get a negative response for the question.

And yeah, Caleb immediately goes on the defensive, just like I suspected he would. His expression flattens out, then twists into one of fierce anger.

"I've had a lot of shit going on, Rex." He's all bristle and snarl, like a wounded wolf snapping at a hunter trying to free it from a trap. "Found out I'm dying, remember."

Unlike the Tate thing, I'm unwilling to let Caleb hide from this. It's too important. His love life I have no right to. His health is something I'm more than happy to break boundaries and be invasive about. Like hell will I allow Caleb to wither away on my watch, even if he resents me for pushing in where I'm clearly not wanted.

"We're all fucking dying, Cal," I growl at him. "Don't lie to me. Don't you dare, not about this."

For about three intense seconds, Caleb looks ready to stand his ground and fight back. If it were anyone else, I'd be afraid of them bolting, but that isn't who Caleb is. It never has been. He'll bite and claw at a problem or threat until he's beaten down and out, every time. Retreating, giving up, just isn't in him.

I expect to be told to back the hell off and for Caleb

to whip out his Moon-brand stubbornness to aid him in some serious glaring. It's some intimidating stuff, I won't lie. Caleb's glare game is on point. Has been since he was a child. I still remember how he looked at Snow that time she interrupted our P.E. lesson to take me out for a talk.

But Caleb surprises me by letting the fury drain from his face, his body relaxing back to a more normal state. His jaw unclenches and his shoulders droop slightly. Rather than kicking out, he draws in closer to me, pressing his forehead to mine and closing his eyes, heaving out a long, exhausted sigh.

"I'm working some stuff out," he admits, voice raw and almost gentle. He reaches across to grasp my hand, threading his fingers through mine like he's trying to bind us into one entity rather than two separate people.

"Gonna tell me about it?" I ask with equal softness. Not demanding this time.

"Yes," Caleb says without hesitation, his eyes still closed. "Just. Not tonight, okay? It's a lot."

"Okay," I relent, afraid of letting go, but knowing Caleb wouldn't say he would tell me if he didn't intend of doing so. I trust him. "Are things good, though?" I ask instead. "With Tate, and Mei? Are they... Shit, I don't even know what I'm on about any more."

"Mei is pissed at you," Caleb answers with frightening speed. "Like seriously. You might get slapped by an ice blast, I'm just warning you." He lets out a genuinely humour-filled snort of laughter. "Tate has become what he hates. He's been brooding over you for months. They need you to come back to us. We miss your stupid face."

"Are you pissed at me?" I ask, already knowing the answer.

Caleb opens his eyes and draws back slightly. He gives me an achingly fond smile and squeezes my hand. "I'm gonna give you a free pass this time."

"Are you just giving me a free pass because you've got bored of talking about our stupid feelings?" I suppress a smile.

Caleb picks up on the joke and plays into it. "There's a saying about gifts and horse mouth that you should probably take some wisdom from right now."

"Got it."

Caleb makes a face, then, like something has just occurred to him. "Is it too late to start our own dentistry business?" he asks, sounding absurdly genuine.

"Yes," I say, letting disappointment colour my tone, "which, I will not lie, that's what has upset me the most about this whole dying thing. All the missed opportunities."

Caleb nods in steadfast agreement, humming sadly. "Tooth Heroes would have been so epic."

"We could have had posters of teeth wearing capes and flying around."

"And we could have hired Lady Mars to be our receptionist slash hype-man," Caleb muses. "She would have brought in all the customers."

I scoff, easily imagining a scenario where Lady Mars would designate herself the face of Tooth Heroes.

"You mean she would have gone around Colbie, blatantly threatening her frightened subjects into setting up appointments with us."

"Yes," Caleb says without inflection, "that is exactly what I mean."

"We could have really done some good in the world." I reply mournfully.

"And instead, we became superheroes." Caleb says in self-recrimination.

"Mis-*take*," I agree.

"Still the biggest regret of our lives, for sure."

Feeling the sudden urge to be soppy and honest with him, I practically crawl on top of him, tugging Caleb into an embrace I don't ever want to release him from.

"I've missed you, mate." I press my face into the crook of his neck, curling into him like a baby monkey. "Like. I know we don't say this shit a lot. But. I don't even want to do any of this stupid life stuff without you."

Caleb doesn't hesitate to reciprocate the intimacy. He wraps his arms around me and holds on tight, tucking my head underneath his chin like we used to do when we were little. I'm reminded of all the times we stayed over at each other's houses as children. The number of nights one of us had a terrible dream and reached out for comfort are innumerable. We did it less as teens, but there were still some memorable occasions where one of us woke up sweating and screaming, desperate for help, and we'd reach for each other in the dark, words unspoken, questions and explanations unnecessary.

"You're my best friend," Caleb tells me, and he mirrors back to me something I once told him, "and nothing in this fucked-up world could keep me from you when you need me. Not even you. Not ever again, right?"

I think, *I'm your brother.*

Part of me always thought we'd die together.

I'm sorry we're going to lose everything one day, and there's nothing I can do to protect you from it.

"Not ever," I vow.

This time, it doesn't feel like I'm promising something we both know is a lie.

Chapter Seven

We Must Go On.
Because We Can't Turn Back

"This is a bad idea," Rohan says, eyeing both me and Caleb with a truly epic level of apprehension. He's standing on the living room side of the island separating it from the kitchen. His arms are crossed almost protectively, and his eyes seem to have darkened, appearing more black than a deep brown.

Ever since he came home from the FISA base, having spent the night working in his lab, he's been acting like a skittish, and moderately suspicious, bird. It's the same way he behaved when I first met him in his lab, right after I joined FISA.

"You are very incorrect," I argue, moving around his

kitchen, gathering up the baking ingredients I asked Caleb to go out and procure for us this morning. "This is a brilliant idea."

Caleb, who is currently snooping and crashing around Rohan's cupboards, searching for the necessary baking utensils, looks over at us and nods confidently. Too confidently, if we're being real, considering what we have planned.

"We are gonna rock this like a Queen song," Caleb pronounces, brandishing a newly found measuring jug like it's a sword he just plucked from some clingy stone.

Rohan does not look in the least bit reassured. If anything, he seems more sceptical than he was before.

"Have either of you ever baked before?" he asks warily, his tone indicating doubt over such a thing being possible, which I take immediate affront to.

"Yes," I say, throwing him an indignant frown, "of course we've baked."

Caleb chimes in from behind me, holding up two fingers with his free hand and flagrantly waggling them at Rohan. "Like a whole twice," he confirms unhelpfully.

"Oh yeah?" Rohan moves forward and rests his crossed arms down on the spotless granite countertop of the kitchen island. His gaze flickers between me and Caleb, stopping on me and hanging there. "And how'd that go?"

"Badly," I admit under Rohan's intense scrutiny, wincing at the memories of birthday cake disasters and cupcake explosions. "Very badly."

Our last attempt had been trying to make cupcakes for the Colbie baking festival when we were young teens.

We overdid it on the baking powder and our cupcakes exploded like small, chocolate-infused bombs. They didn't even stop exploding once we took the trays out of the oven. There was cupcake on the ceiling of Tate's kitchen.

Caleb scoffs dismissively, shooting me a reproachful look, as if mortally offended I would besmirch our baking reputation so easily.

"Get off it, Rex." He comes over and bops me on the head with the wooden spoon he's dug up from somewhere. We'll need to wash it; I think there's a tiny cobweb clinging to it. Caleb gives an overly exaggerated eyeroll. "Nobody even died or got poisoned or anything."

Raising my eyebrows at him, I counter, "Almost certain Jamie got poisoned by our lemon cake that one time."

"He was already sick," Caleb says adamantly, slapping the edge of the island with his dusty spoon. "No one can prove shit." He starts gesturing with the spoon. For emphasis, I assume. "Not Jamie. Not the doctors at the hospital. Not the Colbie town council. Not those melodramatic fucks at the department of health. No one."

Good point, well made.

"No one *can* prove shit," I agree in sarcastic realisation, looking up at Caleb with mockingly wide eyes. "Wow. You know, it really is a high to get away with crimes. We should really do that more."

"Agreed," Rohan says plainly, nodding like that's the first sane thing I've said all morning, "we could always be doing more crime."

He looks a bit tired. I know, like me, Rohan doesn't sleep much even on a good night. But he's been overextending himself lately, working on that drug intel we took from OI. He's spent years trying to find a way to save us, to undo what was done to us by Liquid Onyx, and just like Mia, he's failed.

As dark as it may seem, Rohan's second-best option is to find a way to neutralise our powers if they ever force us to become dangers to our loved ones and the public. I can't blame him for being so hyper-focused on it. None of us know when we could start to lose it. Rohan told me it always happens before the age of twenty-five, but that doesn't mean it won't happen far sooner. The last civilian Liquid Onyx survivor FISA had to take down was only twenty-one when he became mentally compromised.

"And besides," Caleb puts in, "it's not proper baking. We're gonna make Rice Krispie cakes. It's Rice Krispies and chocolate. How hard can that possibly be to smash together?"

Rohan is not impressed. Although, to be fair to Caleb, he rarely is.

"I think the fact you just described it as smashing them together indicates this task will, in fact, prove significantly difficult for you to carry out successfully."

Caleb scowls at Rohan, pressing a hand to his heart and sucking in a dramatic breath, pretending to be very hurt by his assessment of our baking abilities. He points the wooden spoon at Rohan and exhales in a rush, "Shun the non-believer."

I rest my forearms on the countertop and lean towards him, grinning at my friend suggestively, quirking my eyebrows. "Does that mean you want to help?" I ask hopefully.

Rohan's lips twitch at both corners, which mean he

wants to smile but is suppressing it to remain outwardly bored and aloof and some other rich boy bullshit. I swear they must have taught him this stuff at the posh public school he went to.

I'd give almost anything to see a picture of young Rohan in a school blazer. I bet he stared at the school photographer's camera lens like he wanted to make it redundant without severance pay and leave the camera's little camera children destitute on Christmas.

Rohan leans in, too, bringing us closer together than he usually prefers, not just for me, but for anyone. He's grown comfortable with letting me into his space the last three months of us living together. I consider it an accomplishment to have gained his trust in such a big way and try my best not to abuse it.

He tilts his head, black eyes unsettlingly opaque.

"I don't know what it was about our past interactions which implied that I would be in any way interested in helping you fail to make cakes with breakfast cereal, but I can only apologise for the falsehood my behaviour appears to have communicated."

"Apology not accepted." I shake my head slowly. "If you wish to gain my true forgiveness, I require one hour of your time as my baking assistant."

"I can live with your hatred and resentment," Rohan proclaims.

"Yes," I say wryly, "but do you want the constant threat of my revenge plots to hang over your head?"

Rohan snorts. "I'm not afraid of you." His arrogance is appallingly valid in this instance.

"Oh really?" I'm intent on blagging this out, having

prepared ahead of time for his refusal when he was in the shower. "Ask yourself this, Dr Sathe, when was the last time you saw your specially imported coffee beans?"

Rohan looks horrified, his lips parting and a muted gasp of astonishment coming out. "You planned this?" He sounds shocked and outraged at this revelation, like he shouldn't have presumed I would.

"To be underestimated is a great gift when one is embroiled in the fine art of extorsion," I say in triumph.

Knowing he's lost this round, Rohan gives in.

"Fine." He huffs grumpily. Then he points a warning finger at me. "But I'm not wearing an apron."

I settle back, taking my arms off the countertop and crossing them over my chest, looking down my nose at Rohan.

"I think you'll find I make the rules around here, underling."

Rohan presses his lips together and shoots daggers at me. Murderous daggers. Hitmen-ordering daggers.

"Wow," Caleb finally interjects, his voice sardonic and amused. "Is this what the last three months have been like? How are you both still alive?"

"Sheer bloody determination not to be the first to cave." Rohan raises a fist, clenching hard, and shakes it.

"Plus," I say more congenially, "neither of us felt like having to clean up a body and Rohan doesn't trust his cleaning lady enough to keep a secret."

"Excuse me," Rohan drawls, frowning at me, "my cleaning lady has a name."

"Which is?" I ask, happy to call him out on a question I know full well he has no idea what the answer is.

Rohan visibly struggles, searching through his admittedly impressive brain for the correct response. He will not find it.

He does go up in my estimation a little for giving it a solid attempt. "Lu-Ja-Alis... Uh. Charlotte?"

"Okay." I put him out of his misery, even though he doesn't deserve it. "You have two cleaning ladies, neither of them named Charlotte. And I know that, because, unlike some rich arseholes I know, I actually *asked*."

"Hey," Rohan says defensively, looking all ruffled like a disgruntled little bird who just got pushed into a birdbath by some big, mean pigeons, "consider yourself lucky I remember your name."

"Yes, very impressive. I am *impressed*. Look, see, this is my impressed face."

Caleb, having gone wandering off at some point, appears again at my side and interrupts my back and forth with Rohan. He has a thoughtful expression on his face, which rarely means good things for us. He's holding the very large pack of Rice Krispies he picked up from the Spar around the corner from Rohan's building.

"Do you think we need to cook the Rice Krispies before we mix them with the chocolate?" he asks me.

"No," I say flatly, sensing the possible tangle this conversation could become. If Tate were here, I'd suspect him of asking that question just to be irritating, but with Caleb it's possible he's being serious. Of all of us, he is the worst cook.

You know how I once said everyone can make dry toast? Well, Caleb is the only exception to that statement. This man can burn water.

Caleb raises his other hand, the one he had hanging by his side, and shows me a large pan he must have found somewhere.

"Can we use this to melt the chocolate?" he asks, brows drawn.

"That is a wok." My eyes flit to the pan and back to Caleb's expectant face.

He looks at me like the fact it's a wok has no bearing on the question he just asked. "So...yes?"

And, like, does it really matter? Is a wok, at the end of the day, not just a fat-arse pan?

"You know what," I say, puffing out air, "fuck it, yeah, go on then, let's break some rules."

"Epic," Caleb intones. He spins the wok in his hand like it's a tennis racket, tongue caught between his teeth as if he's performing a difficult stunt.

We are doomed.

"Why do you even have a wok?" I ask Rohan curiously. "You never cook anything in it."

"Oh, like I'm the only person to have shit in their kitchen they never use." Rohan rolls his eyes, sounding droll. "Don't come at me, white boy. At least when I buy a spice rack, I know what most of the spices are for."

"Really?" I ask, genuinely surprised at this hidden talent I was insofar unaware of. He hasn't even mentioned cooking a meal since I moved in. We almost always get takeaways or eat snack foods, not proper home-cooked dinners. It's another thing which has made me really miss having meals with my family.

"Yes." He taps the countertop, suddenly agitated. "My mum liked to cook, and she'd insist on me helping her. She said it was so I'd be able to take care of myself if I ever had to, one day."

Rohan grew up in a home where he never had to do anything for himself if he didn't want to. But his mum apparently thought he should know how to be independent. Maybe she always knew he would need to run from her husband, his dad, someday, and wanted him to be prepared for at least some aspects of it.

I can't help but wonder if the reason Rohan doesn't cook, even though he can, is less about laziness or anything like that, and more because it reminds him of his mum. Rohan doesn't take well to being reminded of emotionally compromising things. He'd rather pretend they don't exist.

If Rohan and I were alone, I might ask him about it. I would never do so with Caleb in the room, though. It's not that Caleb can't keep secrets or be occasionally tactful, but this is a territory I know Rohan hates to discuss with anyone, let alone somebody he doesn't trust.

Maybe Caleb senses the change in atmosphere, because he turns to Rohan and asks, "Where's the hammer for the chocolate?"

Rohan takes the out Caleb has either purposefully or inadvertently given him. "I'll go get it," he says without looking at us.

Caleb watches Rohan go, an interested glimmer in his eyes. He switches his attention back to me when Rohan disappears down the hallway. There's another question on his face, and this time I don't think it's about baking.

"No," I cut in before he can ask. "Just. Whatever you're about to say. Don't. Because the answer is no."

I expect Caleb to try to niggle me about it, to ask his question anyway, because that's the kind of bull-headed nightmare he is. But he doesn't, instead holding up his hands in defeat, still clutching the wok and Rice Krispies, so it's less effective.

"All right, mate. Keep the kitten claws in. I'll leave it."

I deflate instantly, relieved I won't have to explain myself about Rohan. We have grown close in the past three months, but it's a relationship I'm not sure how to define. Apart from Not Sexual and Not Romantic. It is something, though. Like a friendship, I guess, but different.

We're the same, is what I mean. We share stuff I can't with anyone else. The whole evil dads who killed our mums deal, and the windstorm of crap which comes along with that. Plus, our powers. The only thing either of us can do with them is hurt people. I'm not sure how to explain, but that does something to you. Having so much power which can only be used as a weapon or not at all.

I can't imagine Caleb understanding it if I tried to tell him what it means to have someone in my life who gets what it's like having the ability to cause pain imprinted both inside the blood I was born with, and the blood I was given.

Sometimes, it feels good to have Rohan just know, without me having to explain the why of it.

I push lightly at Caleb's chest with one hand. "You've been spending way too much time with Tate," I tell him, scoffing. "*Kitten claws.*"

Caleb's mouth opens, releasing a laugh. He doesn't disagree. Prolonged exposure to Tate has left its mark on us all, but if there really is something going on between Caleb and Tate, I can only imagine the carnage. They'll both annoy me to death before Liquid Onyx hurries up and poisons me.

Feeling a twinge of hunger in my stomach, I take the Rice Krispies away from Caleb and set it down on the countertop. I open the box, undo the packet inside, and take out a handful of Rice Krispies. I toss them into my mouth like they're pills.

Rohan reappears a couple of seconds later with a normal workman's hammer, like you'd get in a toolbox.

"What the hell is that?" Caleb looks at the hammer, askance, when Rohan puts it down on the countertop in front of us.

"A hammer," Rohan says, looking perplexed by the question, and a little irritated, like we're being stupid just to poke at him. "It's what you asked for."

"I meant a special cookery-kitchen hammer thingy." Caleb fails to clarify.

"What's the difference?" Rohan scowls, clearly not understanding the problem. "A hammer is a hammer. You just hit things with them, and they break stuff."

And yet again.

"Good point." I tip an imaginary top hat at Rohan. "Well made."

Caleb picks up the hammer and inspects it with slightly narrowed eyes, like he thinks it will reveal *ancient hammer secrets* if he stares at it hard enough.

"Did you just get this from your bedroom or something?" I ask Rohan, unsure how to feel about it if he did. "Why do you even have a hammer?"

I can predict with absolute certainty, willing to stake any amount of money on it, that Rohan has never done any DIY in his life. Rohan might use tools in his FISA lair, yeah, but not a bog-standard one like this.

"I have an engineering degree," Rohan says, like that explains it.

"And, what?" I challenge him. "They hand out hammers now instead of certificates? Has it got your name on it?" I make like I'm going to take the hammer off Caleb to check it for an engraving. Caleb misreads this, yanks the hammer away from me, and holds it to his chest protectively. In the process of snatching his beloved hammer, he accidentally bangs the bloody thing against the wok, creating a loud clanging sound my ears very much regret.

"Don't be ridiculous." Rohan blatantly ignores the unpleasant noise in favour of berating me. "What if I used it to do some of that crime we were talking about earlier? I'm not a moron."

That seems to get Caleb's attention again. He peers at Rohan inquisitively. "What sort of crimes would you commit with your hammer?"

"Construction without the relevant permits," Rohan offers without hesitation.

"Illegal blacksmithing," I add helpfully.

"The usurpation of Asgard," Rohan goes on. "Arcade property destruction."

Been there, done that, Mei has all the T-shirts.

We all went to Weston-super-Mare for my tenth birthday, and there was this claw machine in the pier arcade, with sealife-themed plushies.

Predictably, Mei just about lost her shit trying to win this one shark plushie for me. It was my own fault for showing too much interest in the toy and I took full responsibility for the ensuing carnage.

Mei got so frustrated by her lack of success in taking down her new archnemesis, The Claw, that she kicked the machine hard enough to crack, then break, the glass. Twice.

"Murder for people who have a flare for the dramatic," I throw in, "like that one himbo from the Netflix show we watched last week."

"I'd say hammers are a very himbo weapon in general, really," Rohan muses.

And, like, where's the lie?

Caleb crashes the hammer against the wok again, this time on purpose, and I barely resist the urge to chuck a handful of Rice Krispies at his face in recompense for any potential damage to my eardrums.

"Hey, we're getting off track, people," Caleb says, pretending not to see me glaring at him. "Aren't we supposed to be baking right now, not listing possible future crimes?" Then he hits me lightly on the shoulder with his new pet hammer, Hammy, and asks, "Remind me why we're baking today?"

As much as I'd probably rather stay in for the day and hang out with Caleb, to catch up and plan for my probably dramatic return to Colbie and our family, it's Sunday and I did say I'd go to The Caf. The baking part is me taking my own initiative in making amends to Rani for all the trouble and stress I've caused her, roping in Caleb and Rohan as well.

"I've been a prick," I say, unwilling to go into everything that's happened with Rani and Jatin. "So, I'm making up for it with Rice Krispie treats."

"A prick to who? Is it me?" Caleb asks, sounding weirdly delighted by the prospect. "Please say it's me. I really want free stuff."

"I'm seeing a new, very materialistic side to you today, Moon." Rohan eyes my oldest friend with what appears to be renewed interest.

And because I can't ever not, I inform Rohan, throwing Caleb under the bus without compunction, "Caleb was telling me last night he wants to marry you for your billions. He wants a castle. And dinosaurs. And the Heart of the Ocean. For artistic purposes."

"I don't want dinosaurs," Caleb corrects, but for some reason leaves the rest of it as is.

"Okay, fine," I say, placating him, "they can be your gift to me once you're married and have access to the rich people dino-making technology."

"Hold on a minute," Rohan cuts in, his brows set in a deep, unhappy frown, "if he's marrying me for my money, what am I getting out of it?"

That stumps me for a minute. A fact which does not go unnoticed by Caleb, who appears mildly offended. He clears his throat pointedly and knocks me on the bicep with his wok. Apparently, Hammy is too precious for the likes of me and will no longer be used for casual acts of violence.

Right. Time to sell Caleb into a financially motivated marriage, like a good friend would.

"He's very..." I give it a go, looking Caleb up and

down, gesturing first at him, then to Rohan. "You know. Attractive."

Caleb makes a series of tutting sounds at me, bonking my arm with the wok again, like it helps him make his point somehow.

"Stop flirting with me in front of my new fiancé, Rex, please, it's embarrassing," he says drolly. "What we once shared is over. Have some self-respect."

"Don't start," I warn, already exasperated by a conversation I only have myself to blame for kicking off.

"His arguable attractiveness is hardly enough motivation to make him my trophy husband," Rohan contends, also looking Caleb up and down and giving him another unimpressed face. "I could just get one of those Crescent posters and stick it up in my room or something if I wanted to stare at him appreciatively."

"Hold on, *arguable* attractiveness?" Caleb says, incensed, glaring at us. "Excuse me, I'll have you know I've been voted one of *GQ*'s sexiest men alive two years running. It's in print, which we all know means it is, therefore, indisputable fact."

"And so," Rohan says, splaying his hands in a "there you are then" gesture, "we circle back to me ripping the magazine page out and taping it to my wall."

"He has other desirable qualities," I offer with forced enthusiasm, poking Caleb's chest encouragingly, "Go on, tell him about your five skills."

"You have a *whole five skills*?" Rohan looks at Caleb in open disbelief.

"Oh, shit, yeah," Caleb says quickly, eyes wide in sarcastic recognition. He holds up Hammy and bangs it against the countertop. "Okay. So, number one, I can spell the word supercalifragilisticexpialidocious."

Rohan shakes his head in outright denial. "That's not a word."

"It is. It's from the Mary Poppins film."

Rohan appears to consider that for a moment, squinting like he's trying to bring forth a memory. "Is that the one with the car that has wings and the man who catches unruly children and puts them safely in a roomy cage where they can't bother people with their childlike antics?"

"No, that's *Chitty Chitty Bang Bang*," I say, giving him a concerned look, "and we are really going to need to address your description of the Child Catcher's villainous activities."

Rohan doesn't seem to understand my issue, because he's just like this. "I found him to be quite a sympathetic character."

"I'm very worried about how seriously you just said that."

"I hate children," Rohan grumbles, wrinkling his nose in genuine distaste.

Caleb becomes absurdly excited by this and nods in eager agreement. "They are the worst, aren't they?"

"Right?" Rohan says enthusiastically, seeming happy to have found another child-hater to bond with. "They're so annoying and loud and sticky for no reason all the time."

I look between them slowly, making a humming sound. "Well, at least we know you'd both be okay with a childless marriage."

"We could get a Bengal tiger instead?" Caleb looks at Rohan hopefully.

"All right, fine," Rohan answers with surprising speed, "but you have to take care of it."

Caleb looks a cross between ecstatic and hesitant. Presumably ecstatic at the thought of owning a tiger and hesitant about having to take care of it. Probably remembering the last time he tangled with a big cat. "Can't we hire people to do that?"

Rohan crosses his arms again, looking at Caleb judgementally. "What would be the point in us getting a Bengal tiger to raise if you aren't even going to look after it?"

"We get a Bengal tiger so when we meet people and they start talking about their stupid children, we could turn around be like, *ha*, we have a fuckin' tiger, arseholes, and all you have is a constant drain on your savings, sanity, and freedom."

Now it's Rohan's turn to look positively thrilled. "That is so petty." He gifts Caleb with a proper smile. "I love it. Wait here and I'll go buy you a diamond ring right now."

I mean. What is happening?

I raise both hands, attempting to calm them down before anything insane happens. For the sake of the bro code Tate and I agreed upon when we were twelve, I should stop Caleb from running off and marrying Rohan this afternoon.

That was actually one of the rules of the bro code we came up with; not letting your bro's POI, Person of Interest, marry someone else without at least warning your bro and giving them a chance to win back their POI's affections.

We created our own bro code after we kissed, then promptly agreed to never do so again because it felt mega weird, like kissing a sibling.

It was then I realised how much like real family we'd become. For that reason, among others, my first kiss is a good memory for me.

We were up in a tree, the tallest one in Colbie, because I challenged Tate to a race, betting I could beat him to the top. I was confident of my climbing skills after a lesson of cliffside climbing with Lady Mars earlier that day. Lady Mars had me warm up before our climb and kept telling me to "become the goat, Rexley, become the goat I know you can be".

It was close, but I did beat Tate to the top of the tree, and I was incandescent with victory, in the way only a twelve-year-old can be when competing against a friend to do something ultimately pointless.

Tate looked really dejected, more so than he normally would, never having been a bad loser. I wanted to make him smile, so I said I'd let him choose what we do next, which is always a risky offer when it's Tate. He could very well have insisted on watching some old history documentary or playing footie on the beach. Two things he knew I only did begrudgingly to please him.

Instead, Tate asked if he could kiss me. I think I said yes more out of shock than anything else. And, yeah, curiosity. I wanted to know what it would be like to kiss someone, and Tate was a safer option than most. So, I let one of my best friends kiss me in a tree, which was as awkward as you can probably imagine.

But, despite the undeniable weirdness of the kiss, it was also sweet and with someone I really care about, and I know that's soppy as fuck, but I don't care.

So much that came after, in terms of the physical stuff, was not sweet at all. Which was all mostly my choice, but still. I like having one thing to look back on that is indisputably good.

I flap a hand between Rohan and Caleb to draw their attention away from how well they're getting on. Because bro code is law, bro code is *life*. "Okay, okay, let's not get carried away with—"

Caleb shuts me down by practically thwapping me in the face with his wok. "Rex, shut up, don't ruin this for me. You had your chance, slow poke. Now it is my time to shine in the reflection of the massive diamond I am going to have."

I finally give in to the urge to snatch the wok away from Caleb. He fights me, but I make to bite him, and he relents. Because Caleb knows I don't joke about biting. He learned that the hard way when we were children, and he used to put his hand over my mouth to stop me rambling on for a thousand years.

I waggle my pilfered wok at Rohan and Caleb and make an attempt to return us to something resembling sanity.

Maybe.

I don't know really know what that means.

"As much as I support this whirlwind romance you've both entered into in the last five minutes"—except not really because of the bro ethics involved—"I think we should take a step back and reassess before anyone gets hurt. And by anyone, I mean me. Because it would be me who had to plan the stag party, and we always said we'd do Vegas at least once, but you"—I hit Caleb with the wok, because vengeance—"and Jamie are both still wanted by the CIA. Plus, we can't go to any casinos, anywhere, because Mei would absolutely develop a gambling addiction."

Although, that might be a good way to kick off the countdown to another intervention, so we could all have a second chance at doing it right.

We will never forget the great claw machine incident of my tenth birthday, and how Mei shouted *"ACAB!"* at the pier security guards as she was dragged away by Jian.

"Fair point," Rohan says amiably. He flickers an inquiring look up at Caleb. "Also, aren't you already doing the whirlwind romance thing with Bishop?"

Rohan asks the question without any malice and with genuine casualness, but Caleb looks immediately uncomfortable anyway. And maybe a little scared to be put on the spot, as if he was unaware anyone knew about whatever is going on between him and Tate and therefore has no real idea how to respond correctly.

In an effort to save Caleb by distracting us all from what Rohan just blatantly called attention to, I throw down a conversational gambit of my own.

"Right you are, Cal." I grab the box of Rice Krispies. "We're getting off topic." Like he said three random segues ago. "I'm supposed to be getting to The Caf for around lunchtime, so we need to get a move on if we're not going to piss off Rani all over again by being late."

Caleb takes full advantage of the out I've given him,

pushing away from the counter and giving me a two-finger salute. "Ready and willing to get the fuck on with it, boss."

I shove the wok back at him. "Go on and break up that chocolate, then." As Caleb turns away to do that, I fix Rohan with smile I know will unsettle and irritate him. "And you," I say, "can help me turn your futuristic bastard of a hob on. Last time I tried to do it by myself, it hissed and blew steam at me."

Rohan doesn't look at all moved by this. He does, however, come around the kitchen island to do as I've bid him, which is a genuine miracle, even with the threat of losing his precious coffee beans.

I move to stand beside Caleb again at the other counter, where he has a ridiculous amount of cooking chocolate heaped in front of him ready for smashing. He looks over at me, a small quirk to the left side of his mouth. He reminds me of Jamie when he does that, and my chest aches a little for it.

Caleb offers Hammy to me. "You want the first smash?"

I bump him with my hip, shoving him out of the way a little, and take the proffered hammer.

"You know what?" I spin the hammer in my hand. "Yeah. Yeah, I do."

Chapter Eight

What's in a Name? Everything, Actually

"It tastes like air freshener," Caleb announces in disgust as he hands back the cup of lemon tea to Geoff.

After we finished up with the Rice Krispie cakes, which I'd argue turned out a lot better than they could have done—nothing exploded that much, and I wasn't even afraid of taste-testing the results—we boxed everything up and Caleb tagged along with me to The Caf.

Upon arrival, I introduced Caleb to Rani and she seemed to immediately take to him with a ferocity I did not expect. She led us to the kitchen and, similarly to the last time I was there with Damon, we put the cakes on plates and took them into the hall.

On our way over, I insisted we stop in Caffè Nero and get a lemon tea. I was hoping Geoff would be at The Caf, and if he was, I wanted to have a peace offering ready. My lemon tea debt was way overdue.

I found Geoff sitting on his own at a table near the back of the hall and went to sit with him. He seemed pleased to see me and took the lemon tea eagerly.

Rani and Caleb soon joined us, and I did some more introductions.

We talked casually for bit, until Geoff caught Caleb eyeing his tea like it was a particularly nasty-smelling sock. Geoff offered to let Caleb have a sip of his tea, insisting he would like it if he tried it.

It would seem Geoff was incorrect on that score.

Geoff takes his tea back from Caleb, shaking his head at him like he's just too silly for words.

"How do you know what air freshener tastes like?" Rani asks Caleb, raising her eyebrows at him from across the table. She's sitting next to Geoff, opposite me.

Caleb seems to have a mini panic at having been addressed directly by Rani. He picked up on her Lady Mars energy straight away and modified his behaviour accordingly.

"I don't," he lies.

Oh, no. We can't have lies between us. That's just not on.

"He drank air freshener once when we were, like, eleven." I provide the truth, your honour, the whole truth and nothing but the truth.

Caleb whips around and looks at me, features set in abject betrayal.

"*Judas*," he accuses.

"Why would you do that?" Rani asks, looking mildly

horrified by the prospect of an eleven-year-old drinking toxic chemicals. Funny, that.

"It was a dare," I tell her, damning Caleb further, without even a shred of remorse.

"Someone dared you to drink air freshener?"

Caleb points two fingers at me, and Rani turns a wide, judgemental look on me.

"To be fair," I say, "we were very bored that day and left unsupervised, so…"

"Also, I did dare him to literally jump off a cliff," Caleb says, the words coming out sounding a bit weird because he's roving his tongue around his mouth like he's trying to wipe away the taste of Geoff's lemon tea.

"And did you?" Rani asks me, looking even more worried, despite the fact she knows I've jumped off worst things than a cliff during my time as Wrath.

"Hell yes, I did," I say, like it's a ridiculous question. "You can't back out on a dare once it's been issued."

"Of course you can!" Rani's voice is shrill.

"No, no," Geoff says gently, like he's consoling Rani from a bit of bad news. "He's right. You can't back out on a dare after it's been dared."

"That is the rule," Caleb adds with a sombre nod.

Throwing up her hands in despair, Rani sits back in her seat with a light thump. "Boys," she mutters like it's a curse.

"Nah, nah," Caleb argues. "It ain't just a boy thing. Frost takes that shit dead serious. She's the worst out of all of us."

That is true. Mei is the official Dare Queen. Most of the time Mei is the sensible, level-headed one, but when it comes to dares, she's on a whole other level. She'll do anything, the lunatic. And she comes up with the most insane dares. It was Mei who once dared Tate to climb up onto the life-size dinosaur-bone display at the Danger City Museum. Tate climbed the dinosaur, and he rode it like a cowboy, singing "Home on the Range" to the backdrop of the *Jurassic Park* theme music, which Caleb and I both helpfully played on our phones at full volume.

This earned all of us yet another lifetime ban from a place in Danger.

We are also banned from the Danger City Zoo, because Caleb once tried to liberate an orphan penguin, which is a whole story I am not going to get into right now. Not to mention the pier, where Mei committed shameless property destruction on an innocent claw machine. And our first ban came from Danger's largest soft play centre when we were seven, after I, in their terms, "instigated a riot" in the ball pit.

"Now that does surprise me," Rani says, voice droll. "A superhero who likes to take risks and play the daredevil? I am truly shocked by this revelation."

Geoff nods along in agreement with her, looking to us straight-faced. "You have shaken my belief system to the very core, to the point where I'm unsure it if will ever fully recover."

I can't help but grin at Rani and Geoff, their matching dry tones expertly wielded.

Caleb turns to me again and nudges my shoulder. He leans in and lowers his voice conspiratorially. "I think maybe you just attract sarcastic arseholes and weirdoes, mate. Like, our family, hell, you hooked in *North*, now

Rohan and these two." He jerks his chin at Rani and Geoff. "You are the common denominator, it has to be said."

And he hasn't even met Julia, Elle, or Jatin yet.

His mention of Damon has my body tensing up without my permission, though, and I don't feel as much like laughing any more.

Caleb must pick up on my emotions, because he winces noticeably, perhaps having realised what he's done a bit too late.

Maybe Rani senses the sudden nosedive of our conversation's vibe, the atmosphere tightening around us like a plastic bag, because she gives me a sympathetic look, all cow eyes and downturned mouth, which I try very hard not to bristle at like a duck on grass.

I'm certain not all ducks hate grass, but Maddie does. He avoids walking on it whenever possible and waddles quickly away if we try to herd him near the garden. I swear, he hissed at a patch of grass once and kicked at it, in a very *take that, and that, and don't come back* kind of way. It was more ludicrous to witness than you can possibly imagine.

Rani slowly gets up and grabs a few plates from the table, making like she's going to take them to the kitchen. She nods at some used cups scattered across the table, asking me without words to gather them up and follow her.

I hesitate for a couple of seconds, unsure if I want to have the talk I know is coming if I go with Rani. But in the end, her expectant stare gets to me, and I get to work collecting the cups.

"Back in a sec, yeah?" I say to Caleb. Then to Geoff, "Tell him about your secret identity, Banksy. He's an art nerd and your biggest fan."

"What?" Caleb chirps, scowling from me to Geoff in confusion.

It was Caleb who showed me some of Geoff's street art, ages ago, before I even became Wrath. There are quite a few pieces spray painted on walls around Danger. He's good, really good, and Caleb talked about his work like it was legendary. Of course, at the time, I had no idea who the infamous, mysterious street artist known as Pan was.

I mentioned it to Damon when we were out for patrol one night, and he told me Pan was Geoff. I'd meant to get Caleb and Geoff in the same place at some point before everything got fucked up.

Geoff's mouth twists in consideration. He squints at Caleb, sizing him up, looking at his hands in particular, like he's inspecting them for evidence of his artistic leanings.

I leave them to it, positive my friend can charm Geoff into discussing his work. They'll be swapping tips and comparing shading techniques, or whatever it is artists do, by the time I get back.

Rani leads me through the hall, stopping a couple of times to speak to people she knows at different tables. A few of them recognise me, and I stop to have a chat as well. They're all very nice about the Rice Krispie cakes, no official complaints of attempted poisoning, which is kind of them.

Once we make it to the kitchen, Rani guides me over to their two large dishwashers and put the plates and cups into one of them.

I'm unsure how Rani is going to start, or even what she wants to say, so I keep my mouth shut and wait it out, feeling more nervous than I should. Whatever Rani wants to talk about, it can't be too bad. We did the hardest conversation already.

Rani turns away from the dishwasher and leans back against the counter, looking up at me with her arms loosely crossed. Non-combative, but serious. I can't read much from her expression, but she doesn't seem annoyed or angry, which is a good sign.

I copy her pose, parking my arse back against the counter. There's a polite amount of distance between us, enough that we could lean sideways and bump arms, but not so little we'd do it by accident.

"Do you know why my son calls you Sky?" Rani asks, head tilted up to fix me with a soft, enquiring gaze.

Her question is so out of left field that my brain is tricked into giving a normal answer for once in my life. "No."

Rani nods, like she expected that was the case. She breathes out through her nose and rolls her shoulders back, as if she's holding herself back from being too abrasive or maybe like she's preparing herself for something difficult.

"The night before he died, Polaris came to me a complete mess." Her voice is quiet and uncomfortably sad. "It was the first time he'd ever done something like that. Just showed up at my door in the middle of the night, asking for help."

That would have been after the patrol where Polaris

and I found Lewis dead and Julia half-dead. After our stupid fight. A fight I regret more bitterly now than I did at the time.

I wondered what Damon did that night, if he kept on patrolling, or went back to the base to regroup. I had hoped the latter, but suspected the former was more likely.

Now Rani has presented elusive option three, Damon went to her, even let her see how fucked up he was by what happened. I would never have guessed he did that. It's so *not* a Damon thing to do.

Before I can ask her anything, Rani is talking again. "He told me you two had a horrible argument." She seems to be fully aware how much of an understatement that is. "And he was afraid he'd really messed things up with you."

It's like my brain comes to a screeching halt.

"Wait. He said..." I can't quite process what Rani is telling me, incredulity colouring my tone as a result. "*Polaris* said he thought *he'd* messed up with *me*?"

Are we even talking about the same person right now? Have I travelled to another dimension by accident? What is this absolute crap?

"Yes," Rani says simply, although she seems to realise it isn't simple at all. None of it is. "I'd never seen him so distraught." Her expression shifts into something less placid, more upset and frustrated. "He was wrecked over whatever happened during the patrol, I could see that even though he didn't talk about it. But his argument with you was what tipped him over the edge into coming to me."

"He asked for your help?" I prod, still not able to fully believe it.

Rani dips her head, her brows smoothing out again, although it looks forced to me this time, too much emotion clogging up the muscles in her face, like a teddy stuffed with an overload of cotton.

"To make things right with you. How to fix what he thought he might have broken." Then she delivers the final blow, her voice hardening. "He thought you might never forgive him."

I don't respond immediately, because I have no clue what Rani wants to hear, or why she's telling me this stuff.

Damon and I worked out our shit, or at least we started to, the day he died. Him going to Rani out of fear of losing me is something I might have wanted to know about once. But now? What difference does it make?

I'm not sure what makes me say what I do next. It isn't relevant, and it never would be again. He's dead. His status in my life right before he died is unimportant.

But... For some reason...

I want Rani to know, because maybe she's the only person who will care. She's the closest thing I think Damon had to family, even if he didn't realise it. Rani cared about him, and she was the only person who was there when he needed someone. He went to her because he knew, somewhere deep inside that thick head of his, that Rani would help him. For Damon, that would have been a revolutionary concept, considering how he was treated by everyone else following his parents' death.

"I'm so fucking angry at him," I admit to her.

I say the thing I've been so afraid of admitting, even

inside my own head. I haven't wanted to acknowledge just how pissed off I am at Damon for what he did. For dying on me like that. For taking his life, treating it like it meant nothing to him, like it meant nothing to anyone else, when that couldn't have been further from the truth.

I'm ashamed of how angry I am. It lives inside me like an infected cut, weeping and brittle around the edges. Throbbing continuously, incessant like an adrenaline-fuelled heartbeat.

Somewhere beneath all that rage is the sadness, the devastation. I know that. I can feel it there, waiting impatiently to be felt to its fullest capacity.

But for some reason, I can't seem to move past the anger. It consumes me, so much so that I've been afraid of talking to Rani about Damon because I thought I might be unable to keep it in check.

Rani's expression softens far more easily this time, and she reaches out a hand to gently touch my arm.

"Of course, you are." A knowing smile flits across her lips, like a ghost of the real thing. "I felt the same, when Rajan died. I was so furious with him for trying to play hero and getting himself killed."

Rani stops talking for moment, the words breaking off at the end like she's overcome by the emotions attached to those memories. She presses her lips together and closes her eyes tight, as if she's trying to stave off the intense grief she must still feel over what happened to her husband. Not just the fact he died, but how he died as well. The swift and unexpected violence of it.

Most terrible things happen in an instant. A handful of seconds could change your life.

I don't offer any comfort to Rani. Mostly because I know there's nothing I can do or say to banish her pain. And I'm not even sure if should be able to. There are some things that demand to be felt, and that's okay. We shouldn't always try to eliminate the bad feelings we have.

"But the truth is"—Rani opens her eyes again and looks up at me with a fierceness I've come to expect from this woman—"I was even more furious with myself. Because Rajan was only in that warehouse, working for the Winters, because we needed the money. And we only needed the money because I asked him to help our friend get away from them by paying her debts with our savings."

Lady Mars used to tell me that bad feelings are just our mind's way of teaching us how to understand other people. The more we've felt, the deeper our ability to empathise.

I don't think that's a blanket statement we can make, but in some situations it's true. Like in this one.

Because of course, my anger is directed more at me than at Damon. It feels like I let him down, I let him die. Like I told Snow, he deserved better.

"How did you forgive yourself for that?" I ask her, eager to know, so I can emulate it.

Rani considers my question for a few seconds, her gaze unwavering. She squeezes my arm, then takes her hand away and crosses her arms again, like she's resetting herself to primary. Rebooting the system so it doesn't get overheated.

"Well, at first," she says, huffing out a sigh that sounds almost indignant, "people told me I had to respect that Rajan made his own choices." Her expression twists into a resentful snarl. "But then I thought, fuck that, he made them because of me and pretending otherwise won't help."

She tightens her arms, like she's physically holding on to her temper. I don't know if she's remembering how frustrating it was to be told how to feel by other people, or if this is more a reflection of that same self-imposed anger.

"Next, I thought about how upset I would be if it was me who died, and Rajan blamed himself. Then, I thought, fuck that, too. Hypotheticals don't mean nothin' to me." A little bit of her Danger City accent floods in at the end there, reminding me of Jatin when he gets upset or especially pissed off about something.

Rani lets out another heated breath, dispelling her worn and tattered fury like a kettle blowing out steam. I untangle my own limbs and put a hand on her arm much like she did to me. I'm more hesitant about the gesture than she was, but the sentiment is the same, and Rani seems to take some comfort from it. Her hunched shoulders loosen ever so slightly, and I wait for whatever she plans to say next.

"Honestly"—she meets my eyes, her own filled with a sadness that is clear and profoundly recognisable to me—"the thing that finally stopped me from feeling guilty about what happened was accepting the fact Rajan is dead, and there's nothing I can do or think or feel that will change it. It's just done. And all my guilty conscience was doing was hurting other people I cared about."

From her inflection and tone, it's obvious Rani has finished making the point she was trying to get across to me. The finality is there, like the vocal equivalent of a full stop.

I take a moment to consider what she said. There's a lot to unpack, and I'll need more time and energy than I currently have to properly dissect and apply it how she intends me to.

In short, it seems there's no easy answer, which I already knew. But seeing Rani, someone who has come through the other side of all that pain and guilt, who has managed to process it to whatever extent is possible, gives me a sense of hope I didn't have before.

"He asked me not to hate him. Or myself," I tell her after a few silent minutes of contemplation, where Rani just let me think and stare at the wall.

What I've avoided acknowledging to myself is the fact I've not been trying all that hard to comply with Damon's wishes, practically his last fucking request, because I was too busy being angry, and also being angry about being angry, like the massive forest fire of a person I am.

"Sometimes," Rani says, an explicit graveness in her voice, "the best we can do is own our shit, and let go of what we can't fix."

"It feels like letting go of him," I admit, afraid to speak too loudly, like it's an indictment I'm throwing at myself. "Forgetting him like I did my mum. Like one day he'll just be a memory I can barely see."

I've been scared of what would happen if I let the rage go and the sadness in. Because once the sadness dulls and starts to fade, what then? Holding on to the anger was like holding on to Damon, because as long as I was still furious with him for dying, there was a piece of us that felt unfinished. Yet to come. Something I needed to wait or fight for.

"My son calls you Sky," Rani says, confusing me by bringing our conversation right back to the beginning again, "because he overheard Polaris talking about you to me, months before we met. And one of the first things he said was how blue your eyes were. Like the sky—"

"—when there's no clouds. Epic," I finish on autopilot, unable to help it, a slowly rising tidal wave of suppressed emotion threatening to drown me.

"Yes," Rani murmurs solemnly, "that's right."

I think of Julia, then. Everything she said about sharing memories. About how good it felt to share stories about Damon with her.

Rani isn't a stranger. She knew Damon, maybe better than me. But the same basic idea Julia offered, sharing the weight of remembering with other people, could be applied here.

"We won't let each other forget," I say to Rani. And it's another promise I think it's actually possible for me to keep.

Rani covers the hand I have on her arm with her own hand, her skin warm, the touch achingly kind, as is the soft smile on her face.

"No," she vows in return, "we won't."

Chapter Nine

Confrontation on a Roof; the Remix

I leave The Caf with Caleb feeling better, if more emotionally drained, than I have in a long while.

Caleb doesn't ask about the sudden change to my mood, or what my conversation with Rani was all about. He seems to understand I don't want to discuss it, without me having to outright tell him so, and instead fills the quiet between us with excited chatter about his new artist conspirator, Geoff.

I'm happy to hear Caleb talking so animatedly about something, even if most of what he tells me is shit I do not understand in the slightest. Art-talk is a little beyond me, to be honest. If it isn't, "oh, look at the pretty picture", then I'm done and out.

Caleb is so cheerful that when he gets a text on his

phone just outside Rohan's building and his demeanour changes from joyful to mildly panicked, I'm immediately put on edge by it.

When Caleb pulls us to a stop by grabbing my arm and looks at me with one of his classic guilty expressions, mixed with audacious obstinance, because they always are, I know I'm not going to like what he's about to say.

Gaze darting between my face, the building entrance, and his phone, Caleb makes his stalwart confession.

"Okay, so, please don't be too fucked off about this, because it's too late to change now, and I only did it because I thought it was the right thing for you *and* him."

Oh, Jesus Christ, I think I already know what the tosser has gone and done. It was dumb of me not to assume he would give me up to the one person I've been the most anxious to avoid seeing for as long as I could possibly get away with.

"Cal, you prick, have you told—"

He doesn't even let me finish, blurting out his confession of betrayal without any nail-pulling or blackmail required.

"Yeah, I did." Caleb shrugs helplessly, like the devil on his shoulder made him do it. Or the angel. I'm not sure who would be on my side in his scenario. "I told him where you've been hiding."

"Caleb!" I yelp, giving my friend a vicious glower, the likes of which haven't been seen since my sixteenth birthday when he planted a glitter bomb inside his present and it exploded in my face when I opened the box.

I don't know what your experience with glitter has been, but I'll tell you right now, it is harder to get rid of than any amount of sand or dirt on this earth. Seriously. I had glittery hair for *months*. Caleb is lucky I'm a benevolent and forgiving person, as we all know I am, because otherwise I would have disowned him right then and there.

"I had to," Caleb states defiantly, like I challenged him in court or something. Then he seems to deflate when the glower on my face does not lessen by a single inch. His shoulders give a noticeable slump. "Okay, I didn't have to. But I wanted to. He's my brother, and he's been going mental." He makes cartoonishly exaggerated cow eyes at me. "I couldn't not tell him, Rex. It would've been too shitty."

There are a million things I could say to argue the point, or to rail against him for grassing me up to Jamie, of all people. But it's pointless to get all worked up over it now, if Caleb has already ratted me out. I'll just have to deal with whatever comes from it.

"Let me guess." I sigh heavily. "He's on his way over here."

"Uh"—Caleb looks extra guilty and wary now, which bodes very badly for me, because it always does—"actually, he's waiting upstairs with Rohan. Like. Right now."

Of. Course.

"Fuck me." I run a hand through my hair and tug on the strands caught between my fingers, a new wave of anxiety beginning to wash through me. "Rohan is gonna murder my face with science for all this drama I've brought down on his house like a bloody plague of locusts and blood rain and cow-death and, um, whatever the other ones are, I forget."

Caleb frowns a little, thinking that over for a moment, before coming to a conclusion about it. "I don't think blood-rain is like an *official* plague."

"Nah," I disagree, far too adamantly considering the huge amount of fuck-all I know about this kind of stuff. "There was def a water turned into blood bit in that story."

Caleb's frown deepens. "Wasn't that the creepy wine-magic thing?"

"Different religion, Cal," I respond dryly.

"Right, right." He nods to himself.

"Also, it's 'Rohan' now, is it?" I purposefully raise both my eyebrows at him. "What happened to the strict surname only usage? You're not actually gonna run away to Billionaire Island and marry him, are you? Because if you are, please give me twenty-four hours' notice. People need to know your eloping plans. For reasons."

Caleb ignores most of that, which is either very wise or suspiciously evasive of him. I will have to ponder on it.

"There isn't a billionaires' island," he states with far too much authority for someone who's met exactly one billionaire in his lifetime.

"Has to be," I protest. "Where else would they all go?"

"Anywhere they bloody well want to, I'd wager." Caleb reasons. "They're *billionaires*. They have billions of pounds. That's 'fuck you and fuck off to wherever I like, catch me if you can, peasants' money they have there, isn't it?"

As much as I'm enjoying this little interlude before my fate is sealed and Jamie kicks my arse across Rohan's flat, I can't ramble on about nonsense with Caleb forever. Well, I think my past interactions indicate I could ramble on into eternity regardless of where I am or who I'm with. But Jamie is a smart cookie, and utterly shameless when he's pissed off. He'd probably figure out my plan and just come outside to face off with me in the street.

I don't respond to Caleb's non-question, needing to end the conversation now, otherwise I know I'll get swept up in whatever random crap my brain gives the green light to.

While turning my head to look up at Rohan's building, I feel a growing sense of unease inside my gut. It's like a thousand angry moths are battling their wings in warning. They want out, and the longer I try to keep them trapped in my stomach cavity, the more nauseated I become.

Caleb doesn't miss the ostentatious change in my demeanour, and he follows my gaze. He mutters something, once again, about the fancy-arse block of extremely expensive flats.

Rohan's building is one of the tallest in Danger, and one of the newest. It has that modern, almost futuristic, style, with a twisting double helix design, making it look more like a giant artistic sculpture than a skyscraper.

Caleb lets out a short breath, almost a sigh, and nudges my shoulder. I think he means it to be encouraging, but I can't feel anything beyond the mounting dread.

When I don't react to his gentle prodding, Caleb starts walking ahead, assuming I will gather my courage and follow him more easily if he treats it like it's no big deal, rather than if he tried to steer me inside.

He's right. I would probably have balked if he tried to shove or coax me from my safe spot on the street.

After only a couple of seconds' hesitation, I catch up with Caleb and we walk into the building together.

I get the usual dubious look from the doorman and the other residents who happen to be in the main lobby of the building. It's equally as nice inside the skyscraper as it is outside. Everything is either marble or glass, shining and pristine. It appears more like a hotel on a beautiful island than a block of flats in a busy British city. There are even palm trees and other tropical plants dotted around the place.

If Rohan kicks me out after this thing with Jamie, which he would have every right to do, and probably should for his own sense of sanity, I might steal one of these plants as a gift for Green. She seems like the type to enjoy a bit of light crime in her gestures of affection. I can relate to that, honestly.

Unknown to the pier security guards, Mei snuck back into the arcade later that same day and nicked the shark plushie from the broken claw machine. I still have the toy now, and will treasure Sharptooth always, because I appreciate the fortitude and commitment it took for Mei to obtain him for me.

I give one of Rohan's neighbours, a prim little old woman who wears gold jewellery and posh red dresses exclusively, a jaunty wave. She narrows her dark eyes back at me and does a little upturned nose haughty sniffing thing I had no idea people did in real life until I saw her do it for the first time months ago. Sniffy has her granddaughter with her today, a very beautiful woman around mine and Caleb's age. She looks exactly like the rich girl she is, well put together and dressed in a pretty lace dress.

I give her a wink and another wave. Unlike her grandmother, Lacy waves back and gives me an abashed smile in return. Sniffy notices her granddaughter's reaction, grabs hold of her arm, and steers her away protectively.

Caleb notices this exchange, too, and lets out a short guffaw. He bumps my shoulder again and admonishes me.

"Stop flirting with everyone, you nightmare." His tone becomes wry. "We're all just people, unable to resist the magnetic pull of Rexley Nova."

I bump Caleb back and shrug unrepentantly. "Don't get salty about my epic amount of game, Cal," I joke.

Caleb snorts out a laugh and throws an arm around my shoulders, dragging me to his side and hanging on to me all the way from the lobby up to Rohan's private floor. I allow his Tate-like clinginess, another sure sign those two have been spending way too much time alone together lately, until we're outside Rohan's flat.

When I give him a light shove, Caleb extracts himself from me and takes a step back, respecting my desire for space.

Voices come from inside the flat, low and garbled so I can't make out the words being spoken. One voice, however, I could never mistake as belonging to anyone else. Jamie.

All the nerves and gut-wrenching fear that had been building up inside me since Caleb told me Jamie was here seems to come to a sudden head at the sound of his voice. I feel the urgent need to flee. Or punch something. There's a bit of frustrated anger mixed in with the anxiety, I can't deny. I'm not ready to see Jamie, and I wish he'd waited until I said I was to come after me.

But at the same time, I can't be truly pissed at him, because if it were me, I would have been over here like a shot.

I dig into my pocket for the key to Rohan's flat, trepidation coursing through me as I fish out the key and push it into the lock.

Caleb is watching me carefully, his frame taut and antsy, like he's preparing to run as well. More likely, he's preparing to swoop in for rescue if it looks as though I need it. Jamie must be apoplectically furious with me for Caleb to be this openly concerned for how our reconciliation will go.

He smiles weakly at me when I look at him, turning the key at the same time and moving to open the door.

I twist my head back around to face forward and stride into the flat with as much confidence as I can dredge up from the depths of my psyche.

My eyes are drawn to Jamie, who's standing opposite Rohan in the living room, by what feels like some other-worldly force. He seems to turn his head and look directly at me in the exact same instant. As if the moment Jamie and are in a certain amount of square meter space, we're automatically alerted to each other's presence, unable to deny the strength of the pull that has existed between us for as long as I can remember.

Everything I expected to get from Caleb when I chased him down last night, the fury and the resentment for the choices I made, for running away and hiding from them, both of which were absent from Caleb's initial reaction to seeing me again, seem to ignite in Jamie now.

His expression transforms so quickly it almost looks painful, from placid when speaking to Rohan, to enraged when he catches sight of me. I could swear lightning crackles around his irises like static electricity in one of those plasma balls.

Lightning in a bottle, finally uncapped and unleashed. That's always been what Jamie reminded me of when he'd get worked up over something. When he became properly angry, not just annoyed or frustrated, but truly pissed the fuck off as he is now.

I stare at him without restraint, drinking my fill, not bothering to hide my own mixture of complex emotions, allowing each and every one to play across my face, showing him everything. It seems pointless to hide from him, now he's found me.

I see the truth in him, the raw hurt and ferocity of his anger. If I was under any delusions, Jamie's instant reaction to seeing me has cut them away at the root. I've really fucked up, and Jamie doesn't appear willing to pretend otherwise.

There's no calm before the storm, no promise of reprieve from the onslaught. Caleb's forgiveness came hand in hand with his fear and anger over losing me from his life the last few months. In contrast, it seems Jamie's mercy will be harder won.

It might sound wrong to think, but of everyone I left behind, with the possible exception of Lady Mars, it might be Jamie who has the most right to feel betrayed by my choice to run. I can't really explain why that feels true to me, it just does.

Jamie doesn't look like he's handled the last few

months any better than I have. He's still just as beautiful as he's always been to me, rugged and rough edged and comforting in his familiarity. But there's an unmistakable air of exhaustion to him now, dark circles under his eyes, hair long and unruly, a new scar on his face, cutting across his cheekbone. The facial hair's back, too, although not as thick as it was after that last mission, more scruff than beard.

He's got the wild and unkempt look of a man who's spent months living on the brink, not taking care of himself the way he should have.

It hurts, the fresh reminder of how much I've missed this man kickstarting a cacophony of sharp twisting sensations in my chest and pangs of regret in the hollowed-out cavern of my stomach. There's not a single inch of skin that doesn't buzz, not one cell that doesn't ache, one bloody nerve that doesn't throb in reaction to him.

Jamie mouths my name, like a prayer or a curse, and doesn't bother to act like this is any less than what it is to either of us.

It's like Rohan and Caleb disappear entirely. I knew they're still here, but that no longer computes information I need to take heed of.

I take an aborted step towards Jamie, holding myself back at the last moment. I'm not sure if I deserve to go to him right now. It seems beyond unfair to expect the open arms I'm used to getting from him after all the bullshit I've pulled. Like it would be a show of disrespect to even make out like I have the right to ask for what he's freely given to me so many times before.

The seething anger in Jamie's eyes intensifies, sparks

new life, and takes hold of him like I threw a lit match at a house made of tinder.

Jamie presses his lips together hard enough he must be biting down on the inside of his mouth to stop himself letting go and yelling at me right here and now, in front of Rohan and Caleb, who or may not still exist on this astral plane. Who knows? Not me. Can't know. All my mental energy is being used up trying to interpret what Jamie's next move is going to be.

When Jamie jerks his head at the doors leading to Rohan's balcony, I don't need to guess what he means by it. He must know this, because he walks away from me without a word.

I ignore Caleb's attempt to talk to me as I follow his brother. Rohan doesn't make any attempt to stop me, stepping aside and going to intercept Caleb instead. Some part of my mind is grateful to my newest friend for reading the room correctly and doing me the great favour of handling my oldest friend.

Thankfully, Caleb allows himself to be prevented from intervening and I'm able to escape through the balcony doors after Jamie.

Jamie doesn't stop until he's reached the end of the balcony, where he rests his forearms on the metal railing. He doesn't look over his shoulder to check where I'm at, instead waiting for me to catch up and copy his action, resting my forearms on the cylinder bar.

I keep a few feet of distance between us and look out at the city beyond, my gaze trained on a point in the distance.

Wind whips at our hair and whistles past our ears.

The sounds of Danger rise up to meet us, car horns and people shouting and the usual bustling noise of a large and busy city.

Up here on the balcony, however, there is only frigid silence. Or perhaps the silence isn't frigid at all. It's far too explosive for that.

In all the years we've known each other, I can't ever remember feeling this level of hostility between us. It festers in the atmosphere like stale smoke on fabric. This is so new for me and Jamie. We've had tension before, of course, but never anything this volatile, or as potentially devastating if broken in the wrong way.

Time passes. A lot of it. I don't turn my head to look at Jamie. I think, if I do, it will be like pulling the trigger on a starter pistol, and I'm not ready for that. I'm not ready to apologise or to defend. I'm not ready for Jamie to tell me just how much I've hurt him by doing a runner, for leaving him behind to deal with the mess I left in my wake.

I wait, like the coward I am, for Jamie to make the first move and decide how this whole thing is going to play out.

Jamie is practically vibrating with barely restrained emotion right next to me. He's an arm's reach away, and part of me is elated by this fact, after so long. Some part of me feels this is just like all the times he went away on a mission, the missing him, the fear, the relief when he would come back and we'd collide like atoms drawn together by an invisible force.

Except there's no agency or international enemy to blame. This was *my* choice, and mine alone.

Another part of me wants to remind Jamie of all the times he left me. Of every occasion he chose to go on missions he knew would take him away from our family, from me, for months at a time.

But I won't.

We've both spent far too much of our lives running from each other, in our own ways. This has to be where it ends, or I'm afraid it never will.

When Jamie does finally offer a reprieve from the anticipation, a swoop of dread hits my gut and digs in with talons sharp enough to rip me open and bleed me from the inside.

"I'm sorry, Rex." Jamie's voice breaks slightly on my name like dry wall cracking up under intense heat.

For a moment, I'm not sure if I heard him correctly. "What?"

Jamie's mouth flattens into an inscrutable line, offering me nothing to work with. "You heard," he says, like me not hearing him was my problem with what he said.

"Sorry?" I blink like a concussed owl, gaping at him in disbelief. "What the hell? I thought you were angry at me?"

Jamie laughs, harsh and incredulous, shooting me a look so quelling it hurts like a physical kick to the chest. "Jesus, Rex." He fists a hand in his hair and drags his fingers through it like he's trying to pull the locks out at the roots. He looks at me despairingly. "I'm so fucking pissed at you I can barely stop myself from laying you out and pinning you beneath me and strangling the life out of you. I mean. What the fuck. You left us. You left me. I get why you felt like you had to spend some time on your own, I really do. But. Seriously. You scared the fucking shit out of me, you bastard. Not a word from you. In *months*. Not a single bloody text to tell us you were alive. You got any idea what that did to us? I ain't never gonna forgive you for that."

He sounds like he means it, too, which is what I expected. Definitely what I deserve.

"If you're so upset, then why are you saying sorry?" I demand, becoming furious with my own lack of grip on this conversation. The cogence of my own convictions is already slipping through my fingers and we've barely begun. "I'm the one who messed up, here, and you know it. You just said so."

"Oh, and I suppose you're the only one who gets to fuck up at a time?" Jamie bites out, sardonic and almost cruel. "Not willing to share the limelight? Possessive of our new bad boy anti-hero rep, are we?" He gives my hair a pointed look.

Flames of desperation rise inside me, my chest and throat tight with cloying heat like any minute smoke will come billowing out of my mouth. "Jay, please—"

But Jamie talks right over me like he can't be fucked with whatever bullshit I was going to come out with. Like we don't have time for it, for the game we've been playing for years, the back and forth we've been daring each other with like bait in a trap. The fight I abandoned without bothering to tap out first.

"I'm sorry for a lot of things, Rex." He looks it. He really does, which is somehow worse than anything. Far worse than anger and condemnation would be. "I'm sorry for not being around as much as I should have been these last few years. I'm sorry for what you had to see that night. I'm sorry for whatever I did to make you think you couldn't trust me to keep my distance if that's what you needed. I'm sorry Roux died—"

My own anger flares to life and whips itself into an emotional hurricane of fire, like it's trying to fill a void, an understudy taking its place centre stage now Jamie's rage forgot to show up in time for curtain up. "Roux dying had nothing to do with you, so don't be sorry about it. I can't take that from you, Jay, I really can't." I kick out at the balcony, needing some physical release even if it's only small, even it makes me seem more petulant than anything else.

Jamie doesn't give an inch, his expression hardening again. "Fuck off with that shit. I loved him, too. I know it's not the same, because he was everything to you. You were everything to each other. But we loved Roux. He was ours, too. We *lost him, too.*" He puts so much emphasis on the words each one feels like another blow being brought down on top of my head.

He shakes his head, turning his face away like he can't bear to look at me any longer. He slows down, speaks so low it's more a broken whisper than anything else. "Then I found out Cal, T, and Mei were dying. That you were…" He stops, seemingly unable to finish the sentence, gulping in air like he's been starved of it.

A brand-new wave of guilt crashes through me like saltwater slamming against a cliff face it's slowly eroding, replacing the anger so fast it gives me psychological whiplash. "I'm sorry for running."

"No," he scoffs, but it sounds wet and wrung out,

"you're not." He looks at me again, a level of resignation I don't like on his face.

I glare at him stubbornly, taking my life in my hands. "Fuck off, I am."

"You're bloody not." Jamie makes a noise that would be amusement if he didn't look so bitter about it. "You just think you should be. I know you, Rexley Nova. I know you, so don't bullshit me. Don't lie. It's just going to piss me off more."

I want to tell him he's wrong. I want to scream it in his face. But I can't, because maybe he's right, my regret is flawed, has holes in it the size of a small country. Because there are things I would change if I could. But not everything. Not nearly enough to satisfy Jamie.

And we don't lie to each other, Jamie and me. We don't play that shit, never have before, and I don't want to start now.

"Then what do you want from me? If you don't want an apology and you understand why I left..." I am honestly bewildered by Jamie's response.

"What do I *want* from you?" Jamie explodes, his head whipping around to fix me with a look that somehow manages to appear both scathing and desperately sad. "Who the hell am I to you, Rex? What the fuck kind of question is that? Have I been hallucinating all these years, or are we family?"

"Of course we are!" I splutter out, frustrated at the fact I seem to be losing my grip on this conversation. "How can you even ask—"

Jamie cuts over me. "Then you already know the answer to what I want." He's solemn now, not quite as angry, like he really needs me to *get with the programme.* "It's the same as it's always been."

I don't need to wonder what he means by that. He's told me enough times.

"Hate it, fight it, survive it," I murmur gravely, as if they're the words written on my family coat of arms or something. "You. Me. Us."

Jamie seems relieved he didn't need to spell that out for me, exhaling loudly, shoulders slumping like someone cut the strings holding them up.

"Right, yeah. I told you before, and I'll tell you again now." He's still looking at me with that earnest intensity from before, and it takes real effort not to shrink away from him as he talks. "All you ever have to do is say the word and I'll do whatever you need me to do. You want to take out an entire mafia, I ain't afraid to spill blood on your say-so. You want to blow up every single Obsidian Inc facility, I'll be the only backup you need. You want to run all over the world, risking your life to avoid thinking about everything you've lost, I'll run right alongside you. Rex. I swear. Whenever, whatever, I am *with you.* Get that through your thick skull before I give in to the urge to beat it in there myself."

I turn to the side and cross my arms, although it's more hugging myself as a need to soothe the anxiety I'm feeling at this whole thing. "And if what I need from you is space?" I challenge him. "If what I need is to be on my own?"

"Then fine. I'll respect it," Jamie concedes, tipping his head in acknowledgement. His eyes light up a second later with defiance when he adds, "But you fucking let me know you're okay. You can't just disappear on me, Rex. I let you do it this time, and I'm telling you it almost killed me, but..." His jaw tightens for a second, like he needs that time to rein in the harsher words he wants to let loose. "If you ever leave like that again," he warns, "I won't respect your wishes. I will hunt you down and drag you back and I won't give a single shit how much of a bastard that makes me. Hear this, Rexley Nova. I won't let anyone take you from me again. Not even you." And something in the deep, rumbling way he says it sounds like a condemnation, a threat, and a sentence passed all in one.

There's a moment where it just sits there, all the things he said, in the small bit of space between us, heavy to the point of crushing, like the pressure of sinking too deep into the ocean.

"Okay," I allow tentatively.

Jamie raises his eyebrow at me. "Okay?"

"Yeah. I... Yeah, okay." I loosen my arms from around my chest and let them drop to my sides, taking down the barricade I'd temporarily erected for the sake of public— my—safety. "Next time I go on a suicidal crusade slash property destruction murder spree, I'll extend an invitation."

Jamie relaxes a little bit more, too, as if I've initiated a ceasefire of some kind.

"You'd fucking better. You know what's boring? Grief. Grief makes you want to stab yourself just to escape the tedium. I *wished* I'd had a crusade to focus on. It would've given me something to do with myself."

I make a low humming sound. "Could have just gotten one of your own."

"Excuse me," Jamie huffs, "not all of us have billion-aire benefactors to fund our mental breakdowns, thanks. Check your privilege, Rex."

"Is that the reason you came around?" I ask, mouth pricking up on one side. "To make sure I wasn't selling out and forgetting where I came from?"

"Nah," Jamie says dismissively, "my crash of your runaway train lifestyle is twofold. I've actually come to issue an invitation of my own. Wanted to know if you'd be interested in another off the books mission."

I blink at him, surprised. "Well, I'm intrigued, go on, sell it to me."

"Alright, merc," Jamie says, leaning towards me. "Listen to this. Got an incarcerated Liquid Onyx survivor kid, second gen, who needs rescuing. Found him by accident when I was on a mission for FISA, undercover at an OI black site."

My surprise triples by ten and tips over into outright shock. "Wait, seriously?"

"Yeah," Jamie confirms. "We think it's Connie Lorde's son."

"Hold on," I frown at him, "we think? Is FISA sanctioning this mission?" I ask dubiously.

Jamie's expression darkens. "No, that's the problem. Snow won't give us permission to infiltrate for the purpose of extraction."

"Why not?" I demand, although I've got a pretty good idea already.

"Usual reasons," Jamie says grimly. "Higher ups have clamped down on activity involving Obsidian Inc. They don't want to take the risk based on the intel I gathered in my brief time at the black site."

I bring a fist down on the balcony's metal bar. "Well fuck that. I'm in."

"Figured you would be." Jamie smiles proudly, then he winces a bit as if something just occurred to him. "But...you should know, there's more."

"More, like what?" In my experience, it's never good when people say that.

"The boy, Lorde's son. We know who the father is. He's a Liquid Onyx survivor, too." Jamie explains. "Or was. He's dead now. But. His brother is alive and...he wants in on the mission."

Ignoring the twinge of pain at the idea that another Liquid Onyx survivor died, likely while imprisoned by OI, I can't deny I'm also properly invested now. "Who's his brother?"

Jamie hesitates before answering, "Dan Roth." He seems to brace for my reaction.

It takes my brain a second to compute the information.

"Wait. Sami's boyfriend? That Dan Roth?"

Jamie nods. "Yeah, they're on their way over now. We need to plan. Rohan is on board, too."

I feel like I've spent the last few minutes blinking at Jamie like a befuddled bush baby.

"He is? Why?"

Jamie's pauses are going from ominous to just plain dramatic at this point.

"Because Dan is Rohan's half-brother." He says it slowly like it'll have less impact that way.

"*What?*"

"Yeah." Jamie pulls a face like he just ate something nasty. "Dan's bio-dad is Ian Stone."

"I think my brain is going to explode," I say, scrubbing a hand through my hair and looking around, feeling a bit dazed by all this. "Might want to get out of the splash zone," I warn Jamie.

"Nope, no time for that. We got shit to do." Jamie leans back from the metal railing and grabs onto it with both hands. "Get it together, Rex, we've got a rescue mission to make a shit plan for that we'll barely adhere to once we're on the ground."

As if on cue, Rohan bangs on the window to get our attention. Jamie and I both turn around. Rohan jerks his head at something behind him. I peer over his shoulder and see Dan and Sami both standing behind him in the living room with Caleb.

"Come on, then," I say, nudging Jamie's arm. "We better get in there so I can formally commiserate with Dan over his familial ties."

Jamie tilts his head consideringly. "Because he's related to Ian Stone the evil director of Obsidian Inc, or your new partner in crime, Rohan?"

I beam up at him, charmed by the slight acidic edge to his voice. "Wow, careful, Jay, your extreme jealousy is showing. It's very pretty and sharp, I love it."

I'm mostly joking, but Jamie snorts, serving me a harsh scowl. "I am jealous. You ran off and shacked up with him for months."

"Oh, don't you start." I scoff. "Cal is the one who got semi-proposed to, not me."

"So, nothing's happened between you and Rohan all

this time?" Jamie looks very sceptical of this fact, which given what he knows of me is a fair reaction.

"Well, he's come on to me a few times with legendary, smooth lines such as 'I'm not *not* in the mood'. But. No. We've managed to restrain ourselves from ripping each other's clothes off between my mental chaos spiral and Rohan's allergy to physical affection."

I once asked Rohan if his dislike of touching stems from his fear of losing control and hurting someone with his Liquid Onyx power, or if he feels naturally repulsed by it. Aversion *can be* built from the foundations of negative experiences, but it doesn't *have to* be. Some people are straight up born with their "no touchy" feels already implanted.

Rohan admitted to not being sure, since he can't remember a time when his pain power didn't have some impact on how he thinks about physical interaction with other people.

"Somehow, I am no less jealous," Jamie mutters dryly.

That's also fair.

"We did blow a lot of shit up together, though, which is honestly more significant. I've slept with loads of people before. I haven't blown shit up with anyone else outside of training. It's been a real heart-warming experience."

Rohan starts bashing on the window again, with more enthusiasm this time. Jamie and I share a wry look, then flip Rohan off in almost perfect unison. Rohan clutches at his chest and pretends to be scandalised.

I let out a sharp bark of laughter and start heading towards the balcony doors, half afraid Rohan or Caleb will come out here and make a scene. Caleb, because he can't help himself. Rohan, just to be a prick.

Jamie grabs hold of my upper arm, stopping me from striding away. I look back at him, brows furrowing in question.

He's got this vulnerable air about him he isn't bothering to hide. His grey eyes appear darker than usual, hooded and filled with a fragile kind of bravery.

"After this mission is over, I want to us to go to Colbie together. Will you do that, Rex? Come *home* with me."

I take in a deep breath and exhale slowly. "All right. After this mission, we go home."

Chapter Ten

Let's Rescue a Child Assassin, I Guess

When we get back inside, Caleb is already half out of the door, having been called in for a mission due to some supervillain in Ireland kicking off and requiring the attention of the whole SSS team.

He throws me an apologetic, almost hesitant look, clearly wanting to stay. I wave him off. Immediate world saving still comes first, no matter what. Caleb shares a significant mini stare-off with Jamie that ends with Jamie nodding like he's making a promise. Probably about me. Whatever. It seems to make Caleb feel better about leaving.

Once Caleb is gone, the rest of us congregate together in Rohan's living room and go about embarking on a truly haphazard planning session. There's some arguing, mostly between Rohan and Dan, and some playful mock-ing, mostly from Sami, but we get it together for the most part, perhaps the knowledge of what's at stake allowing for it despite all the obvious uneasiness.

With some idea of what we'll be doing, the group of us head out to the landing strip where Rohan keeps his private jet. I'm thinking Rohan will need to bribe some poor pilot to take us to Germany where Dan's nephew is apparently being kept, but Jamie surprises me by offering to do it.

When I prod Jamie, asking like it's an accusation, "Since when can you *fly a plane*?" his response is to give me a decidedly wicked curve of his mouth and say, "You only *think* you know everything about me, Rex." I flush at the heated drawl in his voice and beat a hasty retreat from the cockpit to take up residence in one of the extra comfy chairs in the main body of the plane.

Sami, having taken his spot as Jamie's co-pilot, laughs raucously at me as I go. I flip him the bird without looking back.

Rohan's plane is small but possessing enough tech-nological advances on the inside to make me think he might have designed the thing himself.

During the flight, Dan indulges me when I ask him about his Liquid Onyx power. He has the ability to manip-ulate glass with his mind. He takes one of Rohan's empty whiskey tumblers from the nearby drinks cart decked out with bottles full of amber-coloured liquid and a half-dozen glasses, and uses his ability to first crack, then break the glass apart into shards. The pieces of glass float between his hands, a neon-green glow around them.

It's extremely cool but frightening to imagine him doing the same thing with a much larger source of glass. He could bring down buildings in this city with a power like that.

"Okay, seriously, people need to stop turning out to be secret Liquid Onyx survivors slash secret family members, I can't take it," I bemoan, pinching the bridge of my nose and closing my eyes, puffing out an exasperated breath.

"Technically it wasn't a secret that I'm related to Satan and triple six over here." Dan jerks his chin at Rohan, voice caustic, face screwed up in mild antipathy.

"Don't be dramatic," Rohan admonishes his brother, his mocking tone holding a contemptuous edge that isn't at all a joke. I know what he sounds like when he's playing, and this isn't that. "I'm the one who's related to a *blond person*. It's embarrassing. At least with Satan there's power and prestige to be taken advantage of. You can't do anything with a blond brother except trade them for camels in Egypt."

Dan shoots one of the glass shards still floating between his hands at Rohan, who just manages to dodge it. The shard pierces his chair, driving in deep. Rohan doesn't look bothered by the sudden attack, sitting back up with a roll of his eyes and a smirk, leading me to believe this is their usual dynamic. Biting and volatile.

It's not difficult to imagine why there would be tension between them. Sharing a father like Ian Stone is hardly the best thing to be bonded by.

"Play nice, children." To head off any more potential barb throwing, or literal glass throwing, I turn to Dan again and ask, "When did you escape Obsidian Inc?"

Dan considers me for a moment, his pale-green eyes seeming to become flinty and distant. It makes him look somehow far older than he is. I've never met any of the Liquid Onyx survivors who OI kept and trained as child-soldiers. My knowledge about what was done to them is surface level, and that's bad enough. OI moulded the super-powered children they kept into assassins, capable of killing with brutal efficiency and a distinct lack of remorse. Roux's voice spindles through my mind like the cold hands of a ghost.

Twelve years old and he tried to kill me like he'd been doing it for years.

"I didn't," Dan admits with a light shrug, his mouth pursing in consternation for a second before he goes on. "Your boy, Moon, he got me out. Stumbled on me by accident during a storm of some OI facility and we recreated a scene from *Prison Break* together."

I dart a glance in the direction of the cockpit, suddenly wishing I could see Jamie's face. As if I'm not always wishing that on some level, right?

"He never said anything," I murmur, not upset by the fact but filtering it into the file I have in my head on Jamie. Maybe he's right. Maybe there's a lot to him I don't know, despite how long we've been what we are to each other. I suppose it's fair. Everyone has secrets, don't they? And as far as secrets go, rescuing a Liquid Onyx survivor who OI spent years torturing isn't exactly the worst he could have.

"Yeah, well, he's like that, isn't he?" Dan scoffs, lowering his voice so Jamie won't hear him. "Likes being the unsung hero. It fits his whole aesthetic."

"What aesthetic?" I ask, grinning at the open scorn on Dan's face. "Revamped James Bond?"

Dan shrugs again, gaze shifting to the glass between his hands again. He idly plays around with them, making the shards dance around him, reminding me for a moment of Damon and his stars. A breath catches in my throat at the memories assaulting me of Damon's stunning face, set in a scowl or less often an amused smile, illuminated by blue star-fire.

Instead of answering the question directly, Dan shifts his attention to me, eyes fixed on mine like he's trying to convey something nonverbally that will better help me to understand the meaning behind what he does say.

"He's a good man."

A ball of razor blades squeezes around my heart, cutting into sensitive flesh from every angle. No escape from the pain, from the bite and slice of it. "I know that."

Dan hums like he isn't sure if I do. He's quiet again when he says, "Might want to zero in before someone else realises it, too, and does a better job of making like they know."

Unsure how to react to that, the very unsubtle hint to get my head out of my arse and do something life-changing about my thing with Jamie, finally, I take a page out of Dan's book and don't reply to it head on.

"How's Sami dealing with what *he* knows is gonna happen to the likes of you and me in the next couple years?" If we're lucky. Could be months. Not like there are actual rules to all this shit. None we can rely on, make plans around, anyway.

Dan's mouth turns down, like a snarl that's been bitten in half and stapled back on all crooked. He shoots a look over at Rohan, whose expression is carefully blank, has been this whole time. Dan shifts his gaze to the doorway to the cockpit where his boyfriend is probably doing his best to make sure Jamie crashes this plane into the ocean rather than landing it in Germany.

Dan releases a slow sigh, his lips taking on a new shape, more of a curl than a jagged cut, eyes filling with a dark sort of humour that reminds me so much of Rohan I can see for the first time the brotherly resemblance.

"By making outrageous demands on dead stars and bribing every fountain in Danger City Park like he's tryin' to fix a prize fight." It doesn't sound as if he's joking, and knowing Sami, he may very well not be.

I make a low noise of disgust, looking between Rohan and Dan before spitting out a rough, "Fuck our dads, huh?"

Rohan snorts at the crudeness of the statement but nods his head in agreement. Dan doesn't respond, though his expression clearly indicates he feels the sentiment is sound.

We lapse into silence after that, the heavy hopelessness of the topic of our almost inevitable spiral into insanity and eventual horrific deaths casting a dark pall over us for the rest of the flight.

Jamie lands Rohan's plane on an empty lot where a load of warehouses used to stand. There's no one around for miles, which means hopefully the plane will sit undisturbed until we can come back for it.

Together, we hike into the nearest town and scout

around until we find a white van big enough for all of us to fit in. Rohan makes quick work of hotwiring the engine and Jamie takes the wheel again, the rest of us jumping in the back.

We're two hours out from the black site, according to Jamie, and the time passes by fast and without incident. Unless you count Sami entertaining himself by singing ABBA songs at top volume and Rohan threatening to murder each and every one of us including himself if we don't make it stop. Dan encourages Sami to sing louder despite the fact he doesn't seem any happier with having the lyrics to "Dancing Queen" shouted into his enhanced eardrums. Because siblings.

The black site is hidden away behind a dense thicket of trees, in a clearing within a large forest. Once we get close enough, Jamie says we need to go the rest of the way on foot. There's only one road in and we can't exactly roll up in our van to ask the OI guard stationed here to politely hand over Dan's nephew.

We park the van behind a cluster of trees so anyone driving past won't notice it on first glance. Rohan sets up in the back of the van with his laptop and another machine he brought with him from the flat which he says will scramble the signal coming from his laptop, shielding him when OI try to track who's hacking into their security system. Much like every other mission we've been on together, the plan is for him to break into the OI facility's security and allow us easy access to every corner of the building with no need for pass codes or some way to fool the thumbprint recognition software OI are fond of using in their facilities.

Rohan hands out comm units to all of us so we'll be able to keep in contact once we're inside. Jamie, having been inside the facility before, draws the layout of the interior using a piece of chalk on the floor of van. We gather around the surprisingly detailed map. He labels each room he was allowed into and gives us a basic rundown of the OI guards' routine both inside the facility and on the perimeter. He's so thorough with his information I figure he must have been on this job for a long time, which is mildly terrifying to me. The idea of Jamie being within reach of OI's brutality makes my stomach churn with a sick feeling I can't shake.

"How long were you posing as an OI guard?" I ask him, unable to help myself, as if I think having more details about his mission will make it somehow less scary to imagine.

Jamie's brows pull together like he either doesn't understand the question or doesn't think I'll like the answer for some reason. But then he answers, "A couple of hours. The mission was aborted at the last minute, and I was pulled away sooner than I should have been."

"Hours? Seriously?" I scan my eyes over the exhaustively comprehensive map he's drawn from memory in disbelief.

Jamie misunderstands me and tries to explain. "They thought there might be leak of intel on my status as a FISA agent, so they pulled me just in case."

I look up at him and shake my head, laughing incredulously. "No, you dummy, I meant did you seriously retain all this after only a couple hours of being inside the facility?"

Jamie pulls a face that's half a grimace and half an embarrassed frown. He shrugs, looking away from me and down at the map like the thing has done something to purposefully show him up. "You know I've always had an okay memory."

Self-deprecation, thy name is Jamie Moon.

I must be staring at him with something like awe on my face because Rohan quickly cuts through that shit by snorting in annoyance. "Yes, yes, Jamie Moon, the wonder agent, best of his generation, can retain basic information and utilise chalk like a five-year-old delinquent in a playground, we are all very impressed."

Jamie immediately flips Rohan off, although his attention diverts to me, that quarter smile I've missed so much quirking at one corner of his mouth. "Is being a competent agent really all it would have taken to impress you all these years, Rex?"

He's teasing, but there's a real edge to the question I could easily cut myself on if I'm not careful in handling it.

"I've always been impressed by you, Jay. Don't need to try, I'm already a diehard fan," I tell him seriously, allowing only a slight lilt so he can take the truth out if he wants to and not engage with the deeper meaning to my response. My own mouth curls up on both sides as I nudge his shoulder and joke, "I was into you before you were famous, skater boy."

Because that's who Jamie is to me. He's like a band I've loved all my life, who everyone else only got into recently, but who I've been obsessed with since the very beginning.

Sami and Dan are on the opposite side of the map,

exchanging glances like they've got some kind of bet going that Jamie and I are about to settle for them.

It makes me feel self-conscious, especially when Jamie doesn't choose to back down and instead shifts forward, invading more of my space and replying in a low voice, "I'll keep that in mind, Avril." He's looking me right in the eye. Gets my oblique references like he does, has always been so good at doing, could read me like no one else, apart from maybe Roux.

Rohan makes a retching noise in the back of his throat and throws the piece of chalk at my head. I see the chalk coming, catch it in one hand, and chuck it back at Rohan twice as hard. He catches it, too, making grumbling noises about our "inappropriately timed eye-fucking".

Part of me really hopes Rohan falls for some poor bastard one day just so I can spend whatever time we both have left on this earth laughing my arse off at him out of spite. I hope there's lots of awful, angsty pining and that he hates it. It's what he deserves, quite frankly.

Jamie brings us back on point, clearing his throat and taking on the role as team leader, eyeing each of us in turn with a more serious expression. "Are we all okay with the plan? We'll get into position and Rohan will take down the facility's security, allowing us to infiltrate." He nods at me. "Rex can blow up the entrance, which will have the added benefit of causing a distraction. Then we'll make our way through the facility until we find Dan's nephew."

We all exchange looks of agreement and voice our okays to go ahead with the plan Jamie outlined. It's basic, but sometimes simple is the best option. OI have no reason to believe we'll be going after them today and, based on my now extensive experience infiltrating OI bases of operation, hitting them hard and fast will likely be our best chance of success in this instance. There was a brief discussion earlier about waiting until dark and going in more covertly, but Jamie negated that plan, saying there are too many security measures to bypass, including more guards scouring the place who would certainly notice four new people.

Jamie said OI have doubled the number of guards they used to have on average patrolling their facilities. He didn't say it out loud, but it was pretty clear he was implying Rohan's and my recent slew of attacks on their properties instigated this change. Although it's caused trouble for us now, I can't help a small slip of satisfaction leaking through at the idea I've got OI scared enough to be calling in reinforcements to protect their assets.

Today's going to be one more hit against them, and I'm nothing but buzzed for it.

With everything settled, we leave the van with Rohan and move through the forest on light feet, keeping quiet to avoid detection. Rohan swept the area for cameras in the trees and found none, which is an oversight of OI. If it were me, I'd have cameras jammed into every other tree in this forest. I know Snow would. She loves a good hidden cam.

Dan and I take point, being the ones more likely to heal from a bullet wound and me in my bulletproof super suit.

Once we find a suitable spot near the facility with a good angle on the front entrance, I whisper a quick message to Rohan over the comms, letting him know we're ready when he is.

The facility isn't overly large and resembles a science research centre, built from metal and glass, shaped like a triangle. It looks oddly out of place in this rustic environment. But the amount of glass is a good thing for us with Dan's ability.

Crouched down behind some thick bushes, we wait for Rohan to do his thing and give us the go-ahead. Sami and Jamie have their guns in their hands, two Sigs, black and held competently like they're an extension of themselves rather than a weapon they needed to have extensive training to learn how to use properly. Jamie has at least one other gun strapped his side, and it wouldn't surprise me if he had another tucked away somewhere.

Growing up, Jamie did well with guns. It was his preferred weapon right from the jump. Much to Caleb's consternation and Hector's proud delight, Jamie became an excellent shot in record time, receiving rare praise from Fiona, who is also known for her killer aim. In another life, he would have likely made a brilliant military sniper.

When Rohan's voice comes through with a sharp "Done", we're off. I look at Jamie, treating him as the leader and asking his permission. He gives me a firm nod and I turn back to the facility's entrance. I summon up my power, blood setting light in my veins, a rush of sensation rippling across the inside of my skin like my bones are thrumming with an electric pulse. Once I have a grip on my power, I push outward, sending it towards my target.

From one second to the next it's as if the world stills,

every person holding their breath in perfect unison.

Then the front entrance to the facility blows apart in a loud and dramatic blast of fire and debris. The large glass wall explodes outwards, scattering shards across the muddy forest ground in the clearing. I can feel the heat of the blast against the skin of my face.

Another moment of stillness, then anarchy descends.

There weren't any visible guards before the explosion, but they come running soon after, flooding from all around like bees desperate to save the hive.

"*Move!*" Jamie barks and we all charge forward into the fray.

There's so much chaos and confusion that at first the OI guards don't seem to notice us. Jamie runs at my side, drawing up his gun and firing off a few expert shots at three OI guards, catching them in the head and taking them down easily. His face is set in grim determination, looking more gunmetal grey than ever before, which I suppose is fitting.

It takes me second to realise why the sight of Jamie shooting three people dead without a hint of hesitation triggers an oddly off-balanced feeling inside my chest. This is the only time I've ever seen him kill someone in person. I've heard about such instances before, of course, from other people and Jamie himself. He called me after he took a life for the first time during a mission. He wasn't as much of a mess about it as he could have been, but there's no denying it deeply affected him, I could tell that from just his voice over the phone. I insisted he come home that weekend, and we spent the entire two days on the beach, not talking much, but sharing each other's space as we read or listened to music, and I like to think it helped him.

Despite this, it cannot be denied Jamie's never had problems pulling the trigger. I knew that, have known that always, but something about *seeing it* hits different. Not in a bad way, necessarily. It just makes me look at him in a new light, more aware of the dangerous man my friend has become in the time we were apart. With every mission, every target, he was hardened and honed into the man he is now, Agent Moon, not Jamie, the boy who used to go around after it rained picking up snails from the path and putting them out of the way so they wouldn't get accidentally stepped on.

Jamie catches my eye, like he knows what I'm thinking, and there's a slight softening around the edges, just for me, a reminder he's still in there, the boy I've loved almost all my life. I give him some of the same back before turning away again.

There are more OI guards now and Jamie and Sami empty their clips firing off head shots when they can and less lethal shots when they can't.

A group of OI agents get their guns out and Dan summons up a load of the glass shards that were sprayed across the ground and raises them like they're zombies from a graveyard. The green glow around them is so bright it's almost blinding. He pushes his hands forward like he's throwing the shards, and they go flying through the air only to slice and cut at the OI guards about to start shooting. Most of them collapse either to shield their faces or due to injuries caused by the larger pieces of glass.

When two OI guards get back up with their weapons

up and aimed at Sami and Jamie as they're changing out the clips in their guns, I summon up my power and explode them in their hands. Blood and bone erupt and fall to the ground along with the smoking remains of the guns.

With most of the OI guard dead or too injured to cause problems, I race towards the gaping hole in the building, metal hot and twisted around it like someone took a bite out of it. My friends follow me, catching up as I run down the main hallway. Jamie takes the lead again, being the one who knows the layout of the facility best.

Jamie takes us down a series of corridors and in each one we come across at least a couple of OI guards. They seem to be spread out through the facility quite evenly. With Rohan's help, getting past the doors linking each corridor is as simple as pressing the green "open" button on the wall beside them. I probably could have blasted through them with my power, but this is certainly the easier, less messy option.

Dan lifted more glass outside and brought it in with him, glowing green glass shards dancing around him as he runs, reminding me once more of Polaris during a fight. Much like Polaris, Dan uses his power to take out any guards too far away to reach who would be the first to get off a shot at us. Between that, Sami and Jamie's well-aimed shooting, and my ability to disarm anyone, we move through the facility quickly, leaving bloodied walls and the slumped corpses of OI guards behind us like crumbs in a fairy tale forest.

When we come to the part of the facility where Jamie saw Dan's nephew locked up in a holding cell, a collective apprehension travels through the group. This is the part where we find out if our hazardous invasion of this OI facility has been worth it. I would say destroying anything belonging to OI would be, but I know it isn't the same for Dan. We all want to save a child if we can, but it must be a little bit extra when the boy is the son of the twin brother you lost.

Jamie stops us outside the door, the facility's cells lying beyond it. "We'll wait here in case more OI guards come out of the woodwork." He tips his head at Sami. Then he nods at me and Dan. "You two go in and grab the boy."

Dan and I follow the order, despite our obvious reluctance to leave the normal humans without our powers as protection. I have to remind myself Jamie has gone on countless missions and survived, that he's more than capable of playing lookout.

We find ourselves in a narrow corridor with more doors lined up on either side. Cells. Each door has a slim rectangular window built into it, allowing someone to look inside at whoever is being held in the cell.

Dan checks each one, with me following closely behind him, and an increased sense of urgency with every empty cell he finds. On the fourth door, he lets out a breath he was clearly holding in, relief flooding across his face in a torrent. I expect him to yank the door open, but he hesitates, his hand hovering over the door handle. He turns to me uncertainly and I try to look encouraging, although the situation is well beyond my emotional capacity, and I think we all know that.

Still, Dan must see something in my expression because he steps away from the door and says, "You go in and get him." At my confused reaction he explains, "I don't want to accidentally hurt him." He indicates the shards of glass still floating all around him. He sighs, adding dejectedly, "Or frighten him."

It's doubtful to me whether someone raised within OI would be scared of much. If Rohan is anything to go by, and Roux's story about the boy who attacked him, this kid is more likely to come out swinging than be cowed by some glowing glass. But there isn't really time to argue back and forth about it. We need to get out of here as soon as, before OI manage to call in reinforcements.

"All right, then," I acquiesce, moving forward to grab the door handle and yank it open.

Inside the cell is a little boy, maybe five or six years old, with thick dark hair and brown skin. He has a lovely face, much like his father and uncle, and a pair of striking eyes the colour of pure violet, which he possibly inherited from his mother.

He looks well fed, at least. Healthy. But that's just the physical side of things. There's no telling what's going on with him psychologically.

The boy blinks at me from his position braced against the left side wall. He's put himself at the hardest place to reach within the small cell, forcing anyone who wants to get at him to enter the cell first and put themselves at risk of being trapped in the opposite corner if he were to strike out. Without knowing what his power is, that's more of a potential for trouble than I'd like. Mia said the boy had the same abilities as his mother, or both of his parents, I suppose, but she didn't say if he had the same power, or if he has an individual power at all. The whole next gen thing is even more new territory than the original Liquid Onyx survivors are.

Bracing myself for anything, I step into the cell, maintaining eye contact with the boy, trying to seem as unthreatening as possible so I won't set him off.

"Hey, my name's Rex. I swear I'm not going to hurt you or anything. I just want to get you out of here," I say, feeling awkward but not knowing what else to tell him.

The boy just stares at me without an expression on his little face for a really long time. The seconds tick by and due to the situation going on outside this cell they feel a lot longer. Every second we spend in here ups the chances of us not getting out at all.

Still, I don't move closer to him, knowing somehow it will only spark off a negative reaction.

In a desperate attempt to make him trust me, if only temporarily, I go outside the cell and grab one of Dan's glass shards out of the air. Dan raises his eyebrows questioningly, but I don't waste time explaining.

When I go back into the cell the boy's eyes dart to the glass shard and his breath hitches in slight panic, but he doesn't move otherwise.

I drag the glass along my neck, angling my throat so he can see the sharp edge break skin and the black blood ooze out from the shallow wound. The boy's brows come together in either confusion at me cutting myself or at the colour of the blood. After making the cut, I drop the shard of glass to the ground so he knows I'm not about to hurt him with it.

"I'm like you," I tell him, calm and certain, trying to sound like the adult I should be rather than the boy I feel like most of the time. "I can take you to a place where people like us are safe."

It feels almost like a lie. I'm not sure if FISA really is safe, or if anything can be considered safe when you have poison inside you which is slowly killing you. But now really isn't the time for that kind of nuance.

I take another step towards the boy, feeling marginally more confident when he doesn't instantly try to make a run for it or attack me with his possible power. "I know you have no reason to trust me," I say, looking him in the eyes, trying to convey my sincerity to this abused child with blazing violent eyes and his uncle's nose, "but if you just come with me, I won't let them take you back. No matter what, you won't ever belong to them again."

There's another pause that seems to last at least fifteen minutes rather than the five seconds it probably is in reality. But then the boy pushes himself away from the wall and throws himself at me in one surprisingly graceful leap. Despite the suddenness, I'm able to catch him in my arms. He wraps his arms loosely around my neck and squeezes his legs around my waist.

"You got a name?" I ask him, feeling mildly concerned he might not. What if OI have done something insane and given him a number rather than a name or something?

The boy assuages my fears by nodding his head and answering in a young, rasping voice, "Nathan."

Nathan. Right, that I can work with.

"Brilliant, Nathan, good to meet you, now let's get the fuck out of here," I say in a rush, feeling the urgent need to run like hell.

I get a tight grip on Nathan and walk out of the cell with him. Nathan doesn't seem phased by the sight of Dan and his shards. If anything, Dan seems more wrong-footed by the sight of Nathan. His green eyes get all wide and fearful, like he's suddenly realised this little person in my arms is his brother's son and he has no idea what to do with the magnitude of that fact.

If nothing else, this facility and these cells must bring back some terrible memories for Dan. Finding his nephew in the same kind of place he and his brother spent their entire childhood must be one hell of a mindfuck.

Unfortunately, we don't have time to slow down for anyone to have a mental breakdown, and if we did, it would be for mine. So...

Nathan stares at his uncle with curious and wary eyes but doesn't speak.

Dan steps up like he's going to reach for Nathan or at least talk to him—I have a sudden flash of memory. Roux. The roof of that safe house. My uncle reaching out for me with shaking hands and a look of severe trepidation on his face—but he backs down at the last second, turns away from him entirely, and strides away towards the exit. "Come on, Nova," Dan snaps over his shoulder at me, "get a shift on before we all have a chance to get dead in this shithole."

I rush to follow him, holding Nathan just that little bit tighter, like I'm afraid he'll vanish into thin air if I don't.

Outside in the corridor we're met with an ongoing fight between Sami and Jamie and a group of OI guards. Fear grips my heart at the chaotic mess of violence it takes my eyes a second or two to compute and parse to under-stand what's happening. My brain catches up just in time to witness Jamie kick the shit out of two OI guards in a hand-to-hand fight that is nothing short of breath-taking.

Jamie punches one of them in the throat and as his hand goes scrambling for his neck, he knees him in the stomach, causing the OI guard to double over with loud gasps of pain. Flowing from one movement to the other, Jamie jabs his elbow backwards into the throat of the OI guard coming up behind him, sending the man choking for air. He spins around and in one fluid motion he grabs the man by the hair and lifts his knee up to smash the man's nose. There's a loud crunch and blood explodes from his nostrils.

Jamie shoves the man to the floor. He whips out his second gun—the first must have been lost at some point during the fight—and spins around to shoot the first man in the head just when he's recovered enough to try to lunge for another ill-fated attack. Then Jamie brings the muzzle of the gun back around to the man he shoved to the floor and lets off another shot, the bullet lodging in the second man's skull. There's the same forbidding mer-cilessness on Jamie's face as he looks down at the man he just killed.

Dan has already moved in to assist his boyfriend with the remaining OI guards, dispatching them with ease be-tween then. When done, Dan pulls Sami to him, checking a wound he's found in his side from where a stray bullet must have caught him. Sami doesn't seem to be struggling with it too much, so it's probably nothing serious.

Jamie catches sight of me staring at him in the

doorway, his frighteningly resolute expression melting away slightly to something kinder, more human. He steps over the bodies of dropped OI guards to stand in front of me and Nathan. The boy tilts his head, regarding Jamie with no fear, like the outright violence he just saw Jamie commit somehow makes him more trustworthy rather than less.

Jamie offers Nathan a gentle smile, smoothing out the hard lines of his face. "Hey, little man, glad to see you again. Told you I'd be back, didn't I?" He has blood splashed across his features, which rather ruins the effect of his softness, but I still appreciate the effort. Nathan must do as well, because he offers a surprising upward twitch of his lips in response to Jamie's smile.

"Not little," Nathan argues with a tiny pout.

Jamie nods contritely, as if he's been corrected. "Too right, actually. You've grown at least three feet since I last saw you. You'll be bumping up against skyscrapers by next year."

Nathan's lips curve into a proper smile this time. "I *will*," he insists, like we'd all be a fool to doubt his ability to grow as tall as any building in Danger City.

I have a sudden wild and entirely inappropriately timed thought, one I've had before, that Jamie could make a great dad one day. Part of me hoped the thing that brought Jamie and Caleb back together again would be if they both had children. Now that won't ever happen, thanks to Caleb's shortened lifespan, and I mourn the loss of a possible future that may or may not have been.

Jamie winks at Nathan conspiratorially, then steps back and casts a look around at the others. "You all right to go, Sam?" he asks his partner, eyes going to the blood seeping from Sami's side.

Without asking permission, Dan stoops down and sweeps Sami into his arms. Sami yelps, whacking his boyfriend over the head in consternation. "That hurt, you prick. I am *injured*." He huffs. "Injured people don't like it when you jostle them around like an armful of dirty sheets for the wash. Unhand me immediately." He narrows his eyes. "Or I will be forced to bite you."

"Now we can go," Dan says, ignoring Sami's indignant squawk to put him down.

Jamie is apparently unwilling to get involved in all that, which is very sane of him, and he jerks his head for us to follow him along the corridor to freedom.

We don't meet any more trouble until we're back outside in front of the facility and at the edge of the forest.

A black van speeds down the road and stops at the end of it, the door on the side opening with a loud crash. Another group of OI's people, likely agents rather than guards and therefore better trained, spill out of the van wearing body armour and holding large, black machine guns.

Excellent.

Jamie moves in front of me and Nathan with his gun up and already firing. It's no use, though, there are too many of them and they've moving fast, way faster than the guards did. Dan had to drop his glass to pick up Sami and, not wanting to risk using my power while I have hold of Nathan, I conclude the only option we really have is to make a run for it.

I grab Jamie's arm and drag him towards the trees. Dan comes with me with Sami in his arms and we all run full pelt through the forest together.

The OI agents give chase, their thundering behind us the total opposite to how we moved through the trees earlier, with no care for how loud they're being. Like a bloody herd of pissed-off elephants. Elephants with guns. There's an image for you.

Bullets starts firing after us, catching on tree trunks and spraying bark all over the place. Lucky for us, the trees are so dense that the OI agents have trouble shooting in a straight line.

Unluckily for us, the trees are so dense we're unable to run as fast as we would like, having to dodge and manoeuvre around the forest like it's a particularly hazardous assault course.

As the machine gun-wielding shitheads close the distance between us, their bullets start hitting trees right next to our faces. Failed headshots get closer and closer with each attempt.

I tighten my hold on Nathan, putting one hand on the back of his head and pushing it down to my shoulder to better shield him from a potential stray bullet. But Nathan fights me, raising his head to look at the OI agents coming for us. I don't have time to panic over the boy catching a shot to the face before *it* happens.

A loud noise, like a burning house exploding, sounds behind us. A tempest of heat hits our backs and almost takes me off my feet with the strength and pressure caused by the blast.

Only just managing to catch myself, I stop dead in my

tracks and whip around to check what the hell's just happened.

My eyes widen in shock at the eruption of fire, violet fire, that has seemingly appeared from nowhere around the OI agents chasing us. It catches them alight with supernatural speed and they immediately begin panicking and screaming as flames lick across their bodies like thick, grasping fingers.

What makes it even stranger is the fact the trees surrounding the OI agents, who are now fully engulfed in fire, seem completely untouched by the violet flames, almost as if the fire is choosing what it wants to burn.

Well, that's interesting.

It doesn't take much deduction to realise who did this. I shift Nathan around so I'm able to get a better look at his face.

Jamie comes up to stand beside us as we watch the OI agents burn and die. We should probably go, but I'm so transfixed by the sight of violet flames eating away at their victims I can't make my feet move.

Other than the last screams of agony from the agents, there's complete silence in the forest.

Until.

Nathan stares at the result of his power being unleashed, his violet eyes raging and churning like gales of fire trapped inside a bottomless pit, and rasps, "Not going back." His voice is so childlike and so serious at the same time it's genuinely chilling.

I dart a quick glance at Jamie, whose gaze flickers away from Nathan and over to me at the same time, and we share a look of mutual disquiet.

Chapter Eleven

Home Is Where the Heart Is, They Say

Once we get a grip on ourselves following Nathan's show of power, we make a mad dash for our waiting getaway van. Rohan is already in the driving seat ready to go and when we all pile into the back, he sets off without asking any questions.

In unspoken agreement, based on the communal need to put distance between us and the now compromised OI black site, we head straight for Rohan's plane and board. Jamie commands the pilot's seat and takes off before any of us are properly sat down and buckled in.

Not long into the flight a conversation starts up about where we're taking Nathan. It seemed obvious to me that we would be going to the FISA base, but Dan immediately fights against that idea.

"I don't trust them," Dan growls, shooting a venomous glare at me, daring me to challenge him over this. "They're a government agency with their own agendas when it comes to the Liquid Onyx survivors. They always have been. Snow didn't create the SSS unit to give supers a place to go out of the goodness of her heart. Everything she does is to benefit the agency."

I can't exactly argue with him there, although I'm not sure it's as simple as Snow wanting to use the Liquid Onyx survivors for her own gain. Thinking back on the argument we had right after Damon's death, it's impossible not to apply more complexity to Snow's motives.

"FISA saved you," I point out carefully, not wanting to have my head bitten off but seeing no real alternative other than taking Nathan somewhere we'll know OI can't get to.

"Bullshit. Moon saved me." Dan jerks his chin at the cockpit. "Against fucking orders. Just like now. Snow didn't want him to help me or Nathan, so she can get fucked, I'm not taking him to another agency so they can lock him up or let their scientists poke at him like he's an experiment."

None of us states the obvious fact Nathan's very existence was in fact an experiment. One instigated by Ian Stone so he could find out what the child of a Liquid Onyx survivor would be like.

I take Dan's point, though. Just because Nathan started out his life as an experiment doesn't mean he should be continually treated as such. No matter what he's capable of, at the end of the day he's still a child in need of protection. He deserves a proper home, not the same cold, lonely life dictated by a sense of duty like

Damon had.

Sami, who I patched up with the plane's generously stocked first aid kit, shifts in his seat, pain lancing across his face, moving closer to Dan. He touches his arm, shaking it a little until Dan turns his head begrudgingly to look at him, giving up his glare-a-thon with the rest of us.

Nathan is up front with Jamie after insisting he take the co-pilot's seat. Rohan agreed, very reluctantly, to have his nephew seated on his lap. He stared at Nathan like he was a particularly bizarre-looking gremlin at first, but when Nathan just stared back at him, entirely blank faced and unnervingly quiet, Rohan seemed to settle into his role as child-holder. Good thing Nathan is old enough not to need things like nappy changes, otherwise Rohan might have lost his nerve.

After a bit of silent communicating between the couple, Dan seems to unfurl a little from the metaphorical corner he behaved like he'd been backed into by the mention of FISA. He turns back to me with a less mutinous expression, although he still seems mildly hostile about the whole thing.

Sami gives me a tight smile, his hand still on Dan's arm, thumb gently rubbing over it in soothing motions. "Sorry, Rex, I get what you're saying, but taking Nathan to FISA is out," he says regretfully.

Well, he's Dan and Rohan's nephew, not mine. If anyone has the right to decide what happens to him from now on, it's his family.

"All right." I dip my head in acceptance of their decision. "What do you want to do, then? Take him to your flat?"

Dan looks unsure all of a sudden, like now I've conceded the main fight he doesn't know what to do with the power of making such a big decision about a child's future. He becomes increasingly distressed, the uncertainty playing out across his face in full technicolour.

"Okay"—I hold up a hand to stop him from having an actual meltdown—"how about we take a step back and regroup somewhere safe, then go from there once you've had time to think properly about everything?"

Dan looks suspicious, eyes narrowing on me slightly like I'm trying to trick him into going to FISA after all. But Sami seems to know where I'm going with this.

"You and Jamie are going to Colbie, right?" Sami prods, brows coming together pensively. "You think we should go with you? Hole up in Colbie for a bit?"

I shrug, shoving away the windstorm of anxiety that begins brewing at the notion of returning home after purposefully avoiding it for so long. "It was a safe place for me and my friends for fourteen years."

Dan and Sami do more of that silent communicating thing, and I wait patiently for them to give the final verdict.

"Okay, let's go play small town boys in Colbie," Dan eventually sighs, the scowl affixed to his face belaying his easy agreement. He sits back in his seat and gives me a droll look. "I'm excited to finally see if this town is as fucking weird as Sami keeps telling me it is."

I refuse to comment. Dan will just have to find out what he's really made of on his own.

*

Jamie flies Rohan's plane back to his private hanger and from there we split up.

Rohan insists on going to the FISA base to continue working on an important project. I suspect it's the chemical he's been working on to stop the progression of the Liquid Onyx survivors' descent into madness and death, but he doesn't want to say so in front of anyone other than me. He never said it was a secret explicitly, but I know him well enough by now to be aware he doesn't like to share half-finished or ongoing projects.

I tell him to keep me updated and Rohan promises to do so.

Jamie picks out one of Rohan's cars, a large SUV big enough to fit us all, and drives the rest of us to Colbie. I take the passenger seat, and the others get in the back with Nathan sitting between them.

Half an hour in, we turn on the radio in the hopes of hearing any news about the supervillain attack Caleb left to deal with. After a bit of fiddling, we find a channel discussing the event. I'm shocked when the people on the radio talk about the Irish superhero Guardian having gone insane and attacking the city she protected for years.

I exchange more horrified glances with Jamie when the reporter says Guardian was killed during the ensuing superhero versus superheroes fight when she went to land a fatal blow against Barricade and Crescent swooped in to save him by killing Guardian.

Holy *fuck*!

If that's true, Crescent must be a mess right now. Guardian was an ally, a powerful and longtime superhero. Add to that Crescent's usual reluctance towards lethal violence in general and it's painfully clear to me how this incident will hit him hard, and possibly at the worst time. He's already been struggling; something like this could send him over the edge. What waits for him on the other side of that edge, I'm not completely sure, but I do know it'll lead to me losing my friend even sooner than I might have otherwise.

Jamie can see me begin to panic over what's going on with Caleb and he reaches across the console to take my hand, his other one tightening on the wheel, a sure sign of his own anxiety. He tries to catch my eyes, looking away from the road briefly. "Stop, Rex. Cal knows you'll be at home waiting for him when he comes back."

Jamie is right. It's not just about Caleb.

I link my fingers with Jamie's and squeeze his hand, using the solid feel of his warm skin wrapped up in mine to keep myself grounded and prevent my thoughts from spiralling in all the worst directions. "It must be Liquid Onyx that made her do it," I say instead of responding directly to his attempt at reassurance.

Jamie scowls lightly at the road ahead but doesn't argue with me. He knows as well as I do the likelihood of Guardian's sudden shift in mental state having come on naturally is extremely low.

There's a palpable silence in the backseat of the car where Sami and Dan are sitting with Nathan. I don't want to think about the possibility that little boy's life will be shortened because of Liquid Onyx, let alone the chance he'll lose both his newly found uncles before he reaches double digits. It's too fucked up to process how unfair that is.

We ride the rest of the way to Colbie with a stilted feeling of discontent permeating the air inside the car. I keep hold of Jamie's hand the entire time and he doesn't once try to pull away.

When we reach the outskirts of Colbie I open my window and breathe in a couple of lungfuls of that familiar ocean air. Other than the sounds of my family bickering about nonsense among themselves nothing reminds me more of home than this. We drive past the welcome to Colbie sign, which still has the words "Beware the Gnomes" spray-painted over it in bright red from when Tate and Caleb decided to step up their knitted gnome reign of terror. That was well over seven years ago, and at the time we had a big town meeting over whether we should remove the spray paint from the welcome sign.

You'd think most people would want to remove it, but this is Colbie, so you'd be wrong. Half the town argued we should keep the new spray paint because it's "art" and "freedom of expression" and "like Banksy". Of course, it was none of those things. It was Tate and Caleb defacing public property for the sake of their teenage amusement. But like hell was I going to be the one to stand up during our town meeting and say that.

Jamie takes us through the tiny streets of my—our— childhood home and it seems almost bizarre how nothing has changed. There's the series of identical cottages dotted around with no real pattern, like they dropped from the sky one day when someone decided to create a town next to the sea. There's the short strip of quaint little shops and the town hall made up of large stones that most Colbie residents will tell you—*lie*—was built over three hundred years ago. In fact, it was built barely seven years ago after Simon McClair tore down the old one by accident with the bulldozer he stole from a city worksite. How he drove that thing all the way from Danger to Colbie without getting pulled over I will never understand.

Simon originally meant to use the bulldozer on his ex-wife's house, because *marriage*, but then decided to destroy the town hall instead because it was where they got married. Honestly, I could appreciate the symmetry of the choice; the marriage is dead, let's kill the place where that marriage was born. Loved the drama.

Point is, everything looks exactly how I left it, and I know I've only been away for a few months, but it feels longer, years and years since I set foot in my hometown. It seems wrong somehow that I'm the only thing from this place that hasn't remained unchanged.

I get Jamie to drop me off at home and tell him to take the others to his house. It wouldn't be right to rock up to Lady Mars's cottage with a whole load of people in tow after having ignored her for three months. Plus, whatever conversation is going to take place between us, I'd rather not have an audience for it.

Jamie seems reluctant to leave my side at first, possibly more because he's afraid I'll run off again than anything else, which is fair and my own fault for making him feel like he can't trust me to stay. I'm under no illusions my family will easily let go of what I did. Forgive, yeah, of course, they love me. But it isn't the same as forgetting.

With Jamie and the others gone I'm left alone at the end of the garden path, staring up at the cottage where I spent most of my life, and suddenly everything seems so much bigger than it did before.

Standing in front of the cottage I grew up in shouldn't feel this momentous. It shouldn't terrify me. It shouldn't make me want to run and hide in the caves on Colbie beach like I did when I was a child.

Reality, however, is hard to ignore.

Much like the rest of Colbie, the cottage looks the same as it did the last time I was home. It's oddly large for a cottage, like it was once meant to be something else and whoever built it changed their mind halfway through construction. It has an unmistakably eerie vibe; the structure itself seems to slant and twist where it should have straight lines. Its corners spike out crudely where any other cottage would have blunt and rounded edges.

There's a path leading up to the front door, a small patch of grass on either side. Flower beds are dotted around in no real design, and where most people would have roses or other such beautiful blooms, Lady Mars prefers odd ones like Bat-flowers and Violet Thistle. She also has thorn-infested vines climbing all the way to the thatched roof on one side of the cottage. It all adds to the creep factor, and never let it be said Lady Mars doesn't know how to set a mood.

It seems to take roughly between five and ten thousand minutes to reach the front door. Time could literally be turning backwards with how every molecule of my body rebels against every step closer to the inevitable oncoming confrontation.

Raising a hand, I take one last calming breath before knocking on the dark-wood surface of the door. In other circumstances I wouldn't bother knocking. I have a key, and besides which Lady Mars never locks her door. None of the townspeople would ever barge inside her cottage without invitation, they're all too afraid of her, and as I've said before, Lady Mars is more than capable of dealing with any intruders via scarf Shibari.

There's a full eleven seconds where nothing happens, and I consider the idea she might not be home. A tiny, cowardly part of me feels glad of this possible stay of execution. But then the door swings open to reveal Lady Mars in all her bizarre glory. Her red curls are in complete disarray and she's wearing a silk black dress with sparkly rainbows stitched into it, her feet adorned in the old dinosaur slippers I bought for her when I was a child. They're well-worn, all but falling apart. She usually only wears them these days when she's looking to comfort herself over something.

For the longest time Lady Mars and I stand there on opposite sides of the threshold, gazing at each other. Her eyes are filled with sadness, deeper than I've seen it before, even worse than the few times she talked to me about her runaway daughter, Sandy.

I'm holding my breath, waiting for Lady Mars's reaction to my sudden reappearance, honestly unsure how she's going to take it. She takes me in like I'm some kind of illusion she's trying to work out the trick to, like any moment a mirror somewhere will crack and the image of me will be distorted and ruined, my existence proven to be a lie conjured up to hurt her.

Finally unable to stand the silence or Lady Mars's endless sad staring, I gasp out a surprise sob of, "It was for me. He d-died to s-save me and I'm s-so sorry and

I'm... I'm s-sorry. I... He's *dead*." My voice breaks and keeps breaking, every word feeling like it's torn right out of my throat with clawed hands coated in acid, ripping at my vocal cords, leaving behind ragged, singed flesh. "He's... I was right *th-there* and I c-couldn't... It was my *f-fault*. I know that. I know. And. I. I'm sorry, I'm sorry, I'm sorry, please, I'm *sorry*, Lady Mars, I'm s-so s-sorry."

Tears, salty and hot, collect at the corners of my eyes, blurring my vision so quickly and so badly I can't make out Lady Mars's expression. It doesn't really matter, though, because she leaps forward and throws her arms around me, dragging me into a fierce hug. A hug which brings up vivid memories of my childhood, when I was a little boy who thought Lady Mars wouldn't wait outside school for me all day just because I was afraid she'd never come back if she left. The days of reading *Treasure Island* at bedtime and cooking odd, sparkly food and taking the piss out of Roux for being the nightmare of a man he always was.

Lady Mars lets me cling to her like I did then and cry and sob and gasp apologies over and over until my throat starts to hurt from overtaxing my voice. My face feels puffy from crying and there's the distinct sensation of snot attempting to leak from my nostrils, which real, ugly crying produces every time without fail. Real crying is nasty, let me tell you. None of that one manly tear nonsense. It's one reason why I hate to do it, especially in front of other people.

When I'm finally done losing my shit all over her, Lady Mars pulls back from our embrace, and I immediately mourn the loss. She looks at me again with wet eyes of her own and blinks them rapidly to dispel the sheen.

"No more apologies," Lady Mars orders when we've both collected ourselves enough to speak properly. Her scowl is as fierce as her hug was. "You're not to blame for what happened. There's only one person who is," she says with true disdain, "and I've been informed she's quite dead. Which is lucky for the bitch, otherwise I'd have got my hands on her and done some real damage. So, you needn't feel guilty for offing her either. Saved her from a worse fate. Got it?"

It's rare for Lady Mars to say such dark and merciless things, but not ultimately a shock. She's protective of the people she loves, a trait I must have picked up from her and Roux both. Lady Mars loved Roux and treated him like a son, thought of him as a son and a best friend and brother. He was almost all things to her, as he was to me. The three of us made a strange kind of family, not one some people would understand, but a family we were. It's why I stayed away so long. No one could understand the loss of Roux better than Lady Mars.

"Got it. No more apologies," I respond hesitantly when Lady Mars's glower intensifies. She searches my face for quite some time until she finds the sincerity she was looking for and appears satisfied by the strength of it.

"You better get in here and regale me with tales of your gloriously violent exploits." Lady Mars grabs at my hand and starts pulling me inside and I can do nothing but docilely follow her, just so relieved to finally, finally be walking on what feels like solid ground.

Chapter Twelve

The Weirdo Brigade Rides Again

Lady Mars takes me into the kitchen, which resembles the outside not at all, decorated in bright colours and eclectic patterns, and we spend the next few hours drinking an inordinate amount of hot chocolate and catching each other up on what we've missed. I omit some details of what I've been doing, not wanting to upset her. Lady Mars seems to be doing the same as she tells me about how she's dealt with Roux's death. When I get up the courage to ask her about his funeral, she tells me hesitantly that she had him buried next to his parents in Danger City's cemetery.

Mercifully, Lady Mars doesn't mention anything beyond that. I'm grateful she seems to be willing to forgive me for not being there. She can't hate me more than I do myself. I already know missing Roux's funeral will be a regret I carry for the rest of my life. I knew it for the months I was gone, but I still couldn't make myself return to the people and the responsibilities I'd run from.

We very pointedly don't talk about my shortened life span. I'm sure she was told about it; what Liquid Onyx will do to us. But there's no reason to dwell on it right now. I'm still riding the high of being home and I don't want my inevitable demise via the poison running through my veins to ruin it. Not yet. Maybe not ever, if I can help it.

Lady Mars brings me up to speed on all the town gossip, which is plentiful and as bizarre as it always is. For example, Mrs Markin, a retired dentist, decided to step up her campaign to make the town eat more healthily by staging a protest outside the local bakery and sweet shop, which just so happen to stand next to each other and are owned by the same man, Mr Colburn. Also, yes, he is the husband of the infamous Mrs Colburn who once made us sit through a PowerPoint presentation about the "unlawful besiegement" of squirrels in our town.

Mrs Markin's protest was a surprising success, mostly due to the bakery's lone shop assistant, Jade White, joining it. Although, to be fair, Jade seemed more interested in getting a pay rise and the protest became very confused, with Mrs Markin dressed in a giant carrot costume and yelling about "killer cavities", while Jade made a haphazard sign with bright-pink lipstick scrawled across a bit of cardboard that read "Give me more dough!" and in brackets beneath it she'd written "(Money)".

The whole town insisted on having a meeting about it afterwards and it devolved into whether Mr Colburn was the cause of cavities because he was cheap and refused to pay his workers a living wage, despite it being well known Jade had a real knack for burning every single bakery item she'd ever attempted to make. Why him being cheap meant he was the cause of cavities, I have no idea. That makes zero fucking sense. The town let him off with a warning, though. Any more cavities and he'll be getting another strike.

Mad, the whole lot of them. Absolutely bonkers times ten.

Eventually, Jamie comes over and joins us at the kitchen table. He tells me he left Nathan, Dan, and Sami at his house to get settled by themselves. It seems like a good idea. They have a lot to sort out between them. I still think Nathan should be checked over by a doctor, one experienced with the biology of Liquid Onyx survivors, and possibly talk to some sort of child psychologist. But Jamie says those things can come later and I guess he's right.

Lady Mars asks who Nathan is and we explain our most recent foray into death and mayhem. She seems uniquely interested in the whole thing, Nathan in particular.

"Do they know where they're going to stay?" she asks, her brow furrowing slightly in concern. "A child like that needs a safe place to depend on." She nods at me. "It's why Roux and the other parents stayed here, together, for all those years."

Jamie gets a thoughtful look on his face, head tilting to one side, grey eyes lighter than they usually are. More cloud than metal. He flicks a glance between us questioningly, eventually landing on Lady Mars.

"Would you be willing to let them stay here for a bit?" he asks her carefully.

The idea isn't a bad one; Nathan would certainly be safer here than Danger City. Before what happened to Roux, Lady Mars wouldn't have hesitated to say yes. But she's been through a lot recently and it would mean taking on a lot all at once. She did the same when I was a child, though, and this situation isn't too different. She'd been dealing with the loss of her daughter when Roux and I came into her life. Perhaps having a new child in need of a home to focus on would help.

Lady Mars seems to agree because she inclines her head, smiling kindly, almost gratefully, at Jamie from across the kitchen table. "If you think Dan and Sami would be amenable to it, I'd be happy to have them here."

"Brilliant," Jamie exclaims in obvious relief, "I'll bring them over and you can have a word." His mouth breaks into a rare *full* smile. He gives them out to Lady Mars more than almost anyone else. It's a good thing he doesn't do it often because it makes him look almost too handsome to live, I swear. He's unfairly gorgeous, just sitting there, dark hair tousled and as wonderfully imperfect as the rest of him, so real it hurts to look at him, smiling with all his teeth, illuminated by the light streaming in through one of the kitchen windows. I spot a speck of blood he missed when cleaning his face after the mission. It's right below his jaw, dark red and indicative of the man who exists below the beautiful surface.

It hits me all over again, and with somehow twice the force, how much I've missed him. He's so Jamie right now and I'm suddenly desperate to let him know what he means to me, the crushing weight and mass of all that meaning making me feel set alight and doused in terror at the same time. Both emotions are powerful, ones I've been wrestling with since the first time Jamie looked at me and I knew he wanted the same thing I did. As insane as everything is, I'm thinking it might be time to be honest about some stuff. Unless we come up with a miracle cure, and soon, I'm going to die young. So...if not now, when? A more selfless choice might be never. But I've already broken so many of my own rules, why not one more?

As I'm thinking about this, the sound of pounding footsteps from outside alerts me to the fact someone is coming. Or multiple someones, more likely. I wonder at first if it's going to be Sami and Dan, coming to tell us Nathan has accidentally set fire to Jamie's house. But then the familiar noise of my family hits my ears as the door slams open and a moment later the kitchen is flooded with all the parents.

I get up from my seat to meet them and immediately find myself engulfed in a series of strong hugs and hard back pats and particularly stinging scolding from Fiona for scaring the ever-loving-shit out of them all by disappearing with no word for months. Even Jian hugs me, and that man does not *do* hugs.

I take it from them, every lovingly meant admonishment and too-tight embrace. There's a stretch of time where it's overwhelming to have everyone so up in my space at once. It's like I've forgotten what it's like be smothered by a large family and all my coping mechanisms are desperately trying to rewire themselves to help me process it.

Pushing my way out of the huddle, I place myself partially behind Jamie, who has also stood up. "All right," I say to all of them, "I get it, you missed me and I'm a bastard for leaving, please don't *eat* me over it."

Jamie plays his role of shield with utmost expertise and crosses his arms over his chest, making like an astoundingly attractive wall. "Okay, let's not scare him off two seconds after he comes home to us." He gives the parents a stern look I cannot believe he has the balls to level at the likes of Fiona and his father, who he shoots an especially scathing narrowing of his eyes. To my bewilderment, Hector gives his oldest son the most ferocious glower of disappointment I think I've ever seen.

I have no idea what any of that could be about until Hector steps away from the other parents, moving closer to Jamie. "Don't think you can use Rexley coming home to pretend like nothing happened, James. We *will* be discussing your recent behaviour."

Oh shit, Hector never calls Jamie by his proper name. *No one* does. I didn't even know about it until Hector got really angry at Jamie one time for sneaking off to a concert in the city behind his back, one of the few times Jamie broke his father's rules, or at least one of the few times he was actually caught, and Hector laid into him as badly as he usually does Caleb.

Jamie reacts to the use of his full name the same way Caleb does when his father uses that particularly condescending tone with him. The Moon brothers are never more alike than when their backs are pressed up against the wall. They come out swinging every time.

"There's nothing to discuss, Dad," Jamie bites out,

his back ramrod straight, shoulders tense and pulled back, making him look even taller than usual. "It was my decision to make, and I made it. I've already spoken to Snow, so it's done."

For a second, I think Jamie is talking about the unsanctioned mission we went on to get Nathan. But then Hector blows that out of the water by levelling a full-on exasperated glare at his son and shouting, "This is ridiculous! You can't quit FISA just like that! To do *what*?"

"That's for me to figure out," Jamie replies with a frigid coldness to his voice I haven't heard in a long while. He sounds like Snow at her most arctic.

Hold on, the contents of Hector's indignant shouting just registered. Jamie *quit* FISA? The hell.

I shift around to get a better look at Jamie's face, staring up at him in genuine shock. "You quit?" I say in disbelief. "Seriously?" When Jamie gives a jerky nod, I demand, "*Why*?"

Hector gestures in my direction as if to say *see, Rex thinks it's ridiculous, too*, while still glaring at his son like he's being accused of committing some heinous sin against his family name.

To be fair, he probably is. After all, *Moons don't quit.* It's a lesson Hector sledge-hammered into both his sons their entire lives. He probably can't fathom why Jamie, the one who seemed to take that lesson the most to heart, is breaking away from it now.

"Yes, please," Hector snaps, "explain your total lack of responsibility, of loyalty to the agency I raised you to respect the importance of, to Rexley, since you seem utterly incapable of explaining them to anyone else."

Fury simmers off Jamie like a blur of heat above a desert sand. Every one of his muscles seems set to burst from his skin from how tightly they're coiled beneath it. Jamie breathes out through his nose, fists clenching and unclenching, clearly trying to remain calm despite his father's hostility.

"Dad, for fuck's sake, I'm twenty-four years old," Jamie snarls, losing his grip on his temper by a few inches. "I've been an agent since I was eighteen. I have done things, things you'll never understand, in defence of my country and in the name of protecting the people of this world from threats unknown to them. I've worked in the shadows for years, trying my best to even out the scales one bloody fight at a time, just so civilians get to complain about their internet speed. I've lost plenty to my work as an agent. Time with my family being right there at the top. You don't get to come in here and talk to me like I don't understand what I've walked away from. I do understand."

Hector doesn't seem to have listened to a single word Jamie said, because he's no less vehement when he tries to argue with him again. "Then if you understand the mistake you've made, why—"

Jamie takes a dangerous couple of steps towards his father, putting them at only a few feet apart. Close enough to reach out and touch. Or, as seems more likely, kick the shit out of each other.

"My priorities have changed." He sounds so bloody angry as he spells it out for Hector, and there's a significance to it that feels different, more vicious, like it's about more than just this argument. "And you know *damn well* why. You keep going on like you don't and I'm gonna start to think Caleb was right all those times he said you don't give a shit about our family. About *him*." Jamie practically gnashes that last bit, like it's more teeth and bite than actual words.

Hector isn't having any of it, though, stubborn to a fault just like his sons. I wonder sometimes how he doesn't seem to know it's his own fault they've turned out so hard-headed. "Don't you dare start with all that nonsense, James! Of course, I care about our family. There's nothing more important to me than what we've built here."

Jamie doesn't relent either, finishing with a hardline, "Then you should understand why I've quit."

Hector seems, for once, unsure what to do or what to say in response during an argument he 100 percent believes he is in the right about. It's a novelty. Someone should be filming it. If Tate were here, he would, then Fiona would yell at him and Mei would sigh loudly and Caleb would laugh in encouragement.

The other parents are starting to shift around uncomfortably like they usually do when Caleb and Hector fight. I take pity on them and turn myself into a loud and sparkly distraction, as is my real superpower.

"So, where's Cal, T, and Mei, then? How long does it take to get back from Ireland these days? I flew to *Germany*, fought an entire black site full of OI guards, rescued a second gen superhuman child single-handed, and got to Colbie to spend three hours catching up on town gossip in less time than this." I shake my head in a show of disappointment at the slow return of my friends.

Of course, there's a good chance what's holding them up is the fact Caleb had to kill another superhero, but that's not the point. The point is to get Jamie and Hector to stop giving each other evils and add some levity back into the room.

It has the desired effect when Jamie abandons his glare-off with his father to arch both his eyebrows at me instead, asking, "Single-handed, was it? Suffering from a bit of selective memory, are we?" He eyes me up and down. "Probably what happens when you don't sleep for three months straight."

"I've slept!" I squeak at him indignantly, and not very convincingly if the worried looks everyone is giving me are anything to go by.

"To be fair, you do look like shit, Rex," Quinton says, frowning at me ruefully. "Blond, muscly shit, to be sure, but shit nonetheless."

"Yeah, Rexley, what happened?" Jian asks, gaze trailing over my broader shoulders and bulkier arms. "Did you go to prison? Is that where you've really been all this time?" He looks askance at the other parents. "That's the one place we didn't check!"

Dawn completely ignores her husband's distress and comes over to me. In her words, "as the resident doctor", she starts poking and prodding at me like she'll somehow divine what's wrong by jabbing it out of me with her blunt fingernails.

"I checked the prison records," Quinton reassures Jian, patting his shoulder, "and he wasn't in there." Then he pulls a face and adds in a comically ominous tone, "Not under his own name, at least."

Jian and Quinton both squint at me suspiciously.

"Did you take on an assumed identity, Rexley?" Jian asks.

"Yes," I respond dryly. "Wow, you've dragged the truth out of me. You might have heard of a vigilante called Wrath. Don't want to shock you or anything. But...I am Wrath." I splay my hands out with sarcastic enthusiasm, "Ta da, reveal!"

Quinton and Jian both feign loud gasps of surprise, because they are amazing.

"Hmm." Quinton considers my response. "I suppose one of us will be kidnapped by a supervillain and dropped from a very tall, possibly culturally significant building now we know your secret." He looks quite excited by the prospect.

"I think that's only if you're a potential love interest," Jian muses. He squints at me. "You'd have to kiss him."

I point at him and warn, "Don't kiss me." Quinton seems to be thinking it over. Fiona catches my eye, and I give her a beseeching look. "Don't let your husband cheat on you with me. I'm not worth it. I mean"—I clear my throat and flex—"I *am*. But I don't want to complicate our relationship like that." Although it would horrify Tate, so that's one point in favour of starting up a love triangle with his parents.

Fiona elbows her Quinton and jokes, "One look at his prison muscles and suddenly you're all about that pretty little white boy arse."

Quinton bursts out laughing, sending adoring eyes at his wife. "Your muscles are the only ones for me, love."

She raises a bared arm and flexes her impressive

bicep. Quinton leans forward and gives it a light peck in appreciation. Fiona beams at him happily. "Should have put that in the vows, too."

"Our parents would have hated it. An opportunity I will regret always."

Then they gaze at each other like two teenagers on their first date.

It just goes to show, kids, there's a weirdo out there for everyone.

Also...

"Wait, you searched for me in *prison!*" I demand, gaping at Quinton.

"You have been getting all criminal-orientated lately," Dawn points out, taking a break from randomly prodding my face for some reason.

Jian comes over to join her and hums in agreement at me. "Laws have become more a suggestion to your super counterparts, you've got to admit that. And prisons are where law breakers go. It's not an unreasonable assumption."

They've misunderstood my reason for being annoyed. I rush to correct them. "No, I meant, you thought I'd be that easy to catch!"

"We did find you in the south of France after only two weeks when you and Caleb ran away that one time," Fiona reminds me.

"It was *three* weeks and were thirteen!" My hands start doing their uncontrollable flailing thing. "You can't hold those same standards against me now."

Fiona snorts as if that's a ridiculous assertion. "Can and will. We found you again this time, didn't we? Four months isn't that much more impressive."

"What? No! You did not *find* me! I went to Caleb by choice, then he blabbed to Jamie." I shove a hand in Jamie's direction, almost whopping him on the arm, not that he would have felt it, the tree.

"Well," Fiona reasons, "involving Caleb again was your first big mistake." Clearly.

"Also," Jamie puts in, eyeing me with far too much mirth considering he was yelling at his dad, like, two seconds ago, "he had a wealthy benefactor this time to keep him hidden with his gadgets and his millions."

Oh, how did I know he was going to take any chance to bring that up?

"Billions," I correct imperiously.

"Oh, I'm so sorry"—Jamie holds a hand to his chest in sardonic dismay—"didn't mean to misrepresent the extensive wealth of your new boyfriend's economic status."

I flip him off.

"Boyfriend?" The parents chorus in tune.

They all gape at me in varying stages of disbelief. Apart from Quinton who, like his son, never misses an opportunity to take the piss.

"Is he the real reason you don't want me to kiss you? Because, just to be clear, I was joking about that." He makes a face. "You are like a son to me and kissing you would be weird and gross." Then he seems to think he might have offended me and rushes to add, "Not because you're gross or anything! You're nowhere near as ugly as Agent Wesley's baby or puppies. I'm sure your secret billionaire boyfriend thinks you're lovely." He frowns deeply. "At least I hope so. He'd better be nice to you or

I'll make sure he never gets reliable internet access ever again! I have that power. You can tell...wait, who is your secret billionaire boyfriend?"

Oh, fuck me, no. I refuse to have this conversation with any of them.

Unfortunately for all of us, Quinton's question unlocks the gates for the others and I'm hit with a plethora of nonsense.

"Is your secret billionaire boyfriend a supervillain?" Jian asks eagerly, looking enthralled at the prospect for God knows what reason.

Dawn frowns at her husband, her lovely face reminding me so much of Mei when she hears Caleb or Tate say something weird. "Why would he be a supervillain?"

"All supervillains are billionaires," Jian explains with a truly absurd amount of confidence. "They have to be, to afford stuff like lasers and uranium and robot butler minions."

"Hard disagree." Quinton butts in, shaking his head obstinately. "Some supervillains go the extra mile and steal their utensils of evil."

Utensils of evil.

Utensils. Of evil.

Fucking hell.

Dawn swoops in to defend me. "Rexley wouldn't date a supervillain."

"He might if he was sexy enough," Jian reasons, disparaging my character without a care in the world. "Remember that one who always had his shirt off? The really buff one with the exploding teacups."

"You mean Rules?" Quinton asks, nodding along in

answer to his own question. "Yeah, he was properly bonkers, that one. Gorgeous, though."

Jian turns to me again and prods, "Is Rules your boyfriend?"

"Rules is in prison," Fiona reminds him, like that would be the only barrier to a possible romantic relationship between me and an insane teacup-exploding supervillain.

"Well," Jian reasons, "maybe that's where they met."

Fiona snorts derisively at that. "What porn video universe do you think we're living in?"

Jian makes a face, screwing up his nose in disgruntlement. "The one where people are still watching porn on videos, apparently."

"In my day we drew our own porn," Dawn says cheerfully. "My mate Tonya made a blow job flip book." Her smile broadens at the memory. "It was epic."

What even is this? What are any of us doing here? I cannot believe how much I've missed this absolute load of nutters.

I'm so distracted by my own dismay and yet another existential crisis, at least the sixth one I've had this year, I tune out the rest of their insane conversation. Focusing instead on making eye contact with Lady Mars and silently asking for help when it seems like Hector and Jamie might be about to start sniping at each other again.

Lady Mars gets up from the table, finally, and circles around to grab hold of Jamie. "Right, young warrior, you feel like introducing me to the child who can set people alight with purple fire? It might be more comfortable for them if we went over there rather than dragging them over here for our first meeting."

Jamie looks reluctant to leave the house, but he agrees with Lady Mars's assessment that it might help make Dan more comfortable if he meets Lady Mars away from her homestead so she can convince/trick him into living with her forever. It's too bad we didn't have the forethought to stage some kind of car accident she could use as emotional blackmail like she did with Roux, but I have no doubt Lady Mars can improvise some other form of manipulation.

Jamie glances over his shoulder at me as he's shuffled out towards the door and I mouth the words "good luck" to him, complete with a discreet double thumbs-up. He flashes me a very quick middle finger in response which makes me laugh a little under my breath.

All the parents make sounds of interest over this new superhuman child and insist on meeting him and his uncle. They go trampling off with Jamie and Lady Mars before I can make the point that their presence will likely overwhelm Dan and Nathan, which we were trying to avoid by having Lady Mars go to them instead of getting them to come here. But I suppose if they do end up staying in Colbie, they'll have to get used to being mobbed all the time and being robbed of their privacy. Best to find that out early than be surprised by it later.

"Hector, come take a walk with me on the beach, yeah?" I say, catching him by the elbow before he can go storming out after his son along with the other parents. He looks down at my hand on his arm. The expression of foreboding on his face might scare off some junior FISA agent, but I'm a pro at bracing against the storming eyes of the Moons and shan't be dissuaded so easily.

Despite his mutinous glower, Hector allows himself to be dragged down onto the beach. I keep hold of him once we're walking across the sand, looping my arm through his so he can't run away. He doesn't throw me off like he might other people. Hector isn't a very physically affectionate person, but he's prone to indulging me, which I take full advantage of now.

For a little while neither of us speaks, letting the mood between us shift from being uncomfortable and stilted to a silence containing less friction.

The wind whips around our faces, blowing our hair about and muffling the sounds of waves crashing along the shore and gulls squawking at each other overhead. Maddie is likely flying around up there somewhere, bossing the seagulls about like the winged overlord he is, taking out his pent-up rage on lowlier birds.

Glancing up at Hector, I am taken aback, like I am every time when we've spent a significant time apart, by how much he looks like Jamie and Caleb. It's almost eerie. That might also be why I give him so much more slack than either son appreciates. I also see a lot of their personalities in him, too. Jamie's dedication and sense of duty. Caleb's loyalty and righteousness.

Hector is the one to break the silence, glancing at me with an uncharacteristic amount of wistfulness. "Do you know what I thought when we first met?" he asks somewhat ominously.

Feeling this can't have a good answer, I press forward regardless. "What?"

Hector's brow creases, like the truth pains him. "That

you'd be trouble for my sons." He sighs tiredly. "The way they both looked at you. It was full speed, high volume, unforgiving intensity from day one."

I take my time absorbing that, pulling it apart and trying to figure out what he really means by it. "You think I've ruined them by leaving?" I guess, squinting at him, still unsure.

Hector is quick to shake his head, negating my fears. "I think you've been their crutch for a long time," he explains, "and when you left, they were forced to stand on their own."

I hum thoughtfully, neither agreeing nor objecting to the idea. "How'd they get on while I was gone?"

"Badly," Hector responds with his typical bluntness.

"I'm sorry." For leaving. For not being there when they needed me. For being there too much before.

Hector doesn't sound angry or resentful when he says, "I know you are."

"They're a lot stronger than you give them credit for," I tell him, defending Caleb and Jamie to their father because he doesn't see them as clearly as I do, just like they don't see him sometimes. "What seems like them struggling without me might just be them figuring their shit out like they should have done ages ago."

I expel a slow breath, squeezing his arm like it will make him listen more closely. "Crutches help you move forward while you heal, they're not meant to be forever. Eventually you have to learn to trust yourself. You need to find out what you're capable of doing on your own."

It's something Phoenix said to me once during a training session and I know Hector will recognise the words as belonging to his wife. One of the worst things about missing the last few months with my family is the fact I didn't get to go on the Moons' yearly trip to visit the site where they scattered Phoenix's ashes.

A complex myriad of emotions passes over Hector's face. There's another beat of tense silence before he speaks again. "I'm glad you're back, Rexley. Not just for the boys' sake. I missed you. We all did."

Hector is so rarely verbal with his displays of care or sentiment it strikes me as especially significant he's doing so now.

Pushing my luck as far as it will go, I bring us to a stop and pull Hector into a surprise hug. He goes easily, letting me hold on to him for a solid three seconds before stepping away again.

"Do you want to just sit together for a while?" I ask hopefully. I like the thought of sitting on my beach and letting the feel and sound and smell of it wash over me.

Hector nods his agreement, and we find a good spot to settle down in companionable quiet, the essence of home like a welcoming hand reaching out to both of us.

Chapter Thirteen

We Are This, Together

Hector sits with me for a solid hour before getting up and heading back up the beach. I don't know if he's going to search out Jamie again. I don't ask. There's a limit to which I'm willing to get involved. Maybe whatever is happening between them needs to play out so they can reach a better place of understanding.

We can dream.

Not long after Hector leaves me, my nice, alone time is extinguished by the arrival of my friends.

Mei and Tate come first, with Caleb hanging back to give us some space. Tate is grinning so widely it looks painful. Mei is marching towards me like she's going off to war on the front lines.

Glancing over their shoulders at Caleb, I can't help

but note how exhausted he seems. He appears somehow slimmer than he did this this morning. A lost quality to his eyes only adds to my concern over his mental state. I ache to pull him aside and talk to him about what happened with Guardian, but Tate does a good job of distracting me by yanking me up off the ground and wrapping me in a hug so tight it makes my bones creak in protest.

"You absolute fucker!" Mei curses at me while Tate makes like a boa constrictor and tries to break my spine.

Twisting my head to the side so I can talk to Mei, or scream for help, I'm stopped in my tracks by the look she is levelling at me like the barrel of a gun. Her expression is an interesting mix of outright fury and bone-deep relief.

Tate buries his face in my neck and takes a loud inhale. He gets choked up when he speaks, lips brushing against my skin. "You scared us, Rexy. You scared us." He somehow manages to sound both vulnerable and young, and too old for his age at the same time.

My stomach drops out at the thick layer of fear coating Tate's voice, guilt at having hurt my friends like a boiling-hot rock lodged in my throat.

Finally giving in to the crushing embrace, I hug Tate back almost as hard. We stay cinched together for a long time, far too long for it to be reasonable or decent. I don't care, though. I've missed the overwhelming size and strength of my most annoying friend.

We don't pull back from each other until Mei gets involved. She steps forward and all but rips me away from Tate. She manhandles me into a fierce hug as well and I go along with it, partially afraid she'll freeze my balls off if I try to evade her. Unlike Tate and Caleb, Mei often runs cold. It feels like hugging a weirdly shaped icicle. But even so, it would be a lie to say I haven't missed this, too.

When Mei releases me, I step away and give myself permission to drag my eyes over them, noting the ways they've changed since I last saw them up close.

It's undeniable that Mei and Tate look different. Not quite as different as Caleb, and their changes are more neutral than his. Mei has shorter hair that barely reaches her chin, whereas Tate's is longer than it's been in a while. He has it twisted into braids and tied back. It looks great, the new hairstyles suiting them, making them appear older, too, like they've come into their own more.

My friends seem to be doing the same as me, gazes raking over me again and again, taking in all the little differences.

Tate talks first. No prizes for anyone who guessed that one.

"Rex, I love you. I love you like crazy. But. Please." He's having one of his rare serious moments, scowling at me like I could be in trouble if I don't give the right response. "Don't ever do that to Caleb again." He lowers his voice to something rumbling and reproachful. "You properly wrecked him by leaving like that. Made it worse for him because he could feel what other people were feeling about you being gone as well."

Shit, I didn't even consider that angle. Everyone grieving over Roux and worrying about me must have put a real strain on Caleb's power, especially with his own emotions to deal with making it harder for him to protect himself from everyone else's.

Catching Mei's eye, then darting my gaze meaningfully between Tate and Caleb, I ask silently if she's getting the same vibe I am off Tate's protective, vaguely threatening demeanour. She nods at me, reading my question correctly and not seeming the least confused. If anything, she seems almost charmed, if a little exasperated, by the whole situation. I wasn't quite sure how Mei would feel about Tate and Caleb being a possible thing. I had no doubt she'd realise what was going on long before they got up the guts to tell her.

I squint at Tate. "Is this you doing the protective boyfriend bit?" I ask, only half teasing.

Tate looks over his shoulder at Caleb, who does a terrible job pretending like he can't hear every word we're saying. Tate seems to get caught up in staring at Caleb for a while, who in turn catches Tate's eyes and stares back, his face flushing in response to whatever nonverbal communication is going on between them.

"Did *he* tell you that?" Tate asks when he turns back around to face me. There's a vulnerable tilt to his mouth I'm intrigued and surprised by. Tate is usually the most confident of us in all aspects of his life. This whatever-it-is with Caleb must have really thrown him for a loop.

It's kind of sweet. And maybe a bit unnerving.

"Will *you* be telling me that?" I counter, exchanging another meaningful look with Mei. She rolls her eyes like she's tired of their bullshit.

"Why," Tate asks sardonically, raising his eyebrows at me, "do I get a shovel talk if I say yes?"

"Absolutely. Don't worry, I'll be giving him one, too." I try my hand at some *very serious* talk as well. "You both better be nice to each other or I'll be forced to kick your arse and his."

Tate does not look intimidated, his eyes taking on an amused shine, which is more like him. "Think you could, little brother?"

"No." I snort, then grin wickedly at him. "But I'll tell your mum, and she'll do it." Fiona would, too. She loves Caleb, has had a soft spot for him since he was little. Her protective mother instincts extend to all of us, but I've always had the feeling there's something a little extra in there just for Caleb.

"Cold, Rex. Cold."

A thought occurs to me. "Do your parents know?" I ask tentatively.

Tate hasn't ever been vocal about his sexuality one way or the other. I think his parents, since he hasn't contradicted them, have assumed he's straight, because people do. Fiona and Quinton are great parents, and they've never had an issue with either me or Jamie, not when we came out initially or any time afterward.

But, as much as they might care for me and Jamie as family, we aren't their sons. Not in the way Tate is. I could understand if Tate was afraid to broach the topic with them just in case it's somehow different when the queerness they're being asked to accept is their own son's.

Tate grimaces and he reaches up to rub at the back of his neck, a signature move signifying his anxiety over this topic. "About my queerness in general," he asks, "or my specific longtime gayness for Caleb?"

Longtime? How long? I'm beyond curious about the timeline of Tate's discovered feelings for our friend, but I can tell now isn't the time to grill him over it. He'll get all twitchy and uncomfortable and I don't want to do that to him. I know how difficult all this stuff is to get your head around.

"Either," I answer cautiously, searching Tate's face for any sign of genuine distress.

"No. I'm still…" Tate gives his head a slight shake, biting his bottom lip then releasing it to continue, "I'm still working up to that."

"Got it." I nod once, letting that be enough for now.

Mei, sensing the need for a topic change, reaches out to punch me on the shoulder. "I can't believe you were with Rohan this whole time!" She huffs, crossing her arms, her mouth forming a displeased moue. "He didn't say a single word about knowing where you were."

"Yeah, that secret-keeping twatclock," Tate grouses, snatching the baton from Mei and setting off with admirable gusto. "Remind me to kick the crap out of him for not telling us."

"No one is kicking Rohan," I say firmly. Not that he isn't fully capable of protecting himself, but I'd rather not deal with the complaining about it afterward.

"Are you two a thing?" Tate asks, wrinkling his nose like he finds the idea an unpleasant one.

I want to tear my hair out with frustration. "No!" I yell. "Rohan is not, has never been, and will never be my boyfriend, for fuck's sake!" I throw my hands out in front of me dramatically. "Spread the fucking word, get a conference set up and make an official announcement, do a bloody *TikTok* vid about it, I do not want to have to say this ever again!"

There's a long pause where I pant like a pissed-off

water buffalo and my friends stare at me impassively in response to my outburst.

Then.

"The lad doth protest overmuch, methinks," Tate muses, sharing a significant look with Mei that makes me want to kick *them*.

I wouldn't mind if it weren't for the fact there's genuinely nothing going on between me and Rohan. For their own sakes, they better not behave like this in front of Rohan. He'll bite them. Seriously. The man's shameless.

"As much as I've missed being thoroughly irritated by you people"—I glare at Tate pointedly, who in return grins at me like I've just handed him the perfect birthday gift—"can we please move on to more important things? Either of you feel like telling me about your mission in Ireland?" At their confused looks, I explain, "I heard about it on the radio."

Tate's expression takes on a dour quality I don't often see on him. His features seem to harden, the angles of his face sharpening like someone took a whetstone to them. Tate's usually warm brown eyes lose some of their jovial shine, becoming opaque. The person I'm looking at now is more Barricade than he is Tate.

Beside him, Mei is pissed off and making no effort to hide it. Her arms tighten around herself, posture rigid, energy taking on a spiked quality you'd have to be braver than me to touch. Her already dark eyes become cesspools of animosity. Although that anger isn't aimed at me specifically, I still feel the power of it.

"You should talk to Cal," Tate says gravely. Mei nods jerkily in agreement.

Glancing between my friends, it isn't difficult to read their mix of grimness and fury and take heed from it. I imagined the mission was terrible, but their extreme reactions confirm just how much. All earlier humour has drained away at the reminder of Guardian's mental break and consequent death.

"I'll come back after, okay?" I promise. "There's so much shit I want to tell you."

"Same," Mei says, reaching out to squeeze my arm.

Tate makes a noise of agreement. "We'll be here when you're done." He looks over his shoulder again at Caleb. He turns back to me with concern etched deeply into his face and lowers his voice so Caleb won't hear. "No matter what he says, this wasn't on him. We did everything we could to save her, but she was too far gone. There's nothing he could have done differently to make things end any other way."

I nod in acknowledgement, noting his less biased version of events than whatever story I'm likely to get from a guilt-ridden Caleb.

"I'll try to sort him out," I tell my friends, who both look more reassured by that than I feel.

Caleb shifts away from the rock he's been leaning against as I approach, a crease between his brows, questions spread across his face.

Without speaking, I grab Caleb's hand and tug him along, heading towards our usual spot in the caves, where we'll have the privacy necessary for this conversation.

Caleb allows himself to be pulled deep inside the cave without a fuss. When we're in the right place, I drop to the ground and yank Caleb down so we're sitting with our backs pressed against the cave's damp walls. Surrounded by darkness and with the sounds of outside muffled even to our enhanced hearing, I feel cut off from the world.

Our equally enhanced eyesight allows me to see Caleb in the dark, which is good because I have a feeling this conversation is going to be difficult enough without the added problem of not being able to see his reactions.

Caleb surprises me by openly asking, "You heard about Guardian?" He sounds almost as exhausted as he looks.

"Yeah, heard it on the radio on the way over," I confirm, keeping my tone neutral. The last thing I need is Caleb latching onto something in my voice that he will undoubtably use to hurt himself with. "Was it as bad as it looked?"

"Nah." Caleb lets out a humourless laugh that cracks in the middle like his vocal cords have a dodgy signal. "Lot worse, mate. Fucking nightmare was what it was." It all comes out in a flurry as if he has a limited time to speak and any second the timer will run down. "Don't think Blue Storm will ever be able to forgive me. Don't know if I'll be forgiving myself, to be honest. Worst I've felt doing something in my life, you know?"

"She would have killed Barricade," I remind him. "You saved his life, the way I heard it."

Caleb pulls his knees up and wraps his arms around them. "I didn't have to kill her." He looks at me, features twisting in frustration. "I just fucking panicked when I saw her go for him like that."

There's the echo of terror in his voice. Almost losing Tate in that moment must have really shaken him.

"Doesn't mean it wasn't the only decision you could have made at the time." Sometimes that's all you're left with.

Caleb's shoulders are stiff from tension. "I should have been able to save her," he mutters harshly. "I should have done more. Tried harder."

I lean into him, pressing our arms together, wishing they were bare so we could have skin-on-skin contact. "You know what we do isn't about saving everyone," I murmur reprovingly. If he starts thinking like that he'll be in a world of trouble every time he goes out as Crescent.

Caleb scowls, shoulders hunching up further. "Yeah, yeah, all right. I already got the 'nobody can save every-one, we're in it to save as many people as we can' speech from Tate, and I know he's right. I know. But that doesn't make it feel any less shit, Rex. It doesn't make me any less of a murderer."

"You made a hard call. We all have. It won't be the last time, either," I tell him bluntly, because it's true. Hiding from it won't help.

"I'm not you, Rex." Caleb huffs angrily. "I can't just kill people and walk it off." His eyes widen the second those words leave his mouth, and he rushes to fix it. "Shit, Rex, I'm sorry. I didn't mean that how it sounded."

I think he probably did, but that's okay. I've always been aware of our differences, just like I was with mine and Damon's. But Caleb isn't Damon, and he won't expect me to adhere to his personal moral code. He knows we don't have to agree on everything when it comes to this whole vigilante gig. It's how we were raised, to see the benefit in a diverse array of people working towards the same goal from multiple angles.

"You never stop feeling it," I tell Caleb, tone muted, "the impact of that choice. But it does get easier to process how it affects you."

Caleb's mouth slants downwards on both sides, conflicting emotions in his eyes, clearly unsure how to take that. "I don't think I want to get used to how this feels, Rex."

"Of course not." I snort. "That's how you know you're still on the right side of things. It's when you start wanting it that you know something has gone very wrong inside your head."

Caleb opens his mouth, possibly to ask if that's what happened with me, but he closes it again without making a sound. I'm glad for it, as I have no idea how I would answer the question.

When he opens his mouth again, he takes a different tack. "You're not making me feel better about this," he complains.

"I'm not trying to make you feel better about it," I say shortly. "I'm just telling you what's true. Take it or leave it, Cal. And if it's help with untangling things mentally you're after, you should talk to Green. It's what she's there for." I give him a small shove.

Caleb shoves me back. "Jesus, you're brutal." He shakes his head. "You've gotten worse, you know? Meaner." He gives me another one of those concerned frowns.

"Lies." I scoff dismissively. "I've always been like this. You've just forgotten."

Caleb looks doubtful about that.

Sensing the need for a topic change before Caleb

starts trying to psychoanalyse me, I bring up something I know will distract him. "Did you know Jamie quit FISA?"

"Yeah!" Caleb's eyes seem to brighten with excitement. "It was amazing! You should have seen Dad's reaction. Went absolutely apoplectic, mate." He snorts. "Figures Jamie would find a way to piss him off more than I ever have when he finally decided to flip the finger at the old bastard."

"I saw exactly how your dad reacted to it when they got into a massive tiff in Lady Mars's kitchen."

"Seriously? Did Jamie belt him one?" Caleb is far too happy about this thing with Jamie and Hector. But I guess I can't blame him. Jamie has been the golden child for so long, leaving Caleb to get all the shit from their father.

"Nah, I played peacemaker before they could go too far." Lady Mars would not have appreciated two idiot Moon boys fucking up her kitchen with nonsense.

Caleb looks disappointed that I stopped his father and brother from getting into it. "You should have let Jamie at him. He deserves it for being such a nightmare to Jamie for wanting to make his own decisions for once."

That is about as close to a proper defence of his brother as I've heard from Caleb in a long time. "Are you and Jay getting on all right, then? Or are you just glad he's pissed off your dad?"

Caleb shrugs, making a face like he doesn't want to admit to being on good terms with his brother for the first time in years. "He's been different since...you know...we found out the truth about Liquid Onyx. We talked about stuff. Stuff we should have probably dealt with a long time ago."

I raise my eyebrows at him expectantly. "So, things are good now?"

"They're *better*," Caleb allows begrudgingly.

"Surprised you're willing to say even that much, to be honest, mate."

"Yeah, well, I'm gonna die soon probably. So, it's kind of now or never. Didn't want to die hating him, you know." He sounds gruff and unaffected by it, but I can tell it's taken some weight off his shoulders.

"Good," I say sincerely. "I'm glad."

Caleb shrugs, awkward, and clearly tries to search his mind for a topic change. "Did Mei tell you she's got a girlfriend?"

"What?" My eyes widen so fast it's painful. "No! Who?"

"Don't really know that part." Caleb wrinkles his nose. "Felt weird *me* asking to meet her, but she'd probably tell you more about her if you asked."

Shit, okay then.

"So, you and Mei..."

Caleb sighs. "We talked our shit out, too."

"Blimey, I've missed everything! I go away for a few months and you lot go all gay and start doing the whole open communication thing! If I knew me pissing off would have helped this much, I'd have done it way sooner. Jesus Christ, wow."

Caleb snorts. "Think it was more about us finding out we're *dying* than you leaving, Rex."

I look at him doubtfully. "I mean, we've always been dying. Now it's just faster. So, I think it was me leaving that helped, at least a little bit."

"All right. Maybe, yeah. Forced us not to be so dependant or whatever the fuck. But I swear if you piss off again, I will kill you before our toxic blood can, got it?"

"Yeah, yeah, bossy knickers. Jesus. You murder one person and suddenly you think you're a scary hardass."

Caleb ignores my inappropriate joke about his murder rampage and very purposefully gets to his feet, dragging me up with him. "Come on, we'd better get back to the others."

"Yeah, all right," I agree easily, going along with him.

But before we can, Caleb stops me with a hand on my arm. He turns to face me in the dark, his expression contemplative. "Hey, do you really think I should talk to Green about what happened with Guardian?"

"Yeah, Cal. She helps me with my shit. But don't tell her that," I warn. "She doesn't deserve to know her plant powers work."

Caleb dips his head in a slow nod, but doesn't respond, clearly thinking it over.

I hope he agrees to do it. He really does need to talk to someone, and that someone should know a hell of a lot more about how to help people with their mental stuff than I do.

Caleb keeps hold of my arm as we walk out of the caves and trudge our way back to our friends, who are sitting in the same spot where I left them.

Tate darts a look between us, a question in his eyes. I give him a discreet nod and Tate all but sags in relief. He grins up at Caleb and grabs hold of his hand the second he gets close enough to reach. Caleb lets go of me and drops to sit between Tate's open legs without needing to be coaxed. He leans back against Tate's chest and Tate wraps his arms around him from behind, his knees drawn up and bracketing Caleb in.

Tate seems glad to have Caleb back within his sights. Caleb looks more relaxed than he has since I found him on that rooftop last night.

They seem really comfortable with each other, more so than I would have expected. There's a presumed intimacy between them that wasn't there before.

It's a bit strange to see them being so openly affectionate, but I'll get used it. Mei doesn't seem bothered, barely glancing at them and instead focusing all her attention on me. I sit down next to her and Mei shifts over to take her standard spot between my legs, mirroring Tate and Caleb, although without the same level of physical intimacy.

Looking out across the water, I'm almost surprised the sun has only just begun its descent into the sea. It's been one hell of a day. With so much emotional upheaval in one twenty-four-hour period, I'm officially ready for it to end.

"How was your mission to rescue the second gen kid?" Mei asks, twisting her neck to look at me.

"It was bloody mad! Jamie flew a *plane*." I glance over at Caleb. "Did you know he could do that?"

"What," Caleb gasps sarcastically, pulling an exaggerated face, "my incredible, wonderful, perfect older brother can fly planes now? What. A. Shock. Look at my face and all this shock I feel at this unexpected, totally unprecedented piece of news." He flaps a hand at me. "Please, Rex, gush more about one of his many, many skills."

And we're back. Some habits die hard.

I pointedly ignore Caleb's sarcasm and spend the next few minutes explaining what went down at the OI facility where we found Nathan. My friends are uncharacteristically quiet through the whole story, until I get to the part about our escape through the forest.

"Nathan killed the OI agents coming after us. He burned them to death with this weird violet fire he can make."

"Sick." Tate nods approvingly, his chin bumping against Caleb's head.

"Did you burn down a forest without us?" Mei asks, sounding affronted we'd do such a thing and not include her.

"He *killed* them?" Caleb gapes at me. "How old is he?"

I answer all three in quick succession. "It was sick. Nathan seems to have control over who or what the fire burns, so the forest got to live another day. Yeah, he straight up murdered all of them, and he's maybe five or six years old."

"Jesus Christ," Tate mutters, frowning to himself like he's imagining a child murdering a whole load of people. Dickhead people, yeah, but people all the same.

Caleb doesn't look like he knows what to do with the information. "That's bonkers, mate."

"Where's Nathan now?" Mei asks, heavy suspicion in her voice. "We didn't hear anything about him back on base."

I shrug. "Dan didn't want to take him to FISA, so I brought them here with us. Lady Mars is going to ask them if they want to stay with her for a while."

"Excellent!" Tate exclaims excitedly. "It's about time we recruited more family members. Plus, this means Sami will officially become *one of us*!" He chants the last part in a low drone like he's conducting a sacrifice in a horror film.

Both Mei and Caleb seem equally enthused by this idea, which is mildly terrifying. At least for Dan, Sami, and Nathan. While I don't disagree with the sentiment, there's still part of me which thinks I should tell Dan to take his boyfriend and his nephew and run very far away from all of us.

"There's a town meeting tomorrow," Caleb states randomly.

"About what?" I ask, dubious of his intent in bringing it up.

"There's been some discord over what the primary school summer play should be about," Mei answers for him. She tucks her dark hair back behind her ear and leans back further against me, like I'm her personal deck-chair. I press my nose into her hair and smell the familiar scent of apples. It's an odd thing to be comforted by, but the fact Mei is still using the same shampoo makes me feel less distanced from my friends. Some stuff may have changed, some of which is even important and needed change, but not quite everything has.

"Oh blimey," I groan, "not again!

"We should take Dan and Nathan," Caleb suggests, revealing his true motives for bringing it up in the first place. "Show them what they're in for if they decide to live here."

"Excuse me"—I give him a disparaging glare—"we actually *want* them to stay."

"Lady Mars is presiding this time. She got a new gavel!" Tate chips in like it's supposed to convince me rather than prove my point.

"Shitting hell." I roll my head back and stare up at the early evening sky, lots of reds, purples, and blues all blending like paints smeared across a canvas. "We are not taking Nathan to a town meeting," I say without looking at my friends. "He's already suffered enough. Come to think of it, *I've* already suffered enough. We're not going. No way, that's final, end of discussion, goodbye."

We will absolutely be going to that fucking town meeting.

Chapter Fourteen

Uncle Roux

I spend most of the evening with my friends down on the beach, talking and sharing stories and going through all the things we've missed out on in the last few months. Eventually we go back up to Lady Mars's cottage where we raid the kitchen for snacks and eat around the kitchen table. It takes much less time than I thought it would to get back into the swing of being together as a foursome. It's been a while, even from before Roux and Damon died, since it felt so good between us. I felt right in the best way to be with them again.

Eventually, my friends leave to travel back into the city for their nightly patrol. They ask me if I want to go with them and a bit of me aches to say yes. But then I think about Lady Mars and Jamie, who would be simultaneously pissed off and hurt if I disappeared again, and the thought of disappointing them again sits in my stomach like a heavy stone, making the choice to say no a lot easier.

Once I'm alone, a sense of desolation begins to set in. Going upstairs, I peek in on Lady Mars to find her sleeping in her ridiculously large, round bed. For a second, I think about waking her, but ultimately decide not to. I doubt she's been sleeping any better than I have lately, so I should allow her any rest she can get now I'm home.

When I plod down the hall and crack open the door to my own bedroom, I'm only half-surprised to find my bed already occupied by Dan and Sami, with Nathan slipped in between them. It looks like Nathan is wearing a set of my old pyjamas. Thankfully my bed is large enough to accommodate both men easily, with room to spare so Nathan isn't squashed in by them. Still, Dan and Sami must have made some headway with him to make the boy trust them this much.

I'm looking forward to finding out how Lady Mars convinced Dan to stay the night at her cottage rather than remaining at the Moons' house. Although it's possible they were driven away by whatever battle likely took place between Jamie and Hector the moment they came into contact again.

Before I can move back and close the door, one of Nathan's violet eyes pops open and looks right at me. He doesn't get up, but his stare is oddly expectant, like he's waiting for me to do something he'll be forced to react to.

I raise my hand off the doorknob and crease my fingers in an awkward wave. Nathan's little eyebrow arches with far too much judgement for a child his age. He brings one of his hands out from under the covers and waves back at me with his own far smaller fingers.

Pressing my lips together so I won't laugh and wake the others, I mouth "goodnight" at Nathan and close the door to my room.

Wandering back along the corridor with the intention of going downstairs to sleep on the sofa, I find myself stopping outside Roux's. After a moment of hesitation, I push open the door and shuffle inside.

Much like the town, Roux's bedroom hasn't changed since the last time I saw it. Same light-blue walls and grey carpet, metal-framed bed and ornate set of drawers and wardrobe. There are photographs on every wall, mostly of the family, but some he took himself when he went through a phase of being an amateur photographer. Part of me was afraid Lady Mars would react to Roux's death the way she did her daughter's departure from her life, by packing everything up and shoving it in the attic, out of sight.

Quite the opposite; Roux's bed seems to have been left untouched. It's decked out in soft pink bed sheets and about two dozen pillows of various shapes and designs, all made by Lady Mars herself. I let myself sink down onto it, a flood of memories hitting me in a rush of the countless times I sat or slept or jumped on this bed with Roux. Jumping up and down to wake him up in the morning as a child. Sitting with him the few times he was sick. Sleeping beside him when we stayed up late talking and I couldn't be bothered to get up and go back to my own room.

My eyes sting with the threat of tears and I blink them rapidly to stave off the flow. In the process my eyes catch on a picture sitting on Roux's bedside table. It's a picture I've seen a hundred times before. The frame is thick and made of wood painted black. Inside is a photograph of our family grouped together down on the beach. The photo was taken the night Jamie left to join FISA. We had a goodbye bonfire party for him.

I reach out, pick it up, and bring the picture close. I use my sleeve to wipe away the gathered dust on the glass and gaze down at the grinning faces of my family. There's so many of us we barely fit into the frame. We all had to sling our arms around one another's shoulders and squish together until there wasn't an inch of space from one person to the next. It was the perfect photograph, made more so with all its imperfections, like the bunny ears Tate stuck up behind my head and Quinton sticking his tongue out at the camera. If anyone ever tried to tell me Tate was adopted, I would not believe them.

My thumb brushes over Roux's still face, his eyes bright with laugher.

As if conjured from the depths, a memory resurfaces that I haven't thought about in a long time.

*

"You look like one of those sad kitten memes," Roux says. "Except weirder. And not as cute."

I will myself to glare at him. Or thump him one on his baby toe. But I just can't find the energy.

I'm too preoccupied thinking about the going-away

party down the beach, and more specifically the person who's going away we're meant to be celebrating.

I should be over there with my friends, but I think my heart might explode if I have to pretend Jamie leaving isn't the thing I've dreaded for years finally coming to pass. There was never any doubt Jamie would go to Danger City and become a FISA agent, just like his parents before him. But now it's actually happening, I can't help feeling completely unprepared for the reality of it.

It makes me a coward, I know, but I slipped away from the fireside party as soon as I could and went to suffer in my angst alone. I wandered into one of Colbie beach's many caves and got lost in the dark, caught up in the need to have one of those "no one has ever been as sad as I am right now" teenage moments.

Unfortunately, it seems like Roux knows me a little bit too well, which is obviously horrifying all by itself.

Roux sits down next to me on the balcony, leaving a small amount of space between our hunched forms. I look over at him. He's got a serious, somewhat grave expression on his face. He's looking up at the cave ceiling like it's done something to personally offend him.

"Why are you here bugging me instead of sitting by the fire bugging other people?" I complain.

Roux's scowl loosens and his mouth twitches up into a small smile. He reaches over to wipe a hand down my face. I make an inhuman pigeon sound and bat at his arm.

"Get off, you inappropriate waste of oxygen!" I struggle when Roux scoots closer and wraps me up in an octopus hug.

"I thought I'd come and spend some time with my favourite pretend-son," Roux coos in my ear.

"You mean kidnap victim," I mutter, giving up on escape for now.

Roux sighs and just hugs me harder. "I know you've grown to love me—"

I scoff. "There's a psychological term for that."

"—and I have grown to tolerate your existence in my life as well."

"Stockholm syndrome."

I do battle with Roux for the next few minutes, both of us flailing around on the sand and screeching at each other. I'd like to say that I win our fight with dignity, but that would be a lie.

Roux shoots me a baleful glare from his curled-up position a few feet away. "I can't believe you bit me." He rubs at his arm where my teeth marks are still visible. "Again."

I bring my knees up to my chest and nudge Roux's shoulder. "I only ever do what you deserve."

"You're too mopey to sound that smug," Roux snipes.

"I am not mopey," I say, which is a total lie because I am feeling very mope-worthy right now.

"Okay, you little liar." Roux pokes my arm. "If you're not up here moping about Jamie then why aren't you at the party?"

I flick his poking finger. Roux snatches his hand away and curls it against his chest protectively. Because he's a massive baby and a half.

"I just wanted some time alone." I stare at Roux meaningfully.

Roux sits up and touches my shoulder gently, ignoring the pointed look. "I know how much it hurts when someone you care about leaves, especially when they're leaving to do something that could be dangerous. But I don't want you to throw away good moments because you're afraid of caring too much."

I blink stupidly at Roux, uncomprehending. Is that what I'm doing? Hiding away here because I'm scared of how much Jamie means to me? Yeah, probably. But knowing that doesn't take the fear away.

"Jamie's..." I discard the word "friend" as inadequate. "He's family," I settle on instead. "The thought of him getting hurt out there, so far away from us, makes me feel like I'm gonna throw up. I hate it."

Roux looks at me with an expression on his face I can't read. I would call it disbelieving, but I don't know what Roux thinks I could be lying about.

"You're assuming that everything is gonna go to shit," Roux says knowingly. "I get that, Rexley. I spent most of my childhood waiting for the other shoe to drop and crush me. I pushed away the people who cared about me, because I thought they made me weak. And I was right. Because loving someone is the scariest thing there is. Loving someone is you choosing to put everything on the line. It means having so much more to lose."

Roux wraps an arm around my shoulders, and this time I let him pull me in close. He tugs gently on my ear like he used to do when I was little and scared of nightmares I didn't understand.

That one small gesture reassures me in a way that any number of words would never be able to.

"You're braver than me," Roux says. He looks proud of that fact, but also sad, like he isn't sure if it's actually a good thing or not.

"Being brave is overrated." I turn my face into Roux's shoulder. "If you were braver then you might not have run away with me to Colbie and we wouldn't have met Lady Mars. I wouldn't have grown up with Caleb, Tate, and Mei. We wouldn't have our family."

There's no other life I want than the one I have because of what Roux did the night my parents died. That's probably wrong; I should want my parents more than anyone else. But all I know is the family I've got. And I love them. I love them in all their insanely weird glory. Even when they infuriate me, I still wouldn't trade them for anyone else, or for any other life than the one I'm living now.

"I just don't want you to be afraid of being close to someone because there's a possibility that you might lose them." Roux squeezes me tightly against his side. "You're the most important person in my life. You have been since the moment I held you for the first time—"

"You said the first time you held me I threw up on you."

Roux makes a disgruntled sound, breath puffing out against my hair. "Yeah, you did, it was gross. You were gross. Babies are gross. Especially you, though, because you peed on me as well."

"I clearly had good taste in people even back then," I say smugly. Roux ignores me and goes on with his original rambling.

Roux's face hardens with grim resolve, making him

look less like the idiot I've known all my life and more like a man who chose to join Obsidian Inc when he was only a teenager, just so he could try to stop his older brother from going too far down a dark path.

"I used to be terrified of fucking you up," Roux admits. "I told myself I had to do right by you—"

I snort, interrupting him again. "Please tell me you haven't been toning down the lunacy all this time. Because I will not believe you."

Roux flicks me on the nose, the anger and pain in his eyes slowly fading away. "Hush, anti-son, I am attempting to fill your pitiful existence with my wisdom. Stop ruining it."

"I can't ruin what doesn't exist," I huff, slapping at his hand.

"I'm trying to be a good pretend-father here," Roux grumbles. "And you're making it very difficult." He gives an exaggerated sigh and goes whinging on, "I don't even know why people have children on purpose. All you ever get in return for your love and constant support is slammed doors, I hate you's, and snark."

"Well, you should have thought about that before you abducted me then," I say. "And I've never slammed any doors. That was always you, remember, Lady Mars took your door away. She hid it in the attic because you never go up there."

"Of course I don't! There are fucking dolls up there," Roux exclaims dramatically. "Hundreds, thousands, millions of dolls, and they all stare directly into my soul. They know my darkest fears, and I refuse to be murdered by an army of dolls. I simply refuse to go out like that."

There are, like, maybe ten dolls up there, but whatever. Roux won't set foot in the attic ever since The Doll Incident.

When I was about seven years old, I woke up in the middle of the night during a particularly monstrous storm. I was frightened so I went looking for Lady Mars. I tiptoed out into the hallway and caught Lady Mars sneaking down from the attic. She was holding three dolls. When Lady Mars saw me, she handed over one of the dolls and told me her plan.

We placed the dolls at the bottom of Roux's bed. Then we hid in Roux's wardrobe and waited.

As Lady Mars predicted, Roux woke up after a very loud bout of thunder. When he sat up and opened his eyes all he saw was three dolls staring at him in the darkness, their faces lit only by the lightning slashing through the sky outside.

I'd never heard Roux scream quite that hysterically before. Which, considering this is Roux we're talking about here, should really say something about just how hysterical it was.

Ever since that night Roux adamantly refuses to go up to the attic. He even hisses at the door to the attic when he walks past it sometimes. Because he is a lunatic. I was raised by a lunatic. It is a bona fide miracle that I turned out even half as normal as I am.

I puff out a breath and lean back to flash Roux a genuine smile. "I'm really glad you're the massive weirdo who kidnapped me," I tell him.

Roux blinks a bit in surprise, but he smiles back at me fondly. "Me, too."

I watch Roux in contemplation for a moment. There's something I've been wanting to ask him, but there's never been a good time until now. I'm still not sure if I should leave it alone or not.

Curiosity wins out in the end, and I ask hesitantly, "Who was it who left you behind? Did you mean your parents?"

I see a flash of something undefinable cross over Roux's face. But it passes too quickly for me to be sure how Roux actually feels about the question. "No, not my parents," he says, his tone deceptively light. "There was someone else. A boy that I—" Roux breaks off and closes his eyes tightly shut, as if warding off unwanted thoughts, and even more unwanted feelings.

"Did you love him?" I ask, watching Roux's face carefully.

Roux smiles, but it's a bitter, sad smile that makes my chest feel tight to see on my guardian's face. "Look, Rexley, love can be wonderful, and it can also be horrific, especially when you're young." He looks me dead in the eye and says with uncharacteristic softness, "Do me a favour, okay...don't be afraid to feel vulnerable with someone who you know cares about you. Don't let a boy you love walk away because you're too scared to show them the parts of yourself that you think no one wants to see."

I let that sink in, making the obvious link between Roux's request and what must have happened all those years ago, back when Roux was a lonely, confused teenage boy.

"All right," I say decisively. Roux looks somewhat relieved until I add, "I'll promise to do that, but only if you

promise to do something for me?"

Roux narrows his eyes at me and huffs, "Are you ex-torting me right now, you sneaky elf? Am I actually be-ing emotionally manipulated by a fourteen-year-old blond child?"

"Yes," I say unapologetically.

Roux crosses his arms, his bottom lip sticking out in a pout. "I can't believe I'm being extorted by my own fake son. Is it my fault you've turned out this way? Where did I go wrong with raising you? Am I a terrible guardian?"

I answer all his questions in quick succession. "Yes. Your entire parenting technique consists of mocking me, teaching me how to beat people up, and setting an exam-ple that I can only assume is meant to be some kind of psychological trick to make me behave the exact opposite of you and therefore become a semi-normal human be-ing. And yes again. You are terrible. In every possible way. All the time."

Roux gasps dramatically and clutches at his non-ex-istent pearls. "Who taught you to be so mean?"

"The comments section of YouTube."

Roux clenches his hands into fists, raises them into the air, and shakes them at the sky.

"Damn the net for corrupting my ugly little elf nephew!"

"The net? The net?" I squeak. "How old are you?"

Roux sniffs. "I am a youthful flower."

"More like a deranged cactus," I mutter. "And I am not ugly."

Roux waves one hand dismissively and says, "I meant ugly in a nice way, God, you are so sensitive."

I pin him with my best glare and hiss, "I hope all of your dreams crumble and die."

Roux laughs mockingly. "Joke's on you, I don't have any dreams." He seems so proud of that for some probably stupid reason.

"Why, do you think you're too old? Because old people can have dreams. I mean, it's too late for you, of course, but that's for entirely different reasons."

"I am not old!" Roux snaps indignantly. "I have been informed that I could still pass for a university student, thank you very much. The people have spoken."

"What people? Who told you that?" I ask. "Because whoever it was, they lied."

Roux slumps defeatedly and holds his hands up in surrender. "Oh, for fuck's sake, go on, then, you evil little nerd, what is it you want from me?"

I arch an eyebrow at Roux but decide to let it go just this once. But only because he's sitting there looking all pathetic and blah.

"I want you to promise that if you ever properly like someone, you'll follow your own advice. That if you get the chance to be happy, you won't run away from it either."

Roux blinks at me in surprise, clearly not having expected that. It takes a handful of seconds before he says gravely, "Okay, Rex, I promise."

*

My sudden need to see Jamie hits me like a brick to the temple. He's probably not gone to bed yet, knowing his bad sleeping habits as well as I know my own.

Fumbling for my phone too fast, I almost drop the picture of us at Jamie's bonfire party. I set the picture back down on the bedside table before opening my phone and shooting off a text to Jamie.

RN: You awake?

Jamie's response is so rapid I suspect him of hovering over his phone, possibly considering sending me a text asking the same question.

JM: Yeah. Come over?

I smile down at the brightly lit screen and type out my answer with equal fervour.

RN: Give me 10.

JM: x

Getting up from Roux's bed, I take another moment to look around my uncle's room. There's not an inch of it that doesn't remind me of him. The pink neon trainers jammed behind the door. The charcoal drawing Caleb did for Roux of me and him practicing our knife throwing together. The old record player in the corner he bought for fifty pence at a car boot sale and spent months trying to fix up so he could play some of Lady Mars's old records. The pack of unopened cigarettes sitting on his desk. The stack of finished colouring books on his bookshelf. Every photo. Every carefully collected memory.

I've never put much stock in ghosts or any kind of afterlife in particular. The thought of all that felt too impossible to be real. But the thought of Roux, my bright and loud and insane uncle, being...gone. Just gone. Well. That's even more impossible to believe, so... For a second I allow myself to believe Roux isn't gone entirely, that some vestige of him remains, that the echoes of his spirit linger in this place.

"I need to tell you something, Roux. I just need...I just really need you to hear me."

One breath. Two.

Inhale.

Exhale.

"I miss you. I miss you all the time. And I know I've messed up a lot lately. But I swear I'm gonna fix that. I'm gonna...I'm gonna be okay."

My eyes close for one beat. Then two.

Inhale.

Exhale.

"I love you, Uncle Roux."

Again. Again. Again.

Chapter Fifteen

Speak Now or Forever Hold Your Peace

Jamie is already sitting on the roof when I reach his house. He sees me coming and indicates for me to join him. The front door is open, so I go right in and climb up to the attic where I'm able to heft myself through the skylight and out onto the roof. It's a nice night, the sky a clear fathomless black decorated with sporadically hung stars. There's a stillness to the air, too, like time has slowed to an abated grind.

Settling myself next to Jamie, I slide my gaze over to discreetly study him. He looks softer than usual, dressed in grey jogging bottoms and an old green hoodie. His hair is a mess, like he's been tugging at it in frustration for hours. A couple of his nails are lightly bloodied, which means he was chewing on them again.

Jamie catches me watching him, filing my attempt at a subtle damage check. His mouth turns up slightly on one side and he raises both eyebrows, daring me to pretend like I wasn't doing exactly what I *was* doing. I bite my tongue between my teeth in response, giving no verbal reaction to his dare, and instead tilting my face up to gaze at the sky hovering weightless and unending above us. I can still feel Jamie looking at me for a lingering second or three, but then he moves his eyes away, returning them to the town spread out before him.

We sit together for a while in the quiet peacefulness of the night. Even when I dip my head and join Jamie in staring out at the town, we keep our comfortable silence going. There's a layer of tension draped across us like a particularly heavy cloak, but it's not the type that feels close to breaking, smashing to pieces and cutting into us in the process. It feels kinder than that. It's the same tension Jamie and I have been wearing since we were both old enough to know what it meant to look at another person and see the possibility of always.

A gentle breeze blows past our faces like caresses from the wind, invisible fingers reaching out to stroke skin and run through hair. Jamie has his legs drawn up and so do I. There's a hole in the knee of Jamie's jogging bottoms. It's small and frayed. I remember how it got there. Last year, when Jamie went running one morning in Colbie and got roped into helping Mrs Denton rescue her pet bulldog from where it got itself stuck up a tree. How did a bulldog get stuck up a tree in the first place? I don't know, as Jamie didn't ask Mrs Denton that question, because he has this thing called self-control and doesn't actively try to invite insanity into his brain.

Jamie climbed this massive tree Mrs Denton has in her garden and managed to rescue poor Balloon, but snagged his jogging bottoms on the way down, ripping a hole in them.

Yeah. Mrs Denton's bulldog is called Balloon, and I know why, because I asked that question when I first found out about it, so now I know Balloon is called Balloon because he apparently likes the staticky feel of having an inflated balloon rubbed against him. So there. You can have that now. Good luck living with it.

There's a loose thread on the cuff of Jamie's well-worn hoodie. You're not supposed to tug on loose threads, but I reach and do it anyway, snapping it off his hoodie and twisting it around my fingers. It cuts into my skin, turning the pads of my fingers from red to white.

Jamie looks down at my hands and idly watches me fiddle with the thread I stole from his hoodie. His gaze eventually travels up from my hands to my chest, then ventures further upwards until it settles on my face. His eyes look lighter, almost luminous in the moonlight. It makes the scar, the one curved around his eyebrow, appear whiter, too, somehow more starkly visible in the night than in the day.

"Your dad home?" I ask him, unsure why I'm asking, although it feels like there are multiple reasons behind it.

Jamie gives his head a small shake. "Nah." He cuts his chin in the direction of Danger. "Went back to the city."

"Did you fight again?" I ask, nonplussed, figuring I already know the answer based on his hair and nails.

Jamie pulls a face I swear I've only ever seen on Caleb before and it's so sudden and jarring I almost burst out laughing.

"Jesus, Rex," Jamie growls, instantly furious, "he just says this shit, right, and it makes me go off on him. He kept trying to use you and my brother against me, and it pissed me off so much."

It is such a direct quote of what I've heard from Caleb at least a million times over the years that I'm unable to stifle my reaction to it.

Jamie scowls at me while I snicker to myself uncontrollably for a good minute or so.

"Why is that even funny, you weirdo?" Jamie prods, still looking rather irate, although probably more at me now than Hector.

I wave him off, unwilling to explain why it's so hilarious to me that both he and Caleb would come out with such similar expressions of anger following arguments with their father after having spent so much time at odds because of him. "You wouldn't get it," I tell Jamie, still struggling not to laugh again at the absurdity of it all. "Trust me, you had to be there."

Jamie squints at me for a handful of seconds, assessing, but seems to ultimately decide it isn't worth poking the information out of me.

"How's Cal?" he asks, his brows wrinkling in genuine concern.

Twisting the length of thread around my middle finger, I contemplate how much to tell Jamie of what Cal and I spoke about. Before, I would have given Jamie a vague response, because that's how Caleb would want it. But if what Cal said is true in regard to their relationship having taken a turn for the better, he might have less of a problem with me speaking about his personal issues with Jamie than he has in the past.

"He's going to struggle with it for a while." I shrug one shoulder. "But that's standard for most people who've killed someone for the first time."

Jamie makes a soft noise of agreement. "The first time I took a shot like that it was a couple days before it really hit me. Everyone kept telling me it would, and I pretended to believe them. But I was young and arrogant as hell and thought maybe I was just stronger than everyone else." He laughs, caustic and self-deprecating, like he can't believe he was ever that stupid.

"You're still young," I point out. Sometimes Jamie talks like he's decades older than he is, a man who's seen too much and lived for himself too little.

Jamie's mouth tilts up again at one corner, doubt clouding his eyes. "Still arrogant, too, right?"

"Yeah," I drawl, grinning slowly at him, "but I like that about you."

"Really?" Jamie's eyebrows rise in disbelief.

"Yeah, it's just part of your whole thing." I wave my hand up and down, indicating his entire self.

Jamie snorts, amused. "My whole *thing*?"

"Yep." I press a hand to my chest. "Like how being a screechy nightmare is part of mine."

Jamie's smile grows, then goes soft. "I like that you're a screechy nightmare," he tells me, all quiet and sincere, like he doesn't know how much his easy acceptance of my lesser qualities matter to me.

"Too right," I quip jauntily, winking and startling another laugh out of him. Then I ask more seriously, "What happened after a couple days, when it properly hit you?"

Jamie grimaces, smile disappearing so fast it's like it was snatched off his face with claws, leaving behind a jagged expression in its place. "I was a complete fucking mess," he admits. "Got the shakes in the night. Threw up bile for hours. Then I had terrible dreams for weeks. Barely slept."

"What helped you get over it?" I ask with interest.

Jamie gets this sad, far-off look to his eyes as he turns his head to stare into the distance again. His shoulders tense up like he's expecting trouble to follow his response. Without looking at me he murmurs apologetically, "Roux."

I'm caught for a moment, confused by the answer, combined with the general feeling of being gutted that any mention of Roux seems to inspire. "How?" I ask timidly, unsure if I really want to start any conversation about him.

"Nothing special," Jamie says. "We just talked. He told me about the first time he killed someone. Then he suggested I speak to one of the psych agents about what was going on with me up here." He taps his temple with two fingers.

"Green?" I ask suspiciously, narrowing my eyes.

"Yeah, actually," Jamie confirms, letting out an amused puff of air and shaking his head a little. "She was brutal with me, but it helped."

Jesus Christ, does FISA even *have* any other psych agents?

I don't respond about Green, knowing I'll just end up ranting that she knows far too much about the people in our family and we might need to ice her one day out of self-preservation. What if Green ever decided to do a villain team-up with Diane Foxley? Her new book is coming out soon and I'm expecting a social media shitstorm to follow. She's been on the news multiple times speculating on Polaris's disappearance. She's somehow made his death into a conspiracy about the government creating some underground bunker where superheroes are being sent to be trained to take over the world. The fact she's half correct about that infuriates me.

Jamie breaks me from my ruminations about how frightening a world with a teamed-up Foxley and Green would be by asking, "What are you scowling about now?"

"Diane Foxley making up random shit about Polaris being"—I let out a harsh breath—"gone."

A complicated expression forms on Jamie's face. I don't know how to interpret it. He doesn't seem angry or annoyed by the mention of Damon, but there's a layer of discomfort, like he isn't sure how to deal with talking about him.

"He was my boyfriend," I tell Jamie, because I haven't told anyone, and he's probably not the best person to tell, but it doesn't feel like it could matter the same way to anyone else. "Before he died. We talked and...he said he wanted to be a part of us."

I think that's one thing I'll never be able to let go of. How ready he was to be folded into my life, into my family's weird bubble. He should have been part of it from the start and it feels like a great unfairness that he wasn't.

"You know—" Jamie releases a short, rasping laugh without any actual humour, like the sound pains his throat to make it. "He probably would have fit."

"I think so, yeah." Maybe I should feel guilty for saying that directly to Jamie's face, but the fact is I did believe Damon would fit in with our family eventually and I don't want to lie about that, especially not to Jamie who would see right through it if I did. "I know you weren't ever friends, but...you were a lot alike, you know. If we'd all grown up together, maybe things would have been different. You might have got on."

There's a long stretch of silence where I let that sit between us.

Without warning, Jamie gets up from his seated position and nudges my hip with his socked foot. I look up at him expectantly.

"Let's go inside." Jamie sighs, looking uncharacteristically nervous. "I need a drink for this conversation."

Wordlessly I heft myself up and follow Jamie as he climbs back through the skylight. He leads me downstairs to the Moons' kitchen. It hasn't changed since Phoenix last renovated it before she died. Light hardwood floors and pale-green cupboards and dark-grey countertops. Hector isn't the house redesigning sort, and beside he's away so much it hardly matters.

Jamie goes to the fridge, coloured a green which matches the cupboards, and opens the door, reaching inside to grab two beers in glass bottles. He digs into a nearby drawer to take out a bottle opener and uses it to pop off the metal caps. Once opened, he turns around and offers one to me.

I move closer to him and take the drink, toasting it against Jamie's before raising it to my lips. Cool, bitter liquid splashes over my tastebuds and down my throat.

Jamie takes a longer swig from his drink and avoids looking directly at me for a good few seconds, gaze darting around the room, lingering everywhere but my face. When he finally does meet my eyes, it feels like a declaration of war, one that's been brewing for a long time and might finally require a call to arms. Going by the flinty edge to Jamie's expression, I might need to conscript some extra brain cells for this battle if I'm going to stand a chance of being in a position to call an eventual cease-fire.

"When I first met North," Jamie says, resting back against the kitchen counter like he's settling in for the long haul, "he asked me about you right off the bat."

I blink at him in surprise. "Really?"

Growing up, I wondered if Damon thought about me as much as I did him. It feels strange to have it confirmed by someone else that I was important to him, too. I don't really know if it's a good feeling, but it's not nothing. It *matters*, is what I mean.

"Yeah." Jamie dips his chin in a short nod. "He wanted to know if you were okay. Then, every time I saw him, he asked the same thing. If you were okay. It was weird, because otherwise he was always so mission focused when we were working together. He was properly intense about it all, you know? Like...*really* intense."

"Hello pot, nice to meet you," I drawl, putting my bottle down on the counter and crossing my arms, "what was that you were saying about kettle?"

Jamie gives me a quelling look and huffs out a frustrated breath, like he thinks I'm not grasping the significance of what he's telling me on purpose. "What I'm trying to get at is, North was an all or nothing kind of bloke. And he always cared about you, even when he didn't really know you. So, to be honest, I think if we grew up together, we wouldn't have been friends."

I frown at that, confused and not understanding the link between the two pieces of information. "Why not?"

Jamie takes another drink from his beer as if preparing himself for some inevitable fallout his answer might cause. "Because, no matter what, there would always have been you between us," he says in a rush like he wants to get the words out before he loses his nerve. He smiles ruefully. "Couldn't have been friends with someone whose boyfriend I was in love with, could I?"

My eyes pop open so wide I think they might look anime-level big. "Jamie…" I honestly don't know how to react.

Jamie must take my response for a denial, or possibly a dismissal of some kind, because he scowls at me and growls angrily, "Nah, nah, let's be real for once, yeah? I'd have never stood a chance with him right there all those years. The fact you two got in deep so fucking fast after you met is proof enough of that, right?"

Hitching my hips against the counter and tightening my arms around myself defensively, I try to make Jamie understand it wasn't that simple. "I didn't know what was going on between us at first. We didn't start talking about real feelings until near the end. I didn't choose him over you. He just asked first."

Blimey, are we really doing this? Are we saying all the shit we've never said before but which we both had to know existed between us for years?

It seems like we are. I'm suddenly terrified of continuing this conversation. Jamie looks equally as terrified of what he's saying, but he doesn't let up or make any move to back down from it.

"Caleb warned me about a month after you joined FISA. He told me to make a move before my next assignment. He told me if I went away on a mission again, I'd lose you to North. I didn't believe him." Jamie makes a choked, bitten-off sound that could be a scoff or maybe a bitter laugh in another life. "I thought you weren't ready to be with anyone long term, so it wouldn't matter even if you did fuck North. It wouldn't get serious, because you don't *do* serious, even with people you have feelings for."

I can understand why he'd think that. It was never a secret that I was romance-averse and none of the people I slept with were meant to last anything more than a night.

Feeling defensive over my relationship with my past sexual experiences, as well as my relationship with Damon, I throw out heatedly, "How could you know I wasn't ready? Based on the men I fucked who I didn't know or give a shit about? Why the hell do you think I'd have treated you the same way I did them? It's bullshit, Jay. I thought you said we were being real. What's the *actual* reason you never told me how you felt?"

Jamie slams his beer bottle down on the counter so hard the beer sloshes out and a few droplets run down the sides of it. "Oh, fuck off, Rex, you know why!" He looks at me with furious eyes, the storm in them raging to life. "I was scared of messing up what we already had. You mean too much to me to risk losing."

I ignore the fact his reasons for holding back are exactly the same as my own, unwilling to give him the win just yet. "How long have you felt this way?" I demand, meeting his ferocity with a fresh wave of my own.

Jamie raises his hand and spears his fingers through his hair in a clear act of anxiety. There's pain in his eyes now, in the furrow of his brow and tightening of his mouth.

"How long have I loved you? Fucking hell, Rex, I don't even know. It's like I can't remember a time when it wasn't there, this thing"—he fists a hand in his hoodie and presses his knuckles against his sternum—"this loving you. It's like it's a part of me. It's like you're a part of me. A vital part that I wouldn't be able to live without, because I wouldn't even fucking know how to." Jamie's storming gaze locks on hard to mine as he tells me, "Breath in my lungs, blood in my veins, thoughts in my head, Rex in my heart. I don't know." He shrugs, at a loss. "Some things just are because they are because they are."

It's too much, then. The intensity of Jamie's admission as well as the tsunami wave of emotion they evoke in me, like a dam breaking and a torrent of all the things I kept walled off and securely hidden away flood through me, destroying every carefully built defence system I put in place to protect myself against this very thing.

"Why are you telling me now?" I choke out painfully, my throat suddenly dry and cracked. I'd reach for my beer if I didn't think my hands would tremble so hard I'd drop it. "If you were afraid of losing me before, what's changed?"

Except I know. I know what's changed.

"I found out there was a better than good chance I was going to lose you anyway," Jamie says, confirming my thoughts. "Suddenly, my reasons for holding back seemed stupid and weak." His voice is harsh, as if berating himself for it. "I realised I would rather tell you the truth about how I felt and risk everything than spend my whole life wishing I was a braver man. The kind of man you deserve."

If I deserve a braver man, then so does Jamie, and if I can't be that forever, surely, I can be it now, for as long as this body and mind infused with poison allows me to.

"It's..." Deep breath. *Don't bottle, Nova.* "It's the same for me, Jay. I was scared too."

Jamie must see how much I'm struggling because he tries to give me an out. "Rex, you don't have to—"

But I can't let him do that. I *need* to do this. For him. For myself. It really feels like it's now or never.

"I can't remember any one moment when loving you became a fact of my life," I tell him, moving away from the counter and stepping towards Jamie. "It's like I was floating in space for years until we met, and something dropkicked me at the atmosphere. The *force* of it." I press my lips together, gazing up at Jamie, trying to convey everything I want to tell him with more than just words. "Smashed right through that shit, yeah? Then gravity got a hold of me, and I went into free fall. I hit the ground and just started running. Couldn't stop. Needed something solid under my feet."

"You love me?" He sounds so unsure it makes my heart squeeze hard enough it probably cracks that shitty, erratic organ right down the middle.

I'm flying high on the release of finally being able to say all the things I've always wanted to tell Jamie. "It's a universal constant. A fixed fucking point in the timeline." I take another step towards him, Jamie watching me with a fragile kind of hopefulness. "Gravity exists. The big bang happened. Once upon a time Rexley Nova fell in love with James Moon and the magic 8 ball he used when he was ten predicted he won't ever stop."

"Did you just talk about yourself in third person right now?" Jamie asks dryly, grinning so wide his cheeks must hurt from it, ruining the moment like a *prick*. "I mean. Wow. Sexy."

I take the final step in his direction, bringing myself fully into his space, the inches separating us becoming an unacceptable concession of living. I glare up at him fiercely. "Shut up and kiss me right now, Jay, or I will poke you in the *eye*, you basta—"

Jamie grabs my face and presses his lips to mine in a hot, possessive kiss. He holds my face steady as his tongue sweeps inside my mouth and easily dominates. I let him, wrapping my arms around his waist and fisting the back of his hoodie. The kiss turns messy and wet in seconds, both of us grasping at each other wantonly, pressing our bodies as close as is physically possible while allowing our mouths to remain locked together.

One of my hands burrows in underneath Jamie's hoodie and makes contact with the warm skin of his back. Jamie gasps into my mouth at the sensation of skin on skin and he moves a hand to my hair, where he fists a handful of it and yanks hard. Pain prickles at my scalp and lights another kind of fire in my groin. My cock begins to stiffen as Jamie stares down at my face, which is tilted up, throat bared and vulnerable.

Jamie tracks my reaction to the tug on my hair with narrowed eyes, the cogs in his mind whirring at break-neck speed. He does it again, pulling my hair in a harsh twist, just to see, like a test to make sure he's not wrong. I moan in response, digging my fingernails into his back as my cock becomes fully erect pressed against his thigh.

As if to push the theory one step further, Jamie wraps the fingers of his free hand around my throat. His hands are large enough to encompass most of my throat, his thumb pushing in at the very edge of my jaw. He squeezes a little, not hard enough to cut off my air supply, but enough to make the threat of doing so implicitly clear. I swallow roughly, wheezing out a breath of excitement ra-ther than fear, letting him know with my eyes and the way I strain to eclipse any remaining space between us that I want this. I want whatever Jamie is willing to give me.

Jamie tilts his head to the side, considering me for seconds that seem to stretch on and on, the wait making me increasingly desperate for something to happen, to be touched and hurt and taken by the man who I've loved al-most my entire life.

Whatever conclusion Jamie comes to seems to please him immensely, and he's moving fast before I can catch my breath or fully compute what's happening. He spins me around and shoves me into the counters, the edge dig-ging into my back painfully. Then he takes my mouth again, his fingers tightening on my throat as he steals the air from my lungs with the slick heat of his mouth and the crushing possession of his hand.

I try to kiss him back, but Jamie's being so rough and unrelenting that I can't really do much else other than to soak up the onslaught of lips and teeth and tongue. When I'm lightheaded from the kissing, Jamie finally pulls back, only to bite my bottom lip hard enough to trigger even my Liquid Onyx level pain receptors. He doesn't hold back at all, knowing my limits like no one else could, having grown up training alongside me. His hot tongue swipes out over my abused lip and he leans back with a satisfied smile at the dazed, turned-on expression that must be on my face.

Jamie's eyes are so dark right now. Darker than I've ever seen them. There's a jagged quality to him I haven't seen, barbed and easy to mishandle. His edges have become more pronounced, no longer blunt and careful, but razor-sharp and dangerous.

"You want me to be rough?" Jamie asks, low and devastating. "You want me to make it hurt?" He releases his hold on my throat enough I'm able to gasp in a breath and speak.

"Yes," I rasp at him, eager and ready to see what this new version of Jamie can do, what he'll be willing to do.

"Be sure," Jamie says in a gritted voice, an inherent note of warning in it, "because I'm mean like this, Rex. Give me permission to ruin you and I *will*."

My answer of, "Good," comes out more a moan than a word, the excitement almost too much to contain, the fission of electric charges shocking their way up and down my spine, along every available nerve in anticipation.

Jamie grabs my chin. "Rexley, you'll tell me if you don't like something. No jokes, no games. You want to stop, you say so, or if I'm choking you out, you rap your fist against my chest or yours, whichever's easiest, right?"

I trust him. I trust him more than almost anyone else.

His fingers tighten on my chin when I don't answer immediately, grey eyes like wet stone hit by wave after wave of ocean water.

"Okay, James." We've been taking care of each other for years. This is just more of the same. "I swear."

Jamie doesn't need any more than that. He strikes fast, mouth on mine again before I have time to draw another breath, invading my space and pressing up against me. His cock is thick and hard and so hot it ignites the answering blaze inside me, flame calling out to flame, stoking them higher and higher until we're both gasping hoarsely into an open-mouthed kiss.

"Bedroom," Jamie growls breathlessly. A statement not a question.

I've wound myself around Jamie like a particularly clingy vine, making it more difficult when he yanks me away from where he had me trapped against the counter and starts moving us towards the stairs. Jamie doesn't help by continuing to keep our lips connected, bringing them back together every other second. It gets more difficult when we make an unspoken effort between us to remove any remaining barriers stopping us from touching each other intimately.

Our journey from the kitchen to Jamie's bedroom is a disaster of tugging at clothes and digging fingers into freshly bared skin.

Jamie kicks open the door to his bedroom, then, once we're inside it, he kicks it closed again and slams me up against it. He kisses me roughly against the door, his hands sliding over my naked body, nails dragging against my torso, thigh, and arse. His nails bite into my hot flesh deep and hard enough to leave visible marks.

He rips his mouth off mine and barks at me, "Head up!", and when I comply, he presses his lips to my exposed neck. He kisses the sensitive skin under my jaw and above my clavicle before finding the right spot to sink his teeth into. It feels like they break skin with how savagely he bites me. It hurts so good, and I groan out my appreciation to the ceiling.

My fingers grasp at Jamie, his thickly muscled arms and broad shoulders, attempting to find some purchase on him, a way to hold on tight so I won't collapse like a building whose foundation has just been blown to bits.

Jamie gives my neck a series of bites, finishing off by nipping at my jaw. His lips return to my mine for another heated kiss before he leans back far enough to look me in the eyes. I expect him to smile or make a joke about what a trembling mess he's turned me into with barely any effort, but he doesn't. He looks me over, raising one hand to run his fingers over the fresh marks on my neck and pressing down purposefully, eliciting more pain and making me gasp out his name. It's a plea. I don't know exactly what for. But I trust Jamie to understand and give it to me.

"Wish I could make these marks last," Jamie laments, a dark carnality to his words, his eyes hooded. "You look gorgeous always, but you'd look extra pretty with my bruises on your skin."

I tilt my head forward, chasing after his mouth for more contact, more volatile kisses and forceful touches. Jamie responds by wrapping his hand around my throat again and banging my head back hard against the door. He tightens his hold on my throat, cutting off my air and using his other hand to grab my wrists and hold them together, trapping them between our bodies.

Jamie leans in close when I start to feel light-headed from not being able to breathe. I can hold my breath for ages, we were taught to during our training by the parents, and Jamie knows how long I can do it for, so I'm not afraid. His cheek brushes against mine as he speaks directly into my ear, his voice a low rumble. "I'm gonna make you cry for me, Rex." It straddles the border between a promise and threat, which sends a fresh wave of static charges racing along my spine.

I open my mouth to goad him into coming at me again, wanting more, aching for it with every fibre of my being. But Jamie moves back and seems to catch on to my plans, because he raises his eyebrows at me in warning, daring me to do it and see exactly what the consequences will be for trying to play games with him. I clamp my mouth shut, automatically responding to Jamie's silent caution.

Jamie rewards me by pulling me away from the door. He swings me around and walks me back to the bed. I fall back onto it and Jamie follows. He encourages me to move up the bed until the top of my head touches the edges of his pillows.

Once I'm in place, Jamie settles between my legs and takes my rigid cock into his mouth. He swallows me down so fast, tells his gag reflex to piss off, and sucks hard on his way back up, and my vision goes funny for a second from the instant hit of pleasure. His pace does relent for a second, his lips, tongue, and throat working my cock with an expertise I'd be jealous of if I had the coherency to think in proper sentences.

When I go to put my fingers in Jamie's hair, he pulls off me to snap in a cock-choked voice, "Hands behind your head, Rex. If you move them before I tell you, I'll hit you hard enough you'll see stars, okay?"

I do as I'm told, although the idea of being smacked across the face is a tempting one. Not many people can do it right. Some are timid and afraid. Others too eager and clumsy. I've seen Jamie fight. See him land blows with the precision of a trained agent. He knows how to hit a man and make it hurt, as well as how to knock them out of the game. There's a decent chance I'd enjoy getting a good, hard smack from Jamie. It's a theory I'll have to test at some point.

Once my hands are safely folded in under my head, Jamie nods approvingly and goes back to sucking my cock, lighting me up like a sparkler in the process. His lips stretch over my pulsing length, tight and perfect. He laps up my pre-cum like he's trying to coat his mouth and throat in it to make swallowing my cock even easier.

I stop looking at him and dart my gaze around his room, trying to focus on anything else, in an attempt to hold off from coming too soon.

Jamie's room is familiar ground for me with the

scorch mark in the middle of the thick green carpet from when he dropped a lit cigarette and accidentally started a small fire, and the dark-wood furniture he inherited from his grandfather, the drawers of which have mysterious bullet holes in them.

There's a mural on one wall that Caleb painted for Jamie's fourteenth birthday depicting the northern lights floating above a series of mountains and forest terrain. It's an amazing piece of art that Jamie was thrilled over, having become a little obsessed with the northern lights after we'd recently gone away together as a family on holiday to Iceland and seen them.

I wouldn't be able to count how many times I've been in Jamie's room and laid with him on this bed, to read or do homework or listen to music.

However, getting a blow job on Jamie's bed is a new and very welcome development.

Jamie performs a particularly underhanded trick with his tongue on the head of my cock and my hips jerk upwards, pushing my needy cock deeper into the hot mouth engulfing it. Jamie grasps my hip with one hand and forces it down, pinning me to the bed. He uses the other to give my opposite thigh a sharp smack with his open palm. The answering pain ripples along the targeted skin like seawater roving across wet sand.

My trapped fingers twitch under my head with the need to grab at Jamie. I want to run my fingers through his dark hair and tug on the strands the way I've dreamed of doing for years. I want to map the taut muscles of his stomach and the myriad scars left behind on his body from missions past with my tongue. There's so much I want to do with him there doesn't feel like any time we have left could ever be enough.

Jamie gives my thigh another well-aimed smack, getting the exact same place as before and eliciting more of the sweet pain I crave. It brings my thoughts back to the here and now, allowing me to mentally designate the future as unimportant to this moment.

When Jamie finally takes his mouth off my aching cock it's somehow both an immense relief and an unacceptable loss in equal measure. I want to demand he keep blowing me and beg for him to do something else. If he doesn't move this along soon, I'm going to say fuck it and risk a split lip just to touch him again.

I'm not sure how, but Jamie seems to be able to read the trajectory of my thoughts and reprimands me for them by sinking his teeth into the sensitive skin of my inner thigh. As before, his bite isn't playful, it fucking hurts, and the sound I make in response is downright feral. I hiss like an injured alley cat and my body tries instinctively to twist away from him. But Jamie's got my hip clamped down against the bed, making it impossible for me to escape without putting some real effort in. Since I have zero desire to move from this spot, being held in place makes me feel more grounded and secure, like I don't have to worry about losing my grip because Jamie won't let go.

"Jay..." I moan, trailing off into inarticulate sounds of pleading and desperation.

Jamie ignores my begging noises and takes his time kissing and biting his way up my body. He's in no rush, stopping at my hard nipples to twist and nip at them with his fingers and teeth. It's not a part of my body I'm usually all that bothered by, but Jamie is somehow able to use them to make my body sing with dual sensations of pain and pleasure.

When Jamie finally reaches my neck, he spends another minute or so lapping his hot tongue over the marks he already made, ones which will fade far too soon. I lament the fact all his bruising will likely be gone by tomorrow. I'd really like to keep them for longer, to watch them change colour and ache in new ways when I press my fingers against them with each stage of healing.

Jamie must feel similarly, because he bites down on the marks to freshen them up again, like he's replenishing them for both of us.

I'm panting with need and excitement and just a little bit of impatience by the time Jamie's mouth takes mine in another punishingly hard kiss. He folds one hand around my throat as he kisses me, squeezing it in a tight grip, forcing my head to stay in place so he's better able to control the speed and thoroughness of the kiss.

Genuinely without meaning to, I disobey the rules by removing one hand from beneath my head to grab Jamie's thick bicep. I just wanted to touch him, to feel the strength of him beneath my fingers, but Jamie goes rigid immediately and pulls back from the kiss. He looks down at me with narrowed, dark-grey eyes. There's violence in them. The good kind that I want a man, and Jamie specifically, to look at me with.

Jamie takes his hand off my throat and uses it to smack me hard across the face, pain instantly blooming like a flower along my cheekbone. It's such a ruthless hit that my head snaps to the side and my eyes begin to prickle with impending tears. He barely lets me recover before landing another blow that has me gasping from the shock of how much it hurts. Tears, salty and scorching like the Mediterranean sea, fill my eyes and begin to track down over my face, which is already burning like someone set the inside of my skin on fire.

Jamie's hand is back on my throat in an instant and he takes my mouth in another rough kiss. He rears back for a moment to lick at the tears on my cheeks before kissing me again, the bitter taste of my tears mingling with our shared spit, enhancing the experience, making it feel more visceral.

One side of my face feels like a massive bruise and my lips are raw and my body pulses with the pain inflicted upon it by Jamie's well calculated machinations. It's amazing. Perfect. Everything I wanted him to do.

Jamie moves his hand from my hip to press a finger to my hole.

Well. Almost everything, then.

He presses a dry finger further into me, not penetrating, just a tease of what could be. He pulls away from our kiss and looks down at me again with watchful eyes. It feels like he can see right inside my head, to all the secret wants and desires I have buried within the folds and corners of my mind.

"I'm gonna fuck you, Rex," he tells me, voice coarse and gritted and sex heavy. "I'm gonna fuck you on your back so you know it's me splitting you open and filling you up, making you mine like we both need me to."

"Yes, please, Jay," I gasp, fresh tears gathering, this time from an emotional kind of pain rather than a physical one. "Please. I want it. I want you. This. Us. I want it so much it's killing me. Please."

Jamie kisses away the new tears, lips brushing my cheek with a tenderness that utterly undoes me. As much as I crave the roughness, each awestruck caress causes its own unique brand of ache. Jamie's face creases up like he's furiously trying not to cry as well. I can't blame him. There's a lot between us worth crying over, both in the good and bad ways.

But he wants to be strong, to appear strong at least, for me.

"Hey." My voice is hushed and intimate. I wait until Jamie is looking at me before telling him, "This isn't a one-way thing, Jay. I want to make you mine, too."

That gets Jamie to smile wanly.

"Don't need to. I've always been yours," he tells me, *stubbornly* sure and *stunningly* fearless now he's got free rein to be honest about it. "Since the moment my brother dragged you into our house and you stood there frowning like a kidnapped pixie with your knitted teapot hat and a massive book clutched to your chest like it was your last line of defence. I asked who you were, and you looked right at me and said, 'Your worst nightmare if you start asking me stupid questions as well. I've already made one friend today; I don't want to do that again'."

I met Jamie the same day I met Caleb, only a few hours apart, when Caleb decided to take me home with him very much against my will. I met Jamie and he was tall and amazing and seemed untouchable to me.

"Piss off," I snort, feeling giddy and bashful at the same time, "I didn't say that, you plonker."

"You bloody did," Jamie argues, still smiling. "Said those exact words. I remember." His voice lowers a few octaves when he admits, "I remember everything about you."

Not knowing what to say in response, I don't give a verbal answer. Instead, I grab Jamie's hair like I wanted to before and tug him back into another firm kiss. Jamie lets me get away with it this time with only a sharp pinch and twist of my nipple. His fingers are like a vice and the skin between them throbs when he releases me from their cruel grip. I moan in protest at the loss of it. Jamie ignores me and moves to snatch a bottle of lube from the bedside table.

Jamie proves himself adept at fingering someone open, with the right amount of care and attention to his partner's reactions. As is becoming a theme, Jamie doesn't rush the process of readying my hole to take his sizable cock. He puts his mouth back on my straining erection a few times as well, to ease the tension. Or possibly to drive me batshit insane. Either one is an option here.

When Jamie finally begins coating his own cock with lube and tells me to grab a pillow from behind me to elevate my lower body to make fucking in this position easier, it takes quite a bit of willpower not to smack him in the face with the pillow in retribution for making me wait so long to feel him inside me.

Jamie must catch the frustration in my eyes when he gazes down at me, because a tiny smirk quirks his lips, and if I wasn't so desperate to be fucked by him, I'd be kicking his arse for being such a smug prick.

Getting Jamie fully seated inside my hole is no easy feat given the size and girth of his cock. He kneels between my spread legs, one hand guiding it into me and the other grasping my bruised hip, his fingers digging into the bruises to add another welcome layer of sensation.

Jamie grunts with barely hinged restraint as each inch of him breaches me, disappearing inside my body like a dirty magic trick.

Once Jamie bottoms out, he curls over me, pressing his mouth to mine like it's his way of sealing the deal. Completing the circuit we've created. His tongue is slick as it strokes along mine and I'm moaning into him again. My hands twitch at my sides where he told me to keep them while he was opening me up for him.

Now, though, Jamie pulls back far enough from our kiss to give permission. "You can touch me, Rex." He doesn't need to tell me twice. I run my fingers along his shoulder, his torso, his back, whatever piece of him I can reach, scratching at him with my blunt nails and silently encouraging him to move. I'm ready. I'm so ready it's not even funny.

Jamie drags his cock slowly out of me until only the head is stretching my hole, then pistons back in with a sharp thrust that fills my lungs with air in one violent inhale. He sets a slow pace after that, pulling out then thrusting back in and grinding his thick cock deep inside me, bottoming out each time. He manages to hit my prostate more often than he misses with each precise roll of his hips.

Jamie's heat born from the exertion of holding himself in check as he fucks me permeates the air between us, overwhelming my senses, making me gasp and claw at him. No matter how much I beg with my hands and eyes for him to speed things up, Jamie refuses to act on my silent pleas. He seems content to take his time with me, to let the tension build and build into a truly spectacular eruption.

Even knowing it will be better to wait, I can't keep my mouth shut forever. I want faster, harder, meaner, but when I ask for it, Jamie warns me to stop pushing. When I ignore him and carry on demanding he let loose, Jamie gives me another hard smack to the mouth in punishment. It's a backhand hit this time and feels a harsher reprimand for it. When I suck on my bottom lip, there's blood.

Luckily for me, the sight of my split lip and the resulting groan the taste of my own blood drags from my throat seems to spur something on inside Jamie. He pounces on me without warning and kisses my injured mouth without any pretence at gentleness. My lip stings sharply and throbs with a burning pain that has me groaning even louder.

Our breaths mingle, my enhanced sense of smell picking up on the distinct tang of iron from my blood, and salt from both my tears and Jamie's sweat and faint traces of the alcohol we drank earlier meshing as we kiss.

Jamie rips his mouth off mine and presses our foreheads together, my hands cupping his neck, holding on for dear life. His cock is still firmly speared inside me. We pant hot puffs of air into each other's faces. He brings a hand up to wrap around one of my wrists, backing off slightly. His eyes are open and staring into mine with an intensity I can barely stand to look at it's so strong and all-consuming.

"You're so fucking gorgeous," he tells me in a husky growl, "I feel like I could spend a thousand years looking at you and never stop wondering what the hell I ever did to deserve your attention, never stop breaking my own heart every time I'm forced to look away."

I choke off what might be a sob, overcome suddenly with emotion, but all I can do is hold on tighter to Jamie and hope it's enough. There aren't words big or emphatic enough to describe what he does to me, what he's always given to me just by existing in my life.

Jamie pushes the fingers of one hand into my hair and fists a damp clump of it, pulling harshly so my face tips back, my throat bared to him. He presses his mouth to the underside of my jaw and breathes me in. With him holding me down and pinning me with his body and hands and cock and mouth, it's almost too much. It feels possessive and primal. It all screams "mine" without him having to say it.

Jamie speeds up after that, pistoning his cock in and out of me, pushing in harder and harder each time, reaching new depths and hitting my prostate like a jackhammer pummels pavement. He takes hold of my leaking cock at some point and begins jerking me off at the same time he wrecks my hole raw with his thrusts.

All the while, Jamie retains eye contact. His eyes rage with a storm like no other, more catastrophic and wonderous to look at, the sort some chase and others want to bottle and most take cover from.

A steady pressure builds up at the base of my spine,

the precursor to an oncoming orgasm. Jamie returns his free hand to my throat and squeezes hard, cutting off my air again.

When I come in an explosion of intense sensations, I'm lightheaded and the scream that should be ripped out of me at the overwhelming feeling is strangled by Jamie's hand around my throat. I feel set alight by him, a firework set off to light up the sky, a comet scorching its way through space, the very sun itself exploding into life, giving new hope to a cold universe.

My mind wants me to drift into another state of being, to let go of all control and float away on the feel of Jamie fucking me into the mattress, but I fight the urge, wanting to stay present in the moment and soak up everything, to see and feel Jamie come apart inside me.

Jamie's orgasm is like a lightning strike, the thunderous warning beforehand as he shouts, then the impossible heat and terribly beautiful sight of it lighting up the fathomless dark. It's incredible. Jamie is incredible.

He fills me up with his cum and half collapses on top of me, catching himself at the last moment so he's got one arm braced next to my head.

For a while afterwards we just lie there breathing in each other's space. There's a cloying heat in the air from our fucking and it feels like there isn't enough oxygen in the room. Jamie looks down at me the entire time, just staring and staring, eyes half-lidded, but still hyper focused, like he's afraid to lose sight of me in case I disappear on him again.

I stroke my hand down over his side, soothing him wordlessly until his chest stops heaving quite so rapidly.

He takes my hand in his and brings it up to kiss my palm, giving the skin a light press of his teeth, almost a bite. It makes me smile up at him, cheeks hurting from the stretch of it, my cheek still sensitive from where he hit me. It's fading too fast when all I want to do is hold on to every piece of him.

Eventually, Jamie slips his cock out of me and gets up, reluctantly leaving me to grab a wet flannel from the bathroom and clean us both up. The few minutes he's gone feel far too long and when he comes back and fin- ishes cleaning away our cum, I all but throw myself at him, wanting to tangle our bodies together into one entity.

Jamie lets me wrap myself up in him, doing the same in return. He moves us under the bedcovers and pulls them over our heads so we're hiding under them like we used to do when we were children, back when we liked to pretend a single sheet could protect us and the secrets we whispered to each other from the outside world.

It's like we're fused together by the damp heat of post-sex and a cloying sense of fear we might be forced apart without warning. Our position—lying with our sides facing one another, limbs either tangled or wrapped around each other, chests and torsos pressed together—is uncomfortable and awkward and I want to stay exactly like this, with Jamie, forever. For always. Until the sea dries up and the sun stops burning.

Until I die feels like a flimsy promise in comparison.

Into the ensuing silence, Jamie asks, "Did you love him?" He doesn't have to say who he means. There's no rancour in his voice. No condemnation, just a simple question with a far less simple answer.

"I don't want to tell you that."

Jamie frowns a little then. "Why not? It's okay if you did. I know I said a lot of stuff in the kitchen, but I never hated him for wanting you. I was only ever angry at myself for realising how much braver he was than me."

"I don't want to tell you because I didn't tell *him*, and Damon should be the first one to hear how I feel about him." But now he never will, so I guess I'll be taking that answer into the dirt with me.

Jamie opens his mouth like he's going to keep pushing for an answer, but when he clocks the expression on my face he immediately backs down. "What made you want to come over earlier?" he asks instead.

"Maybe I just wanted to see you," I say evasively.

He gives me a look like he's offended I'd think he would ever even pretend to buy that. "Rex."

Sighing, I drop my head forward and sigh in defeat. "I was in Roux's bedroom, thinking about a memory I have of him making me promise not to walk away from someone I love."

Jamie inhales sharply, a flinch creasing his face at the mention of Roux. "We all miss him, Rex." He squeezes me tightly in his arms. "It's not been the same for any of us without either of you."

Now I've started talking about it, I can't stop myself from pouring out the rest of it to him as well.

"I was thinking about how much I let him down. Both of them, actually. They expected more from me, and I've been doing things neither of them would be proud of me for. I should have been better. Shouldn't have let losing them and...the idea of losing so many other people, break me. I'm stronger than that." I scowl to myself. "They made me capable of being stronger."

There's a long pause, then, where Jamie holds me and searches my face in the dark. He leans forward and presses a heartbreakingly soft kiss to my temple.

"It's okay to be sad," he tells me in a low, quiet voice. "About Roux. About Damon. About dying. You don't have to pretend all the time."

"I really fucking love you, Jay," I whisper to him, unbidden and unprovoked.

I thought telling him how I feel would be difficult. I thought it would be one of the hardest things I would ever do. But it wasn't. It was easy. Easier than breathing even on the good days.

"I really fucking love you, too, Rex," Jamie whispers back, and it's everything. Just...in this one moment, it's everything to hear him say that to me.

Tomorrow, other things will matter. Tomorrow, the world and all its problems will exist again.

But for right now, there's not a single thing I care about other than the man I love, who loves me back.

Chapter Sixteen

Town Meeting ft. the Fam

At some point in the night Jamie and I fall asleep in bed together, only to be woken up by just about the worst thing there is.

Nosy lunatics.

Nosy lunatics we, unfortunately, love and therefore cannot murder. Jamie insists.

I don't know when my friends came back from Danger, but they seem wide awake and ready to irritate when they come tumbling into Jamie's room shouting and jumping on the bed like a couple of children on Christmas Day.

"Holy fucking shit!" Caleb all but screams into my bloody ear after falling down on top of me. "The apocalypse is nigh! The end is here! Jamie and Rex finally got their shit together!"

"The *Princess Diaries* song is right," Tate says, pretending to wipe away tears as he grins from his place standing over us, "miracles really do happen when you believe."

"Fuck my life," Caleb says, shaking his head, "I thought there was a better chance of Genovia being a real country than you two idiots getting together before we all die." He pokes Jamie in the cheek. "I mean, come on brother, talk about leaving it till the *last possible moment* to make a goddamn move."

Jamie swats playfully at his head, which Caleb narrowly misses by pressing his face to my duvet-covered shoulder. "Piss off, Cal. At least I knew I liked dick without needing to be hand-held into it by one of my best mates."

Caleb makes a highly scandalised noise, eyes widening at Jamie in shock. He darts a mildly bashful look up at Tate, who looks incredibly smug in return. Very slowly, Caleb turns his head back around and raises his middle finger at his brother. Jamie's only response is to laugh, the sound a welcome one that dissipates my anxiety over my friends catching us in such an intimate moment of ease.

During the night, Jamie and I unclenched, shifting into a more comfortable position. When my friends came in, we moved even further apart. Now, though, I reach across to clasp Jamie's hand above the covers, linking my fingers with his and squeezing. Jamie looks over at me with a smile as soft and beautiful as morning sunlight. His hair is messy, stuck up like a hedgehog on one side, and his mouth is still red and chapped from use. His chest is bare and there are marks on his skin from where I dug my fingers in.

Jamie squeezes my hand just as hard.

I find myself smiling back at him too widely. I probably look ridiculous. We probably look ridiculous. It hits me all over again how mad this is. How mad it is that I get to just *have* this. This thing I've always wanted and did absolutely nothing to deserve. Is this what feeling lucky is like? If so, I could really get used to it.

Without looking, I know Caleb and Tate are exchanging amused glances, plotting how next to annoy the shit out of me and ruin everything, like they always do, perfectly in sync and without having to discuss it out loud. I can't believe I never saw how perfect those two idiots are for each other.

Mei, the merciful soul she is, distracts them by clambering into the middle of the bed and lying down on her stomach. She beams at me and Jamie, her bright gaze switching back and forth between us like she doesn't know who she's more pleased for.

"This is good," she pronounces.

Tate and Caleb make noises of agreement and all three of them give one another meaningful glances.

Suddenly suspicious, I narrow my eyes at my friends and demand, "Did you three fucks make a bet on this?"

I swear, if they made a bet on whether Jamie and I would get together I will kick *off—*

"Nah," Tate says, looking offended, as if they've never made bets on my love life before. He gives both me and Jamie a smile that's far gentler than usual.

"We wanted to," Caleb says, gesturing between himself and Mei, who nods in apologetic confirmation. "But T wouldn't bet."

I look back at Tate with raised eyebrows, silently questioning him.

"No point." Tate shrugs, like it's obvious why. When he realises we don't get it, he sighs and explains, "There's no fun in betting on a sure thing."

Ha. Dru was right, Tate really *is* the smart one.

*

Eventually, Jamie and I are bullied out of bed so we can join the rest of our family at the town meeting. I would have begged off, but Caleb enticed me by revealing Lady Mars had managed to convince Dan and Sami to bring Nathan to the meeting, and I wanted to see the little boy again. I also wanted to see how Dan handles a town meeting.

We're about two minutes in, the meeting hasn't even been called to order yet, and the answer seems to be "not well".

"Is that a ladle? Is that a bin lid? Is the town witch who threatened to adopt me banging a ladle on a bin lid like it's a judge's gavel? What's *going on* here?" Dan demands, half getting up from his bench seat. "I want answers! Explanations! To wake the hell up from this nightmare!"

"Shh, shut up." Sami whacks his boyfriend in reprimand and drags him back down onto the bench. "It's starting."

"What's starting?" Dan whips his head around the town hall fearfully. He lowers his voice to a frantic whisper. "What's going to happen to us?"

This man grew up in Obsidian Inc custody where he was tortured and forced to be an assassin since early childhood, and he's scared of a Colbie town meeting after having only spent one day in this red pill of a town. Read into that what you will.

Colbie's town hall is big enough to accommodate most of the town, and cavernous, loud and quiet voices alike echoing off the walls. It's set up more like a courtroom with a large podium up at the front and benches stacked all the way to the back for the townspeople to sit on. Unlike most town halls I've seen, Colbie's isn't decorated in soft browns and creams, but rather in technicolour with dashes of manic sparkle, like the appropriation of a pride float.

Behind the excessively large podium stands Lady Mars with her ladle held aloft, calling for order. More accurately, calling for us all to shut the fuck up and sit down so the meeting can start.

My family are all gathered in our usual seats near the front. We take up a lot of space, especially when every single member of the family is in attendance like today. It's rare that happens these days, which is maybe the reason why the rest of the town keeps giving us not-at-all discreet stares of interest.

Based on past town meetings, things will likely descend into chaos rather quickly. I should have prepared Dan better for that eventuality. Sami's been to a town meeting before, so he knows, but it doesn't seem as if he saw fit to warn his boyfriend about what he's about to endure. I can't tell if Sami is just insane enough to see no problem with what goes on in our town meetings or if he wants to see exactly how het up Dan can possibly become in reaction to experiencing it for the first time.

I have Nathan sitting on my lap. He's wearing my old clothes again, a pair of simple jeans and a white T-shirt with a turtle on it wearing glasses and reading a book. His previously loose black curls have been expertly wound into multiple braids by Fiona.

Nathan seems very intrigued by what's going on around him. His violet eyes keep darting around like he's analysing the situation, searching for possible threats and planning exit strategies. He doesn't appear afraid, though, which is either a good thing or a terrible indictment against the previous insanity OI has heaped upon him. You decide.

Once everyone in the hall is quiet, Lady Mars leans forward on the podium and calls out in a booming voice, "Okay, first order of business will be discussing the choice for the primary school's end of year production."

Lady Mars points her ladle at Mrs Devon, a teacher at Colbie Primary who usually runs the school plays, and Mr Wong, the headmaster. They're seated at the front of the hall. Mrs Devon shares a nod with Mr Wong and stands up to speak.

"Thank you." She tips her head respectfully at Lady Mars, then turns to address the gathered Colbie residents. "This year, we have two options which the headmaster and I have agreed upon. Option number one; a retelling of *Beauty and the Beast* with a modern twist. Option two; alien invasion the musical."

There's immediate chatter amongst the townsfolk, everyone voicing their opinions at once. The fact every single person seems to have an opinion they think is worth arguing over in the first place is already mind-blowing.

Mrs Colburn stands up first, because of course. She's a short woman with long grey hair and a long face like a horse. A horse with a lot of weird opinions.

"What's the modern twist going to be for *Beauty and the Beast*?" she asks suspiciously, little eyes narrowed.

Mrs Devon, having come prepared, easily answers this question. "Some of the children want to do rapping instead of the usual musical songs." Unfortunately, her answer reassures absolutely no one.

There's some more chattering, louder and more vehement this time from a few people.

"Hm," Mrs Colburn hums thoughtfully, making a face, "is that really appropriate? I don't think we should be encouraging the children to swear."

Mrs Markin, an angry beanpole of a woman, stands up next. She's a few rows ahead of Mrs Colburn. Ever since the incident with the bakery, the two women have been pitted against each other, using any excuse to argue in town meetings, regardless of the topic.

"And *I* don't think we should be limiting the children's right to free expression!" She shoots a glare at Mrs Colburn. "Let the children swear if that's how they're feeling they need to communicate through performance."

Mrs Devon exchanges a harried glance with Mr Wong, turning wide eyes back on the rest of us. She tries to reassure all the parents who are looking increasingly concerned about the turn of this debate. "Just to be clear, the raps would be written by the children as a group, and we would of course be moderating the words used in the songs. There would be no swearing."

But Mrs Colburn completely ignores Mrs Devon, too busy glowering viciously at her rival. "This is just typical of you, Linda," she says scornfully to Mrs Markin, "encouraging radical behaviour in young people. Just think about how badly it went last time when you corrupted our poor, impressionable Jade." She flings her hand out in Jade's direction, who seems surprised to have been singled out, having previously been hunched over her phone, her fingers flying over the screen too fast for the human eye to track.

"You can't do rapping without some well-placed swears!" Mrs Markin scoffs. She swings around and gestures at Tate, who's sitting a little way down the row from me. "Tate, tell them you can't do rapping without swears. Culturally speaking, I mean."

Fuck me. Almost every single person in the room turns to stare expectantly at Tate. A couple of parents look ready to make up their mind about their young children saying "motherfucker" on stage if Tate gives the go ahead, probably in the name of seeming "inclusive".

Tate, unfortunately used to having this kind of question thrown at him, takes it in stride. "Culturally speaking," he says dryly, leaning back in his seat with his arms crossed, like he's a cool professor about to give a lecture, "I think there's room for interpretation in this case. But I wouldn't be the best person to ask, given my predilection towards hip-hop. Quite a lot of contention between the Black rap community and the Black hip-hop community, you see. I'd need to confer with The International Hood

Consortium to get a more concrete answer on that for you."

Caleb is sitting next to Tate with a jumper-covered hand pressed to his mouth to stop himself from outright laughing in response to the drollness in Tate's voice. I use Nathan's head to hide my own smirk, elbowing Jamie when he snorts too loud. Mei rolls her eyes so hard I'm surprised they don't pop out of her head.

Mrs Devon and Mr Wong are staring at Tate in open horror, whereas almost everyone else is either frowning in confusion or nodding along as if they're taking Tate's response literally. It's either politeness or insanity with those people, and considering this is a British seaside town, you'd never know which it was.

Before anyone else can co-opt the discussion, Mrs Colburn swoops in with another question, thankfully changing the topic away from the ethics of eight-year-olds wearing teacup costumes while rapping about a tale as old as time. "What would the alien invasion musical involve?"

Mrs Devon looks very reluctant to answer that question given how badly things went last time, but she rallies soon enough when Mr Wong reaches out to give her an encouraging pat to the hand. Terrible choice on his part, though. Now the entire town will be speculating that he's sleeping with Mrs Devon. That won't end well when it gets back to Mr Devon, otherwise known as Philip the postman. He might wind up heaping everyone's post together in a big pile and setting it on fire again in a jealous rage, like last time when everyone kept saying Mrs Devon was sleeping with his arch nemesis, Ted, the milkman.

"There will be a dance battle," Mrs Devon says

hesitantly, "The children chose some TikTok dance challenges they'd want to include."

Everyone chatters away about that for bit, mostly complaining about the absurdity of TikTok dances and the plague they have beset upon the youth of today, until Lady Mars gets bored and bangs her ladle against the bin lid to get our attention. When we're all quiet, she points her ladle at a young woman named Charlotte who has been patiently waiting with her hand up since the town meeting began.

Charlotte, who is best known for always dressing like she's in an eighties music video despite having been born in the nineties, stands up and we all collectively groan. "How about *Grease*?"

There's an uproar at that. She does this every year.

"We're not doing *Grease*, Charlotte," Ted the milkman huffs, not even bothering to turn around so he can glare at her, which is pretty mean since she's his wife, "get over it."

Charlotte slowly sits down with a dejected look on her face, clearly on the verge of tears. Again. She cries every year, too.

Mrs Colburn makes a face at Mrs Devon and asks critically, "But really, what do aliens invading have to do with summer? Shouldn't we pick something more summery for our *summer* school play?"

Charlotte begins softly singing through her tears. "S-summer lovin', h-had me a b-blast—"

Ted interrupts her furiously, throwing his hands up all dramatic. "The answer is *no*, Charlotte! The answer is *always* no!"

Charlotte bursts into loud tears again.

Mrs Markin huffs, frowning down her nose at Mrs Colburn. "This is so typical of you, Rebecca, constantly trying to stifle the creative flow of any group discussion with your rules and logic." She shakes her head in disgust. "You have no imagination!"

Mrs Colburn makes a scandalised gasping noise and grasps at her real, live pearls. "How dare you!" She hits her husband on the side of the head. "Richard, are you going to let her speak to me like that? Tell her how free-spirited and creative I am!"

Richard, who had previously been dozing in his seat, blinks back into alertness with admirable speed. He also does a very good job of pretending like he has any fucking clue what we've been talking about. "Um...your squirrel PowerPoint was very creative. I mean. You created it. All on your own. And there were photographs. Of the squirrels. Photographs are art. Art is creative." He looks very pleased with himself for that last bit.

Unfortunately for Richard, this does nothing to calm his wife.

"Richard!" Mrs Colburn scolds incredulously. "How many times must we go over this? They were not merely photographs, they were *surveillance* photos. They were not art, they were *evidence*!"

Mrs Markin scoffs, eyeing Mrs Colburn in disgust. "They were faked. Fake photos to further your agenda against the beauty of mother nature."

Mrs Colburn points a shaking claw at her and screeches, "Fuck you and your conspiracy theories, Linda!"

Lady Mars bangs her ladle again and calls out to the crowd over the sound of Charlotte's continuous sobbing, "We'll hold a vote, my lovelies." Mrs Colburn goes to argue but soon shuts the hell up when Lady Mars shoots her a quelling look over the podium. "Everyone who thinks we should choose to be invaded by aliens please make your best *whoooo* sound. And anyone who wants the fairy tale rap video please shout your least favourite brand of tea to the sky!" She looks around the room at us and asks, "Has anyone got any last statements to make before we begin the voting?"

Charlotte raises her hand again and waves it around some. Lady Mars points at her again and gestures for her to speak. We all stare at her and wait.

There's a long pause where we can all hear Ted muttering, "Charlotte, I swear to fucking God—"

"What about *Grease 2*?" she asks hopefully.

"Charlotte!" Ted yells, face going bright red. He turns around to look at her beseechingly. "Why are you *like* this?"

Lady Mars bangs her ladle and shouts, "All in favour of aliens!"

A small portion of the gathered townsfolk make "whooo" sounds.

"And all in favour of the swearing teacups?"

There's a cacophony of people shouting out different tea brands. This then leads into another loud series of muttered arguing between everyone over which tea brand is really the worst one. People have some very strong opinions on this subject, as you can imagine.

Lady Mars waits for fighting to die down before

winking at Charlotte and calling out, "Okay, last one. All in favour of *Grease*?"

As they do every single year, Tate and Caleb both spring to their feet.

Tate clears his throat and sings, "Well, this car is *automatic*—"

Caleb slings his arm around Tate's shoulders and sings, "It's *systematic*—"

They both grin at each other and sing in unison, "It's *hydromatic*—"

Then, as is tradition, our entire family throws our heads back and sings at top volume, "Why, it's greased lightnin'!"

Sami immediately begins clapping and whooping his support. Dan looks at his boyfriend in abject fear.

Nathan is, somehow, enthralled by it all and copies Sami, clapping really fast, eyes darting around at us and shining with excitement.

Charlotte bursts into fresh tears.

Everyone else groans.

Lady Mars bangs the ladle down a couple more times and calls, "Votes are in, and *Grease* wins again!"

For the tenth year in a row.

Because fuck Ted.

When my phone rings, I almost miss it due to the rancour going on inside the hall as the town attempts to mutiny against Lady Mars's decision. They do this every year, and every year Lady Mars rises victorious, so I'm not at all worried.

I'm surprised to see it's Elle calling. She very rarely calls, preferring to text, and even then, we mostly converse in the form of sending weird memes.

Jamie furrows his brows at me when I shift Nathan off my lap and into Sami's instead, who takes him easily, too distracted by the town's nonsense to comment.

I mouth "Elle's calling" at Jamie and get up from my seat, moving along the row. Jamie gets up as well, coming after me. I think about turning back and telling him not to, but we haven't left each other's sight since last night, and as co-dependant as it sounds, I want him with me all the time, until we're literally forced to be apart again.

Once I'm outside the hall I answer the phone.

Elle's voice comes down the line in a panicked rush of words it takes me a couple of seconds to parse and understand.

"He's gone! She took him!"

Fear seizes my heart despite my confusion, responding automatically to the real terror in Elle's voice.

"Hey, what's going on? Who took who, Elle?"

I turn around and make eye contact with Jamie, who's looking at me in concern.

"Jatin!" Elle gasps, sounding close to crying, "This blonde woman attacked us on the street and she took Jatin. She tried to take me, too, but Jatin stopped her and told me to run! I'm sorry! I'm so sorry! He told me to run and I was scared and I'm sorry!" She's so obviously distressed it's difficult to understand exactly what she's saying, but I get the gist.

My stomach drops. Jatin. Some blonde woman took him?

Some blonde woman.

First things first. "Don't be sorry," I tell her firmly,

meaning it, "you were absolutely right to run. Don't ever be sorry for protecting yourself. Are you safe now? Where are you?"

Elle seems to calm down at least a little. "Yeah, I'm safe. I'm on my way to The Caf to tell Rani about Jatin. Me and Jatin were on our way there when it happened, it's only a few streets over."

Fucking hell, Rani is going to lose her shit. Woe betide whoever this woman is who's taken Jatin. Rani is going to beat her to death with a frying pan when we find them. I'd feel a bit of sympathy if I wasn't so eager to rip the world apart to get Jatin back myself.

"Okay, good. You stay with Rani when you get there, don't go anywhere without her." There's a slim chance this is a Winters family thing, and I don't want whoever took Jatin to get another chance at picking up Elle. When Elle doesn't respond, I push her, "Elle, promise me right now you won't go after Jatin and you'll stay safe with Rani."

There's a long pause.

"All right, I promise," Elle agrees. She sounds put out and vaguely seditious, but that isn't my problem at the moment.

"Good, thank you." I let out a relieved breath. "Now, what about this woman? Can you remember anything else about her? Her vehicle? Was there anyone else with her?"

"Yeah," Elle says eagerly, "she was short and had blue eyes. She looked kinda like you, actually. I didn't see anyone else, but I'm not totally sure. There weren't any plates on the van she wanted us to get into."

No plates? Wherever they were going must have been

a short trip, then. Maybe Rohan can hack into the cameras in the surrounding area and find out where the van went. It takes a handful of seconds for the other thing Elle said to fully compute, my mind so preoccupied with thinking of ways to track Jatin down.

She looked kinda like you.

Andy.

No. No way. It can't be her, can it? I haven't heard anything from Andy since that night at the warehouse. Why the hell would she suddenly resurface now, only to kidnap Jatin? She doesn't even know about my connection to him. Unless someone told her. Unless she made it a point to find out.

But even if that's the case, why would she do that? It doesn't make any bloody sense.

I stay on the phone with Elle for another few minutes until I'm sure she's told me everything and she's outside The Caf, about to be safe inside with Rani. No matter how upset she is, I know Rani will look after Elle.

When I hang up, Jamie moves towards me, questions piling up on his face alongside the worry. "Rex?" he asks. "What's going on?"

"I think Andy took Jatin," I tell him, my voice a confused croak.

Jamie's eyes widen, my own shock and confusion reflected back at me.

Before Jamie can respond, my phone rings again. At first, I think it's Elle calling back, but when I look at the screen, it's Jatin's name displayed there.

A mishmash of dread and hope crashes and soars inside me as I answer the phone, locking eyes with Jamie again as I do it.

"Jatin? Shit, is that you? Jatin?" Please tell me it's you. Please say you got away somehow and need me to come pick you up. Please, please.

"Hello, Rexley." And it's been months, but despite having only met once, there's no chance I wouldn't recognise Andy's voice. Her tone is conversational and cool, like this is completely normal and there's no cause for concern. It chills me more than if she'd screamed down the phone.

I don't waste time trying to play nice with her. "Where is he?" Forget why, I don't care about why right now. We can worry about why once Jatin is safe and back with his mum.

"Assuming you mean Jatin," Andy replies dryly, "he's with me."

"Where are you?" I demand, feeling a creeping sense of helplessness. She sounds so reasonable. So much like her mother did.

"I'll tell you that, Rexley. I will. I want you to come here." Andy's voice takes on a more ominous note. "But first, I need you to promise me you won't bring anyone else with you. This is important, okay. You come alone and everything will be fine. I know how this seems to you, but this doesn't have to end badly. I'll only hurt the boy if you make me, all right? I swear it."

"Don't hurt him, Andy." I want it to be a warning, but it comes out more like a desperate plea. "If this is a revenge thing, then okay, I probably deserve it. But Jatin doesn't. He's just a bloody *kid*. Let him go and we can talk, no need for any of this dramatic bullshit."

Andy sighs. "This isn't about revenge. If I wanted to hurt you, kill you, kill the people you care about, I could have done that easily in the last three months." It's horrifying how sure she is about that. "This is about something far more important."

"What?" I ask warily.

There's a pause where my sister and I breathe together.

One. Two.

Then…

"Redemption." It's a whisper that plays more like a scream.

"Andy—" I try, but she interrupts before I can get any further.

"Come to the Hazard industrial estate, warehouse fifty-six. Don't bring FISA or your superhero team." I endure another heavy pause before she adds, "If you do, people will get hurt, and I really don't want that, okay?"

No. Not okay.

"Andy—"

"*Okay*?" Andy barks, and it's so earnest I almost believe her. I almost believe she doesn't want anyone to get hurt. But because she's also my sister and she's too much like me and we're both too much like our father, I think she probably does want to hurt someone. I think she wants to hurt *me*.

I'd want to hurt me.

"All right, fine, I hear you, just please don't—"

"You have four hours."

The line goes dead.

Chapter Seventeen

Nova Vs. Nova

One problem with promising Jamie I would take him on my next mission is the fact he expects me to actually do it.

"She said I needed to go alone." I try for the third time to convince Jamie he should stay behind and let the others know what's going on rather than coming with me to meet Andy. I've been attempting to dissuade him while he marched stubbornly on through town to his car, propelling me forward with a hand on my back.

Jamie opens the driver's side door and gives me his most withering look from across the car roof. "Yeah, okay, in what world is that happening? Because, let me tell you, it ain't this one." He doesn't even bother to let me respond, climbing into the car and closing his door, clearly waiting for me to join him inside.

I make a frustrated noise and drop into the passenger seat, grumbling obscenities in his direction. It takes a lot of effort not to cross my arms and slump in my seat like a petulant teenager with a strop on.

Jamie ignores me and starts up the car, backing us out of the Moons' driveway and onto the road in record time.

I'm mostly surprised we managed to get away from the hall and up to Jamie's house without anyone noticing. I'd imagine it will take the others about three seconds to start a town-wide search as soon as they realise we've disappeared off somewhere. When they find out I've taken Jamie with me and not them, my friends will be so pissed. Caleb will probably seethe in jealousy for weeks. It's going to be so *annoying*.

Once we're outside the town limits, Jamie breaks the tense silence. "Any idea what she wants from this?" He darts a glance at me.

"All I can think is wanting to get at me." I sigh, scrubbing a hand through my hair. "But she said it wasn't about that, so she must at least *believe* she has another reason worth kidnapping a child over."

Jamie's expression becomes pensive, but he doesn't offer any theories straight off. After a few minutes he glowers out at the road ahead; whatever conclusions he's come to about what Andy might be up aren't good.

I can't stop imagining Jatin, possibly hurt and locked up somewhere. He'll put a brave face on, because that's the kind of person he is, but he'll still be scared. He has to know I'm coming for him, that I always would. But what if Andy does something to him before I can get there? It makes me feel sick, physically sick, to think about something bad happening to that kid.

Jamie reaches across the console and grabs my hands. I didn't realise I was anxiously wringing them as thoughts of what could happen to Jatin pervaded my mind like some kind of planned assault by my subconscious.

"We'll get him back, Rex," he tells me, like it's inevitable, a fact of the universe, like any other outcome is near on impossible.

It shouldn't make me feel better, because Jamie doesn't know any more about what Andy has planned than I do, but somehow his ironclad confidence that we'll be able to see this thing through calms my nerves and gives me genuine hope the dread I'm feeling is misplaced. Just the conjuring of my fearful mind and nothing based in reality.

"I know," I say, letting myself believe, if only temporarily, that it's true.

My phone rings again and it's Rani. I contemplate answering it but ultimately decide not to. If I answer, Rani's going to want to know where her son is, and I won't be able to tell her. I feel like a bastard, ignoring her call, but I don't want to lie and if I told her the truth, nothing I say would deter Rani from rushing off to the Hazard estate. As much as I wish Jamie was safe back in Colbie, at least I know he can handle himself in a potentially lethal situation. Rani would be vulnerable to whatever Andy has planned and I don't want another person to worry about getting hurt.

Jamie must sense how distressed I am, because he takes one of my hands in his, the way he did yesterday when I was upset about Caleb. It works just as well as it did then to keep me grounded in the moment, incapable of going into an anxiety spiral.

The journey to Danger City somehow manages to feel both extraneously long and too short. It takes ages to get across town due to the terrible city traffic, and more than once I consider getting out and legging it instead. Only Jamie's calm presence at my side stops me from popping off like a shaken bottle of fizz.

When Jamie parks one street over from the Hazard estate, in the name of giving us the chance to do some basic recon, I'm almost too relieved to feel nervous about what we're walking into. We get out of the car and hustle into a nearby alley, not wanting to be out in the open for too long, just in case.

"We can't be sure if she's working with anyone," Jamie says, peering out from behind the corner and scanning the area around us like he's trying to spot hidden cameras or potential threats. "Our best bet is to loop in from the back way, climb over the fence rather than taking any of the main entrances or going in by roof."

He's right, flinging ourselves from roof to roof will be too conspicuous, especially as it's still light out.

I nod in agreement as we set off, sticking to the shadows as much as possible, taking the long way around so we'll pick up on any obvious signs we're being watched. As far as either of us can tell, we aren't, but that doesn't reassure me. There's only so much we can do, though, without people taking notice, and around here, in an industrial district, two strangers are already going to be pinging some people's radar as odd.

Since I have more experience sneaking around the Hazard estate, Jamie follows my lead. We find a discreet place to climb the fence surrounding the estate and make our way towards warehouse fifty-six, sticking close to the walls and checking there's no one waiting for us before we go around each corner.

There's a fire escape bolted onto the back of the warehouse. Jamie suggests using it to give ourselves some element of surprise. He pulls out the gun he was keeping stuffed into his waistband and insists on taking point. He gets his Moon stubborn face on when I try to argue, forcing me to give in and settle for sticking closely to his back as we move quickly up the metal stairs.

The fire exit has a lock on it, but the lock is rusty and made of an inferior metal, so I'm able to break it without too much trouble.

Inside the warehouse is a series of tall shelves, all of them empty and unlikely to provide any cover. Limited with choice, Jamie leads us down one aisle in the middle. He moves slow and silent, his footsteps barely making a sound on the concrete floor. I remain at his back, alternating between fear over what we're going to find in here and frustration that I didn't have time to grab my suit from Rohan's flat. I let him take it after our mission to rescue Nathan, thinking I wouldn't need it again until I returned to Danger officially.

At the end of the aisle Jamie stops to check around the corner. After a moment he encourages me to take look as well.

Beyond the empty shelves there's an expanse of the warehouse containing nothing other than what appears to be an open trap door. Upon closer inspection there seem to be stairs leading downwards into a space below the warehouse itself.

That's...odd. Why would a nondescript warehouse like this have a secret basement?

I catch Jamie's eye and he jerks his chin at the stairs, asking nonverbally if we're expected to use them. I shrug in response but move forward anyway. There isn't much choice, here. Jatin could be down there; Andy almost certainly is. Either way, it's not like we can do anything but take the risk of going down into the warehouse's basement.

Jamie follows me without protest, likely making the same assessment as me. The steps are just about wide enough for both of us to descend side by side. Jamie keeps his gun up and pointed straight ahead as we climb through the darkness into the space waiting below. We travel down for quite a while, leading me to believe whatever's here was made a long time ago. The warehouses were probably built on top of it way afterwards. Danger has more than a few underground bunkers, one of which FISA took over and made use of.

At the bottom of the stairs there's a short corridor with a metal door at the end of it. The door is cracked open, bright UV light filling up the gap.

Jamie and I exchange another extended look. This is it. I nod at Jamie and he returns it, moving ahead of me again and using his foot to nudge open the door wide enough for us both to fit through.

Beyond the door is another large, cavernous room with a high ceiling and a set of long UV lights bolted to each wall, illuminating the otherwise dim space.

My immediate attention is caught by a machine in the centre of the room. It's a large, metal hoop with some kind of symbols scratched into the surface of it sitting on a platform. The hoop is thick and appears to be mechanical, but I can't be entirely sure since I have no what it is. There is a set of controls with a few buttons and a lever on it not far away, and logic would dictate that would be how someone works the machine.

In front of the platform is Jatin. He's tied to a chair with metal chains, which is overkill for a twelve-year-old, but okay. His mouth is covered by silver tape, and he has a black bit of cloth covering his eyes. Behind him is Andy, holding a knife to his neck, close enough all she'd have to do is jab slightly to break skin. The knife is short, but sharp, with a thick handle.

My heart lurches at the sight of Jatin, eyes scanning him frantically for injury. He looks unhurt from what I can tell, although the fear on his face is its own kind of damage. There's no chance he's coming out of this without material for nightmares. Jatin stiffens in his chair when Jamie and I come in, possibly able to see us even through the black tie, hope cresting over his pinched expression, smoothing out the line between his brows. His fear seems to lessen instantly, like he really thinks everything will be okay now that I'm here. I wish I could be even half as sure of the outcome of whatever Andy has planned.

Andy herself looks, in a word, exhausted. But it's the *manic* kind of exhausted I am more than personally familiar with. Her pale-blue eyes are rimmed with a red hue, the purple bags deep. Although there's a frenzied gleam to her eyes which sets me on edge. Her hair is messily pulled up into a ponytail, white-blonde wisps curling up around her face.

"Are you all right, menace?" I ask, trying to sound confident so Jatin won't panic.

Jatin nods his head as much as Andy will allow. One of her hands is in his hair, her fingers curled up in it, to give her leverage, presumably so she can jerk his head to the side to make it easier to plunge the knife into his neck.

I'm trying desperately to pretend I don't see the knife, because the idea of Andy potentially using it fills me with so much terror and dread I won't be able to remain calm if I imagine her hurting Jatin.

"We're gonna sort this out right quick," I tell him with faux casualness. "You did a really good job giving Elle the chance to run." Jatin looks relieved at this, which is why I told him, knowing he would be worrying about his friend. "I'm proud of you." I'm grateful my voice doesn't break. "You'll be able to see her and your mum soon, okay?"

Jatin nods again, pulling lightly against his chains, frustration becoming clear on his face when Andy tightens her hold on his hair in warning.

Jamie spins around suddenly, so fast he's almost a blur, his gun raised and aimed behind us. I'm startled and confused until Dru steps out of the shadows, a gun held in a tight grip and pointed at Jamie. I was so focused on Andy and Jatin, I didn't notice Dru hidden in a darker part of the room.

Dru appears better off than her girlfriend, eyes bright behind her glasses, holding her usual intelligence.

Although there seems to be some disconnect in how she's looking at us that wasn't present any time I've interacted with her before. All traces of warmth or familiarity are absent. Whatever's going on, Dru is obviously on board with it. I can't decide if that's reassuring or if it makes all this seem more disturbing.

"It's good to see you're all right, Dru. We've been worried," Jamie says coolly, grey eyes watchful and resolute, but I can see the discomfort in them. He'll shoot her if he has to, but I can tell he really doesn't want it to come to that.

"It's good to see you too, Jamie," Dru responds, but as with Jamie there is a slight downturn of her mouth, the slope of her shoulders and looseness of her finger on the trigger which suggests she's equally as reluctant to cause physical harm to in this standoff.

It takes me a second to remember their history. Jamie was the one who brought Dru into FISA. He chased her all over the world until he eventually found her in a Cyprus hotel. She threw a vacuum cleaner at him and broke his nose. Jamie was partially responsible for getting Dru a job at the agency. With that taken into account, this must be weird for both of them.

Andy speaks for the first time, stealing my attention away from Jamie and Dru. "I told you to come alone." She narrows her eyes at me, calculating and cold, not bothering with any pretence at niceties.

"Hey"—I raise my hands as if in surrender—"you brought your girlfriend to this kidnapping, I should get to bring my boyfriend. Fair's fair."

Jamie twitches imperceptibly in my direction at the

word "boyfriend". He retains his stance, however, arms held unwaveringly steady. I can't blame him for reacting, though. We haven't exactly talked about the finer details of this thing between us. Now is really not the time to be defining things, but I'm not sorry for saying it either.

I expect Andy to berate me for bringing Jamie some more, but she seems to accept my bullshit response at face value. I'm not sure if it's because she really doesn't care, or if she's too het up about whatever this is and wants to get on with it. If she's anything like me, it's probably the latter. As I've said before, patience is not a virtue historically held by Novas.

"Come on then," I push, my own agitation bleeding into my voice. "We're here, what's this all about?"

"After you killed my mum, I..." She stops, breathing too loud, gathering herself as pain and grief cascades over her face. My gut clenches at the sight of it. But she continues before I can respond in any way. "After you killed her, I went through my mum's files. She wrote about her plans with the Mages, detailing her thoughts and reasons for everything she did. It took a while to get through it all, but after I did, I realised she was right. Not about killing the Liquid Onyx survivors, but that something needs to be done to stop them from becoming a danger to civilians. Mum kept trying to come up with a cure." She takes a shaky breath, and when she speaks her again, her voice has a solemn cadence. "But failed at every turn." Then Andy fixes me with a hard look, her chin jutting out stubbornly. "I think she was wrong to look for a way to reverse the Liquid Onyx process. What we really need is to find a way to, for lack of a better word, upgrade it. We need a better version to replace the old one, a new chemical which will debug and update the system. In this case the system is the Liquid Onyx survivors' biology."

She pauses, folding her arms behind her back in an attempt not to fidget under my heavy gaze.

"I looked through my mum's files," she says, "trying to find the chemical equation for Liquid Onyx, so I could begin working on tweaking it, to improve it. But she must have destroyed any trace of it, just like Dad did. At first, I didn't know what else to do, but then I realised the best way to get the information on how to make Liquid Onyx is to go ask the very people who made it."

Andy looks over at Dru for a moment, and whatever she sees on her girlfriend's face must imbue her with more confidence, because she returns her attention to me and pushes on, explaining, "Dru and I have spent the last few months building this machine." She gestures at the me-chanical hoop.

"What is it for?" I ask, dreading the answer.

Andy takes another fortifying breath, setting her shoulders back as if bracing herself for my reaction. "It's meant for interdimensional travel."

Whatever I expected her to say, it certainly wasn't that.

"Interdimensional travel? You mean, like, going to other universes? Is that even possible?" I glance over at Jamie, who spares me a brief look, his brows furrowed with the same trepidation that I'm feeling.

It's not that I'm unaware of the theory. Hell, anyone who's seen a sci-fi film or read a comic book knows about the multiverse idea, but, for all this world's weirdness, I haven't heard of anyone coming close to proving that theory correct, which is almost bizarre, since it's exactly the kind of thing I'd imagine some supervillain scientist would do just to fuck with us.

"Not using technology alone," Andy says. "It's a mix of tech and magic. Those symbols"—she indicates the ones carved into the metal ring—"allow the machine to connect us with our other selves. We can travel to any universe where another version of ourselves exists, alive or dead."

I hold up my hands. "Okay, putting aside the complete insanity of everything you just said...why do you need me for this? I'm assuming you want me to come on this mission of lunacy, right? I'm also assuming there's a reason. What the hell do you need me for, Andy?"

Andy sighs loudly, her mouth turning down in annoyance. "I can't be sure if I go alone I'll wind up in the right universe. I need one where Liquid Onyx was created, so for that I need a universe where you were definitely born."

"What?" I stare at her, confused. "Why?"

Distantly, the voice of Mia echoes inside my head.

It was all for you.

Now Andy looks properly irritated, like I've just asked her to help me tie my shoelaces or something.

"I'm guessing Uncle Roux never told you this," she says bluntly. "But when you were about three years old, you got really sick. You were taken into hospital and they ran some tests. Those tests showed you had leukaemia. It was aggressive, a rare sort the doctors told your parents they likely wouldn't be able to combat effectively. In short," Andy's voice pitches low, grave, "you were going to die."

"No." Shock hits me square in the chest. A stinging sensation forms behind my eyes, and I'm not sure if it's born from anguish or straight up rage-denial. "No way. That's not—"

"Of course, our dad wouldn't accept it," Andy interrupts as though I hadn't spoken. She sounds angry, her voice clipped, when she says, "You were his son, and our dad was a genius. If he couldn't use his genius to save his son, what the hell was the point of it? So that's what he did. He started working on something that would save you. He roped my mum into it as well, and together they created Liquid Onyx." Andy's mouth becomes a jagged, cruel sneer, and she looks at me with so much resentment I can practically feel it burning from her eyes. "All of this"—she gestures with both hands—"everything that's happened since, to the other children OI experimented on, came from our dad doing whatever it took to keep his baby alive."

All right, that's enough.

"Fuck you, Andy." I glare at her, feeling that toxic, guilt-ridden monster in my stomach gnash its teeth and writhe, snarling to be set loose and wreak its usual havoc. "Jesus Christ, fuck you."

"It's the truth." Andy clenches her fists, jaw set, that same righteous anger exploding across her face. "I remember it all happening. You can keep on thinking our dad was some villain if you want, but he loved you. He loved you more than anything or anyone. He broke *every rule* to save you, did something *incredible*."

I take a furious step towards her. "Don't fucking say that like this somehow makes what he did redeemable. Lots of children get sick. He had no right to destroy the lives of hundreds of people to save his own kid." My voice breaks on the last word, a tempest of emotion rampaging through me.

"No," Andy agrees coldly, "he shouldn't have done it. He should have let you die. That would have been the right thing to do." She narrows her eyes at me. "But if you think almost any other parent with a dying kid would make a different choice, you're delusional. Your mum knew about it. Your mum, the pretty as a princess nurse, paragon of virtue, let him do it."

No, that's...that's too much.

"She ran from him when she realised what he'd done!" I argue fiercely, because it's just... It's just too much, isn't it? After everything, to find out my mum was complicit in all that horror Alex Nova caused.

Andy makes an exasperated noise. "Only *after* you were saved by it! It's easy to feel regret over something when you've gotten what you wanted from it!"

"For bloody hell's sake!" I shout at her, officially done with whatever the hell this is supposed to be. "I'm not going to fight with you about this. Whatever our parents did, they're all fucking dead now, aren't they? I'm tired of drowning in the shadows of what our father did. If you expected me to feel guilty for being the reason Liquid Onyx exists, you can piss off! I wish he'd made a different choice. I wish my friends weren't dying. I wish my parents had been brave enough to let me die rather than force loads of children and parents to suffer on their behalf. But

I can't change any of it."

Emotional fucking growth, hallelujah. I'm really, really sick of feeling guilty for things I have no control over. At least now I know why I've always felt responsible. My subconscious mind probably remembered that I was sick and influenced my feelings about it all these years.

"If you were hoping to use that guilt to manipulate me into coming with you to another goddamn alternate universe, you're shit out of luck," I tell Andy. "The answer is no. Now, you absolute nightmare, let that child you have chained to a fucking chair go." I point at Jatin. "You wanna fight about how mental the idea of going to another universe is to, presumably, find alternate versions of our parents and get them to help you make an upgraded chemical of Liquid Onyx, we can do that without the threat of child abuse."

"You think this is a joke?" Andy looks apoplectic with rage, glaring fiercely at me now. I glare back at her, undaunted. "We're doing this today, whether you want to or not. Don't you want to save your friends? This is how we do it. It's the only way and you know it!"

I ignore all of that, because *obviously* I have to, otherwise my brain might genuinely explode from exasperation.

"Please tell me you are not threatening to knife a literal child right in front of my face for...reasons?"

"If you won't do it for your friends," Andy sounds so solemn, so resigned to some fate only she knows the existence of, it gives me pause. "Then maybe you'll do it to save the boy. This is your chance to prove yourself right," she bites out acidly. "How much like our dad are you really? How brave are you? Brave enough to let the boy die?"

"Come off it, Andy. What, are you really going to fatally stab a kid in the neck?"

Everything I know about Andy tells me she won't do it. She's nothing like that Winters family lackey who would have killed Julia. No matter how forbidding she's pretending to be, I don't believe her capable of such overt violence against an innocent person, let alone a child.

Andy's mouth presses into a grim line, and it hits like a warning shot. "No, I won't stab him. I don't need to."

"Okay, wanna explain that?" I eye her warily. "You're coming off very ominous and unhinged, right now, just so you know, sis."

Andy ignores my blithe tone. "When I was going through my mum's things, I found something inside her lab, locked inside a box in one of the fridges. She must have saved it, maybe for further experiments."

"Andy." That sense of foreboding from before roars in my ears. "Saved *what*?"

She hesitates for a moment before answering, "She had a vial of Liquid Onyx."

It takes my brain far too long to connect the dots on that one. When it does, I can still barely believe it.

"No." I'm shaking my head, taking a few, stumbling step backwards. "Shit. Fucking shit. Andy. Please, God, no. Please tell me you didn't. Please tell me you didn't *do this*."

Andy's expression doesn't waver as she shifts her blade to press it into Jatin's skin, just above his exposed collar bone. When she cuts him open, I inhale sharply along with Jatin, jerking forward a few steps again, instinctively moving to help him. I come to an abrupt stop when Jatin's skin splits and blood trickles out of the new wound.

Black. Not red. His blood is *black*.

At the same time as my mind is attempting to detonate itself with this information, Andy lets go of Jatin's hair to yank off the black cloth, revealing his eyes.

Jatin blinks at me with cobalt-blue eyes. I have such a strong flash of memory it almost cripples me mentally. Memories of a different pair of eyes set in a different face. Jatin's irises are the exact same colour Damon's were. It's almost surreal how similar it makes them look at first glance. It's one hell of a gut punch, too.

With the knife no longer held at his neck, Jatin twists his head to throw a ferocious glare in Andy's direction. He makes a few angry noises behind the tape covering his mouth, and I'd put good money on them being a series of viciously barked swears, most beginning with the letter *f*.

"Jatin," I say, my voice cracking right there in the middle of his name. He tears his new eyes away from his captor and looks back over at me. He makes another few noises behind the tape, seeming to get even more frustrated when all I do is stare back at him blankly, not understanding.

My gaze flickers back up to Andy again. She seems to have faltered slightly now her grand reveal has been performed. I stare at her, my eyes so wide they sting from the lack of blinking, in frayed disbelief. How could she do this? "Jesus *Christ*, Andy! What the *fuck*?"

It's like I can't be any more coherent than that. All I want to do is yell at her, scream in her face for doing something so insane and cruel to a *child*. To Jatin, because yes, it does feel especially gut-wrenching to think this is my kid. Mine as much as any kid could be without being my actual son. He's my mentee, my friend. He was mine to train. Mine to protect. We chose each other, like Roux chose me, like Lady Mars chose us, like me and my friends and their parents all chose one another.

This, more than what my father did, I am responsible for, because I made myself responsible for Jatin.

Guilt and horror spreads through my body like a drug, like Liquid Onyx must have rushed through Jatin's veins, twisting and changing him on a biological level. He and I are more alike than we've ever been. He'll share more genetic similarities with me now than he does his own mother. Oh, God, Rani. She's going to murder me, and I'm going to *let her*.

Beside me, Jamie has gone rigid. He can't turn around, because Dru still has her gun trained on him, but I can feel his desire to do so like it's a physical thing. He darts a quick glance at me, concern shining in his eyes. He looks afraid for me, and he should, because I'm afraid, too. I'm afraid of what I'll do to her if Andy tries to justify this decision.

Everything this will take from him, his autonomy, his health, his mind. Everything he'll never get to do, finish school, fall in love, find purpose in his life, figure himself out, become the man he's meant to be. Like Damon. She's taken Jatin's future away from him, just like her mother took Damon's.

Jatin won't have as long as even my friends and I do. Most children over the age of ten injected with Liquid Onyx barely make it a couple of months if they manage to survive the initial injection.

My rage bumbles over into a white-hot eruption.

"Do you know what you've done to him?" I could kill her for this. "Look at him!" I fling an arm out, gesturing at Jatin emphatically. "He's a fucking *kid*!"

I don't realise I'm practically screaming at her until I see the startled look on Jatin and Andy's faces. I'm so angry I don't even know what to do with myself. How dare she do this. How dare she steal Jatin's life from him just to get at me. I can't even make myself remain calm for Jatin's sake. Unless Andy explained to Jatin before she injected him, he likely doesn't understand why I'm quite as enraged and heartbroken as I am.

Jatin is looking at me with wide eyes, looking lost and confused, like he doesn't know how to feel or react. He finally settles on an emotion. Empathy. He's worried, not for himself, but for me. It's clear on his face. He can see that I'm in pain and despite not understanding why, he wants to help. It makes my chest hurt how brave this kid is. How good. How strong. I might have been the one to train him, but I see Damon in the determined set of his shoulders and the selfless fire in his eyes.

"A kid you were training to become a vigilante!" Andy scoffs, scowling at me, unimpressed. "Don't pretend you're some saviour, you bastard. You're more of a killer than everyone else in this room combined!"

I knew it. I knew this was, at least in part, about what I did to her mum. Even if Andy doesn't know it, she chose

Jatin, she did this to him, to hurt me. To punish me for killing Mia.

One day she's going to realise that, and I hope when she does, she's more forgiving of herself than I am.

In the aid of putting off whatever argument she and I need to have about all this, I push down my own roiling hostility and choose to focus on the other part of this absolute lunacy.

"You really think we can save the superhumans by going to another universe and getting our parents to help create some 2.0 version of Liquid Onyx?" I ask, forcing myself to genuinely consider it for the first time.

I still think it's barmy. Ruining Jatin's life hasn't suddenly changed that. But if Andy feels this strongly...she must think she can save Jatin. It's the only thing that makes sense. I would never have thought her capable of hurting a child like this, let alone outright killing them. She has to really believe she can fix, or upgrade, the Liquid Onyx in his system before it causes his death.

Andy pulls up short, blinking owlishly at me, all the suppressed fury that was ready to erupt on her face vanished now I've backed off and she has nothing to burn down with it.

"I do," she confirms, giving her head one decisive nod. "I wouldn't have done all this if I didn't think it was our best option at this point. If we want to save everyone, we need to go. Now."

"Does anyone else know about this thing?" I gesture vaguely at the big hoop, scowling at it like it's done something rude by existing.

Andy gives me a more thoughtful look, seeming to

have calmed down some, like she's reassured now I seem to be taking the idea seriously.

At the very least, we should be running this by FISA. I can only imagine Snow's face if she found out we'd created a dimension transport machine and used it without any government oversight.

But Andy is also probably right in that if we wait around for permission, it likely won't come in time.

Plus, do we really want the government to have access to dimension travel? I don't want to speak for everyone, here, but I wouldn't trust most of our government with supreme power over a sharp spoon. I make a mental note to convince Andy to destroy this thing once we're done with it.

I cannot believe I am seriously considering any of this nonsense.

As if on instinct, Jamie chances a look at me just as I'm turning to do the same and we lock eyes. He seems as conflicted over it as I am, although that might be more about him being afraid of what could happen to me. Fuck knows what that machine might do to us, really, or where it might take us. We could wind up almost anywhere. I doubt Andy has any real control over the machine beyond close your eyes and shoot. You'll definitely hit something, but whether that's your target or some poor bystander is down to luck.

I'd rather not depend on something that flimsy when I'm being sent to another dimension.

"Jay," I murmur, asking for help or reassurance or some way out of this.

Jamie's hand tightens on his gun, which does not go

unnoticed by either Dru or Andy. He ignores them and gazes at me pensively. He takes his time thinking it over.

"Whatever you choose," he says gravely, eyes dark and holding a profound sincerity, "I'm with you. In here. Out there."

I dip my head in acknowledgment of his promise, the repetition and meaning behind it. "You and me," I murmur, and despite all the shit I'm dealing with up inside my head, a warm smile spreads across my mouth. "Us." I give myself a handful of seconds to stare at him, to catalogue his features, every freckle and scar and imperfection on the face of the man I love.

Somehow, beyond all reason, having him here makes everything seem survivable, possible, worth fighting for.

One breath. Two. Again. Again. Again.

Turning back to Andy, I sigh heavily, nodding at her. "All right, then. What do we have to do to make this work?"

Andy meets my eyes with an assessing look on her face. Maybe wondering if I really mean it. There's so much of me that wishes I didn't.

Jatin is frowning at me, dark brows pulled in severely, his disapproval clear. He looks just like his mum when she's telling me off.

Still seeming suspicious, Andy explains, "All we need to do is start up the machine and jump through the portal it will create inside the hoop."

"How do we get back?" I ask, brow furrowing. That part's kind of important. No point in doing any of this if we can't come home afterwards.

Dru answers that one. "I'll set up a timer. We'll have

a set amount of time to do what we need to do before the portal opens again and we come back through it from the other dimension. It'll open up wherever the portal drops us, so we just need to get back to that point within the predetermined timeframe."

"Which will be?" I ask, looking from Dru to Andy.

"We think about six weeks should be long enough," Andy says.

Six weeks? Jesus. My family are going to murder me.

There's a pause where I digest that information. It obviously sounds simple enough, if we're willing to put aside the insanity of the very concept itself.

"Okay, fine," I bite out caustically. "Sure. Jump through the fucking magic hoop to another dimension. Brilliant. Looking forward to it, let's go."

Jamie makes a low humming sound, slight traces of amusement in his voice when he mutters, "Rex, the silky-skinned wonder, jumping through a hoop." He slides a discreet smirk at me. "Been training those arms your entire life."

"Jay, please," I huff irately. "People are dying."

Jamie doesn't look repentant in the least and stage whispers, "This is your *moment!*"

Since I am an adult and this is all very serious and me and Jatin are slow burn dying right now, I resist the urge to flip him off. I am growing as a person, yes, thank you.

Andy must come to a decision about trusting me, because she turns her attention to Dru and motions with her hand, silently telling her to stand down.

Dru complies immediately, lowering her gun. She waits, unmoving, and it takes me a second to realise she wants me to do the same with Jamie. I hesitate. Just because we've come to a tentative agreement doesn't mean I want Jamie to make himself vulnerable. I glance back at Andy, who gives me an impatient look in return, like this is all so *inconvenient* for her.

God, my sister's such a dramatic bitch. She would have got on so well with Roux. My lips threaten to twitch at the mental image of Andy and Roux screeching at each other over something ridiculous. I have to shove those thoughts aside, because they're making me ache for things that can never happen, not now. We're so far past that point we might as well already be living in a different universe.

Jamie tilts his head at me, asking for my permission to drop his arms. I breathe out, expelling my nerves through my mouth, and nod. Jamie slowly lowers his weapon, although his grip remains steadfast, and I know from seeing him in action he can have that gun back up and firing at breakneck speed.

Now no one is pointing guns, there's an air of relief in the room, the tension between us lowering to a more manageable level. Enough so I feel comfortable enough to ask Andy, "Can we please unchain the child now?" I jerk my head at Jatin, who sits up straighter in response to the idea he might be freed.

Andy doesn't respond straight away, her face creasing, obviously unsure whether that would lead to trouble. She exchanges a glance with Dru, who seems far less conflicted. "Let the kid go, Ands," she says.

Andy looks back at her girlfriend obstinately and for

a second, I think she'll refuse anyway. But then she sighs heavily and sticks her lightly bloodied knife into a sheath she has attached to her belt. She takes a key out of her pocket and undoes the padlocks keeping Jatin's chains in place. Jatin doesn't hesitate to yank the chains off and leaps out of the chair. He uses a free hand to rip the tape from his mouth.

I'm striding towards Jatin and pulling him into an aggressively tight embrace before the last of the chains hit the floor. Jatin slings his arms around me and hugs back, pressing his face into my shoulder. He's got taller since we last met. It makes my heart thrum painfully to think of him never growing to his full potential height as a man. I squeeze him too hard, harder than I would have when he was a normal boy. Jatin squeezes his arms around my middle, not realising his own strength, causing me to grunt as my ribcage creaks from the pressure.

Andy backs away from us, stepping up onto the platform behind her. She grabs a decent-sized backpack up off the floor where it was leaning against the hoop and slings it over her back.

Jamie is there beside me and Jatin within seconds, his large form seeming to envelop us all together in the same space, blocking off everyone and everything else. He puts a hand on the back of my neck and presses his forehead to the side of my head. His other hand mirrors the same position on the back of Jatin's neck. Holding on to us both. He murmurs words of comfort to us, nonsense things that are more about the reassuring tone than the actual words he uses.

When Jatin moves back enough so that I can see his

face, his blue—so *blue*—eyes are too shiny. He isn't crying, but there's a wet sheen to them that says he might want to.

I'm suddenly hooked by the urge to drag him out of here and make a run for it, to protect him from the nightmare he's been pulled into. Everything in me screams to do whatever it takes me keep the boy in my arms safe. I have to wonder if this is what Roux felt all those years ago on that rooftop. Did he look at me and see what I do now? A child worth risking everything for?

I want, so badly, to do what Roux did, take the kid and run. But even the most frenzied and panicked part of my mind can't pretend taking Jatin away from here would save him in the long run, not with how things have been going out there. No one's offered a possible solution to the threat Liquid Onyx poses to those injected with it, and Jatin doesn't have the kind of time me and my friends do. Andy has made sure of that.

Andy interrupts my rambling thought-spiral by asking, "You ready?" She looks at me expectantly.

What ready is supposed to mean in this case, I've got no idea, but whatever I'm feeling now will have to do. "Yeah, okay, let's do it." I grab hold of Jamie's hand and pull him up onto the platform with me. He comes easily, stuffing his gun into his back pocket and staying close to my side.

I'm not in the least surprised when Jatin springs up onto the platform. "I'm coming, too," he says, fiercely adamant. "This is my life, too."

When I open my mouth to argue, Jamie stops me. "Rex, he's right. This is his fight, too, now. Besides, if we're gone for six weeks, we might not get back in time before...." He doesn't finish, but his meaning is clear. Jatin could be dead in less than half that. He has to come with us.

"Okay. Fine. Rani is going to murder me. But fine. She was already going to murder me for getting her son turned into a superhuman, so. Fuck it, I guess. Might as well go all in." I sigh, wrapping an arm around Jatin's shoulder and tugging him into my side.

Jatin beams up triumphantly at me, then shoots Jamie a grateful look for aiding and abetting him. Jamie gives Jatin a discreet fist bump. I glance between them despairingly. If these two start teaming up on me, I'll never win another argument again.

Andy eyes us with a tiny frown, like she doesn't know what to do with what she's seeing. After a moment she seems to shake off her pondering. "We're ready to go, Dru," she calls out to her girlfriend.

"On it," Dru says, moving forward to stand beside the machine's control panel. She presses a couple of buttons and there's a low, rumbling mechanical sound like a large computer warming up as the machine turns on. In turn, each of the symbols on the hoop begin to glow with a pale brightness.

From one second to the next, the empty air within the confines of the hoop seems to become a tangible substance, like soap inside one of those bubble blowers you get at children's parties.

In the centre of the hoop a small pocket of light appears. A second later, that light expands, a blast of roiling whiteness exploding outward until it fills the hoop. It's so bright I have to squint, my corneas putting up more than a token protest.

There's a faint feeling of compressed air against my skin that grows and grows until it becomes a sucking sensation, like if you put your hand over the end of a vacuum cleaner hose. It sucks at our hair, whipping it back like we're standing up against a stiff wind. The strength of it isn't enough to pull us in, but I grab on tighter to Jatin and Jamie just in case it suddenly grows more powerful and tries to consume them like a black hole sucking stars and planets.

Dru does whatever she needs to do with the panel, then rushes to the door we came through and closes it. She turns a lock on the door, which I'm guessing is to make sure no one gets in and messes with the big stupid hoop before we get back.

There's another backpack near the far corner by the door which Dru snatches up before jogging over to us. She jumps onto the platform and takes Andy's hand.

The machine is emitting such a loud whirring noise that even with my enhanced ears I can barely hear her when she shouts, "*We need to jump in three!*"

I nod back at her in understanding, letting go of Jamie and moving quickly to tug Jatin so he's standing between us. I grab Jatin's hand and Jamie does the same on his other side. Turning my head, I meet Jamie's eyes over the top of Jatin's head and give myself a split second to stare at him, on the off chance something goes wrong and this is my last chance to do it.

Jamie gazes at me with eyes illuminated a pale grey by the light blazing from inside the hoop. He mouths,

"Love you."

He could tell me that a million times and it would never feel anything less than the best thing. Just the very best thing.

I hold my free hand out for Dru to take so we're all linked up. I don't know if it's possible for us to get separated, but I'd rather not take the risk.

Andy counts us down.

"*One!*"

breath

"*Two!*"

breath

"*Three!*"

Together, the five of us jump through the hoop and get swallowed up by the light.

About BL Jones

BL Jones is a twentysomething British author who spends all her free time reading and writing and taming her three little brothers. She lives in Bristol with a temperamental bunny named Pepsi. She's been writing stories since she was five, rarely sharing them with anyone except her numerous stuffed animals. BL has had a difficult journey into discovering and accepting her own queerness, and therefore believes that positive, honest, and authentic stories about queer people are very important. She hopes to contribute her own stories for people to have fun with and enjoy.

Email
bljonesbooks@yahoo.com

Facebook
www.facebook.com/bl.jones.33

Twitter
@BLJONES18

Website
www.bljonesbooks.wixsite.com/website-2

Other NineStar books by this author

Liquid Onyx Series
Novas Got Nerve
Make Like Mountains
Drowning in Danger

Connect with NineStar Press

Website: NineStarPress.com

Facebook: NineStarPress

X: @ninestarpress

Instagram: NineStarPress

BlueSky: NineStarPress

Threads: @ninestarpress